Sweet Adelaide

JULIAN SYMONS

PENGUIN BOOKS

Penguin Books Ltd, Harmondsworth,
Middlesex, England
Penguin Books, 625 Madison Avenue,
New York, New York 10022, U.S.A.
Penguin Books Australia Ltd, Ringwood,
Victoria, Australia
Penguin Books Canada Limited, 2801 John Street,
Markham, Ontario, Canada L3R 1B4
Penguin Books (N.Z.) Ltd, 182–190 Wairau Road,
Auckland 10, New Zealand

First published in Great Britain by
William Collins Sons & Co. Ltd 1980
First published in the United States of America by
Harper & Row, Publishers, Inc., 1980
Published in Penguin Books in the United States of America by
arrangement with Harper & Row, Publishers, Inc.
Published in Penguin Books 1981

LIBRARY OF CONGRESS CATALOGING IN PUBLICATION DATA
Symons, Julian, 1912–
Sweet Adelaide.
1. Bartlett, Adelaide Blanche de la Tremoille, b. 1855—Fiction.
2. Bartlett, Edwin, 1845–1886—Fiction. I. Title.
PR6037.Y5S9 1981   823'.912   81-1714
ISBN 0 14 00.5792 7   AACR2

Printed in the United States of America by
George Banta Co., Inc., Harrisonburg, Virginia
Set in Video Gael

For
Elizabeth Doherty
and
Diana Jagoda

Now Mr Bartlett the grocer he was looking for a wife,
and to a girl named Adelaide said, Will you share my
    life?
Then she replied, I'll marry, but please know my
    situation.
Before I truly am your wife I'll complete my education.
    Oh Adelaide, sweet Adelaide,
    Sure she was a pretty maid.

So Adelaide and Edwin lived as became their station
Until a clergyman they met who completed her
    education.
Oh, the Reverend Mr Dyson in the pulpit was all virtue,
But out of it he said, Come now, a kiss or two won't
    hurt you.
    Oh Adelaide, sweet Adelaide,
    The things she did, the trouble she made.

And when Edwin says now come to bed, just come
    and keep me warm,
She answers him, Just drink down this for it won't do
    you harm,
And after you have taken it, why then I'll come to
    bed.
But when poor Edwin's drunk it, then he finds that
    he is dead.
    Oh oh oh oh that Adelaide,
    Wasn't she a naughty maid?

Victorian Street Ballad,
sung at Adelaide Bartlett's trial

CONTENTS

9

ACKNOWLEDGMENT

I owe a debt of gratitude to Dr John J. Gwilt in America and Dr Richard Jack in England for their expert guidance in relation to medical problems and possibilities regarding the mystery of Edwin Bartlett's death. Their help has been most valuable. They are in no way responsible, however, for any errors in the suggested solution.

SWEET ADELAIDE

AFTERWARDS (I)

She opened her eyes, and was surprised to know that she had slept. How was it possible that she should have fallen asleep at such a time, she wondered, and in the next moment thought: what *is* the time? She got out of the easy chair in which she had been sleeping, as she had slept many nights before, and without looking towards the bed made her way in the velvet darkness across the room.

The clock stood in the middle of the mantelpiece, but the fire had died to a mere red glow, and she could not see the clock face. She did not at once light the gas, but shovelled some coals on to the fire, which began to burn up again, small green and red flames shooting upwards with a faint hiss. By their light she discerned what the yellow clock hands said against the black face: a quarter to four. She had been asleep for nearly three hours.

She stood beside the fire warming her hands and feeling the cramp fading from her arm, for perhaps half a minute. Then she pulled the gas chain and the mantel lit with a faint *plop*. The soft light shone around the room, but the bed remained concealed by the piano, in its alcove by the window. She said gently 'Edwin,' and when there was no reply, went round to look at him. He lay on the little iron bed with face turned away, and did not respond when she spoke his name again. She put an arm round his shoulders,

and pulled him over so that he lay on his back.
His expression was peaceful, the mouth slightly
open. She poured some brandy from the bottle
on the central table into a wineglass, returned
to the bed, and let a little drip into the open
mouth. It dribbled out on to his chin and down
to his nightshirt. One hand was outside the bedclothes, and she took this hand. It was cold. She
pulled back the nightshirt, felt his heart. Nothing
fluttered. His blue eyes, open, stared at the ceiling,
and she gently closed them. It was over.

'Adelaide Bartlett,' she said softly as she looked
down upon the figure in the bed, then: 'Adelaide
Blanche de la Tremoille.' For more than ten years,
she thought, I was this man's wife, I shared his
home and his life. Now it is finished. My destiny
was always different from his, and the tragedy is
that we did not both understand it earlier. Life,
Madame Blavatsky had said at their one memora-
ble meeting, life is nothing if it is not the fulfilment
of one's destiny. Now she must face that destiny,
must be a bereaved widow as she had been a loving wife. Do we not all play many dramatic parts
in our lives?

As she opened the door and stepped out on
to the darkened landing, she admired her own
composure. She went up to Alice Fulcher's room
and knocked on the door. She could hear the servant snoring like a pig.

'Alice,' she called urgently. 'Alice.'

The snoring stopped, the door handle turned,
and there was Alice wearing a flannel chemise,
and looking a fright.

'Alice, you must go and fetch Dr Leach. I think
Mr Bartlett is dead.'

PART ONE

In the Beginning

'She was the unacknowledged daughter of an Englishman of good social position; and he, or his agents, arranged the marriage.'

SIR EDWARD CLARKE,
Leaves from a Lawyer's Casebook

The first thing she remembered was a gold watch. It seemed to hang motionless above her, she stretched a hand and caught hold of the chain, a voice made clucking noises, there was a sound of rumbling laughter, she tightened her grip and was aware of a pleasant smell as the chain came nearer to her and the watch grew so large that she could see nothing but gold. Then fingers detached her grip, the watch and chain disappeared.

At that time she must have been very small, and the recollection had the quality of a dream. Indeed her early years were altogether dreamlike, and they ran into each other confusingly. There were rooms so big that they seemed to have no walls, lights so bright that she wished to hold them as she had held the gold chain, a rug or carpet so soft and delicate that she longed always to be placed upon it. People she remembered by smell, although she identified them later as men and women. There was a sour strong smell, not pleasant, a smell that had some delicate scent like gar-

17

den flowers, a warm rich smell that made her kick
out her legs in excitement. Wetnurse, mother, father, those were the identifications she made later,
but she could not be sure that they were right
because at this time she never knew mother or
father. Perhaps she had dreamed them, or made
them up. Later in her life she found that she was
good at making things up.

She remembered also people speaking, speaking endlessly, sounds that she could not understand and that seemed to concern her yet to
ignore her, so that she cried. Many things made
her cry in this early time. There was a memory
of being bumped up and down, up and down,
on something hard and painful. Then, as a varia-
tion on this, she was rolled about, over and over,
round and round, until she banged her head and
cried for that. There was more bumping and
thumping, her existence for a time seemed to be
made up of it, and sounds that were meant as
consolation, but these sounds were associated with
smells that she disliked, the sour smell, a strong
cheesy smell, the smell of oil. There was an occasion when somebody picked her up, she felt a
rough cloth against her cheek, and she wept for
the soft carpet.

Later, when she was in her teens and had been
told something of her past, she interpreted these
memories. Her name was Adelaide Blanche de
la Tremoille, she had been born at Orleans, and
when she was two or three years old had been
brought to England to live. The lights, the scent
of garden flowers, the rich masculine smell, belonged to her time in France. The bumping and
rolling came from her journey to England by

coach and ship. Those were her interpretations, but she never knew whether they were true, for that early time remained cloudy in her mind, even though the clouds were broken by a few scenes of great clarity.

In one such scene she was being carried bundled up across an open space at night. She was conscious of the stars, and stretched up hands towards them in pleasure. Voices chattered all about her, then she was indoors and it was warm, she was put beside a fire and held out hands again to its yellow and red richness. In another scene she was again wrapped in a bundle, and taken out of some kind of carriage—it seemed that in memory she was always travelling—and into a house. This time there was no fire, and she did not like the place. A woman's voice said, *Not here, she cannot stay here*, a man spoke soothing words in reply, but the woman was not pacified. *I will not have her in the house*, she said, and the child began to cry. Did she cry at the words, Adelaide wondered afterwards, and decided that she could not have done so because she did not understand their full meaning. It must have been the tone, bitter and unrelenting, that made her weep. Or perhaps these things were not memories, perhaps her later self had dreamed or invented them all. She could not be sure.

The first things she really remembered were Patty and the cottage. It was as though she had been born then, at a time when she was perhaps four years old. The cottage stood in a field and had three rooms, a kitchen with a range, a sink, and a dresser which held cups, plates, and a jar of variously coloured sweets which was placed just

too high for her to reach it. There was a table
in the middle of the kitchen, and a little window
with a ledge on which she used to sit or kneel
for half an hour at a time looking out, although
there was nothing to be seen but fields, and occasionally sheep or cows in the farther of them. The
kitchen contained three chairs, a rocking-chair for
Patty and two old horsehair chairs which had the
stuffing coming out of them so that they tickled.
A little ladder led up from the kitchen to the bedroom under the thatch. The bedroom had no window, and so received light only from below, but
there was a carpet on the floor of which Patty
was proud, telling her that it was a real Turkey,
so that when she learned what a turkey was she
expected for a long time that a real turkey would
spring suddenly out of the carpet's faded reds and
blues. Patty's bed was at one end of this room,
her own box bed at the other, and an old oak
chest in between held their clothes. Then there
was a third room down below which was used
for stores, wood for the range, the brooms with
which the cottage was swept out and the brush
used on the carpet every day, and shelves containing the jams and pickles that Patty made in summer and autumn.

Here she lived with Patty until she was quite
old. For a time she thought that Patty was her
mother, and one day asked whether this was so.
Patty stared.

'Your mother? No, bless you, child, I'm just Mrs
Patton. Patty, that's all.'

'Then where is my mother? And my father?
she added as an afterthought, although that did
not especially interest her.

'Both dead, my lamb. That's why Patty's looking after you.'

'Have you always looked after me, Patty?'

'Why, no.' Patty paused in rolling the pastry for a fruit pie. 'I got married, see, and my Thomas he went off to be a soldier and I never heard word of him again. So I went into service at the Hall. I was a housemaid up there, and then looked after the children. Then I had the rheumatics in my knee, and couldn't do so much kneeling, and then you was left alone and I came here to look after you.'

She knew about Patty's rheumatics, and had often helped with floor scrubbing when Patty had said she couldn't manage on her own, but she sensed a mystery in what she had been told. 'Where was I before you started looking after me, Patty?'

'How can I get on if you keep asking questions? You just go out and play.'

'What is the Hall, Patty?'

'A big house. Ever so many rooms.'

'A hundred?'

'I expect so. I never counted.'

'Is it far away?'

'Over there.' Patty waved a broad hand. 'A long way.'

'Is that where the baskets come from?'

'Yes, it is.' And now Patty positively pushed her out of the door. It was all very well to be told to play, but what could she play at? She had a cart that could be pulled along, and a doll with button eyes that she kept pulling out as fast as Patty sewed them in, but she did not care much about playing with them. She had been told not

to stray beyond the fields around the house, but
there was little to play at in those fields beyond
picking wild flowers. She tried to pull the handle
on the well that gave them water, but found it
too stiff, so she went across to the gate that opened
into the next field and swung on it. Then she saw
Ethel coming across the field with the basket, and
ran to meet her.

The basket came every week. Sometimes Ethel
brought it, and sometimes Phyllis. Ethel was always good-tempered, Phyllis was often cross. The
basket, which was covered with a white linen
cloth, contained mostly things to eat. There might
be a piece of beef or ham, there was often butter
and cream, sometimes fruit. Patty grew her own
vegetables in a patch at the back of the cottage.

Phyllis would often just empty the basket and
trudge back across the fields, but Ethel mostly
stayed for a cup of tea and what she called a bit
of a natter. She was much younger than Patty
and her face was a little shiny, as though she
scrubbed herself clean every morning. She wore
mostly a blue and white striped dress, and this
was always spotless. Adelaide liked to perch on
the window-seat and listen to Patty and Ethel talking about the Hall and what went on there, what
Mr Barrow thought about the Master being away
so much, and the hard words Mr Barrow had
heard spoken by the mistress when he came back,
and how Mr Barrow put all the trouble down to
somebody whose name sounded like Mr Chase
A Man. Why should he want to chase a man? It
was a long time later that she learned his name
was Mr Casumain.

For most of the time the women gossiped as

if Adelaide was not there, but occasionally Patty
would put a finger to her lips, or say something
like 'Little pitchers have long ears.' Then Ethel
might stop, but more often she would ask what
Addy could possibly understand about it, poor little mite.

'She's sharp, is Addy. Not much she misses.'

'But who's she going to tell then? You wouldn't
tell on your Ethel, would you, my duck?'

'I might,' she said. 'I might tell Mr Barrow, and
then he would send Mr Chase A Man away.'

'I declare,' Ethel said, and laughed.

'If Mr Barrow did that the Master and mistress
would be happy again, and none of the lovely
things would get broken.' On an earlier occasion
Ethel had told of hearing voices raised in a place
called the Oak Room, and had gone in to find a
plate broken on the floor, and the mistress crying
out that the Master had broken it deliberately
because he knew it was precious to her.

'You'd best keep a padlock on your tongue,
Ethel. Didn't I say she was sharp? She doesn't
miss a thing.'

'She's a caution. Goodbye, my duck, and here's
something for you.' Ethel bent over to kiss her,
and produced a handful of sweets from a pocket
at the same time.

If it was true that she remembered everything,
was this not because she had so little to forget?
They saw few people. Occasionally a shepherd
would pay a visit and stand talking to Patty for
a while, but otherwise nobody came for weeks
except Ethel and Phyllis. On Sundays she walked
with Patty across the fields to the road, and then
down the road to the church. The church was

on the outskirts of a village, so that they passed a number of small houses and cottages on the way. Sometimes there would be people at the doors and they would greet Patty, but she never stopped to talk. In church she knelt when Patty told her to do so, and tried to sing the hymns without knowing what the words meant. She listened to the preacher, and although again she did not understand him, she received a general impression that there was somebody who lived above the sky, and was kind to everybody as long as he was good. She liked the idea of this universal kindness, and disliked Satan who it seemed was trying all the time to stop people being kind and good. Was Mr Chase A Man a friend of Satan's, she asked Patty, who told her not to be silly.

There were always a lot of people in church. Patty knew some of them, but again she rarely exchanged more than a few words before they started for home. Only once or twice did the people they spoke to make any reference to Adelaide. One matron—the butcher's wife, as Patty told her afterwards—said, 'So this is the little girl, your sister's daughter. What's her name?'

Patty said briefly that it was Addy, and when the butcher's wife went on to ask whether she was ever taken up to the Hall, said that they must be getting on home.

On the way back that day she asked, 'Were the Master and mistress there?'

'Bless you, no. They go to another church.'

'Do Ethel and Phyllis go there?'

'Everybody up at the Hall, yes.'

'Why don't we go there too?'

'Wouldn't do,' Patty said briefly, and then

added, 'Too far away.' On the next day Patty put
on her best clothes, consisting of a black dress
with a white lace collar, took the stick she always
used for walking, and said that she would be away
an hour or two and Addy was to be a good girl.

'Are you going to church again?'

'The things you ask,' Patty said, and bent down
to kiss her. 'It's Monday. No church service today.'

'Are you going to the Hall?' After a moment's
hesitation Patty said yes. 'Can I come too?'

'No, love, it's too far.'

'I could walk all the way. I should like to go
with you, Patty. I promise I wouldn't get tired.'

'Then you can't,' said Patty almost harshly, and
turned away. Adelaide watched her until she was
out of sight. She did not cry—it seemed to her
later that she must have got all crying out of her
system when she was very small—but she felt
cheated. When Patty returned after more than
three hours she asked no question about the visit.

Not long afterwards they had a visitor, a man
who rode up, tethered his horse and came into
the kitchen. He was a big, hard-looking man, with
rough tweedy clothes and a billycock hat which
he did not take off. He greeted Patty with a brisk
good day and asked how she was keeping, to
which she replied that she was pretty fair. The
man sat down in Patty's rocking-chair, and looked
at Adelaide.

'So this is the little girl.'

'My sister's daughter, yes. Adelaide Harris.'

'Just so,' the man said, and went on looking at
her. 'Adelaide Harris. You wouldn't be making a
cup of tea now, would you, nanny?' There was a
kettle on the range, and while Patty warmed the

pot, the child considered the man with as much curiosity as he had been staring at her. Something about his red cheeks, thick brows, and the way that his dark eyes looked boldly and almost jeeringly from one object in the room to another put a name into her mind.

'Are you Mr Chase A Man?'

'What's that? What's the child talking about, nanny?' Patty leant over and whispered. The man laughed.

'My name's Jabez Wilson, little Adelaide, what d'you think of that for a name? Come here then, I ain't going to eat you, come and sit on my knee.' But she thought nothing of the name, and did not want to sit on his knee. 'A bit of cake goes down well with a cup of tea,' Mr Wilson said.

Patty said there was no cake, although Adelaide knew that there was a fruit cake out in the pantry, and she added that Mr Wilson had better say what he had to say and be done with it.

'Well then, the answer is no.' Mr Wilson's gaze moved with a kind of glee from the old woman to the child.

'And who was it said that, who decided?'

'It was the Master himself as told me.'

'Then he ought to be shamed, it's what shouldn't be. What's to happen to her, is she to stay here all her life?'

'As to that I couldn't say, not seeing that I'm just a messenger. The Master he said, tell nanny I've every confidence in her doing her best for all concerned. And with that, seeing you ain't a bit of cake to offer a man, I'll be gone.' He raised his hat, said, 'Good day to you, little Adelaide,' and left.

Had he not been Mr Chase A Man after all,

even though he would not admit it? Patty dismissed the idea impatiently, and said he was the bailiff.

'What's a bailiff?'

'The man who looks after the estate, makes sure the cottages are in good order, sees the tenants pay their rents. To send a message, just to send a message by Jabez Wilson.' At moments of excitement or emotion a drop formed on the end of Patty's nose, and one was there now. But for this warning not to ask any more questions, she would have tried to discover what was meant by an estate, and tenants. Later on, however, she could not resist asking what might have happened if a message had not been sent by Mr Wilson.

'The Master might have come down himself. Or at least—' She hesitated. 'If not that, he could have written a letter.'

'Shall we go up to the Hall and tell him so?'

'Shall we—' Patty repeated, then stopped, gathered Adelaide into her arms and burst out laughing. 'You're my little love, my Addy.'

'But shall we go there, Patty? I would like to see the Hall.'

'Perhaps you will one day. But I'll tell you something. If you go to the Hall when you're not asked, Mr Chase A Man might get you.'

'What would he do?'

'He'd huff and he'd puff and he'd blow down your neck like *this*.' At that Patty blew a gust of breath down her neck. 'And he'd say, "I like to eat little girls for supper," and after that he'd eat you all up.'

She screamed with pleasurable terror, and asked what Mr Chase A Man would do next, but Patty had gone into a kind of dream and did not reply. And nothing more was said about going to the Hall.

The next day Patty told her to get the stool that was kept in the pantry, put it against the chest of drawers, stand on it, open the top left-hand drawer, and take out the books she found there, together with her spectacles. The spectacles were small and had metal rims. Adelaide had seen Patty wear them only once, when she had been reading a letter that came with the weekly basket.

The books had pictures of children on the covers and inside, and Patty said that she should learn to read them. They began with one that had pictures of things she knew, a shiny red apple, a black and yellow bee, a comb for the hair, and she learned that A, B and C were for apple, bee and comb. Patty said that she was quick, and certainly before long she was able to read the words in the alphabet book, and began to try whole sentences. The book that fascinated her, so that she looked at it again and again, was called *The City Apprentices: or, Industry and Idleness Exemplified*. There were pictures on every page, with rhymes under them, and they told a story of two apprentices named Francis Goodchild and Thomas Idle. Francis was always good, and became Lord Mayor of London. Thomas was always idle, and went from bad to worse until in the end he was hanged at Tyburn. There was a picture of the gibbet, which moved her even more powerfully than the verse beneath it:

> The hurrying crowd, the tolling bell,
> The frame of death erected nigh,
> All, with a fatal meaning, tell
> Yon wretched culprit comes to die.

Patty read this to her first of all, stumbling over some of the words, but she came to disapprove of Adelaide's absorption in it, and in the end took away the book. The picture of Thomas Idle with the rope round his neck, however, remained fixed in her mind. Where had the books come from?

'I used to read them to Master John and Master Robert. The Master's sons, that was.' 'And the mistress, was she their mother?' 'Of course,' Patty said, and gave her a sharp look. 'But Master Robert he's down from Oxford now, and John's at his school, no need for an old nanny.'

'Did they learn their tables properly, or were they like Thomas Idle? What are tables, Patty?'

'Tables, why, that sort of table's multiplication and division. They had a governess come to teach them tables.'

'I know they're multiplication.' And she quoted from another of the books in the drawer:

> 'Multiplication is vexation,
> Division is as bad,
> The rule of three doth puzzle me,
> And practice drives me mad.

When shall I learn multiplication, Patty, and what's the rule of three?'

'That's enough questions.' Patty's lips began to move in and out, and the drop started to form on her nose.

Soon after she had learned to read, she discovered that they were less lonely than she had thought. If you walked, not in the direction of the Hall but the other way, and went across two big fields, one a meadow which sometimes had bulls in it and another with a stile which could be climbed over or wriggled through, there was the cottage where Charley Frim lived, and the one beside it that housed the Pargoe sisters, Sally and Jane. There were other cottages also, and if you knew which way to go over the fields it was easy enough to walk to them. They did not see other people, as she slowly realized, because Patty did not want to have anything to do with them.

It was on a fine day in spring that she first saw Charley and the Pargoe girls. Patty was doing washing, and Adelaide was imagining a scene in which she met Mr Chase A Man and told him that he must stop making the Master and the mistress angry with each other. Mr Chase A Man's response was to say that naughty little girls must be taught a lesson, they had to be eaten up. With that, he began to chase her as she ran over a field. Then she stumbled so that he almost caught her, and he followed her into a small clump of trees. She did not dare to turn round to look at his face, but she could feel his breath on her neck and hear his panting, which was remarkably like that of a dog. She screamed and buried her face in a mass of ferns, but the panting became louder. Then Mr Chase A Man's tongue began to lick her neck.

'Rover,' a voice said. 'Come off, Rover.' She turned over and saw a boy and two girls looking down at her. With them was a big brown dog, who jumped up at the boy and then sat down panting. 'Who you?' the boy asked, or that was what it sounded like.

'My name is Adelaide Harris.'

'She talks funny,' he said to the girls, who giggled. 'Where you live then?'

She made a gesture in what she hoped was the right direction. The taller of the girls whispered something to the other, and then both whispered to the boy.

'You live with old Nanny Patton, that right?' She said that she did, and there was more giggling from the girls. 'I'm Charley Frim. This here's Sally, and the little one's Jane. We'm playing hide-and-seek. You want to join in?'

She said that she did, and they hid and were found in the little wood. The seeker was assisted by Rover, who tended to follow those who hid, and stand beside them wagging his tail. Adelaide, however, put her arms round his neck and drew him down beside her. She had never before been so close to a dog, and there was something exciting about the heart beating beside her own. When she told Rover to be still he obeyed her, and it seemed that a long time passed before she was found. She played without thought of time passing, and afterwards she walked back with them to their homes, which were cottages much less neat than Patty's. A woman came out from one of them and asked who she was. When they told her she called to her neighbour, who came out from the adjoining cottage. The two of them stood looking at her as if she were a curiosity. Then Charley Frim's mother, a big woman with a nose curved like a bird's beak, said to her neighbour, 'What d'you reckon?'

Mrs Pargoe merely said, 'Ay.'

'Who's your mother then, little Addy?'

'My mother's dead. That's why I came to live with Patty.'

'So that's what they told you. That's what they

told her,' she said to Mrs Pargoe, who responded with another 'Ay.'

'You'd best be off home then. Charley, you see her back.'

So they went back together and Charley, who had unruly hair that wouldn't lie down, and wore knickerbockers that were both dirty and torn, told her about himself and his family and the Pargoes. He was the youngest Frim and had two brothers, both of whom worked on the estate like his father. His father was an under-gardener and one of his brothers was a gardener's help, while the other did odd jobs. There were half a dozen Pargoes, including two younger than Sally and Jane. Their father had hurt his leg in an accident, and helped to look after the horses. The oldest Pargoe boy, Johnny, was also working in the stables, and May was in the Hall kitchens, and hoped she might be taken on as a housemaid.

'I'll be going too, soon's I've finished school. Don't like school. Teacher hits I on the hands. Why'n't you go to school?'

Adelaide shook her head to show that she didn't know. 'Where do you all live?'

'What you mean? All live at home, where else? 'Course, if Tom goes away, which he's always talking about, I'd like that.'

'But is it big enough for all of you?'

'Don't talk daft. We got nowhere else, always lived there. Who else lives at Dip Cottage?'

'Just Patty and me, nobody else. There wouldn't be room.'

'Wouldn't be room?' He guffawed at that, and the tufts of hair stood up straight as spikes. Then she asked if he had seen the Hall, and he had.

He had been in the stables and helped to muck
out the horses, and in the kitchens where he had
been given meat pie, but the Hall itself he had
seen only from outside. How big was it? Big, bigger than anybody could imagine, larger than this
field they were walking through, and with rooms
in it that you couldn't see from one end to the
other. It was May Pargoe who had told him about
these rooms and the things they contained, great
tables all loaded with pieces of silver that shone
in the lamplight, silver plates even that they ate
their food off, and so many things to eat, sometimes twenty different dishes brought in at a meal,
great turkeys and hams and sides of beef that big
it took two men to carry them in. That was when
there were parties, sometimes thirty or forty people there to dinner, and a dozen or more staying
in the house. When she asked if May had ever
seen Mr Chase A Man, he asked if she took him
for a loony, there couldn't be anyone with such
a name. She told him that she and Patty had a
basket sent down from the Hall each week with
ham or beef or other meat in it, but at first he
didn't believe her. When she asked if his family
or the Pargoes got a basket too, he turned a cartwheel in delight at her foolishness.

'Us don't eat meat 'cept on Sundays. 'Course
Dad does, working at Hall, May too. They gets
leftovers, sometimes brings back bits for us. Us
has bread and scrape mostly, sometimes jam. And
a' course we has taters, I likes a nice baked tater.'

They had come to the rise from which the cottage could be seen between the fold of two hills,
and she saw that it was well named. Charley Frim
turned another cartwheel, and ran off back along

the track they had come without saying goodbye.
Soon he began to hop on one leg, then on the
other. Just before he went out of sight he turned
and waved.

When she went in, Patty scolded her, said that
she had asked her not to go out of sight of the
house, and asked where she had been. Her nose
seemed to come down so that it reached her
mouth—or perhaps her mouth moved miracu-
lously upward to meet her nose—as she heard
about Charley Frim and the girls, but she said
nothing. Adelaide was full of questions which tum-
bled out on top of each other. Could she go and
play with Charley, Sally and Jane tomorrow?
When was she going to school? Why did she and
Patty get a basket every week and Charley never
got anything at all except leftovers? Why didn't
they have more people living with them, when
Charley and especially the Pargoes had ever so
many? When could she go to the Hall and help
with the horses like Charley and have meat pie
in the kitchen? When could they have a dog like
Rover? At this point she ran out of breath.

Patty said she had best sit down and eat her
supper. She did so, although she could not help
squirming with impatience. While she ate, Patty
sat in her rocking-chair, moving back and forwards. The drop began to form on the end of
her nose. Her lips moved, but she did not speak.
Then afterwards Adelaide sat in the old chair with
its horsehair stuffing tickling her legs, and Patty
began to talk.

'What you need to understand, little Addy, is
that you are a girl in a privileged position.' What
was a privileged position? She did not know, but

did not dare to ask for fear that Patty would stop.
'That Pargoe, he's no use to anybody, never was.
They only keep him on out of kindness.' When
Adelaide said he had hurt his leg in an accident,
Patty sniffed. She had a tremendous sniff, full of
contempt. 'Fell off a wall when he was drunk,
broke his leg and it never mended right. No use
to himself or anybody else is Pargoe.'

'Is Mr Frim any use to himself?'

Another sniff, less decisive. 'Nothing against
Frim that I ever heard. But they're not proper
children for you to be playing with.'

She considered this. 'Where are they then,
Patty?'

'Where are who?'

'The proper children. I should like to play with
them.'

At that Patty's head sunk on to her chest so
that Adelaide might have thought she was asleep
but for the fact that her eyes were open. 'It isn't
right, it's what shouldn't be,' she said. Adelaide
waited for her to say something more, but she
showed no sign of doing so.

'Perhaps,' Adelaide said, 'the proper children
are at school, and if I went to school I should
meet them.'

At that Patty got up, turned her back to Adelaide for a moment, and then said, 'Time for bed,'
in what the little girl thought of as her 'You're
aggravating me' voice, because Patty sometimes
used those words when there was to be no more
talking. When they had gone up the ladder, however, and Patty was tucking her into the box bed
in which she was so cosy, she was emboldened
by the darkness of the little room in which the

candlelight showed only the outline of Patty's head, into repeating what she had said about school. The reply came in a harshness of tone that she had heard only on rare occasions, much worse than the 'You're aggravating me' voice.

'You won't be going to school and there's no use asking. Nor there's no use asking about other children. There's nobody right for you to play with here.'

When Patty blew out the candle and retreated down the ladder, Adelaide did not cry. She plucked instead at the thatch, as she had often done before, finding comfort in running her fingers along the reeds which were rough but warm. Then she began to whisper to herself, and in the darkness whispered all those things to Patty that would have been aggravating if she had said them out loud in Patty's presence. 'I *shall* see Charley Frim again and Sally and Jane too, and I shall go up to the Hall and sit at that table with the pieces of silver and eat with the silver knife and fork off one of the silver plates, and I shall find a dog and bring him home and call him Rover, and everywhere I go Rover will come with me.' Then she thought that there could not be two dogs called Rover and that her dog would be named Frisky, which was the name of a fox terrier in one of the books she read with Patty. Thinking about Frisky she fell asleep.

In the course of that summer, however, she did not find a dog nor go to school, nor eat with a silver knife and fork off a silver plate. She did, however, see a good deal of Charley, Sally and Jane, and she did see the Hall.

She said nothing to Patty about seeing the chil-

dren. She met them in the afternoons, because
they went to school in the morning. Sometimes
they met in the wood where they had played hide-
and-seek on that first day, and sometimes she went
to the cottages. She went inside these cottages,
and found that there was very little furniture in
them, and some of that was broken. The four biggest Pargoe children slept in a room no bigger
than the little room under the thatch, and the
two young ones slept with their parents. One day
Mrs Pargoe had a black eye and a big bruise on
her arm, and Sally said that their dad had whacked
her last night. Then there had been a fight between their dad and Johnny. Adelaide was
shocked, but Sally and Jane seemed to think it
rather a joke. When Dad had drink in him, they
said, there was nothing he wouldn't do. After that
they went into the fit of giggles with which they
tended to finish any conversation.

For the most part they played in the woods
and fields, between the cottages and the village.
There was a little pond good for catching tadpoles,
trees to climb, and games to play like prisoner's
base and touch and leapfrog and knuckle-bones,
as well as hide-and-seek which was the game that
Adelaide liked best. Later on she had a vision of
herself at this time, and in it she was always running down a green hill to collapse in a bundle
at the bottom, rolling over with the pleasure of
smelling the fresh grass, or she was hiding in one
of the dozens of places to be found among the
woods, buried among the ferns with Rover by her
side. She liked Charley Frim very much and was
friendly enough with Jane, but she did not like
Sally's continual whispering. It was as though Sally

had a secret which she was keeping from Adelaide. She was always daring the others to do things. One day in the woods she dared Charley to show them something, but he shook his head and said he didn't want to.

Sally danced round him saying 'Cowardy cowardy custard,' went off into a fit of giggling with Jane, and then said, 'We seen our Johnny's, ain't we, Jane? He shown it to us, shown it to May too. Asked us to touch it, our Johnny. His was a whopper, bet yours is just a little tiddler, throw it back in a pond I would. Go on, Charley. Show us, we'll show you. Addy, you'll show him, won't you?'

She shook her head, although she did not know what Sally was talking about. Sally began to shout, 'Charley Frim's a fraidy cat, Charley Frim's a baby,' and Jane joined in. Charley went red in the face and then suddenly pulled open his trousers revealing something like a thin white worm, which he tucked away again immediately. Sally and Jane shrieked with laughter and pulled down their drawers to show him their bottoms, but Adelaide refused to do so. That day she ran home, but a day or two later she saw them again, and nothing more was said about showing things.

They were all interested in her life with Patty, and in the contents of the baskets from the Hall. One day, after a lot of whispering, Sally asked her who her mother and father were. When she told them that her mother was Patty's sister and her father had been a seaman, and that Patty looked after her because they were both dead, Sally giggled.

'T'ain't so. My ma says you're something to do

with the Hall. She reckons you're a bastard, got
to be kept out of the way, like.'

'I'm not,' she said, although she did not know
what a bastard was.

Charley said, 'Shut up, Sally Pargoe. Don't take
no notice of her, Addy.'

'Just a little bastard, that's all she is,' Sally repeated, and at that Charley jumped on her and
pulled her hair until she said she was sorry.

Adelaide knew somehow that it would be unwise to mention this to Patty, and in fact she said
nothing to her about seeing the children, although
she sometimes thought that Patty knew. No questions were asked about where she went in the
afternoons, although sometimes she was scolded
for coming home dirty. On Ethel's visits Adelaide
was now always told to go out unless it was raining,
but sometimes Ethel let her walk back part of
the way, and answered some of the questions she
asked about the Hall, although she would say nothing about the Master. It was a wonderful great
house, Ethel said, and she was lucky to be there.
Ever so many servants, and Mr Barrow the butler
was the kindest gentleman as long as you did what
you were told, although Mrs Deacon was a bit
of a tartar. She was the housekeeper and had control over all the women servants, which meant
that she was important, although not so much so
as Mr Barrow. The Master and mistress of course
were much higher yet, so that it was no wonder
Ethel did not speak of them. It turned out indeed
that she'd never spoken to the Master, nor he
to her.

' 'Cause you see I'm only a laundrymaid, I ain't
a housemaid, it's only housemaids and ladies'

maids and like that are supposed to be seen by
Master and mistress and their friends.'

Naturally Ethel had not seen Mr Chase A Man,
although she had heard of him. She had seen the
Master, however, although all she said about him
was that he was not very tall and that his voice
was quiet, not like that of the mistress. Rose, who
was a housemaid and shared a room with Ethel,
had told her that the mistress would go on and
on at the Master, calling him all sorts of names
and swearing that she would leave him if he didn't
mend his ways. And the Master, very quiet, put
up with it all, never saying anything even when
she called him a country bumpkin and said that
it was so long since he had been in London that
he wouldn't know how to behave there.

One day as they walked along immersed in one
of these conversations, which Ethel seemed to enjoy as much as she did, they went farther than
usual, and as they reached the end of a footpath
Ethel said, 'There 'tis then, that's the Hall.'

And there it was! Adelaide did not know what
she had expected, but she was not disappointed.
They were on a small rise, and the great building
stretched out away and below. She had thought
it might look like the church, but it had no spiky
bits, and no tower. It was much bigger than the
church, however, with a great front entrance,
pieces at either side of the entrance that seemed
full of windows bigger than any she had seen,
and then other parts that made the shape of the
house like a capital letter E with the central bar
of the letter missing. All around were gardens,
laid out as though on a map, with lawns, hedges
and neat gravelled paths. Men were at work clip-

ping one of the hedges. Was one of them Charley's father? She was too far away to see.

'I shall go to work at the Hall,' she said. 'I would like to be a housemaid.'

Ethel burst out laughing, said she was a caution, and then looked alarmed. 'You run home now, little Addy, I wasn't supposed to bring you this far, you just run straight home. And don't you say anything to Mrs Patton about my bringing you here, will you?'

'Mustn't I see the Hall, then, Ethel?'

At that Ethel became confused and said that folk were silly and she couldn't see it mattered, and that Addy was a good girl and was to run along home. She did as she was told, but she remembered every turn along the way, and repeated over and over as she ran, 'I shall go to work at the Hall then, I *shall* go to work at the Hall.' When she got back she did not tell Patty how far she had been, and she never again walked so far with Ethel, but in the course of that summer she went a dozen times as far as the rise, and there lay in the grass looking down. More than once she saw a horseman ride up, dismount, hand his horse to a groom and go in at the front entrance, and once two ladies were handed down from a carriage and made their way into the house, skipping delicately as cats on the gravel. The horses were led round the right side of the house, and she supposed that the stables were there. Once she saw a figure that looked like Mr Wilson the bailiff making his way in that direction, slapping his thigh with his whip as he did so, and often there were girls round that side, moving between the house and what she realized must be the dairy because of the trays of butter and cans of milk taken out of it. It was all like a scene from one of the fairy-tales she had read, one in which she longed to take part.

It was in the autumn that Patty began to have nosebleeds.

They seemed at first to be comical. Adelaide was reading to Patty one evening, for she had become much more proficient than her teacher and now had no difficulty at all in reading anything put before her, when the usual drop began to form at the end of Patty's nose. Adelaide read with one eye on the book, which was a tale about a faithful servant who saved his master from attack by highwaymen at the cost of his own life, and one eye waiting for the drop to fall on to Patty's blouse or skirt. When this happened Patty would say 'Drat it,' and draw her sleeve across her nose. The drop duly fell, but this time there was something different about it. The drop was red. It was succeeded by a splatter of other drops, a little flow. Patty looked at them in surprise and said, 'Drat it, my nose is bleeding. Fetch me a handkerchief, there's a good girl.'

She brought a handkerchief, which was soon stained red, and then another. Patty put her head back, and when the bleeding did not stop climbed the ladder to her room and lay on the bed after Adelaide had undone her clothes. After half an hour, in which time three handkerchiefs and a large cloth had been soaked, the bleeding stopped as suddenly as it had begun, and Patty fell asleep. On the following morning she got up at the usual time, and made no reference to the nosebleed. A week later the same thing happened again. Adelaide asked her the cause.

'Drat the girl, how should I know?' Patty had recovered, but her face was white as chalk. 'Doctors say it's good for you, sometimes bleed you theirselves. Won't have to do it with me, will they?'

'Does it mean you've got too much blood?'

'Ay, that kind of thing. Have you been seeing that Charley Frim?' She spoke sharply, nose and chin approaching each other in the familiar way.

'Sometimes.'

'I told you not to play with him. And them Pargoe girls, you see them too?' Adelaide nodded. Patty sat and rocked in her chair, then spoke as if to herself. 'Got to see somebody, I told the Master so. Should have gone to school.'

'I wanted to go to school.'

'So you should have done.'

'Why didn't the Master want me to go?'

'Because—' Patty said, and sighed. 'He thought you were too good for the village school. But it's no use being cooped up with an old woman like me, you ought to see other children.'

'I like Charley Frim.'

Patty's head had been drooping, but now it jerked up. 'Has he touched you?'

She was puzzled. 'Yes, sometimes when we play touch, we all try and touch each other.'

'I mean has he touched you here?' She indicated the area which Adelaide associated with squatting over the pot at night. 'Or asked you to touch him?' She shook her head.

'You must never let anybody touch you there. Nobody. And never touch men if they ask you. Now you're growing up to be a woman you must be careful. It's a sin against the Lord God, remember that.'

She said that she would remember, although she could not imagine why any person should want to touch another in such a place. She would have liked to ask more about it, but Patty's manner was so forbidding that she did not dare to do so. She wondered also what Patty had meant by saying that she was growing up to be a woman, and asked how old she was.

There was a pause as though Patty was making a calculation. Then she said, 'Going on eleven.'

'Is that being a woman? You said the other day that Ethel was only a girl, and she is ever so much older than me.'

This conversation took place in her little room one night, and she was in bed. The candlelight played upon Patty's face, which looked like that of a witch in the volume of the *Arabian Nights* stories down below. Her eyes had heavy lids, and these now drooped so low over the eyes themselves that she might have been asleep. When she spoke the tone was harsh.

'No mother,' she said. 'That's the trouble, little girl, no mother.'

If she was a little girl, then surely it could not be true that she was growing up to be a woman? But she did not mention this. 'My mother died, didn't she?' Patty said yes. 'And she was your sister, that's right, isn't it, Patty?'

'Has anybody said different? What's Charley Frim been saying?'

Charley Frim, she answered truthfully, had said nothing. She did not repeat what Sally Pargoe had said about her being a bastard, because she sensed that Patty would not like it. 'You've been my mother, haven't you, Patty?' Patty made no answer. 'Is it bad then, not to have a mother?'

'For you it was bad.' With this Patty blew out the candle, so that her last words were spoken in the dark. 'You were born under an unlucky star.'

In her little bed she felt the comforting thatch, and tried to think what the words meant. She had stood outside in darkness looking upwards and had seen the stars shining, at first only a few and then as her eyes became used to them dozens, perhaps hundreds. They were beautiful, but were some of them unlucky? And what did it mean, to be born under one? It hardly seemed the same as being in a privileged position. She was aware that there was so much that she did not know, and that Patty would not tell her. It seemed useless nowadays to ask her questions, because the answers were often short and testy. When Adelaide had said that she would like to be a housemaid and asked if Patty knew how she could manage it, the answer had been that she should stop talking nonsense and help with the washing. She had learned to wash clothes, to bake bread and to do some cooking. She had learned also that the Hall was a subject to be avoided.

She went there on an afternoon in late autumn.

In the morning Patty had spent a long time out in the privy, which she often seemed to do lately, and came out looking poorly. Then after dinner, which that day was only tea-kettle broth— that was, bread with lard on it and then hot water poured over to make it soft—and a bit of bacon to go with it, Patty fell asleep in the rocking-chair. Adelaide was reading again an *Arabian Nights* story which frightened her, about a wicked Princess who ate only a few grains of rice in the day-time but fed at night off human flesh, when she heard a choking sound. She looked up, expecting that Patty was having a nosebleed. Instead she had half-risen from the chair, had a hand pressed to her breast, and seemed to be trying to speak. Then she gave a gasp, fell to the floor and lay still. Her lips were a blueish colour, and she made a rattling noise as she breathed. When Adelaide spoke she did not answer, although her eyes were open.

The doctor had visited the cottage only twice, once when Adelaide had a bad sore throat, and once when Patty scalded herself. Each time Patty had asked Ethel or Phyllis to get him, so Adelaide supposed that he lived at the Hall. She ran out of the cottage and along the path that led to the Hall. Not until she went beyond the point at which she had lain in the grass looking down, and began to descend the slope that led to the Hall itself, did it occur to her that she was doing something forbidden.

When she was down the hill she ran along the wide gravelled drive to a place where it divided, the main drive leading on to the front courtyard and another path going off to the right towards the dairy. She stopped, heart beating fast with so much running, trying to decide which way to go, when a voice called, 'You then, what do you want?' Jabez Wilson the bailiff was scowling down at her from his horse. 'What are you doing here?'

'I'm Addy.'

'I know well enough who you are. You've no business here. Be off home.'

She was upset, but she did not cry. 'I came for

the doctor. Patty fell down. She's lying on the floor and won't speak to me.'

The bailiff stared at her, then said, 'Right, you'd better come with me.' He bent down and lifted her, placed her in front of him on the horse, and so she came to the Hall.

Jabez Wilson took her to the stables, where there were more horses than she had ever seen at one time. There he said to a boy he called Johnny (could it be Johnny Pargoe?) that he should ride down to the village and tell Dr Martin that Nanny Patton at Dip Cottage had been taken ill, and he should call on her as soon as may be. After that he stood looking at her as though she presented a problem he could not solve, and told her to come with him. She followed him through a big oak door and down a long stone-floored passage which had rooms leading off it at either side. So many rooms! What were they all, who was living in them? Where was the kitchen in which Charley Frim had been given meat pie? There was no time to ask questions for the bailiff strode on, thwacking his thigh occasionally as if he were in a terrible temper, and she had a job to keep up with him. The passage turned sharply, and at last Mr Wilson stopped, tapped on a door and went in.

There was a good fire in the room, and a man sat beside it with a half-filled glass, and a flagon with liquid in it on a small table beside him. He wore a jump jacket which was unbuttoned, a pair of breeches also unbuttoned, and stockings with high boots that had tassels on the tops of them. A pair of small pince-nez was perched on his nose, and he was reading a newspaper. This he put down, to stare in astonishment at the two of them. He had large cheeks which swelled out a little when he spoke, as though they were inflated by bellows inside his mouth.

'Upon my word,' he said. 'Upon my word, Mr Wilson.'

'Sorry to intrude, Mr Barrow, but needs must,' Jabez Wilson said. His manner lacked the authority with which Adelaide had heard him speak before.

'You are aware of the time, Mr Wilson?' From somewhere in the jacket Mr Barrow produced a half-hunter, consulted it and snapped it shut.

'I know you ain't on duty, yes.'

'And who is this young person?'

'That's just the point. This here is Addy. Lives with Nanny Patton. Seems she's been took ill. I've sent a lad down for the doctor. Addy here says nanny she can't move.'

Mr Barrow buttoned up his breeches, slowly hoisted himself out of the chair, removed the pince-nez, and examined Adelaide carefully from head to toe as if she were a new species of humanity offered for his consideration. After that he spoke.

'Well, Mr Wilson, this is a pretty kettle of fish.' Mr Wilson nodded. 'You was right to bring her to me, right to disturb me, even though I was a-having my afternoon rest which it's my right to have, and the occasion for being disturbed don't arise more than twice a year.' Mr Wilson nodded again, his hard eyes looking somewhere between Mr Barrow and Adelaide. '*Someone* will have to be told.'

'That's what I thought.'

'And you acted right and proper in bringing her to me.' Mr Barrow's cheeks swelled out more than usual at these words, as though the bellows had had a double puff. 'You are the master in your field, which concerns everything out there, but within the Hall is my province.'

'Just so. I'll leave her with you, then.' And the bailiff, giving Adelaide what was perhaps meant to be a reassuring tap on the shoulder, made his exit. Mr Barrow muttered a little, and then asked Adelaide if she was hungry.

When she said that she was, he took her down more passages until they came to a room that was the biggest she had ever seen. She recognized by the copper pots and pans on the wall, the huge range that seemed to go almost along the whole of one wall, and the cupboards containing all sorts of jars with labels on them, that this was the kitchen. Some maids in caps and aprons were sitting at a big table in the centre of the room. Among these faces turned towards them in surprise, Adelaide recognized that of Ethel, and was suddenly aware of her own loneliness and wretchedness. She ran to Ethel, telling her that Patty had fallen down and was ill, and that she could not make her move, and that also (which was really the worst thing) her eyes were wide open. Ethel made comforting sounds, but stopped when Mr Barrow spoke.

'Now then, Ethel. Just a minute, if you please. I am going to leave this young person with you. She tells me that she would like something to eat and drink, and Mrs Walker I am sure will so provide. And you, my girl, you do what Mrs Walker tells you, and you'll come to no harm.'

Mrs Walker had a face red as a fine sunset, and arms thick as rolling-pins. She said that she'd see the girl didn't starve, and with that Mr Barrow withdrew.

The hours that followed were the most exciting of her life, so that she almost forgot poor Patty lying on the floor in the cottage. There was food, more food than she had ever seen as they all sat down to a meal, thick and clear soup, and then beef or meat pie (she thought of Charley Frim), and then fruit jellies, and tea to drink with it. There were people, so many people coming in and out that she lost count of them, men from the garden and stables and girls from the dairy, all sorts of maids and footmen wearing different uniforms. Mr Barrow reappeared briefly, quite transformed in a tail-coat, white waistcoat and high collar, above which the bellows blew his cheeks in and out with every word. And the housekeeper Mrs Deacon appeared, long-faced and sharp-nosed, with what Adelaide was later to know as a châtelaine round her waist, from which was suspended a host of keys, a pair of scissors and a thimble case, all of which made a jangling noise when she walked. She could not remember anything that Mrs Deacon said, but was aware of a disapproving aura spread around the maids' sitting-room, where Ethel took her after the meal. It was later, too, that she realized that she herself was an object of curiosity, and some of the coming and going was because various people wanted to see what she was like. At the time her senses were overwhelmed by the size of the place, by all the people arguing and chattering, and by a wave of tiredness that overcame

her in the maids' sitting-room in front of the fire.
She must have fallen asleep there, because the
next thing she remembered was Ethel putting her
to bed in a room that had two other beds in it.
She saw that it was dark outside and said to Ethel
that she must go home to Patty, but Ethel said
Patty was being well looked after and would understand.

Then it was light, it was morning, Ethel was
shaking her and she saw that both Ethel and Phyllis, who shared the room with her, were already
dressed. At breakfast she asked about Patty. The
girls looked at each other without speaking, and
at last it was Mrs Walker who said that Patty had
been brought up to the Hall last night on doctor's
advice. When Mrs Deacon appeared, preceded
by her jangling noise, Adelaide asked boldly (although inside she was frightened) whether she
could see Patty. Mrs Deacon looked at her, the
nose looking as though it might descend and cut
a small child in two, and then asked if she understood that Mrs Patton was very ill.

'I am sure she would like to see me. And I should
like to see her.'

The keys jangled ominously. 'What you would
like is not important, but it is true that she has
asked to see you. Ethel, take the child to Mrs Patton. Child, you understood me when I said that
she was ill, did you not?' Adelaide nodded. 'The
doctor says that she will die. It will benefit you
to look upon such a scene, the soul preparing to
leave the body. When the girl returns, Mrs
Walker, give her work to do in the kitchen so
that she does not mope. Idleness is of no use to
anybody.'

Then there was another journey through passages with Ethel, and not only through passages but up many stairs, wide stairs with rails at the side that Ethel said were called balusters, nothing like the ladder at the cottage. They went up and up and the stairs became narrower, and at last Ethel opened a door, and there in quite a small room Patty lay in bed. Adelaide at first did not like to approach closely, for fear that Patty should still have her eyes open and yet not be able to speak. Then the figure in the bed stirred and whispered her name, and she knew it would be all right to go near.

She thought that Patty looked much the same as she had done before she fell down, although there was a funny blueish line round her lips.

'Are you getting better, Patty?' she asked. 'I expect you're pleased to be in the Hall. I had a wonderful dinner last night, lots and lots of things to eat. Then I fell asleep. I was in the same room as Ethel and Phyllis.'

Now that she looked at Patty's face more closely, she saw that it had changed. It was as though the flesh had been taken away from it leaving only bones, two cheekbones with hollows on either side of them, a bone beak for the nose, and a pointed bone chin. The blue-white lips parted and Patty spoke. 'Have you been a good girl?' she asked, and Adelaide said she had been. Then Patty's worn rough hand moved over the bedcover, searched for and found hers.

'My little Addy,' she said. 'What will happen to you, my little Addy?'

She closed her eyes at that, and although she opened them again when Adelaide kissed her and said that she would see her tomorrow, Patty said nothing more. Afterwards she asked why Ethel was crying, and was told that it was because Mrs Patton was very ill.

'Mrs Deacon says she is going to die. If she dies, shall I stay here? I should like to stay here.'

At this Ethel's tears turned into a flood and she said that Addy did not understand what she was saying, although it seemed clear enough to Adelaide. She was not surprised to be told on the following day that Patty was dead, and although of course she was sorry, life at the Hall in those first days was so exciting that she had no time to think about the past. She became used to the immensity of the rooms, and learned to distinguish one of the long dark passages from another, and to know that the butler's room (to which she had been taken by Mr Wilson) was next to the footmen's sitting-room, and that Mrs Deacon's room was down another passage, next to the housemaids' sitting-room. They had their meals in the kitchen to which she had been taken on that first day, and this was next to another even bigger, over which Mrs Walker presided, and where Addy worked at peeling vegetables and washing dishes.

Then there was the whole vast world outside, the world of stables and kennels of which Mr Wilson was the supreme ruler, although he had a number of underlings who looked after particular horses or had special care of the dogs. The Master did not hunt, so there were no hounds, but there were almost a dozen dogs about the place and she made friends with them all, even with a wolf-hound named Rough, who was said to be so fierce that he would bite any stranger. She saw Charley

Frim's brothers and Johnny Pargoe, and also May, who worked as a kitchenmaid, and she was aware of the whispers that went on in the kitchen and elsewhere, and that these whispers had something to do with her. With so many exciting things happening she rarely thought about the life with Patty, except that it was over. It seemed that she had been at the Hall for ever, although the time must have been little more than a week, when she was taken to see the Master.

Before this, however, Mrs Deacon asked to see her. The housekeeper had a voice that perfectly accompanied the sharp nose.

'I have been told that you are able to read and write,' she said. 'Is that correct?' When Adelaide said that it was, the housekeeper took down a book from a shelf, found a place in it, and told her to read. Adelaide had not been told that she might sit down, so she stood in the middle of the room holding the heavy book and reading at the place pointed out by the housekeeper's finger, which said 'St Luke, Chapter VI.' She began well enough, 'And it came to pass on the second sabbath after the first,' but then there were words that she did not know like 'Pharisees' and 'an hungered' and she stumbled over them, so that Mrs Deacon told her to stop.

'Have you not read the Bible, girl?' She shook her head. 'You will reply when you speak to me, and say ma'am.'

'No, ma'am. I don't think Patty had it. I learned to read from books with pictures. The one I like best is *The Two Apprentices.*'

Mrs Deacon gave a prodigious sniff. She then gave Adelaide a metal pen and an inkhorn, and said that she should write her name and the first words of St Luke VI. This she did, sitting at a desk in the corner of the room and taking care not to make a blot with the scratchy pen. Mrs Deacon picked up the piece of paper with an air of distaste, and again commented only by a sniff. She asked if Adelaide knew her tables, and at the reply that she only knew tables with four legs told her not to be impertinent.

On the following day she saw the Master.

She was taken by Mr Barrow, who was wearing his tail-coat and white waistcoat, and in addition had on his hands a pair of white gloves. She had thought the Hall was immense before, but this journey (it was hardly anything less) with Mr Barrow was a revelation, for when they passed a door covered on either side with green baize, it was as though they were in another land. The passages in the parts of the house she knew had floors of stone, but here there was red carpeting everywhere, so thick that a foot made no sound.

They came to a great hall which had in it suits of armour similar to those she had seen in picture-books, but although she would have liked to stop and look at them Mr Barrow moved on at his stately pace. In the hall were two footmen who stood so still that they might have been made of marble like the statues she had seen along the way. They went up a staircase so wide that half a dozen people could have walked up it together without touching elbows, and then seemed to go on and on until at last Mr Barrow tapped upon a door and opened it when a voice from within said, 'Come.'

This room was not as big as the hall but still it

was very large, with books in cases around the walls, and a table covered with papers at one end, beside a window looking on to the garden. A man sitting at this table sprang up at their entrance, pushing back his chair. He was a small man, clean-shaven and quite bald. He had thick dark eyebrows and a wide full-lipped mouth that turned up at the corners, as though at any moment he might break out into a laugh. Above the mouth was a snub nose with wide nostrils, and over the nose large and slightly mournful dark eyes. Could this man, about whom there seemed something familiar, be the Master? Adelaide thought he looked less impressive than Mr Barrow.

He came round the table walking jauntily, as though there were small springs in his boots. 'So here you are then, here you are, Blanche. Eh?'

Mr Barrow made a sound too slight to have been called a cough. 'The young person's name is Adelaide, sir. Adelaide Harris.'

'Bless me, yes, what am I thinking of?' The Master stood there rubbing his hands together, then quickly put them behind his back. 'Thank you, Barrow. Adelaide Harris, eh? Come along then, come over to the window, Adelaide Harris, so that I can get a good look at you.'

She did as she was told and stood beside the window, which looked out on to lawns, while the Master put one hand up to his chin and contemplated her thoughtfully, but always with that air of being about to laugh. Then he told her to sit down in one of the armchairs beside the fire. She did so, and saw that Mr Barrow was no longer in the room, although she had not heard him leave. The Master walked up and down, sometimes holding his hands behind him, sometimes briskly rubbing them together, once or twice touching his bald pate.

'So you've been living with Nanny Patton for a while now, ain't that so? And she's looked after you, seen you lacked for nothing.'

'Yes,' she said, and added 'Sir,' because if she was to call Mrs Deacon 'Ma'am' she should surely call the Master Sir. Then, since he seemed confused about her name, she told him that she was the daughter of Patty's sister, and that both her mother and father were dead. 'It was very kind of Patty to bring me up. And very kind of you to send a basket to us every week with things to eat. We were never hungry.'

'A basket, eh? Well well.' The Master seemed at a loss how to go on. He suddenly plumped himself down in a chair beside Adelaide and stared at her for a few moments before speaking again. 'Nanny Patton has passed away, you know that. She looked after my boys, Jack and Robert, when they were small. And I hear Nanny taught you to read and write.'

She said that was so, and he went on, 'I've got two little girls, Elinor and Sophie. They have a nanny to look after them, but it's time they had a little schooling. What would you say to teaching them as Patty taught you?'

'I could show them how to read and write, but nothing else because, you see, I did not go to school.'

The Master gave her a glance from his large dark eyes. 'That was unfortunate. But they are only five and three, the little girls, so that if they learn their letters that will do for the present.

And you'd see me, wouldn't you like that? I'd be keeping my eye on you, no naughtiness or I'd get to hear of it.' And his mouth turned up in more than a smile, a smile that broke out into a laugh. She thought it polite to laugh too, although she did not really know why. 'Now one more thing, little Blanche. Adelaide. My lady is away at present, on a round of visits. When she comes back mum's the word, eh?' He placed a finger to his lips, and although she did not know quite what was meant by 'mum's the word,' she agreed. Then the Master rang the bell, and one of the footmen came and led her back through the green baize door.

Later she told Ethel what had happened, and asked her who 'my lady' was. Ethel said she was the Master's wife of course, and that it was right Addy should be going to the schoolroom and nursery, the kitchen was no place for her. Adelaide asked why not. 'Is it because I am a bastard, is that the reason?'

Ethel put her hand to her mouth. 'Whoever said such a wicked thing to you?'

'It was Sally Pargoe, and she said the Master was my father, but that can't be true because my father was married to Patty's sister, and anyway the Master is much too old. What is a bastard, Ethel?'

'It's a word you must never use, I can tell you that. And I'm not saying any more, not if you was to ask me till Doomsday.'

To reach the nursery and the schoolroom you went through the baize door, but they were at the back of the house, separated from the part in which she had seen the Master by another baize

door. After going through this door you went up
two flights of stairs and along a corridor into the
west wing, and there were the nursery and the
schoolroom. Next to them were Mrs Foskett's sitting-room and bedroom, and next to that was the
nursery bedroom where Adelaide slept with the
two children and Grace, who like herself was
called an under-nurse. Mrs Foskett was the nanny,
who had always to be called Mrs Foskett.

Life in the nursery was not at all what she had
expected from that talk with the Master. She and
Grace were woken up at six-thirty by the nursery
maid Millie, and at about the same time John,
the footman who looked after the nursery, came
up to light the fires. At seven o'clock the under-
nurses got the children out of bed and dressed
them, which often took some time with Sophie,
who was inclined to be fractious. At eight o'clock
breakfast was brought up from the kitchens, and
after breakfast either she or Grace took the children for a walk if it were fine, or on wet days
played with them indoors.

Then there were lessons in the schoolroom until
lunch, which was at one o'clock. Lunch seemed
to last for ever, because the children were supposed to eat up all their food, and both of them
disliked the milk puddings that came up three
days in the week. Then the children's morning
clothes were taken off, and they had to be settled
for an afternoon nap. At four o'clock they were
wakened for tea, and afterwards put into afternoon frocks mostly of sprigged muslin and taken
down by Mrs Foskett to be seen by their parents.
For these visits, which lasted an hour or a little
more, Mrs Foskett always wore a black silk dress.

The children then had to be bathed and put to bed, but the day's work was by no means over, for there was the ironing, washing and running in of ribbons to be done. The nursery and schoolroom made up a world of their own. She saw nothing more of Ethel, and missed the lively talk of the kitchen. The Master must have forgotten his words about keeping an eye on her, for he did not come to the nursery. The only people she saw were Mrs Foskett and Grace, Millie and John, and of course Elinor and Sophie. She became fond of Elinor, who learned her alphabet, was able to count her beads up to ten, and liked listening to stories. She did not much like Sophie, who was constantly whining, sometimes threw her food on the floor, and wet herself half a dozen times a day.

She spent four years as under-nurse and she was paid £5 a year, receiving one pound five shillings each quarter. How had the time passed, how did the days differ from each other, was something that puzzled her in later years. Soon after she had left the Hall the whole time became blurred, days running into each other like writing that has become damp. Only a few incidents stood out clearly, and they were burned on her mind for ever. There was the day when she understood what Patty had meant about growing up to be a woman, the day when she saw the portrait, the day when Jack came into the nursery, the day she left the Hall forever.

She was doing some ironing one evening when she felt something warm around her legs. When she saw that this warmth was blood she felt faint and called out to Grace. 'Help me, Grace, I think I'm dying.'

When she was lying in the corner of the nursery, curtained off from the children, where the two girls slept on little truckle beds, she said just what had happened. Grace was a couple of years older than herself, and was unable to read or write. Perhaps she was jealous of Adelaide's accomplishments, perhaps her language was naturally crude. Adelaide listened in horror while Grace told her that this sort of thing would happen to her every month, and would continue for three or four days unless she was going to have a baby, when it would stop. Grace went on to describe with relish the way a man got on top of a woman to give her a baby, but Adelaide did not believe her, and quickly stopped listening. She consulted Mrs Foskett.

The nanny was in her sitting-room, with a glass of hot toddy in front of her. Adelaide had been told by John and by Grace that Mrs Foskett drank, but she did not know what the word implied until this evening. Mrs Foskett was short and wide, and inclined to peer because she could not see well, and would not wear glasses. 'Whaddyousay?' she asked now. 'Blood, what do you mean blood, where is it?' Adelaide told her, and Mrs Foskett laughed. 'It's your monthlies you're talking about, is it? Suppose you thought you were too grand to have them? Suppose you thought I'd say do please go and lie down, m'lady, if you're faint, shniff—sniff these smelling-salts and you'll feel better. Not the way things are here, my girl. Doesn't matter if you get pains or feel faint, you'll just do your work and say nothing about it, understand?' A wail was heard from the nursery. 'Drat it, you've woke that child up.'

'She was asleep when I left.'

'Don't you answer back, miss, I won't have it.' Mrs Foskett rose, took a quick sip of toddy, and moved a little uncertainly to a cupboard, from which she took a bottle. The bottle said on the label that it was Dr Grundy's Elixir, and below the name recommended the Elixir as a cure for insomnia, rheumatism and all forms of neuralgia, and added that it could safely be given to infants when teething or troubled by wind. It was certainly marvellously effective in sending the children back to sleep if they woke up, but Mrs Foskett gave much bigger doses than those recommended on the bottle. Now she disregarded Sophie's complaints about having a pain in her tummy, poured a generous dose of Dr Grundy's Elixir into a glass and gave it to the child, who drank it greedily and within five minutes was asleep again.

'There,' Mrs Foskett said. 'You woke the little angel up. I've sent her to sleep. As for you,'— she peered at Adelaide as though uncertain of her identity—'do your work properly and forget all that nonsense. Remember, I won't have impertinence.'

Once a week Mrs Foskett went down to dinner with Mrs Deacon. They had a dinner of several courses served by one of the housemaids, and accompanied by wine and ale. From these evenings the nanny would always return extremely unsteadily, having had as Grace said one over the eight. Once she had come into the nursery, woken them all up, and insisted on the under-nurses joining her in dancing a jig. The children also woke, and were got out of bed in their nightclothes to join in, which they did with gusto until Sophie knocked her head on a table, started crying, and was put to bed with Dr Grundy's Elixir.

Then one night Mrs Foskett was brought back by two footmen who carried her. They were accompanied by Mr Barrow, whose cheeks were puffed out more than usual by the bellows. He woke Adelaide and Grace, told them that Mrs Foskett had been taken ill and must be put to bed. Adelaide had seen, but had not spoken to him since that day when he had taken her to the Master. Now he recognized her, paused in what he was saying, and told Grace to get along and do what he had said. When Adelaide moved to accompany Grace he checked her.

'Adelaide, isn't it? How are you getting on, Adelaide?'

It was a question to which she hardly knew the answer, but she thanked him and said that she was getting on well.

'Very good.' Mr Barrow went on puffing out his cheeks. 'But let's suppose you wasn't getting on well, that there was something you might, in a word, want to complain of, what would you do then?'

The idea of complaining had never occurred to her, but she said that she would ask to speak to Mrs Deacon. She knew by now that in case of any kind of trouble, Mrs Deacon was a final court of appeal for all the women servants.

'Very good again. But Mrs D. now, she can be what you might call uncommon short at times. Indeed she can.' Mr Barrow sighed, as if he had experienced the shortness. 'So I tell you what, little Adelaide, if you've got some question that's a bit too knotty for you, whatever it may be, just you bring it to me. How's that?'

He was so friendly that she made bold to ask

when she was to see the Master, and confided
to him that when she had been made an under-
nurse the Master had said that he would be able
to keep an eye on her, but that since then she
had never seen him.

They were in Mrs Foskett's sitting-room. From
the bedroom next door protesting noises could
be heard, as Grace helped the nanny to bed. Adelaide moved to help, but Mr Barrow said that
Grace could manage. Then he told her to sit down,
and said she was an uncommon rum little girl.
'The Master now, he's very busy. A lot to do, the
Master has. And then in the Season he has to be
up in London part of the time. Hates it, so he
says, but my lady insists on it. Very hot on being
up in London during the Season, my lady is, and
on travel. Often he lets her go off on her own
but sometimes he has to come up to scratch, do
what's expected of him, know what I mean?'

She had learned a little about the Season, that
it was a time when fashionable people were in
London, because Mrs Foskett would have liked
to be there too, and said it was a crying shame
that the little angels were left down here in the
country. But that was not the point, as she tried
to explain.

'Of course the Master cannot see me when he
is in London, but I know he spends most of the
time here at the Hall. I have not once seen him
in all that time. If he does not want to see me,
why did he let me stay here and put me in the
schoolroom so that I could teach his daughters
their letters? He could have sent me away. Perhaps it would have been better if he had sent
me away.' This was one of the rare moments when

she felt like crying, but she did not give way to the impulse.

'You've got a way with you, little Adelaide, I must say you've got a way with you. You leave it to me, and I'll see what I can do.' They had been standing during this conversation, but now Mr Barrow bent over. His left eye closed and then opened again in a prodigious wink. Then he continued in a solemn voice. 'Remember this, little Adelaide. Happiness means doing our duty in whatever sphere of life it has pleased the Lord to call us.' He might have continued, but at that moment Sophie's distinctive wail could be heard. Adelaide went to the cupboard, and Mr Barrow asked what she was doing.

'This is a medicine Mrs Foskett gives if the children cry. It makes them go back to sleep.'

Mr Barrow held out a large hand, and she placed the bottle in it. He read the details on the label carefully. 'She gives them this?'

She nodded, impressed by his gravity. 'Quite a lot sometimes.'

'They are not to have it. I will speak to Mrs Deacon.'

'But, sir. How am I to get Sophie back to sleep?'

Mr Barrow looked at her solemnly. 'That is for you and Grace to manage. But I am taking this medicine away. I shall speak to Mrs Deacon about it.'

Within a week Mrs Foskett had gone. She was replaced by Mrs Prynne, a thin pale woman who was a great stickler for everything being done to the minute. This included the children's visits to the w.c., where they were sent every morning after breakfast, to stay until they had done their business. There was no more Dr Grundy's Elixir, but liquorice powder was given three times a week to help cure constipation, with sulphur tablets to cleanse the blood. Mrs Prynne liked Adelaide's teaching, although she thought that the children ought to have more improving books. There was a piano in the schoolroom and Mrs Prynne would play it, nodding her long thin head gently in time to the music. She played simple pieces and songs, some of them adapted from the Irish poet Tom Moore, and encouraged the children and the under-nurses to accompany her. Adelaide enjoyed these sing-songs, and she learned from Mrs Prynne a rudimentary idea of how to play.

But all that happened over a period of time, and long before it she had seen the Master in the Oval Room, and had been shown the portrait.

One afternoon, a drowsy lazy afternoon when the children were having their sleep, John the footman came in and said that he was to take her to see the Master in the Oval Room. They made part of the journey she had travelled before, but this time did not go up the great staircase but stayed on the ground floor. John tapped on a door, and when the Master said, 'Come,' just as he had done before, she went in.

The Master was in the room, and another man with him, but although she saw them both, her first impression was of something different. It was that the room was filled with gold. The day was dull, but all the furniture appeared to be covered with gold, the table in the centre of the room and the little tables placed beside chairs, the chairs themselves, the cupboards and cabinets round the

walls. All of them shone golden, their sheen illumi-
nated by the light from oil lamps that seemed
themselves made from some golden substance.
Years later, when the room was no more than a
memory, she learned that the furniture was boulle
and the tables marquetry, and that what she had
taken for gold was mostly brass bindings and ornamental inlays, but at the time the goldenness overwhelmed her.

The Master was just the same, jerky in his movements. He jumped up and sat down again, put
his hands behind his back and then the next moment brought them round to stroke his jaw. 'Here
she is,' he said to his companion. 'This is Blanche.'

The other gentleman leaned forward, put up
a monocle to scrutinize her, then dropped it. 'I
see what you mean,' he said. 'It's a demned awkward problem, no doubt about it.' He laughed a
little, silently, head down into his high collar in
a way that emphasized the sharp lines of his face.
Everything about him seemed to be at an angle.
His forehead sloped back, and his sharp nose was
at an angle to his mouth and chin, which receded
back into his neck. Above the mouth was a moustache almost as thin as a pencil line, which
sprouted at the ends a long way on either side
of his face. His clothes fitted very tightly, so that
when he bent his knee the angle between upper
and lower leg was acute. Even his fingers seemed
to be angled, so that the thumb stuck out away
from the rest of his fingers.

'I have been told that you would like to see
me,' the Master said.

She was overwhelmed by the room, but not by
the people in it. During her whole life she was

never greatly in awe of people. 'When you saw me last you said you would be keeping your eye on me, and would know if I had done anything wrong. But I have not seen you once. And my name is Adelaide Harris, I told you that before.'

The Master's hand pulled at his chin. 'You see what I mean, Casumain.'

So this was Mr Chase A Man. Before she had digested the shock of it, the thin man had spoken. 'I see your meaning. She is obviously an intelligent girl. I think she shouldn't be kept quite in the dark.'

The Master said eagerly, 'Then, my dear fellow, if you would be kind enough to undertake—thank you, thank you.' And the Master left the room without even looking at Adelaide, his movements so jerky that he might have been a toy. Mr Casumain said nothing, but beckoned her to him with a finger. She moved until she was within a foot of him.

'Turn around.' She did so. 'Walk over to the wall.' She did that also. Then he picked up one of the lamps, and stood beside her holding it. 'Look at that picture.'

She looked, and gasped. She was facing the portrait of a woman in what she later came to know was an Empire dress, cut low, but at the time she did not look at the clothing but at the face. The painter's subject had dark hair done in long ringlets, full lips, and a well formed but determined chin. The painter had evidently set out to be truthful rather than to flatter, for the eyebrows were thicker than was fashionable. The eyes were beautiful, large and dark, eyes with a hint of some quality that did not belong to the everyday world, but suggested reserves of mystery or

passion. Those eyes were familiar to her, and so
was the rest of the face. She had often seen it
in a looking-glass.

'The resemblance is remarkable, is it not?' She
made no reply, but went on looking at the picture.
'She is not related to you. Her name was Emily,
and she was the Master's mother. The portrait
was painted when she was twenty years old.' Still
she continued to look, until he took her by the
arm, led her back to the centre of the room and
told her to sit. Then he sat himself, legs tightly
but somehow elegantly crossed, and asked if there
was anything she would like to know. She stumbled over the words.

'If we are not related—'

'Why do you look like her? I am going to tell
you. Perhaps you should have been told before.
You were not born in this country, but in France.
Your name is not Adelaide Harris. You were chris-
tened Adelaide Blanche de la Tremoille. Your
mother was a Frenchwoman. I shall not tell you
her name, but she was a member of one of the
noblest families in France. She died when you
were born. Your father—' He paused, put in his
monocle, and looked at her.

'The Master is my father.'

He nodded approvingly. 'I thought that you
would not disappoint me.'

'Is that what they mean by saying that I am a
bastard?'

He let the monocle drop. 'Who says that? Do
they say it here?'

'It has been said to me.'

'And I see that you know what it means. You
should know also that the word is not used in
polite society. There is an old phrase, natural

child. You are the master's natural child. You not only resemble his mother, you resemble him.' She understood now why he had looked familiar when she first saw him. 'He has your welfare deeply at heart.'

'Indeed? Why does he not tell me this himself?'

'The Master likes everything to be pleasant. He tries always to avoid—how shall I put it?—anything disturbing. We are old friends, he and I, and for years I have been his man of affairs. You may call me his adviser.'

'And what was your advice about me?'

Mr Casumain's thin nose twitched. 'You are perceptive. My advice was that you should be put into the care of friends a long way from here, that it was foolish and dangerous to keep you living so near. It was unfair to you also, for it was not possible that you should attend the local school, where the resemblance was bound to have been remarked. And to have you at the Hall was an excess of folly. If the Master's wife learned that you were here, teaching her children, she would—' He hesitated.

'She would throw things at him and break plates?'

'Again, I see that you have heard gossip. Yes, she has a temper. It would have been better for everybody if you had been sent away. But the Master is a man of complicated character. His wife is a sick woman.' He paused, as though choosing his words carefully. 'It is in his mind that in certain circumstances it might be possible for him to acknowledge you as a relation, that you could be introduced as a distant niece.'

There stood beside her a little table of various coloured woods, bound with brass. She touched the metal, her fingers moved over the delicate woods. It seemed to her that this was the most beautiful room she had ever seen, and for a moment the thought that she might be the mistress of the Hall teased and delighted her. Then the many absurdities of such an idea became clear.

'You are speaking of what might happen if his wife should die?' He inclined his head briefly, watching her. 'But it is ridiculous. The servants know me. And I have no education. The Master cannot be serious. If he had been serious, he would have sent me away to be educated.' She noticed with wondering detachment that she said 'the servants' and not 'the other servants.'

Mr Casumain's thin lips twitched in the ghost of a smile. 'Precisely. You have the knack, my dear Blanche, of coming to the nub of the matter. The idea is ridiculous, and the Master is not serious about it.'

'But then—'

'Why does he keep you here, why say things he does not mean to do? In part it is because you remind him of the lady who was, at least in memory, his one true love. But chiefly it is because although the Master is a most agreeable man, he is not a serious person.'

'I do not know what you mean.'

'When your brows draw together in that way you look remarkably like him. I mean that he does not care to think about the serious things of life, or to be troubled with them. It is a kind of dream he has, that the daughter of his true love will one day live here with him, and he does not care to be reminded that it is no more than a dream. Do you know why he calls you Blanche?'

'Because that was my mother's name?'

'You are quick,' he said. He put in the monocle. 'And perhaps you can guess the reason for this interview?'

His look at her was hard and straight, and somehow she understood its meaning. 'I am to be sent away.'

'Yes. You will go to a family where help is needed in looking after the children. They live in London, and it will be altogether livelier for you. You will have time free to go out into the world.'

'It is my wish to be educated. I can read and write, but I have no education.'

'I see no reason why that should not be possible. You can speak to Mr Mitten about it.'

'And I am to be disposed of? I have no choice in the matter?'

Mr Casumain uncrossed his legs, then crossed them the other way. They stuck out like sticks. 'You have a strange way of putting it. This is an arrangement that will be to your benefit. You surely would not wish to stay in the nursery here all your life?'

'Is Mr Mitten a friend of yours? Or of the Master's?'

'He is known to me in the way of business. I am sure you will find him an estimable gentleman.'

'And when is this to happen? When am I to leave?'

'There is no tremendous hurry. The Master's lady is away at present, having treatment at Harrogate. Her latest doctor seems to think it may help to cure an internal complaint she has. But she will be back here in a few weeks, and before then something should be done. I give you the information now because I am here on a visit.'

'And the Master does not wish to tell me himself?'

Mr Casumain's shoulders moved up and down, he touched the waxed ends of his moustaches. 'Upon my word, I admire your frankness.'

'Thank you for telling me. I am grateful to you,' she said, and got up to leave. Before she could do so Mr Casumain took her small soft hand in his thin dry one, expressed his admiration of her, said that he felt sure she would make her way in the world, and that he did not suppose they would meet again.

In this he was wrong.

She lay that night on her low truckle bed, staring up into the darkness and listening to Grace snoring a few feet away. She was conscious of profound discontent, a discontent that was to remain with her for the rest of her life. It was linked with a vision of that golden room, and of the portrait that seemed in memory to shine with the reflected glitter of the gold. The Oval Room was where she belonged, there and in the rest of the Hall on the other side of the green baize door. An accident of birth had prevented her from taking her proper place, from wearing the kind of fashionable clothes that she had glimpsed at a distance when visitors took tea in the garden on summer afternoons, or were handed down from their carriages on arrival at the Hall, the foulard skirts and muslin bodices with fine French lace round throat and wrists, the black velvet mantles embroidered with silk and topped with elegant little lace-trimmed bonnets, the splendour of a full evening dress with a long ornamental train, which she had never seen but only heard about from the ladies' maids.

This accident had kept her also from attending the dinners and dances and balls at which she would have glowed with an inner light like the woman in the portrait. She had been deprived of all this because she was a natural child and because the Master was not a serious person. She knew, because she had heard it so often in church, that it was proper for men and women to accept the circumstances into which life had cast them, yet she could not help feeling that there was something wrong in her own situation, that whatever might have been suitable for Adelaide Harris, it was not proper for Adelaide Blanche de la Tremoille—to use the name that had been given her instead of the Master's own—to be a nursemaid. These feelings did not affect her work. She helped to dress and undress the children half-a-dozen times a day as she had always done, she washed and ironed clothes and folded them with the neatness that was natural to her, she taught Elinor and Sophie their lessons and tinkled on the piano. And she waited, not impatiently, for that move to London where she would have more freedom and where an education might be possible.

One morning Grace had taken Sophie for a walk in the garden, and Adelaide was in the schoolroom reading a story called *Richard Careless: or, the Certainty of Punishment by God for Crime* to Elinor, who had a liking for tales in which naughty children suffered some awful catastrophe, when the door opened and a fresh-faced young man put his head round it.

'How is my favourite sister?' he asked. Elinor cried out with pleasure, and flung herself into his arms. This was Jack, the Master's younger son. Adelaide had seen him sometimes in the stables after he had been out riding, but had never spoken to him. Now she sat with eyes downcast upon her book while Jack positively got down upon the floor and pretended to be a lion, chasing the shrieking Elinor from one corner of the room to another. Then he suddenly seemed to become aware of Adelaide's presence, got up and said with a grin, 'I'm sorry, I have interrupted a lesson. Please go on reading.'

He flung himself into a chair. Elinor sat on his knee, put an arm round his neck, and said, 'Oh, please do, Adelaide, I want to get to the part where Richard goes to prison and repents.'

She started to read again, at first in a low voice, but then with her usual verve as she forgot this unexpected audience. When she had finished the chapter Jack clapped. 'Bravo. It's the most awful rot, but you do read beautifully. I only wish my reading were half as good. You're a lucky girl, Elinor. I think I shall come and listen to Adelaide's next reading, so that I can find out what happens.'

'Oh, will you, Jack, will you?' Elinor danced up and down. Mrs Prynne, who had just come into the room, said, 'Adelaide, you are letting Elinor become excited.'

'I'm afraid it's my fault,' Jack said. 'I can see I'd better make myself scarce. By Jove, I remember this old schoolroom, and trying to learn my letters. Very slow I was, too. I didn't have a teacher like Adelaide.' He looked at Adelaide, frankly stared at her. A lock of hair had come down over his forehead in the game with Elinor, and he brushed it back carelessly. He seemed to Adelaide the most beautiful person she had ever seen.

The next day he appeared again, and after that he came regularly, playing games with the children, and coming out with them on walks through the grounds. Elinor adored him, and even Sophie wailed less than usual when he was there. It was impossible for Adelaide not to see, however, that although Jack liked playing with the children his real interest was in her. He talked to her about himself, and she learned that he was seventeen, and would soon be leaving school and following his elder brother Robert to Oxford. He was not looking forward to the prospect.

'The guv'nor says I've got to read Classics, but I think it's all a lot of rot. Can't stick Latin, and Greek is worse, don't see the point of it, do you? I forgot though, of course you wouldn't know. Don't you think it's dashed odd, Addy, that we were both of us taught to read by old Nanny Patton? Makes a kind of link, wouldn't you say?'

By this time he knew that she had been brought up by Patty in Dip Cottage, which it turned out he had never seen. Did he know that she was the Master's natural child, had he noticed her resemblance to the portrait? It did not seem to her that he looked much like his father, although there were occasional gestures which reminded her of the Master. He began to come up in the afternoons, when the children were resting. He would throw himself down in the chair, in what she learned to be his characteristic way, or else sit on the edge of a table, and talk ramblingly about himself and his future.

'If you ask me it's dashed rotten luck being a second son. There were two after me, you know, but they both died, Clarence and George. Somehow I feel it would be better if they were around, I shouldn't get bossed about so much. My mother's always going on about the kind of thing I should do and about having a purpose in life, but I tell her a fellow ought to do what he likes if he's got money. I like hunting, and I like playing cards if it's with a jolly set of fellows, and I like billiards. A few of us sneak out at night from school and go down to the public house and back ourselves to beat the locals at billiards, devilish good sport that is. You should have seen Higgins's face, that's their champion, when I beat him in a hundred up. Mind you, there was a fearful row when a couple of us were caught down there, we got no end of a wigging. I say, Addy, you're fearfully pretty.' And with that he slid in one easy motion off the table, clasped her round the waist, and planted a kiss on her cheek.

When she had freed herself, he said, 'But Addy, why won't you kiss a fellow? I mean, where's the harm in it?'

She did not quite know where the harm was because it never occurred to her that a young man should not kiss his half-sister, but she knew that if Mrs Prynne happened to come into the room there would be what he called a fearful row. Yet when his arm encircled her, when his hand touched her arm either by accident or intention, such a tide of feeling went through her that she found herself short of breath, and felt sure that she must be blushing. Mrs Prynne was concerned only with the children's doing everything at the right time, going out into the garden, changing their clothes, accompanying her at the piano, being taken down after tea, and she noticed nothing apart from saying that it was good of Master Jack to spend so much time with his sisters, but Grace was another matter.

'Mr Jack, he's sweet on you, Addy, you want to look out.' She liked Grace well enough, but after what she had learned from Mr Casumain she could not regard herself as upon the level of a servant, and she asked rather coldly what Grace meant. 'What I mean is, you don't want to let him have his way with you, otherwise you'll be finding you've got a bun in the oven.'

Adelaide had heard the phrase before, and understood that it meant having a baby, but the process by which that happened was vague to her. It was connected no doubt with the touching against which Patty had warned her, and with a man lying on top of a woman in the way she had been told about, but there must be something more than that. Jack had touched her, was always trying to touch her, but that surely could not mean that she was going to have his baby.

So throughout that summer, which was a long one, with the head gardener shaking his head and saying that they needed rain, must have rain, a summer in which the grass grew brown and two of the streams near the house became mere trickles, she saw Jack two or three times a week, and glimpsed him more often than that as he gave his horse to a groom after riding, or pushed his mother about the grounds in a wheelchair. She was so wrapped up, even on these hot days, that it might have been a shapeless dark bundle of washing he was pushing along, except that he leaned forward occasionally to speak to her, his blond head bent over the chair. Sometimes his brother Robert would take a turn at pushing the chair. Robert was bigger, and looked much older than Jack. His expression was grave, and he cultivated a moustache, side whiskers and a luxuriant beard.

It was when she and Grace took the children down into the garden that Jack made his most determined attempts to do the touching against which Patty had warned her. He would join them, in an apparently casual way, play with the children for a few minutes and then try to get Adelaide away, leaving Elinor and Sophie to play with Grace. Hide-and-seek always provided a good excuse (how long ago it seemed that she had played hide-and-seek with Charley Frim), with Jack taking her hand and leading her into one of several small thickets. There they would crouch together, and he would put his arm round her preliminary to kissing her neck and cheek, until a cry from Elinor would say that they had been seen, or a rising howl from Sophie suggest that it was necessary to come out. There was one occasion, just one, when she let him pull her down to the ground. He lay on top of her breathing quickly, and his fingers fumbled at the buttons of her dress. Very close to her was his neck, and it was so smooth, white and beautiful that she thought she would faint with pleasure when she touched it. But there was something more than pleasure in such encounters, there was the feeling that they removed her from the servants, and were a hint of the world in which she would move as of right in the free air of London.

It was after one of these brief passages that she said she would meet Jack that night in the summerhouse beside the croquet lawn. There were three summerhouses or gazebos in the grounds, all of them with a number of rooms, so that they more truly resembled pavilions. The one beside the croquet lawn was used for storing the mallets and balls, but also had a room from which ladies could watch the game..

She waited until she heard Grace snoring before she put on the dress that she had left ready, opened the nursery door and ran down the stairs to the back door that led into the garden. An almost full moon lighted her way down the path. The summerhouse door stood ajar. She pushed it open, whispered his name, and a dark shape moved towards her. Then she was in his arms, and he was leading her towards the sofa on which she had seen fashionably dressed ladies sitting, laughing, sipping tea.

The sofa was deliciously soft, much softer than her own bed. Jack was on top of her muttering incoherently, his fingers busy. It occurred to her that this was exactly the position against which she had been warned. Perhaps, she thought, it would be all right if she were lying on top of him, and she tried to move her body so that their positions changed. Then his hand touched her breast and the fingers stroking the curve, touching the nipple, gave her such pleasure that she cried out. At the same time his head was bathed in a beautiful light, almost a halo such as she had seen round the heads of angels in church. The light shone upon the glory of his neck, and she put out her hand to stroke it wonderingly, as though it were

something sacred. Then the light moved so that
it shone upon her own face instead of on Jack's
neck, and a voice cried out harshly: 'Enough!' Jack
gasped, and fell or slid to the floor. She looked
up and saw behind the lantern the face of Robert.

The events of the next hours should have been
unforgettable, yet she could never remember anything more than fragments of them. She recalled
a blow on the face, but whether it had been struck
by Robert, or whether she had simply hit her face
in the attempt to get out of the place as quickly
as she could, of that she was unsure. And she remembered Robert saying terrible things to Jack
in an utterly contemptuous voice, although somehow the contempt seemed reserved for her, since
he spoke to Jack as a being of a superior kind
and of her as a person too low to be addressed
directly, except when he told her to get back to
the house. Her shoes had come off in the scuffle
on the sofa, and she did not wait to put them
on but ran across the wet, and as it seemed slightly
scented, grass holding them.

Then back to her room to find Sophie crying
so that she had to light a lamp, Grace waking
and asking why she had outdoor clothes on. And
then—was it five minutes later or half an hour?—
the appearance of Mr Barrow at the door, dread-
fully solemn, not speaking but beckoning her with
his forefinger. Nor did he speak, not a word, while
he led her to a room she had never entered before,
and of which later she could remember nothing.
She recalled only the three figures in it, the Master
standing beside the mantelpiece teetering uneasily from soles to heels, the large hostile figure of
Robert standing behind a big chair, and in the

chair a crumpled lady with a thin grey face, and
faded blue eyes that looked at her consideringly
from top to toe. Then the lady spoke to the Master
in a voice thin and jarring as a saw on metal. It
was typical of the way Adelaide herself was ignored as a person throughout these hours that
the lady did not mention her by name or regard
her, after that one long raking look.

'How could you bring the wretched girl to live
here, when you promised that you would do no
such thing? Look at her, look at the resemblance,
think of the vile gossip that has gone on among
the servants, imagine the ideas that must have
been in the creature's head. That you should have
allowed her to be near my lovely children, to look
after them! Why, the very contact with her will
have meant corruption. And then to set herself
at our own son, so that if it had not been for Robert
she would have entangled the innocent boy in
some way. Oh, it is filthy, filthy. And it is your
responsibility, you brought her into the house. Has
she besotted you also, is there no limit to your
wickedness and folly? I have always known that
you were weak and foolish, but I have never until
now believed you to be evil.'

'You must not upset yourself,' the Master said.
'You know how important the doctor said it was
that you should not upset yourself.' He scratched
the top of his bald head in that slightly comical
way he had. 'I agree that it is all most unfortunate.'

'*Unfortunate.*' The little grey-faced woman got
into the word a scorn such as Adelaide had never
heard.

'But happily nothing has happened, or so I understand from Robert.'

Robert, behind the chair, spoke in a voice deeper than his father's. The gravity of his manner was such that he might have been the parent, and the Master an erring son. 'I had seen Jack attach himself to the girl—yes, Mother, there must be no flinching from it, he pursued her like some farmyard animal. Then I heard him leave his room tonight, saw him in the garden and thought it right to follow him. If I had not done so—' He shook his head to show what might have followed.

'But nothing happened,' the Master said almost perkily. 'And arrangements are all in hand for Blanche to leave, she is going quite away from here to a man Casumain knows, he has the whole affair in hand. Blanche is quite agreeable, ain't you, Blanche?'

The invitation to speak may have been kindly meant, and she would have liked to say that she loved Jack, or at least that he was the most beautiful person she had ever seen, and also that she did not know what wrong she had done. If she had been alone with the Master she might have said such things, and might have asked also whether Jack too had not done wrong and how he was to be punished, but in the presence of the little grey woman she was unable to do more than whisper 'Yes.'

'She must go tonight,' the woman said. 'She must not sleep in this house another night.'

At this Robert expostulated, telling his mother that what she asked was not decent or reasonable. It was settled between them that she should leave on the following day. Everything was done without reference to her, and without the woman looking at her. She felt the injustice of it but what

she felt most keenly of all, after the bell had been
rung for Mr Barrow to lead her away, was that
the Master had never spoken a word in her de-
fense. She remembered what Mr Casumain had
said, that the Master was very agreeable but that
he was not a serious person.

What happened after that bore no correspondence to anything in the life she had known. A
trunk appeared from somewhere, and into it she
packed her few possessions under the eyes of
Grace, and in the presence of the children. Mrs
Prynne looked in once, seemed about to say something, then thought better of it and went out. John
came in, said with a smirk that he heard she was
leaving, asked if he could help, and tried to put
an arm round her. Grace kept repeating that she
had told her to watch out, and that it was an awful
thing to happen, so that Adelaide felt bound to
reply that she did not mind in the least, and that
she was going to a house in London where she
would have a great deal more freedom and be
able to see anybody she liked, anybody at all. At
that Grace shook her head in wonderment, and
Sophie began to cry.

Then she was escorted by Mr Barrow, looking
as solemn as if he were presiding over the sentencing to death of Richard Careless, to the victoria
that would take her to the railway station. She
recognized the driver as a man she had seen at
the Pargoes' cottage, and he must have known
her, but he made no sign of doing so. Her trunk
was put up beside him, Mr Barrow held open the
door of the victoria and handed her in, and then
to her surprise shook her hand.

'I hope that the future will treat you kindly,

Adelaide,' he said. She felt the pressure of something other than his hand. 'I have been asked to give you this.' Then he closed the door, and they were away. When she looked to see what had been given her it was to find a small leather purse containing ten golden sovereigns. She had no doubt that they came from the Master.

Then there was the train. Had she really travelled in a train in the time that she could hardly remember? At any rate she was in one now, a chugging steaming monster, that shrieked and stopped and shrieked again like a human being when it restarted. She sat in a carriage with four other passengers at first, but the train stopped often, people got in and out, and they talked so much and there were so many of them that she began to feel tired and closed her eyes, listening to the train wheels that seemed to say: 'Left the Hall for *ever*, left the Hall for *ever*.' Then the rhythm changed and the wheels said 'Adelaide *Blanche* de la Tremoille' over and over. Listening to this rhythm, she must have fallen asleep. When she opened her eyes the train had come to its terminus in London. There were people rushing about everywhere, more people than she had ever seen and then there, as he had told her he would be, was Mr Casumain coming along the platform towards her, monocle dangling and a walking stick in his hand. He did not speak, except to greet her, until he had summoned up a porter and a cab and they were clip-clopping through the London streets. Then he screwed in his monocle, and contemplated her with what might have been repressed amusement.

'A devilish awkward scrape you've got yourself

into, Adelaide, my girl. There's been a fine flurry, with telegrams going back and forth, saying kindly do this and please arrange that. From what I hear you've been a minx.'

'My name is Blanche,' she said, for she had determined that she would be known by her mother's name.

'Not in Mr Mitten's house. They have been told you are Adelaide.' He gave her one of his sharp looks—although it was difficult for him to give anything but sharp looks when his features seemed composed of cutting edges. 'If you are wise you won't mention matters related to our last conversation. Mrs Mitten has been told nothing of such things, she knows only that you are an orphan, the niece of an old retainer, and that the Master in the goodness of his heart wished to place you in a respectable household. If you are wise you will say nothing of the other story.'

'But the other story, as you call it, is the truth.'

'It is not always advisable to present the truth in what might be called its raw state. Sometimes a coat of varnish over it makes the truth much more acceptable. You must learn the way of the world, Adelaide, which is that the most comfortable thing is to do what is expected of you.' He put his chin on his stick and looked at her. 'You do not agree with me?'

'I do not know. But at Mr Mitten's house I shall have freedom? And receive an education?'

'I should think so.' They were rattling over cobbles, and he removed his chin from his stick. 'Although I have found that the best education is obtained from life itself. We are nearly there.'

They pulled up in a narrow street, before a house that seemed to her—but then she was accus-

tomed to the Hall—small and mean. She saw also
that there was no green anywhere, nothing but
buildings all around and paving stones under the
feet. The door was opened by a girl in cap and
apron, and they were taken to a drawing-room
that was much smaller than the Oval Room and
the Master's study, and that seemed crammed to
overflowing with furniture, photographs and
trinkets. There were knick-knacks on the mantelpiece, shelves containing china vases and memen-
toes, and family photographs in silver frames
about everywhere. Every possible inch of wall
space had been covered with pictures, ornamental
plates and dishes, which were secured to the wall
by metal hooks. Mr Casumain sat down in one
of the chairs, made a gesture to indicate that Adelaide should sit in another, put in his monocle,
looked around, and then dropped the monocle
with one of his brief cutting smiles that might
have signified anything. He rose when Mrs Mitten
entered the room, and Adelaide stood up too.

Mrs Mitten did not in the least resemble the
ladies she had seen arriving at the Hall. She was
dark, thin and tall, and everything about her
seemed to be under some sort of strain. Her pat-
terned brown dress fitted very tightly, her hair
was pulled up on to the top of her head and there
appeared to have been forced into an unnatural
form from which it was trying hard to escape,
and she walked in a manner that suggested the
wearing of very tight shoes. Her hand gripped
the reticule she carried, so that her knuckles
showed white. When she spoke the words fell rapidly one after another, as though she were in a
great hurry.

'Mr Casumain, how do you do? We have met

before, have we not? And this is the girl you wish to place.'

Mr Casumain offered the sketch of a bow. 'I think Mr Mitten may have told you of the circumstances in which Adelaide finds herself.'

'Parents dead, and now aunt who was looking after her dead too. Most unfortunate.' She spoke disapprovingly, as though the lack of parents and aunt were Adelaide's fault rather than her misfortune. 'And the girl has worked in a nursery, I am told.'

'That is so.' Mr Casumain mentioned the Master's name, and continued. 'Only unforeseen circumstances of an unhappy kind—I am sure that I need not enter into details with a lady of your perceptions, Mrs Mitten—could have induced the family to part with Adelaide, and as you see they were concerned to find her another place.' Adelaide recognized this as an example of what Mr Casumain had called varnishing the truth. Mrs Mitten opened her reticule and snapped it shut again without taking anything from it.

'Very well. These will be your duties, Adelaide. I like everything run by the clock. A minute late is a minute wasted. Five-thirty you get up. Light nursery fires, clean fireguard. Seven o'clock call Mrs Waters. Breakfast for children at eight. At ten take out prams, return at twelve-thirty sharp. No loitering, no escorts or followers. Luncheon at one, afternoon walk, tea at four. Water carried upstairs for baths at six. Washing and ironing in your own time. Bed at nine-thirty. No gossiping with other servants, that I will not have. Prayers before retiring, and they must be said in a proper frame of mind. Gossip breeds wrong thoughts.

Wages twenty pounds a year, as much as any employer in London.'

Adelaide looked at Mr Casumain, but he was staring fixedly across the room at a willow-pattern plate on the wall.

'May I ask, ma'am—'

She heard the reticule snap again. 'Well?'

'I can read and write, but I lack education. Shall I have the chance of learning figures? And perhaps something about history? And other languages?'

Whatever Mrs Mitten might have been inclined to say in reply was checked by Mr Casumain's sudden storm of coughing. He drew out his handkerchief and put it before his mouth, but the paroxysm continued. Mrs Mitten rang for a housemaid and told her to bring a glass of water, but before it arrived Mr Casumain was on his feet saying that he had an appointment, and rejecting Mrs Mitten's half-hearted offer of refreshment but saying that there were a few words he would like to speak to her in private. The maid who had brought the water was told to show Adelaide up to the nursery. Before she left the room Mr Casumain took her by the hand, and said that he was sure she would do very well providing she remembered his advice.

She was taken to the nursery, which resembled the nursery at the Hall except that the rooms were smaller, and the children more numerous. Mrs Mitten had seemed old to Adelaide, but still she was young enough to have four children, of whom the eldest was six years old. There were two boys and two girls, and the youngest child was a boy of eight months. Mrs Waters was the head nurse or nanny, and there was another nursemaid, an

Irish girl named Eileen whose brogue was so strong that Adelaide found it hard to distinguish one word in three.

In every way, as she quickly discovered, life was harder than it had been at the Hall. The food was inferior in quality, badly cooked, and often came from the kitchen half-cold. The work took more time because there were more children, and the only alleviations of the dismal routine were the walks to nearby Holland Park. The Mittens lived in an unfashionable part of Kensington, and although the streets leading to the Park were respectable enough, there were no elegant gentlemen or finely dressed ladies to be seen in them. She went to the Park generally with Eileen, sometimes with Mrs Waters, and occasionally young men came up and spoke to them while the children were playing on the grass and the nursemaids and nannies sat on nearby benches with their prams. Most of them, however, were young men of the labouring class and Adelaide did not enter into conversation with them. She remembered that her name was Adelaide Blanche de la Tremoille, and she retained that vision of her own future life as she had seen it in the Oval Room, a vision of fine clothes and dinner-parties, and romantic moonlight evenings on which words of love were whispered. The vision was one of the few consolations she had, as days of drudgery stretched out into weeks, and weeks into months.

She saw little of Mr Mitten. Like his wife he was tall and thin, and he had an air of melancholy as though he were suffering from an incurable but not quickly fatal disease, so that he saw nothing but years of grief ahead. His very step was a weary one, and he seemed always to be carrying about bundles of papers, which were no doubt connected with his occupation as a solicitor. For some weeks Adelaide hoped, and almost expected, that something would be said about furthering her education, and when nothing happened she spoke to Mrs Mitten. The Mittens, of course, kept only a small fraction of the staff employed at the Hall, but still there was a housekeeper, and in order to obtain an audience with Mrs Mitten Adelaide had to speak to Mrs Waters, who in turn spoke to the housekeeper, who conveyed the request to her employer. So it came about that early one evening, after the children had been put to bed, she found herself in the cluttered drawing-room. Mrs Mitten, whose hands were always busy, was working at some embroidery on a frame, and she did not cease while she heard what Adelaide had to say, nor when she replied.

'There are books in the nursery. You may read them in your spare time. I make no objection.'

'But those are children's books, ma'am. I understood that I should be allowed to improve my knowledge.'

Mrs Mitten's fingers moved faster. 'Are you idle, girl? Nothing to do? If so I will speak to Mrs Waters.'

'I have enough to do. But I was promised—'

'Promised, miss? By whom? Mr Casumain, I suppose. But he is not your employer.'

At this moment, as it proved fortunately for Adelaide, Mr Mitten entered the room. He had evidently just returned from his office, and he was holding a sheaf of papers done up with pink ribbon. He hesitated when he saw his wife and Adelaide, but Mrs Mitten spoke to him. 'Adelaide tells me some tale about an arrangement by which she should have the chance of what she calls improving her knowledge. She says that Mr Casumain spoke of it, but I told her that he is not her employer. It is we who pay her wages, is that not correct?'

'That is correct.' Mr Mitten made his way to a chair, lowered himself into it and placed the papers on his knee, actions which seemed to involve infinite effort on his part. 'But perhaps it should be said that some mention of this was made in my discussions with Mr Casumain.'

'*Discussions*, what discussions? I understood that we were obliging Mr Casumain by taking the girl into our home. If you have made some arrangement behind my back which affects my running of the household I could not consent to it, Mr Mitten. I have enough difficulties at present, and if you do not approve of my arrangements I should have to relinquish all attempts to run household affairs. Goodness knows I should be happy to be relieved of the burden. Perhaps you would care to be responsible for it yourself.' While these words were spoken her fingers did not cease to move at the frame.

During the speech Mr Mitten drooped lower in his chair, until by the end of it he resembled a question mark. He made one or two feeble attempts at interjection, saying 'My dear' and 'If you please,' without any success in stopping the flow. When she had done he spoke in a voice that was exceptionally low and dismal even for him.

'If you will do me the kindness of permitting me to explain—'

'Very well. Explain.'

'Mr Casumain is, as you know, a valued client.

It is true that he made some mention of Adelaide—ah—improving herself, perhaps by attending classes of some kind—'

'And you said nothing of this to me, Mr Mitten? You did not tell me that the girl expected to be a lady of leisure.'

'If you will allow me to finish? I replied that the desire for such self-improvement is no doubt admirable, and that we would do whatever was possible to help, but that anything of the kind would have to fit in with your household arrangements. "And Mrs Mitten's arrangements are run to the minute," I told him. "Everything is run quite perfectly to time, and I think it unlikely that time can be spared for the enterprises you suggest, laudable though they no doubt are." Anything of the kind must be done, I said, in Adelaide's own time and not in Mrs Mitten's.'

In the course of saying all this Mr Mitten attained for a sentence or two something almost resembling liveliness, but by the end he had distinctly drooped again, and his voice had taken on its customary dispirited tone. When he had done there was silence. Then Mrs Mitten said, 'You may go, Adelaide.'

While standing in front of them, however, Adelaide had felt indignation rising in her. There was no doubt that she had been betrayed, or at least deceived, by Mr Casumain, but he had at least mentioned her desire for education, and Mr Mitten had given a qualified promise to help. And then of course there also moved in her the knowledge that she was of high birth, and that Mr Mitten was not much more than a tradesman. She addressed him rather than his wife.

'I beg your pardon. May I say something?' There

was no positive denial. 'Mr Casumain promised that I should be educated, and that I should have free time. I do not think it is fair that I should be refused.'

At this Mrs Mitten positively stopped work on her embroidery. She spoke.

'You are impertinent. I cannot keep an impertinent girl in my house.'

Mr Mitten's head rose. 'Mrs Mitten, let us not be hasty. There is Mr Casumain to consider.'

'And what, pray, has he to do with my dismissal of a nursemaid?'

Her husband said quietly, 'Perhaps you will tell Adelaide that she may retire to her quarters, and that we will send for her again.'

She returned to the nursery, and half an hour passed before she was summoned again to the drawing-room, where she found Mrs Mitten alone. That lady told her that Mr Mitten, out of the extreme kindness of his heart, had said that she might be relieved of her duties and permitted to use his library on Wednesday afternoon each week. She could read the books on the shelves, but must not take them away. Mrs Mitten ended:

'I can only hope you will profit from what I feel myself to be Mr Mitten's foolish good nature, and that it will not give you ideas above your station in life. You may go to the library at two o'clock after luncheon, and you will leave at six. I will give the necessary instructions to Mrs Waters. I shall be watching your work carefully, and I wish to hear no more of this stuff about education. Reading and writing is quite enough, indeed perhaps too much, for a girl in your position.'

Mr Casumain's name, then, had obtained some

concession after all, and from that time on she
went to Mr Mitten's study every Wednesday afternoon, sat at a little side table away from his paper-
cluttered desk, and took her pick of the books.
They were mostly dry works connected with the
law, but there was a set of shelves containing a
number of medical works, including one called
The Family Doctor, which she read from cover
to cover in the hope of finding out more about
the birth of children. What she learned, however,
did not seem to make the process much clearer.
There were also books about religion, which she
read although she often found them confusing.
All in all, the library was not much help to her
education.

If only she could write to Mr Casumain she
would tell him this, but she lacked an address.
She had been using the library for some time before it occurred to her that it might be among
the papers on the desk. Curiosity had moved her
to glance at the inch-thick pile of foolscap documents on the desk, but they concerned legal cases,
and the language in them was unintelligible.
There were also, however, books in various pi-
geonholes, and one of them contained the ad-
dresses of what were perhaps Mr Mitten's clients.
Among them was that of Mr Casumain. He lived,
or perhaps it was only an office, at an address in
the City.

Now that she had the address, what could she
do with it? She could write to him, but what good
would that do? She saw clearly enough that she
had been placed with the Mittens to get her out
of the way. She could go to see him, but she did
not know how long it would take or whether he

would be there, and since Mrs Mitten gave her
servants no free time she would certainly be
missed. Or she could leave this drudgery for good,
find a room, and write from there to Mr Casumain,
telling him that she insisted on receiving the education that had been promised her.

This was obviously the most attractive possibility, but the difficulty in carrying out such an idea
lay in the fact that she knew nobody in London.
She might have done nothing at all, but for a conversation she had with Bessie, one of the nursemaids whom she met in the Park. Bessie was a
great talker, particularly about her elder brother
who had gone to work as salesman for a firm of
stationers at a place near London called Kingston,
where he was doing very well.

'You should see him when he's out calling on
customers,' Bessie said. 'I wouldn't have known
our Ernie, he looked such a swell. He's a real gent
now. And you should see the place he lives, ever
so nice it is.' Adelaide asked if he had a room.
'Not just a room, nor it isn't one of those new
flats either. It's what they call an apartment with
service, that means someone comes in and cleans
it, does the washing and all that. And you eat your
meals with the family that lives there, breakfast
and supper. They calls it dinner, not supper, just
like real toffs. Suits Ernie, 'cause of course he's
single. You'll give it up when you're married, I
says to him, and he says, I'm not getting spliced,
no fear.'

Adelaide listened and said little, but asked questions. She learned that you could get to Kingston
by the railway, and Bessie also told her the address, which was Glenfield Gardens, Kingston.

The cost of staying there would be thirty shillings a week. She counted up her savings. In addition to the ten sovereigns given her when she left the Hall, she had another seventeen pounds, the rewards of her service there and at the Mittens. The money would last quite long enough for her to decide what to do next. She was conscious of the tremendous step she was taking, but still she determined to do it.

Bessie also told her the name of the man who owned the house in Glenfield Gardens. It was Charles Bartlett.

'Dear me,' Mr Casumain said. 'You leave me at a loss for words, Adelaide, quite at a loss for words.'

'My name is Blanche,' she said. They were in the sitting-room of her apartment in Glenfield Gardens, a pleasant room with a view of the lawns which sloped gently down to the Thames.

'So it is. Upon reflection it is perhaps a pity that you were ever told of the fact. It seems to have given you hopes that life is unlikely to fulfil.'

'I do not understand you,' she said with composure.

Mr Casumain sighed a little. He was wearing a suit in a rather loud herringbone pattern, perhaps because he was not in town but visiting one of London's outer suburbs, perhaps because it was an unusually fine day in early spring. His monocle looked a little incongruous with such clothes. Adelaide herself wore a simple blue dress that she had bought to celebrate her freedom from the Mittens.

'I think you have still in mind the thought that the Master might acknowledge you, and that you will return to the Hall. That is not possible.'

'If one day he should be free—'

'He is free. His wife died shortly after you left.'

'But then—'

'The Master intends to marry again. The marriage is arranged, it will take place this year. You must accept that he will never acknowledge you as his daughter.' She made no reply to that, and he considered her as she sat on the other side of the room. She was small and almost dainty, not a beauty and certainly not pretty with her jet black hair, thick brows and strongly marked features. Yet there was something exotic about her gestures, and the way she held her head, it might even be said something aristocratic. Her voice had a faintly foreign intonation in speaking certain words, although of course her English was perfect. Her black eyes were large and lustrous, her chin determined. Now that she no longer wore a servant's uniform she had, no doubt about it, a certain charm. Mr Casumain knew what had to be done, but he wished to do it as gently as possible. When he said that he wished she had not left the Mittens she flared up.

'It was drudgery there, drudgery. I was alone, and you had left me with no way of reaching you. I had to search among his papers for your address. You deserted me, quite deliberately you deserted me.'

'When you had the address you could have written.'

'Would you have come to see me? I do not believe it. Anyway—' she shrugged—'I left that drudgery. I came here.'

'Very pleasant. But you will not be able to stay here long.'

'I expect you to help me.'

'Ah.' Mr Casumain dropped his eyeglass, and looked at her with his cutting smile.

'I was promised an education.'

'You must listen to me, and listen carefully. The Master wishes all that is best for you. I thought that the Mittens would be more helpful to you than they were—'

'Helpful,' she said derisively.

'Please do not interrupt me. The Master wishes to see you settled in life. He is willing to provide money for that end. But if money is provided there must be no more running away, no more complaints.'

'The money will be for my education?'

'That is so.'

'I ask nothing more.' She flung her arms wide. 'Afterwards he may forget that Adelaide Blanche de la Tremoille ever existed.'

'There is a condition attached. Supposing that you receive this famous education, and within six months of its end you are writing to me to say that you are desperate, starving and so on? Useless to tell me that this would never happen, it might well do so. I said that the Master wished to see you settled. There is only one way of making sure of that. You must be married.'

She stared at him. 'And who is to be my husband?'

'He will be chosen by me. With your approval.'

'Oh, that is very kind. What if I should say no to the gentleman of your choice?'

'If I thought you did so unreasonably I should advise the Master accordingly. I think that he could not then be expected to provide for you further, certainly I should advise him against it.'

'You are saying that I must be married to some-body you choose. Tell me this. Will my husband be a gentleman? I have a right, surely, to expect that.'

Mr Casumain was not a susceptible man, but the gaze of those large dark eyes almost undid him. He found it better to look away from her as he spoke the next, necessary words.

'I am afraid that is not possible. You have no family who can be acknowledged, and that would be indispensable for the kind of marriage you have in mind. And your station in life is not such that you would be likely to meet a gentleman on equal terms. I shall try to ensure that your husband is a good and honest man, one to whom the money that will come as your dowry is important. When you have married him, the Master will feel that he has done his best to help you.'

'So I am to be given away, with a money prize for the man who takes me.' She stood up. 'Very well. Please leave me now.'

He got up too. He felt that he had mishandled the interview, although he did not see in what other way he could have faced her with the facts. 'You have not told me whether you find the idea acceptable.'

'Acceptable? What choice is there? You may marry me to anybody you wish, young or old, bachelor or widower, with one leg or two, a squint or a humpback, I do not care. Just one thing I insist on. Before married life begins he must allow me to complete my education.'

He began to say something in protest, but she made it unmistakably clear that she wished him to leave. For a girl who was practically penniless

her attitude was, he thought, wonderfully cool.
He prided himself upon his dispassionateness, and
in a dispassionate way he admired her, yet there
was an intensity about her that made him uncomfortable.

Mr Charles Bartlett awaited him in the parlour.
He was, as Mr Casumain had discovered by dis-
creet enquiry, the son of a jobbing builder, an
up-and-coming young man who was making his
way in the world. He had begun well by marrying
a widow who had come to the estate agent's where
he worked to ask for advice on managing her
property, and had gone on to manage it himself
by dividing the large house she owned into two
parts, one for family living and the other for letting as service apartments. He had apparently
worked this so well that he was now launching
out into other property, to be used for the same
purpose.

Mr Casumain did not care for up-and-coming
young men, believing as he did that both men
and women should remain in the stations of life
to which God had called them, but he was aware
that they had their uses. He greeted Mr Bartlett
in a way that measured the social distance between them, yet was polite and even genial.
Charles Bartlett said that he hoped Miss de la
Tremoille was happy with her rooms. It was a
privilege to have a real lady in his establishment,
and if there was anything he could do to be of
assistance at any time, Miss de la Tremoille had
only to call on him. All this was said with an air
of hand-washing unction that Mr Casumain noted
with contempt and amusement, but he thanked
Mr Bartlett and said that Miss de la Tremoille

seemed very happy with her accommodation. Asked whether she would be staying long, he replied that her plans were not yet settled.

At that moment there came a tap at the door, and a young man opened it. He was obviously a brother to Charles, with the same blue eyes and gingery hair and beard, but he was broader and stockier. When he said 'Beg pardon, Charles, I didn't know you were occupied,' Mr Casumain recognized also that his speech was more common than his brother's, lacking Charles's thin veneer of gentility.

'Mr Casumain, may I introduce my brother Edwin.' Charles Bartlett accompanied the words with a slight hand-washing gesture. Mr Casumain asked whether Mr Edwin Bartlett also lived there, and the young man laughed heartily.

'Oh no, sir, just on a visit for the day. I've got a grocery shop to look after, and it doesn't lie in this part of the world, it's at Herne Hill.'

Mr Casumain repeated the name, wondering just where Herne Hill might be. Then he recalled that it was one of the southern suburbs, the kind of place one never visited.

'Edwin went in as assistant behind the counter, but it's Baxter and Bartlett now,' Charles said. 'And he's expanded the business.' Expansion, Mr Casumain thought, that's the thing nowadays. 'I'm expanding too, bought another couple of houses nearby, and when they're done up they'll be tip-top apartments I can tell you, places fit for the Queen herself to stay in.'

'Most enterprising. And are you also starting up new branches, Mr Bartlett?'

Edwin laughed again, and as he did so Mr Casumain received two contradictory impressions. One was of an unaffected gaiety and vitality, and the other was that the laugh showed a mouthful of teeth, some of which looked black and decayed. 'A chance would be a fine thing, sir. Baxter and I, we'd like to do it, and I've got all sorts of plans. It's just the capital that's lacking.'

Mr Casumain said casually, 'No doubt your wife is a help to you in your business.'

'Would be if I had one, I dare say. Charlie's always telling me I ought to get spliced. Plenty of time I say, I'm waiting for Miss Right to turn up. Till she does, many thanks, but I'll stay single. See more of the world that way.'

Mr Casumain got up to leave, said that in future Miss de la Tremoille's bills might be sent to him, and asked whether Mr Edwin Bartlett had met the young lady. This also was casually said, but an enquiring look in Charles Bartlett's eye told Mr Casumain that he sensed something behind the question. Edwin answered heartily that he had met the young lady, and she seemed delightful.

With that Mr Casumain took his departure. On his way back to his place of business he pondered whether it was really possible that a girl like Adelaide should marry a grocer, however respectable. By the time the journey was completed, he had decided that it was. On the following day he wrote a letter to Edwin Bartlett, which he sent care of his brother Charles, and another letter to Adelaide.

He received a note from her in return. It consisted of two words and her signature. The words were 'I agree'. The other letter brought an astonished Edwin Bartlett to his offices. The young man—he proved to be twenty-nine, but could have passed for five years younger—kept repeating that he could not understand what was behind the remarkable proposal in the letter.

'It is not necessary that you should understand every detail,' Mr Casumain said patiently. 'It is sufficient that you should know it is necessary for Miss de la Tremoille to marry—'

'I beg your pardon.' Mr Casumain frowned. He did not care to be interrupted. 'But is it possible that, I don't know how to put it—'

'Miss de la Tremoille is not *enceinte*. Nor has she a lover. She is a virgin.'

'Then I'll be damned if I understand it,' Bartlett said. His naturally ruddy colour turned to brick red.

Mr Casumain's manner became chilly. The angles of his face grew even sharper than usual, the lips almost disappeared. 'I must ask you to moderate your language. The proposal seems to me quite straightforward.'

'You think so? I'm to be married, and then not live with my wife, she's not to be my wife, for how long is it, two years? Seems a funny kind of marriage to me. You say she wants to complete her education. I'm not an educated man myself, wish I was, though I had schooling up to twelve, but what I say is, if you get married you get married, and husband and wife should be together.'

'Remember that she is very young, only nineteen.'

'Lots of women bringing up a family by that time.' Really, Mr Casumain thought, he is a deplorably coarse and vulgar man. 'Then you say my family's not to know till it's happened. Father won't like that, something hole-and-corner about it. Does she like dogs?'

'I beg your pardon?'

'I breed St Bernards, and it would help if she liked dogs.'

'I am afraid I have no idea.' That the grocer might ask questions and try to make conditions had not occurred to Mr Casumain. 'I would remind you that the material benefits offered are considerable. They should be of great help to you in extending your business.'

'Oh, I understand *that*, all right. Getting paid for taking her on, ain't that so? Nothing *wrong* with her, I suppose; sound in wind and limb, is she?' Mr Casumain felt a fleeting pity for Blanche, or Adelaide, but suppressed it. 'Very well then, it's a bargain. Here's my hand on it.'

They shook hands, and then Mr Casumain said drily that he would also like Mr Bartlett to read the document he had drawn up, and then sign it. So it was settled.

On April 6th, 1875, Thomas Edwin Bartlett, who gave his age as 'Full' and his occupation as 'Grocer', was married to Adelaide de la Tremoille de Thouars de Escury, a spinster, the ceremony being conducted by the Reverend W. Wilks. Mr Casumain did not attend, but one of his clerks did so and signed the register as a witness. The bride and groom then departed to Miss Dodd's finishing school at Stoke Newington, where a place had been booked for the bride to attend as a student. Edwin kissed her chastely upon the cheek, and then left to explain to his family that he was now a married man, and was also much richer than he had been before he signed the register.

AFTERWARDS (II)

So much to be thought of, so much to be done. Yet the most important thing of all (this too Madame Blavatsky had said at their all-too-brief meeting) was not *doing* but *being*. If you attained a true state of being, a state that fitted your personality, then the shape of all that happened must be not only beneficent but also beautiful. It was without fear that she climbed a further flight of stairs after waking Alice, knocked on the door of Mr Doggett the landlord of the house, and asked him to come down because she feared that her husband was dead.

He came down with his hair awry, wearing a blue dressing-gown. They had never spoken before, but she saw from his first action, which was to look at the clock, that he was a precise, fussy man.

'Ten past four, Mrs Bartlett, to the minute. Always like to make a note of time on any important occasion, learnt the value of it in my work.' His work? She had momentarily forgotten that he was a local Registrar of Births and Deaths. The fire had flared up and he stood before it for a few seconds warming his hands, before going round to the bed. She followed him and stood watching as he felt for the heart, then asked what he thought.

'I don't *think*, Mrs Bartlett, I know that your husband is dead. Two or three hours ago, I should say. He is quite cold. Were you asleep?'

'Yes, I had fallen asleep with my hand round his foot.' When he stared, she said, 'He liked me to hold his foot through the clothes, said it helped him to sleep. Then I woke with a pain in my arm. He was lying turned away from me, and I moved him back. And I closed his eyes. I truly knew that he was dead, I asked only because I hoped—'

'Of course, I understand.' His head was raised, he was sniffing. 'There is some sort of smell, I can't place it.'

'Perhaps the brandy. I tried to give him some.'

She indicated the wineglass, and Doggett picked it up. 'I don't know if it comes from this glass. Smells like paregoric. Or ether.'

He stood looking down at the bed, at the wine-glass, at the central table which had tumblers on it, together with a glass water jug and a bottle containing carbonate of soda. He might have been making an inventory of the room. All this, she knew, had to be borne, and so had the arrival of nosy little Mrs Doggett, who asked whether she had given her husband the drops she had been talking about earlier, to which she replied that she had given him nothing.

This is New Year's Day, she thought, and the start of a new life.

She could feel that they were not friends as he still stood looking round the room, and Mrs Doggett asked when she had made up the fire, adding meaningfully that it had burned up remarkably in a very little time. Neither gave any expression of sorrow at Edwin's death. She did not fear them, but still she was pleased by the arrival of Dr Leach, young round-faced portentous Dr Leach, who entered with a rush, came

straight to her, took her hands and said, 'Mrs Bartlett, my dear Mrs Bartlett.'

She did not resist, she allowed her hands to be
encased in his fleshy ones, while landlord Doggett
continued to make his mental inventory, and his
wife stood watching the scene with an air of suspicion. It was a comfort to know that in whatever
lay ahead, Dr Leach would be on her side.

He went round to the bed, and was there for
what seemed a long time. Mrs Doggett approached.

'Such a shock, Mrs Bartlett. And him so much
better last night, so cheerful, saying he'd like a
haddock for breakfast. I'm quite faint myself with
thinking of it. Why don't you come down to the
kitchen, and I'll make us both a pot of tea?'

She shook her head, and landlord Doggett
joined in. 'Might be better, Mrs Bartlett. There
are painful duties to be performed, as I well know.
I'll stay to help the doctor, you go down with the
wife.'

'I shall stay here with my husband. That is my
place.'

She spoke the words without emphasis, but Mrs
Doggett went downstairs. Her husband stayed,
and did not speak to Adelaide again. As she stood
there, almost in the middle of the room, she had
the strange sensation of seeing the room and its
contents as though she were outside and above
it, in the disembodied state of which Madame Blavatsky had written. Or perhaps she saw it like a
stage set, the little bed with its head to the wall
in the shallow alcove between window and mantelpiece, the vases on the mantelpiece, two large
and two small, the clock between them, the photo-

graphs of Edwin and of Georgius Rex. The piano
had been placed, since Edwin's illness, to conceal
the bed from the rest of the room.

Then there was the central table beside which
she stood, and which indeed she touched now as
though to make sure of her own presence there,
the table that had the remains of supper on it,
and the brandy bottle, the carbonate of soda, the
jug and glasses. Only the gas lights near the bed
had been turned on, and beyond in semi-darkness
lay the glass-fronted case with her books in it, a
whatnot with ornaments on the shelves, the sofa
placed almost against the folding doors that led
to the inner room. She saw these things clearly
but as though she were not there, not part of them.
She was acutely aware of sounds, the gas hissing,
the fire crackling, the clock ticking. She started
at the sound of the doctor's voice.

'Do you know that when the maid came round
I hardly believed her, I thought it was another
of her notions. But you must be brave, Mrs Bartlett, your husband is dead.' She whispered *yes*.
'Did you try to give him brandy? There is damp
on his nightshirt and chest.'

'Yes,' she said again. 'But he could not drink.
That was when I knew.'

Doggett coughed. 'Can I be of assistance, doctor?'

'I don't think so. What had you in mind?'

'I'm the local Registrar, often have to deal with
this kind of thing. Thought you might like help
in getting him straight. Once rigor has set in it
can be the devil of a job.'

'I am well aware of that. But—very well.' They
went round to the bed, and curiosity impelled

her to watch as the dropped jaw was tied up and
the legs straightened and tied together.

'He'll be more comfortable now,' Doggett said,
as though Edwin were alive. She wanted to say
that Edwin's spirit had departed to whatever Nir-
vana awaited him, and that only clay was left,
but she forbore. 'I'll be down below if needed,'
Doggett said, and went. She was alone with Dr
Leach, and with that capacity she had for going
straight to the heart of a matter, she asked the
vital question.

'What did he die of?'

'I am not sure.' He went round the room, smelling the glasses that had been used. 'This was the
brandy you tried to give him?'

'Yes.'

'I can't account for it, not at all. He mentioned
that he was friendly with a wholesale chemist,
Mr Morton I believe. Could he have got poison
from him?'

'I am sure he has not.'

'It is not prussic acid, I should distinguish the
smell. Digitalis perhaps, one of the alkaloids? Did
he have anything like that in his possession?'

'I do not know what they are, but he could have
had no poison without my knowing it.'

'Strange.' He noticed the little bottle of chlorodyne that stood on the mantelpiece. 'What is this
doing here?'

'Edwin used to rinse his mouth with it at night.
He said it helped to ease the pain after having
so many teeth out.'

'Rinse his mouth.' Dr Leach raised his plump
hands. 'He must have swallowed some, that is the
explanation.'

'I am sure he did not swallow it.'

'If he rinsed his mouth and spat it out, then it must be—' He knelt, pulled the chamber pot from beneath the bed and put it back again. 'Nothing. You understand, chlorodyne is a dangerous substance. It contains one in eight of pure chloroform.'

'But doctor, I don't think it is possible. Edwin used a little only, he never put much into his mouth, only rubbed his gums.'

'Certainly chlorodyne has a distinctive smell, and I do not perceive it. But if he used only a little, it cannot be responsible.' He looked hard at her, then shyly down at the carpet. 'There is nothing more you wish to tell me?'

'I don't understand. Of what kind?'

'He seemed to me a strange man. He had fancies. There was no quarrel?'

'Nothing at all. He went to sleep while I held his foot. He liked that.'

'That is what I mean by his being a strange man, that and other things. I have to tell you, Mrs Bartlett, that since I cannot explain his death there must be a post-mortem.'

'Does that mean an inquest?'

He patted her hand. 'It means what I said. A post-mortem does not necessarily imply an inquest. This is a case I should report to the coroner, but I shall not do so because I have no doubt, no doubt at all, of the death being natural. It is simply that, on making this cursory examination, I cannot explain it.' Dr Leach's round face was almost preternaturally solemn. 'I shall not undertake the post-mortem myself, I shall ask Dr Green the pathologist.'

'As soon as possible, please. Can it be done to-day?'

He looked startled instead of solemn. 'I think not today. Possibly tomorrow. To resume. The pathologist will find the cause of death, and a certificate will be issued. My own belief is that we shall find death was caused by the rupture of some vessel, possibly in the brain, but we must await the pathologist's verdict.'

'You understand why I should like to avoid an inquest. The publicity.'

'Of course I understand. This has been a terrible shock. If I may say so, Mrs Bartlett, I admire your courage more than I can say.'

'I do not show my feelings easily.'

'And your devotion to your husband, I admire that also. Nobody could have had a more faithful nurse, day and night. Now I think you should sleep. I can give you—'

She said almost reproachfully, 'Doctor, it is nearly half past five in the morning, almost daylight. There are things to be done, so many things. Do you think that I can possibly sleep?'

'It was thoughtless of me. Forgive me.' She gave him a brief smile of forgiveness. 'I shall write a prescription to be taken tonight. You must have rest, it is essential. And be assured, Mrs Bartlett, that if I can help in any way you may call on me. I must leave now, but I shall be back very soon.'

With that he was gone. Things had not happened as she expected. She had not thought that Dr Leach, who admired her and was her friend, would hesitate in giving a death certificate. Edwin had been ill, he had died, and the doctor had said he felt no doubt about the death being natural, so why not give a certificate? But no doubt these were rules and regulations, things she had never understood, and they must be observed. In the meantime, as she had said, there were people to be told, not all of them her friends. Telegrams to be sent: one to her particular enemy, the Old Man.

PART TWO
The Wife

CHAPTER 1
ADELAIDE'S JOURNAL

It was in the days at Kingston that Adelaide began to keep a journal. The idea had entered her mind when she saw in a local stationer's a volume bound in red leather, with brass lock and key. When she asked its purpose the assistant, after a preliminary astonished look, said that it was a journal, a book in which you wrote privately, and kept safely locked away from curious eyes. She was enchanted by the idea, and bought the book at once. Thereafter she wrote in it occasionally in bursts of interest and enthusiasm, indignation and despair. Was what she wrote always accurate? Did she sometimes record things, not quite as they were but as they might have been? Such questions would have seemed to her irrelevant, for the journal was an expression of her intimate thoughts, a record of her emotions. Here it seems necessary to put down only a few extracts from the period before her married life truly began, starting with what she wrote on her wedding day.

6 April Today I was married. No, no, not married, I was sold. I, who have been given the name of a French family instead of my *real* name, which is one of the noblest in the whole of England, was sold to a grocer who was paid as a gift for

taking me I don't know how many thousand
pounds. Oh miserable and disgusting Fate.

We came here after the ceremony, the grocer
and I, and I met Miss Dodd for the first time.
Miss Dodd! What a dried-up English spinster,
mincing and decorous, and concerned that her
other pupils—who are all, she said, 'gels of very
good family,' suggesting that I am *not*—shouldn't
know that I am married, and to a grocer. So I
am to be called *Miss* Bartlett. To all this the grocer
agreed and I agreed also, eyes cast down. I shall
be taught deportment, needlework, music, painting and sketching, also a little English literature. Very well. I hope they *teach*, for I wish to
learn.

13 April There is no point, there is no point!
That is already my conclusion. To be taught vari-
eties of stitching and how to sing a song at a drawing-room entertainment, to balance books on my
head so that the back is always straight and the
head erect, is that schooling? The fussy old ladies
who instruct us are concerned with manners, not
learning, they want all their pupils to be nice gels.
My manners are naturally good, for I am an aristo-
crat. The other girls are middle class, their fathers
are something in the Army or the law. Silly sim-
pering things.

I say and show none of all this.

24 April A letter from the grocer. It is agreed
that he shall not pay visits here, because the sim-
pering gels would ask questions. He has opened
a new branch in Dulwich. Such, for him, are the
rewards of marriage.

27 July The end of the term. What have I
learned? Something, I will admit, things that I
did not know before of the ways in which people
behave in polite society. But of what use will that
be to me when I shall not live in such society,
but merely be the wife of a grocer?

And now the school term is ended—my very
first term at school where I longed to be—and I
am living with the grocer. Not as his wife, oh no,
not that. It was agreed, it was all in the papers
drawn up by that evil man Mr Casumain, that I
should not properly become his wife until my
twenty-first birthday. So he has taken a furnished
apartment in Dulwich, conveniently near to the
new branch, and here I shall live in the holidays.
There is a woman who cleans the place, and I
am learning to cook. He goes off early in the morning, returns for dinner. We have separate rooms.
He has agreed, although reluctantly, to call me
Blanche.

29 July Today I was taken to meet the family.
What a collection! I will describe them. First the
father, whose name is also Edwin. His face is red-
der than his son's, he has great coarse hands with
broken dirty fingernails (he is a carpenter, or
something of the kind), he spits disgustingly. Then
his wife, who is something of an invalid, I hardly
noticed her. Then the eldest son Charles, who is
at least polite, and a sister named Elsie, who did
not care for me nor I for her. She seemed to think
I had forced myself on her brother. I should have
liked to correct her, but said nothing. And then—
very much the best of them—the youngest
brother Frederick, whom I met once or twice

when I was at Kingston. *He*, now, has a fine head, and his hair curls most charmingly. And when he laughs he does not, like the grocer, show a mouthful of teeth that are misshapen or decayed.

Among his family the grocer is different. When alone with me, he may be crude but retains some dignity. With his family, however, he clumps about like a great schoolboy, playing tricks and making stupid jokes which they, the old man especially, cap by jokes even more stupid. Then they all laugh. Just before we took tea, the grocer pulled away the chair from behind Frederick, so that he sat on the floor. I thought they would never stop laughing at that, even Mrs Bartlett, poorly as she looked. Then at tea old Bartlett began to talk about my name. (Nobody mentioned the secrecy of the marriage or the fact that I did not yet live with my husband. For *that* at least I was thankful.) 'Blanche,' he said. 'What kind of name is that, then? Sounds Frenchified.'

I said that was natural enough, for I had been born in France.

'Means white in French, I believe.' That was Charles.

'Real Frenchified,' old Bartlett repeated. 'I never heard of a girl being called by a name like that.'

'It is what Blanche wishes to be called,' the grocer said, as though it were *not* my name. 'Her other name is Adelaide.'

The old man was eating, but that did not stop him from speaking too. Crumbs flew out of his mouth on to the table. 'Adelaide, that's a proper name. A real English name is that. I shall call you Addy.'

I looked at my husband, but he said nothing. I told them that my name was Blanche.

Old Bartlett gave a chuckle. 'I'll tell you about Blanche, Addy my girl,' he said. 'Blanche is no name for anybody. I'll tell you what it is, it's what we do to almonds when we skin 'em.'

There was a roar of laughter at this 'joke', in which even Frederick joined. I was bewildered at the time, although I understand now that to blanche something is to make it white, and that the word is used for skinning almonds and revealing their whiteness. It has nothing to do with my name, and seems to me a very poor joke.

But afterwards they all called me Adelaide or Addy. When I spoke to my husband he said that he would call me Blanche, but that his family would never manage it.

31 August   The holidays are over, I return to Miss Dodd. Tonight my husband the grocer spoke to me of our future. I should not think that my life would always be like this, he said. He had agreed that we should not live together as man and wife until I reached maturity, and he would keep his word as a man of honour. He continued: 'This is not an easy thing for me. There are men's passions, Blanche, which women know nothing of. I have to exercise restraint, and with God's help I have done so. But I fear for what may happen if we are together for long under one roof.'

I did not properly understand what he meant, and he explained. He wished me after the end of the next term to live abroad. I should stay there in the holidays, so that he would not be exposed to temptation. He had arranged that I should go to a convent in Belgium, where he had been told that the education was good. Secretly, I suspect that this had all been arranged by the vile Casumain, from whom I have heard *not one single word* since my marriage. What should the grocer know of convents in Belgium?

Tonight I said that I would accept the name Adelaide, as I have accepted so much else. But to myself, in my secret heart, I am Blanche.

27 December I have now been at the Convent of the Holy Trinity, in this little village thirty miles from Brussels, for two weeks. How changed are my surroundings, how changed I am myself! It is another world from the frivolity and foolishness of Miss Dodd and her gels. Here all is peace and goodness, and the awareness of work that should be done well for the love of God. Now, for the first time, I understand the Lord and what he means for mankind. We have classes here, and instruction is given in serious things. The teaching is in English, for almost all of the nuns come from Britain (oh yes, I detect the cunning of Casumain's hand), and we are taught literature and poetry, especially the sacred poems of Vaughan and Traherne. I had never read anything like Vaughan's lovely poem that begins 'I saw Eternity the other night.' Oh yes, I said as I read it aloud to Sister Ursula, oh yes, I have known Eternity too.

1 January 1876 A New Year. And I am a new person. My resolution: to feel with charity towards everybody, to love all humanity. Sister Ursula and Sister Mary say that my development already is remarkable. Sister Ursula teaches literature, Sister Mary mathematics.

17 January   A letter today from Edwin, in reply to mine. Kindness and generosity breathes in every line of it, in the warmth with which he expresses pleasure at what I say about the Convent and the teaching. If I look back over the pages of this journal I am ashamed of my sarcasm and my pettiness. To have called Edwin 'the grocer' in that way, a man who wants nothing more than to love and cherish me, and to have been made angry because I am called by one name more than another, what do such things matter? I know that in God's name I am Blanche, that will always be my name. But in the world I shall be content to be called Adelaide Bartlett.

Tomorrow I shall write Edwin a loving, dutiful letter, saying that I look forward to the time when I truly become his wife.

23 February   Today Sister Mary said that my ability in mathematics was remarkable. Most of the girls find it difficult, but then they are not truly interested. I have a head for figures—not my words but Sister Mary's.

Wrote my weekly letter to Edwin. He may pay a visit here in the summer. I said how much I should look forward to that.

17 April   Today I felt, as I have done more than once in recent weeks, a weariness of spirit which I cannot resist, but of which I am ashamed. At such times the life here seems to me hard and narrow, and the restrictions unreasonable. There are twelve girls who have come here to complete their education, and also perhaps to become novices in the order. I have little to do with any of them. There is a barrier between us, for they are mere girls while I am a married woman. Is it not time for me to take up my life as a woman and a wife?

18 April Spoke of my doubts and spiritual weariness to Sister Ursula, who is my favourite among the nuns. She is always kind and gentle and looks beautiful, with a glow of goodness that seems to surround her like a halo. Sister Ursula said that I might learn in the Convent lessons that would teach me to resist the temptations of the world, and that what I learned would also help me in carrying out my wifely duties, burdensome though they might be. Afterwards we prayed together, and I knew peace.

19 April But what is meant by wifely duties being burdensome? Is not the marriage state ordained by God? I put this question to Sister Ursula. She said that was true, and that it was true also that we must accept the condition of life in which God has placed us, knowing that he has done so in his infinite goodness and mercy.

28 May Edwin has paid a visit, lasting two days. I had forgotten his appearance. I cannot say it pleased me. There were beads of perspiration upon his forehead, his hands are large and clumsy, and his teeth are unpleasant. These are bad thoughts, for he is my husband, and he spoke kindly. He talked much of our future life, of the shops which are flourishing, and of the dogs he breeds, in which he hopes I shall take an interest. I said all that seemed right, and think he was pleased.

19 September I have not written in this journal since Edwin's visit nearly four months ago. What is there to write? Life here pursues an unvarying routine (I had almost said a dismal routine). Every day is the same as the next. There is nothing that seems worth recording, except to say that I receive regularly letters from Edwin, and send just as regular replies.

Three days ago I was talking to Margaret, who is one of three new students. She spoke of being kissed by men, and of their attempting familiarities. I asked about the nature of these familiarities, and she told Sister Ursula that I had questioned her about sexual acts. She attributed to me words I never spoke, questions I never asked. Sister Ursula spoke to me as she has never done before, with a harshness that I thought not in her nature. She took me to see the Mother Superior, who rebuked me, said that I was troubled by a diseased imagination, and that I should ask the help of God to cure it. I prayed to God as I was told, but how glad I am that I have only to pass a few more weeks in a place that has become hateful to me.

27 September Sister Ursula behaves towards me with a coldness and unkindness that I can hardly bear. I asked today what I had done to offend her. She said that it was not she, but the Lord God, who was offended by my licentious thoughts and words. Afterwards, alone, I wept.

14 November In a few days I leave the Convent for ever. Today wrote my last letter to Edwin. In it I said that I should do my best always to be an obedient and loving wife.

CHAPTER 2
OLD BARTLETT

MR EDWARD CLARKE, Counsel for the Defence:
Did you disapprove of the marriage?
EDWIN BARTLETT SENIOR: I certainly did not
much approve of it, but I did not disapprove
of it.
MR CLARKE: I believe you were not present at
your son's marriage with the defendant?
EDWIN BARTLETT SENIOR: I was not.
Evidence at Adelaide Bartlett's trial

I never liked her, I don't mind admitting it.
The whole thing was wrong, from that day in '75
when Edwin strolled along, calm as you please,
to tell Mother and me he'd got married that morning. At first I thought he was joking, a rare one
for a joke is Edwin and he can keep a straight
face with it, but then I looked and saw he was
in his best clothes, and I knew something was up.
So when he'd broke the news, about getting
hitched to this Frenchy with a funny name, and
told how they wasn't going to live as man and
wife till she was twenty-one, and Mother had cried
about not meeting her and not going to the wedding and said she'd never heard the like (no more
had I for that matter), I took Edwin into the parlour and put it to him straight.

'Edwin,' I said, 'I'm your father, and I've always
said what I had to say straight out. There's more
in this than meets the eye, and don't tell me anything else.' He admits that's so. 'She's got a bun
in the oven, is that it?'

He looks at me with the little twinkle he gets when he's having a joke and says very solemn that no, that isn't so. What's the secret then, I asked?

'What would you say, Dad, if I told you Baxter and Bartlett would be opening up a new shop next month?' I didn't know quite what to make of it, but I said that'd be good. 'And if I said we might open another three or four in the next twelvemonth?'

I stared at him. Then he hitched up his coat tails, took out a bit of paper and showed it to me. There was a sum mentioned in it that was bigger by a long chalk than what I'd earned in the whole of my life. Edwin tucks it away again and asks if that don't put a bit of a different complexion on things.

'D'you mean to say—' I starts, but he stops me.

'I don't mean to say anything, Dad, no details. But there's no flies on your son Edwin, you can be sure of that.'

And that was all I got out of him. I can't say it left me happy. I'm a man who likes to know what's going on, and there was something hole-and-corner about this that I didn't see there was any call for. And when Edwin did bring her home she was what I'd expected, a Frenchified miss full of airs and graces who thought herself much too good for the likes of us. She came to tea one day, calling herself Blanche. I took her down a peg or two on that, and when she left the convent place she was at in Belgium and came to live with Edwin at Number Two Station Road, above the Herne Hill shop, she called herself Adelaide which at least isn't a Frenchified name. Didn't like it when I shortened it to Addy, my word she didn't. The looks she gave me sometimes out of those black eyes.

Some said she was a beauty, but I could never see it. She had these big eyes which were as near as you like black, and her hair was black as a darkie's, and thick and coarse as a horse's tail. Then she had great thick lips—she had no mother or father that I ever heard of, and I wouldn't be surprised if there was a touch of the tar brush somewhere—and a pasty face. Give me a nice English rose complexion any day. She looked *foreign*, that's all I can say.

Although, mind you, as far as I was concerned she was all milk and honey at first. It was 'Father' this and 'dear Father Bartlett' that, and 'You should ask your father's advice about such things, Edwin,' and so on. I never believed in it from the first, but there was nothing to put a finger on. And you couldn't say she didn't look after him. There were three shops by this time, and Edwin went to them all every day. He was up, had his cold bath (every day, summer and winter alike, always clean and bright my Edwin), eaten his breakfast—like me he was very partial to a steak or a mutton chop—and in the Herne Hill shop before half past eight, which was opening time. She looked after all that, made his breakfast, seemed to get on with the daily help.

Then at a weekend the family would often come to Sunday dinner, Charles and his wife from Kingston, my youngest Fred who was doing some kind of job with Charles, and of course Mother and myself. There was chaff and games and a bit of the horseplay that Edwin enjoyed as much as

I did, and Adelaide sat there smiling as though butter wouldn't melt in her mouth. So there was nothing to complain of, but somehow I knew things weren't right. I knew she was two-faced.

It was at one of these Sunday dinners that she says she's heard from an aunt who wants her to go to stay in the country for a week, 'Oh no,' I says. 'You've got some relatives after all, have you, Addy? And are we going to see this aunt of yours? I suppose she's French like you, but she might like to see what a real English home is like.' Then Fred takes it up, laughing fit to bust, and after that Charles and his wife do, and Adelaide says nothing but she looks like thunder, and then she gets up from the table and runs out of the room. Edwin started after her, but I told him she'd have to learn to take a joke, and he sat down again. Fine kind of joke it turned out to be.

Very soon after, Mother died. She'd been ailing a long while, and it was a blessed relief for her to be released into a better world, but at the same time a death means grief for those that are left, and problems too. Edwin was the best of sons, and when Mother was lying on her last bed of sickness he says to me: 'Father, I want you to know this. Where I have a home you shall have one.' Those were the words of the best son a man could wish for.

And what did Adelaide say? She'd been away on a second visit to this aunt of hers, who was supposed to live somewhere near Bournemouth, when Mother died. After she learns the news she puts her arms round me, kisses me, and says that whatever Edwin wishes is what she would want. Then she adds that of course the spare room is

very small, but she hopes I will be comfortable
in it, and that all my belongings must go into it
because the house is too full of furniture as it is.

They say my temper's on a short fuse, and at
that I flared up and said I wouldn't go where I
wasn't wanted. Edwin says it was just an unfortunate phrase, and she said it's their Christian duty
to give me a home for as long as I should wish
it. Then she takes my hand (she had pretty ways
about her when she liked, but I was brought up
to distrust such ways) and leads me up to the room
I'm to have, which as she says is very small. 'Well,'
I says, 'I don't know that it's big enough to swing
a cat in, but as I shan't be swinging cats in it very
often it will do for me.' A joke of course, but she
doesn't laugh. Foreigners have no sense of hu-
mour.

So I move in with them. And a couple of days
after I've done so, Edwin takes me out to the
back where the dogs are. These dogs are all St
Bernards and Edwin's been crazy about them for
a year or two. To me a dog's a dog, and if you
keep one it's to frighten off burglars, but Edwin
he goes in for breeding them and belongs to some
club or other. And to my surprise she takes it
up, can't have enough to do with the dogs, exer-
cises them, gives them physic and I don't know
what else. Edwin feeds the St Bernards and talks
to me while he's doing it. I can see he doesn't
like what he has to say, and for a couple of minutes
I don't understand what he *is* saying. Then I understand he's asking me not to spit when I'm in
the drawing-room, which is the name they give
the parlour. She gives it rather, for I never heard
Edwin use the word before he married.

'Edwin,' I says in reply, speaking quite solemnly, 'you are referring to the habit of expectoration, which I was told by my father, and have always impressed on you, is healthy and necessary. The saliva gathers and you must get rid of it. "Never miss the chance of spitting," my father said to me. "But make sure that a spittoon is in place and that your aim is accurate." Which I have always done.' I can see the boy doesn't know what to say. I asks if it comes from her, and he agrees that it does. 'Then you ask her whether she's ever known me to miss my aim.' He says that isn't the point. 'Very well then, ask whether she'll come along with me to a doctor, any doctor, and ask him whether frequent expectoration isn't a healthy habit.'

'Adelaide doesn't like it.'

'Then she'll just have to lump it, won't she,' I says cheerfully. 'You tell her instead of bothering her head with things she knows nothing about, she should be studying how to make me a grandfather.'

Edwin says nothing to that, but throws the last bits of meat to the dogs.

A couple of days later it happened. I'd been working on a job in Streatham, and didn't get to Herne Hill till around seven at night. I found Edwin there. He was frantic.

'She's gone,' he said.

Gone, I asked, what do you mean, gone? Where was she? With this aunt she'd been visiting? Edwin said he supposed so, but he didn't have the address.

Here was a fine kettle of fish. If it had been me I'd have said good riddance to bad rubbish, but I suppose it was natural he shouldn't see it like that. He said her feelings had been hurt, he thought she might have gone to his brother Charles at Kingston, and nothing would do but that he should go down at once. Right, I said, if you're going I'm going with you. Down we go to Kingston, but Charles has heard nothing of her. Then Charles leaves Edwin talking to his wife, and takes me aside.

'Father,' he says, 'Fred's gone too. And it's not the first time.'

I'd no need to ask what he meant, his face told the story. He said then had I never noticed the way she looked at Fred, and I told him no. We were always chapelgoers, the Bartletts, and my mother and father would never have believed such a thing could be, not in the family, they'd have thought it unnatural. So do I, if it comes to that.

I says to Charles now, 'The woman's a Jezebel. A whore.' At that he says we shouldn't be hasty, we should look at the dates. So then we look at them, and it seems that on one of those visits to the 'aunt', Fred had been away too.

'You're his elder brother,' I said to Charles. 'He's been living in your house, in your care. Why didn't you tell him he was breaking one of the Ten Commandments, coveting his brother's wife?'

At that Charles says something about the world being different from what it was in my young day. 'Are you going to tell me you're not your brother's keeper?' I ask him, and he doesn't answer that but says we can't be sure of anything and that if he'd known how I'd take it he wouldn't have told me.

'How do you expect me to take it?' I asks. 'As for being sure, I'm sure enough. Edwin must be told. And we must get the police after them.'

Then Charles says leave it for a bit, and maybe Adelaide will come back. He says this in a way that makes me think he knows where they are and I puts this to him straight from the shoulder, as my way is. He says he's got no knowledge of where they are, none at all. I didn't believe him then, and I don't now.

We stayed the night at Kingston, and I told Edwin. He was angry. I don't know that I ever saw him angrier, not with the whore but with me, his own father. He said I'd always been against her, never accepted her as a good wife for him. And has she been a good wife, I asked, has she given you a son? At that he raised his hand. I think he might have struck me if I hadn't reminded him I was his father.

'There must be one thing clear, Father,' he says then. 'Adelaide's my wife, and I won't hear a word against her.'

So no more was said, and nothing about calling the police. What conversation Edwin had with Charles I don't know, but the next day we returned to Herne Hill, and twenty-four hours later Adelaide came back. The next thing was I had a letter from Fred, no more than a couple of lines, saying he had prospects in America and was going off to try his luck there. It's been said that I had no proof of what I said, but what proof do you need more than that?

When Adelaide came back she was said to be ill, and kept to her room for a couple of days. Then she took up her life in the household again, but hardly spoke to me. That didn't worry me, as may be guessed, but to see her with Edwin made my blood boil. There he was, my son and a fine man of business, and this French piece could turn him round her little finger. I won't deny that I said some things in her presence she didn't like, such as asking whether she'd noticed that the new lad in the shop was uncommon handsome. I always said these things in a joking way, mind you, but I could see they riled her. And I won't deny either that I told other people, people who might come in touch with her, what she'd done. I didn't mention Fred's name, because of the disgrace to the family, but I thought it my duty to tell anybody who might have dealings with her what kind of woman she was. I'm a straight man, and those I spoke to won't have been in any doubt of my meaning.

One day Edwin says to me that this has got to stop. I ask what he's talking about.

'I'm talking of the tales you've been spreading about Adelaide.' My son says more to me than that, he calls them *filthy* tales. He says that to me, his father.

'As God is my witness, Edwin, I have said nothing but what is true.'

'Father,' he says, 'I said to you that you would always have a place in my home and I meant it, but if you are to stay there must be no more tales told about Adelaide behind her back, and no more insulting her to her face.'

Insult, I wanted to say, can you insult a whore? But Edwin is my best-loved son, the one most like his father, so people say. Therefore I agreed that in future I would be silent on such matters. But that was not enough. I must make a written apology, he said, and it must be signed and witnessed before a solicitor. Nothing else would do, he said, by which I knew he meant that *she* had said nothing else would do.

And so I did it. For the sake of peace, not with the French whore but with my loved son, I put my hand to a document I knew to be a lie.

I did it in the hope that all might be as it had been in the past. My reading of the Good Book should have taught me different. Whoever touches pitch, he shall be defiled. Whoever strays from the path of truth, he shall be punished. As I have been. First the French whore set out to separate father from son, then she destroyed the son.

CHAPTER 3

FROM ADELAIDE'S JOURNAL

27 July 1878   I must put down what has happened. I must put it all down.

I have tried, I always try, to be a good and dutiful wife to Edwin, but the Old Man makes it almost impossible. His habits at the table are like those of a dog—no, the St Bernards are gentlemen compared with him. He picks up bones to gnaw them, licks his fingers afterwards, then belches and pats his stomach. And his spitting. Edwin spoke to him of it, but with no effect. I removed the spittoons from the drawing-room, with the result that he makes hawking noises in his throat, looks round and then, grumbling some abuse, goes out to spit elsewhere. In half an hour he does the same thing again. Much of this, I know, has the deliberate purpose of causing me distress and annoyance. A few weeks ago I felt that I could bear it no more. I made the excuse of going to an aunt, packed two cases, and went to stay for a few days in a small hotel at Brighton. The weather was fine, the gentlemen in the hotel were—well, quite simply they were gentlemen and the attentions paid to me as a woman alone were always polite—and I had blissful days of peace. This month I did the same thing again after a *scene* with that awful Old Man. A scene in which Edwin *did not take my side.* He said that his father was old, set in his ways, I must make allowances. Oh, I have made so many allowances! I packed my things on the following morning, took the train to Victoria, stayed in the same small peaceful hotel.

Last night I returned, to find the household in an uproar and vile insinuations being made. Edwin was kind as always. He reproached me for leaving without a word and said that I had done it to punish him, but he asked no questions. He has the instincts of a gentleman, although unhappily not the speech or the manners. I see that it was cruel and thoughtless of me to leave as I did, and not to write. But the Old Man! It seems that Fred has taken it into his head to try his luck in the United States. Good luck to him, and may God go with him. But the Old Man suggested, no, more than suggested, that Fred and I had been together. I shall write down no more of this, it is so vile.

10 August The Old Man is telling everybody of what he suspects. He insults me in front of the family.

17 August Still the same. I have said to Edwin that it cannot go on.

30 August Today I was in the shop, helping with the accounts. There were two women customers, giggling and peering at me as though I were a freak in a sideshow. Spoke again to Edwin.

10 December I can bear it no more. Today I said to Edwin that if his father is to stay under our roof he must apologize to me, and in such a form that the apology is *public*. Otherwise, as I well know, he will mumble a few words to me (spitting between them no doubt) and go away and repeat his calumnies.

31 December Triumph! Today the Old Man signed an apology drawn up by our solicitor, Mr Wood. Edwin has had it printed, and if ever the Old Man repeats his words the paper contradicting them can be shown. Here is the complete document:

Having made statements reflecting on the character of Mrs Adelaide Bartlett, the wife of my son, Mr Edwin Bartlett, junior, which statements I have discovered to be unfounded and untrue, I hereby withdraw all such statements, and express my regret for having made them. I also apologize to the said Mrs Adelaide Bartlett and Mr Edwin Bartlett, junior, and acknowledge that all such statements are altogether unfounded and untrue. I authorize Mr Edwin Bartlett, junior, to make what use he pleases of this apology.

I trust that will be the end of it. I have no malice now in my heart towards the Old Man. I shall always try to behave towards him like a Christian.

Tomorrow I shall kiss his cheek and wish him a Happy New Year.

4 March 1879 At last, *at last* I have persuaded Edwin to go to the dentist. His decayed teeth are getting worse, and that makes his breath horrible. For the past three days he has been complaining of toothache, and last night got up and walked about the room. We tried oil of cloves dropped on the teeth, and hot towels put round the head, but nothing did any good. Edwin is frightened of going, and would not consent to it unless I accompanied him. So the appointment has been made. This afternoon we go to Mr Blossom, who is said to be a very fine dentist.

I suggested at breakfast, which poor Edwin was hardly able to touch, that it might be best if some teeth were removed, and he had a plate made. At that the Old Man said, 'That wouldn't be too comfortable, I'd say.' Edwin answered immediately, 'Depends on the size,' and the Old Man said: 'Breakfast or dinner?' Then Edwin: 'Just about manage tea, that might fit.' At that they both roared with laughter, while I looked from one to the other bewildered, until Edwin explained that it was a joke about whether a dinner or tea plate would fit into his mouth. I do not understand such jokes, and never shall. And that Edwin should be able to make them when he has toothache!

The Old Man and I are now polite to each other, but sometimes I see him looking at me with hatred from the corners of his mean little eyes.

5 March Oh, the troubles of those *teeth*. I will write down what happened.

Edwin had asked particularly that I should go in with him, and Mr Blossom made no objection, so I saw everything that happened. Mr Blossom is not a young man, and he has a habit of neighing sometimes like a horse. He probed about in Edwin's mouth, snorting once or twice, and then said: 'Crooked they are, those teeth in the lower jaw and several decayed. Have 'em out, Mr Bartlett, have 'em out, they're poisoning the whole system.'

Edwin moved in the chair, as though to get up. Mr Blossom pushed him down again, and said that he would do it now. I asked whether he thought that a plate in the lower jaw would be a good thing. He was enthusiastic.

'Very good, ma'am, excellent idea. Just one little problem.' Snort snort. 'These teeth here—just come over and see for yourself, ma'am—very crowded, very crooked, never get a plate to fit round 'em. What's the answer? Simple enough, ma'am. File 'em down, saw 'em down, till you get to the level of the gum. Then in goes your plate over 'em, fits comfortably, no more trouble.'

'I will think about it,' Edwin said. Again he made to get up and again Mr Blossom pushed him down, saying that the decayed teeth must certainly go, and he might as well do the whole job at once. I must confess that I agreed, in part because I hoped it might cure Edwin's fetid breath. If I had known the suffering entailed I might have said no. In the end Edwin submitted.

Mr Blossom called in his partner Mr Horner, and they started. I asked whether they would give an anaesthetic—Edwin was like a dumb ox, saying nothing—but Mr Blossom said no, easier without. Easier for them, perhaps, but not for poor Edwin.

First they pulled out the decayed teeth and that was not so bad, although the gums bled a lot. But then they did the sawing or filing, and that must have been agony. At some times Mr Horner had to keep Edwin in the chair by force, while Mr Blossom worked away with his little saw. Edwin bore it bravely for the most part, but there were times when he shrieked aloud. I found it hard to watch, but when I got up to leave the room Edwin made desperate gestures for me to stay. At that moment Mr Blossom broke one of his saws, flung it down, cried 'Damn the teeth,' and then apologized to me. The thought occurred to me that if the teeth were so hard to cut down perhaps it was wrong to touch them, but I did not care to say this.

At last it was over. Edwin had been in the dentist's chair for more than two hours, and his gums were bleeding badly. I think Mr Blossom himself was concerned. He gave Edwin a drink of whisky, and said that in half an hour he would feel as fit as a fiddle. That was not at all true. A cab took us home, and then Edwin went straight to bed.

6 March   Edwin still poorly. Stayed in bed. Worried about the shops.

9 March   Edwin got up yesterday. He is better, although his gums are still very sore. He can eat only soft foods, and tends to mumble his words because of the lower teeth missing and sawn off. The Old Man of course blames me for allowing the sawing to be done, but Edwin could have refused. Edwin himself does not blame me, nor does he complain. This morning he was blending and tasting tea as usual.

11 March Today Edwin has his new teeth! He was nervous of going to see Mr Blossom again, which is not surprising after what he has suffered. He asked me to go with him, and of course I did so. We took a cab and asked the driver to wait, but on this occasion such precautions were not necessary. The plate fitted perfectly, and the teeth are beautiful, white, gleaming and regular. And now that the decayed teeth have been taken out, the bad smell has gone from Edwin's breath. Perhaps it was worth while after all!

On our return spent the rest of the evening with the St Bernards, Edwin instructing me in points to look out for, as they are approved by the National St Bernard Club. The nose should be large and black with well-developed nostrils, the expression must show intelligence and dignity, the legs should be perfectly straight and the tail set rather high, and in our rough-coated variety the coat should be dense and flat, fuller round the neck. It is most interesting, but as I said to Edwin I love them all, especially our two finest dogs, Golden Hero and Golden Glory. Afterwards I played for Edwin. He listened intently, and said I had a true gift for the piano. The Old Man was away. When he is present I have noticed that Edwin listens much less to my playing, saying that he is too busy, or making some excuse. He seems to think that to listen appreciatively in the Old Man's presence would be a sign of weakness. This was a happy evening. The new teeth are beautiful.

CHAPTER 4
MARY GOVE NICHOLS

'From 1845 to 1853 she contributed extensively to the New York *Water-Cure Journal*, published *Lectures to Women* on *Anatomy & Physiology* (1846), *Experience in Water-Cure* (1849), and several novelettes, and became well-known in reform circles for her advocacy of mesmerism, spiritualism, Fourierism, temperance and dress reform . . . When the Civil War broke out, Mrs Nichols and her husband left America for England, where they spent the remainder of their lives.'

Dictionary of American Biography

On the fine September day in 1879 when she first saw Adelaide Bartlett, Mary Gove Nichols was in her late sixties, but she was still a lively and eloquent woman. More than thirty years earlier Edgar Allan Poe had noted the keen intelligence of her dark eyes, and had praised the enthusiasm of her conversation. All her life she had been an enthusiast for new ways of thinking, feeling and behaving, for spiritualism and socialism, temperance and mesmerism, and above all for hydropathy or the water-cure. She had become what she called a water-cure physician as long ago as 1844, and most of her abundant energy had been given to propagating the idea that all illness was the result of eating unsuitable food and drinking harmful liquids.

Her first marriage had foundered on these beliefs, but the second, to Thomas Low Nichols, had

been from the first a perfect union. It had flour-
ished and so had they, writing books and editing
journals to advance their views that love should
be free, that all humans should be vegetarians,
and that food and drink reform was the way to
health. At the time Mrs Nichols saw Adelaide Bartlett these two energetic Americans had been living in England for nearly twenty years. They had
established a hydropathic institute at Great Malvern to spread the excellence of Malvern water,
and then Dr Nichols (as he called himself, although his degree came from New York and he
had no licence to practise in England) founded
his paper *Herald of Health,* and it became convenient to live in London. Now they were installed
in Earls Court, where Dr Nichols wrote his articles. His wife saw patients, and gave classes for
students in food reform and hydropathy.

Mrs Nichols rose from her desk as the visitor
came in, and warmly clasped the hand offered
to her in both her own. From the animal magnetism flowing from one body to another she could
often tell the emotional condition of a patient.
Sometimes the magnetism did not flow, but the
hand she took now gave back a strong reaction,
telling her that the visitor was tense with suppressed emotion. Her approach was always direct.
She sat again at her desk and said, 'You have a
problem.' The reply came in a low voice. 'Yes.'

'And you have been advised to consult me.'
Shake of the head. 'You saw my name in the paper?' Mrs Nichols's classes were advertised in the
popular press.

'Yes.'

'Do you wish to consult me about your health?'

'Not exactly.'

Mrs Nichols saw that the woman's hands were trembling slightly. What else was there to notice about her? Black hair, thick and coarse and in its own way remarkable. Thick lips, almost negroid. Clothes that seemed merely conventional to Mrs Nichols, who favoured loose garments imposing no restriction on movement, and on this afternoon was dressed in a white robe vaguely resembling a Roman toga. With a smile consciously full of warmth and sweetness, she began to talk.

'You must help me a little, you know, or we shall never get on. I have not asked your name, or anything else about you, because I do not know if I shall be able to help you. When you believe that, then it will be time to ask for names and such things. Now, you have a problem and you find it hard to talk about it. I shall ask questions, and I want you to answer as freely as you can. Will you do that?'

'Yes.'

'Are you suffering from poor health?'

'No, not exactly.'

'Then is it some personal unhappiness that makes you want to see me? Something to do with your husband? I notice the ring, you see.'

'Oh no, my husband is very kind.'

The English was perfect but a slight accent was noticeable. 'I think you are not English. French, perhaps?'

For the first time there was a response, a smile that matched her own. 'That is clever of you. Yes, I was born in France and my family is a noble one, although—' she hesitated a little, then went on—'although I have lived here almost all my life. I did not think that my accent was so obvious.'

'I guess I notice it because I'm not English either. American and proud of it. I love the British, but I wouldn't want to talk like them. It's not your health, and your husband is very kind, so what is it? I'm running out of guesses.'

'May I ask something foolish? Would you turn away from me?'

'Sure, why not?' Mrs Nichols turned to face the photograph on the wall behind her, which had been taken in the 'fifties and showed a group of subscribers to their magazine *Nichols' Journal*, on a picnic.

In a low voice but clearly, the visitor said, 'I wish to know the means of producing children, the way it happens, all about it. I am ignorant of such matters.'

'Can I turn around now?' There was no reply, and when Mrs Nichols turned she saw that her visitor's head was bent as though in shame. 'That's nothing to be ashamed of or worried about. You'd be surprised how often I get asked that same question.' This was true, although it was not often put so baldly. 'I don't think you will have read my husband's book.'

'No. But I should like to.'

'I will give you the book to take home with you, and one of mine, but let me tell you first what my beliefs are in relation to love and the making of children. The first of these is freedom. There must be freedom to love, a free union of one soul with another, one body with another. Without such freedom marriage is a tyranny and love cannot exist.' The words were those which

Mary Gove Nichols had written and spoken many times before, but her eyes shone as they had done in youth when she first made this statement of her faith.

'Free,' the visitor echoed a little dubiously. 'I am not sure that I know what you mean.'

'And, as you are too polite to say, I am not answering what you came to ask,' Mrs Nichols said, laughing. 'But believe me—I think I may now ask your name.'

'Mrs Bartlett. Adelaide Bartlett.'

'I shall call you Adelaide. Believe me, Adelaide, your plight is not uncommon. Thousands of young women get married without knowing the reproductive details that are essential. My husband and I—Dr Nichols is a great and good man who thinks just as I do—have devoted our lives to remedying this and all other kinds of ignorance. You must read his great work, which has sold many thousands of copies in the United States and in this country, and I will give you also my own book about marriage. Take them away with you, read them, show them to your husband if you wish, and then come to see me again. You will have questions, and I shall try to answer them. Perhaps you will wish to join my class of students, and to read our paper, the *Herald of Health*. Now, let me tell you some details.'

Half an hour later Adelaide left the house in Earls Court. She had with her *Marriage: Its History, Character and Results*, written by the Nicholses in collaboration and published long ago in America, and *Esoteric Anthropology: The Mysteries of Man* by Thomas Low Nichols, which had first appeared in America but had recently been reprinted in England.

That was the beginning. From past experience
Mrs Nichols knew that many ladies who, like Adelaide, asked for advice on intimate domestic matters, did not return. But Adelaide came back,
came back with a list of questions that she had
written out in a flowing copperplate hand in case
she should forget them. Mrs Nichols answered
them all with her usual frankness, and she referred
Adelaide often to her husband's work, which was
always called The Book.

On sexual congress she advised Adelaide to consult page 98: 'Once a month is the period in which
a woman requires sexual union, and it may be
doubted whether any greater frequency is not a
violation of natural law. At this period, however,
when in a healthy condition, she is full of ardour,
has a great capacity for sexual enjoyment, and is
seldom satisfied with a single sexual act.' She
warned Adelaide, as the Doctor warned in The
Book, that sexual intercourse during pregnancy
was dangerous to both mother and child. When
Adelaide said that she rarely felt the enjoyment
mentioned, Mrs Nichols shook her head and replied sadly that this was all too common. She referred to a passage in The Book which said that
for many women continence was no virtue, because they were not attracted to sexual connection, but she advised Adelaide that if she truly
loved her husband she would in the end find enjoyment. And what exactly was masturbation,
Adelaide asked, 'the solitary indulgence of ama-
tiveness,' which in The Book was called a disease,
in some cases hereditary, from which many a child
sank into the grave, and which at the least was
likely to cause loss of memory and mental power,
eruptions of pimples, a creeping sensation in the

spine, and in cases of great indulgence insanity
or idiocy? Mrs Nichols gave details of the practice,
while advising strongly against it.

After Adelaide's second or third visit, Mrs
Nichols found herself becoming interested in the
young woman. She no longer thought her a little
negroid and rather plain, but had discovered a
fascination in those puzzled frowns and hesitant
wide-mouthed smiles. There was about this grocer's wife from suburban Herne Hill something
unusual and attractive. More than that, Mrs
Nichols became convinced that Adelaide was one
of the few people with mesmeric power. To believe something was, with her, to talk about it.

'Have you heard of Auguste Mesmer?' Adelaide
shook her head. 'He was a great man who lived
a hundred years ago, one of the true discoverers.
He taught that there is a kind of bodily electricity,
he called it animal magnetism, which flows from
one person to another. It flows through touch,
especially the touch of hands. Mesmer used it to
cure patients of all sorts of illnesses through the
touch of his hands, and the passes he made with
his hands in front of them. Animal magnetism is
a natural gift. I have it, and I believe you have
it also.'

'To cure people?'

Mrs Nichols laughed. 'Not like Mesmer. A Mesmer comes only once in a century, and then he
is not always appreciated. But I am proud to count
myself a humble pupil of his. I have practised mesmerism, and I know that I can influence people.
I think you are like me.'

The conversation ended there, but Adelaide did
not forget it, nor did she forget Mesmer's name.

Once or twice she saw the doctor, a benevolent white-bearded figure, but she never spoke to him. She joined briefly the class taught by Mrs Nichols on the way to complete health through a reformed diet and the water-cure, but attended infrequently. Her interest was in her own marital affairs, and it was intense. How much should wives discourage their husbands from sexual congress, she asked, and what was the best time in a woman's life to have children?

'It says in the Bible that marriage is for the purpose of procreation and not of lust,' she said in a questioning tone.

'The Bible, my dear, must not always be taken literally, but upon the whole The Book says that this is true. If you have read the chapter "Morals of the Sexual Relation"—'

'I have read it, but it is not quite clear to me.'

'When in doubt remember that freedom in love is the rule, the joyful acceptance by two people of one another.'

'Supposing, however—' Adelaide stopped herself, frowning. 'Supposing that what is freedom for a husband is not so for the wife. Supposing that the husband wishes—' She stopped again.

'For marital relations when the wife is unwilling?' Mrs Nichols's eyes shone with the militant ardour that impressed her students. 'That is unreasonable and unfair, I would even say unloving. The truly loving husband will wait until his wife is ready. Making love is a co-operative exercise. The man must exercise restraint.'

'Even if he says that he has desires which must be fulfilled?'

'He must exercise restraint,' Mrs Nichols repeated firmly. And she quoted decisively from The Book. "It is to be observed that the natural period for sexual union is when it is demanded for the purpose of procreation; and that the use of marriage or the sexual act for mere pleasure, and using any means to avoid impregnation, are unnatural." You have read that passage?'

Mrs Bartlett said that she had. She did not seem quite convinced by the quotation, but moved on. 'What is the best time for having children? I should like them, but I am afraid.'

'There is no need for fear, and no need for a doctor. Childbirth is natural, and if you follow the directions given in The Book nothing will go wrong. It is as natural for a woman to bear children as it is for an apple-tree to bear apples.'

'Have you had children yourself?'

'Certainly. It is part of a woman's function in life, without which she is not complete. I have had two children, one by my first husband and the other by the Doctor. Of course they are adults now, and living their own lives. You may take my word that there is nothing to be concerned about in the bearing of a child.'

Not long after this discussion, in February 1881, Adelaide announced that she was pregnant. Mrs Nichols was delighted, and was pleased also to be told that Adelaide was holding faithfully to the directions in The Book. The weeks went by, and Adelaide's fears seemed to have gone. Her husband, she said, was fully in agreement that no medical man was required. They would proceed according to The Book, and in due time she would ask Mrs Nichols to arrange for a midwife.

A month before the confinement was due, Mrs

Nichols did just that at Adelaide's request. She arranged for a nurse named Annie Walker to attend the expectant mother. Later Mrs Nichols heard that the child had been stillborn, and wrote a word of sympathy. She could not forbear to say that Adelaide's loss had been occasioned by her failure to adhere to vegetarianism and the water-cure. She received no reply to the letter, and never heard from Adelaide again.

CHAPTER 5
ANNIE WALKER

MR EDWARD CLARKE: Was she attentive and affectionate towards her husband?
ANNIE WALKER: Most affectionate.
Adelaide Bartlett's trial, April 1886

It was in October, 1881, that I was asked by Mrs Nichols to attend a Mrs Bartlett, a patient who was expecting her first child. I say 'a patient,' but it was all rather unusual because Mrs Nichols wasn't a doctor. Her husband was, but he occupied himself mostly with writing articles and editing a magazine, and she wasn't a doctor but saw the patients. However, that was none of my business. I took my things and went out to where Mrs Bartlett lived, at Herne Hill.

I liked her from the moment I saw her. She was a little bit of a thing and there was something unusual about her, perhaps because she was partly a foreigner. She was, I don't know what you'd call it, withdrawn I suppose. But not with me. The second day I was there she took hold of my hand, fixed me with her great mournful eyes, and said, 'Annie, do you know what I long for most of all? A friend. I haven't got a friend in the world.'

'Come now, Mrs Bartlett,' I said. 'You must have plenty of friends, a lovely young lady like you.' Then, when she shakes her head, I says, 'For a start, there's your husband.'

'Edwin is very good to me, good and kind, but I cannot talk to him. Will you be my friend, Annie?'

I don't approve of that maundering sort of talk, but still there was something about her that made me say yes, I would be her friend and help in any way I could.

It was an unusual household. There was the husband, who was partner in a chain of grocery shops, one below the apartment where they lived and three or four others, all in south London. Very bright and breezy he was, up early in the morning and down in the shop below, then on to the others so that he did the full round each day. And very affectionate. First thing he did when he came home in the evening was to kiss his wife and ask what sort of day she'd had, then he'd put up his head and sniff and say something like 'Is it honey, is it jam, or do I smell good English lamb?' Then when they had apple pie there'd always be cheese on the table, and he would say, 'Apple pie without cheese is like a kiss without a squeeze.' At that he'd get up, go round the table and try to squeeze her. It seemed to me she wasn't always best pleased by this. He was a very affectionate man.

Then there was his father, who was a cheerful enough old fellow in his way, but there was no love lost between him and Mrs Bartlett, perhaps because the father and son were close. Anyway, he was always getting at her whenever he could, making little remarks like saying he'd never heard of getting a nurse in four weeks before the baby was expected, but maybe they did things that way in France. In the evenings she would play the piano and sing. She played most beautifully, I thought, but the old father would stamp out of the room muttering that he'd sooner listen to cats on a roof, or something like that. Mostly he would say such things under his breath so that Mr Edwin couldn't hear, because if he *did* hear he took them up and was sometimes quite sharp. But Mr Edwin himself would fall asleep often as not, and begin to snore. Then when she'd finished he would say, 'Beautiful, my dear, beautiful.' She said to me that he didn't appreciate her playing or her embroidery, which she did most delicately and cleverly, making the prettiest chairbacks and such. And I'm afraid it was true.

She told me once that she came from a family that was one of the greatest in the land, but that for special and particular reasons they couldn't acknowledge her as their daughter. She said also that there was a mystery connected with her birth, but I don't know if that was true.

Of course what I was there for was to help Mrs Bartlett with the last few weeks of her pregnancy, so I'll come to that. She had been a patient of Mrs Nichols, and had total faith in her. She said to me the first day: 'Mrs Nichols says that having children is as natural as apples dropping from a tree, and I only have to follow the right treatment and it will all be quick and easy.' Now, I know from my own experience, which is fourteen years,

that isn't always true, but of course I said nothing
except that we'd do what Mrs Nichols said. I'd
attended one or two other patients of hers, and
everything had been all right. And Mrs Bartlett
went religiously by the Doctor's book *The Mysteries of Man*, which was on a table in the living-
room.

This was the treatment. She had a bath every
morning, not cold but not really hot. Then a wet
bandage over the abdomen to give it support, and
a sitz bath each day, this to be a cold bath because
cold was said to have a strengthening effect. Everything was done to invigorate, and she seemed
to respond well. She never had a great deal of
colour, but said she felt extremely fit. She was
co-operative to anything I suggested, and didn't
object to use of the vagina syringe, which according to Dr Nichols's book also had a strengthening
effect. Then the book recommended a daily injection to move the bowels, but this wasn't necessary.

At this time she ate no meat, again on instructions, although she cooked it for her husband and
normally ate it herself. Nor did she drink alcohol,
I like a drop of porter with my meals, and Mr
Bartlett considerately had it sent in, but she took
nothing. Mr Bartlett and his father drank a little
beer, not much. The old fellow would say he never
heard such nonsense as keeping off meat, and that
as soon as the little fellow had teeth he would
get them into a good rump steak. Both father and
son seemed certain the child would be a boy.

So everything went on as well as could be, and
I grew to feel a great attachment to Mrs Bartlett,
and she to me.

'Oh, Annie,' she said to me one day, 'I am so

frightened. Is it very cowardly of me?' I said it was not, it was quite natural, but that she had faith in the treatment. She said that she had, and that Mrs Nichols was a wonderful woman, but she was still afraid. 'You'll be here when the time comes, and you'll help me, won't you?' Of course I said yes to that. 'And I shan't need a doctor.' What could I do but agree, although I had my doubts?

I ought to say that Mr Bartlett had no doubts at all. For one thing he said that he didn't want any man interfering with his wife, no matter if he was the cleverest doctor in the world. Then once I found him and his father studying the drawings in *The Mysteries of Man* and laughing over them. I think these were drawings of the child in the womb. There was more laughter, and a lot of jokes, when the family came to Sunday dinner. I could see Mrs Bartlett didn't like these visits, though she bore up well and smiled a lot. And some of the jokes, well, I suppose they were harmless enough, but they were more the kind you expect to hear at Collins's or the Alhambra or some other music hall. The old man made a lot of them. I can only remember one, but I'll put it down because it was like a lot of the others.

'Suppose it's twins,' he said, and at that they all laughed as people do, though why twins should be thought funny I don't know. 'Supposing it's twins, what would be the first thing one said to the other?' Nobody had an answer, of course. 'He'd say, "Does your mother know you're out?" '

As I say, they all laughed, and Mrs Bartlett gave a wan little smile. Afterwards I said it was only fun, they meant nothing by it, but she said old

Mr Bartlett hated her, always had. In the past, she said, he had told terrible stories about her, and Mr Edwin had made him swear in front of a solicitor that he'd never repeat them.

Mrs Bartlett—Adelaide I called her to myself, and that was what she asked me to call her too— took all this coarse joking without complaint, and with a sweetness that was truly typical of her loving nature. I only once saw her upset in those days before the birth, and then it was with her husband. There is no doubt in my mind that Mr Edwin truly loved her, but like all the family he was a coarse-grained man who could not understand the delicate instincts of a high-born lady. I forget the exact occasion of the remark except that it was something trivial, like perhaps the fact that his slippers were not laid out ready to put on, but he said: 'I'll tell you what, a man needs two wives, one for companionship and one for use.' His father, who was there, improved on it by saying no need to stick at two, why not half a dozen like they had in Turkey? Then Mr Edwin said something more, about that being a good idea, you would have one to take out, another to run the household, a third to tend the dogs, and so on. It was all meant in fun, or at least I think it was, but it was not kind, especially with Adelaide in her condition. She said nothing, but got up and left the room.

When she'd gone Mr Edwin spread out his arms and said to me: 'Now what have I said, Annie? She must know it was in fun, she's heard me say the same or suchlike before now.' It was not my place to comment, but I followed her up the stairs to the bedroom. She wasn't crying, I never saw her cry, but she burst out into what you might almost call abuse of old Mr Bartlett, saying that he was determined to wreck their marriage, and was a wicked man. I put this down to her being in the last month.

Perhaps it was a slightly unusual household, but not an unhappy one. There was no doubt Mr Edwin loved his wife—and who could help loving her, she had such pretty ways? And all went well, except for little ups and downs, until she began to have pains. At first she was pleased. 'It's coming, Annie, my baby is coming,' she said, and I said yes, it was on the way, but she should be patient. Then she began to quote *The Mysteries of Man*, which she called The Book and parts of which she seemed to know by heart, to say that sometimes labour lasted only fifteen minutes. That's not been my experience, but I didn't say so.

Then the labour pains began in earnest, and they were bad. She began to cry out when they came, and then to say that God was punishing her for her sins.

'Don't go on like that, my love, it's all natural,' I said. I knew Mrs Nichols and Dr Nichols were very much against using ether or anything else like that, because they said the natural way is the best way. And so perhaps it is, but not when it means pain such as this poor lady suffered.

The labour went on for hours. She screamed when the pains were bad, and she was losing the strength to go on pushing, so that I got worried. Mr Edwin had come in to see her once or twice, to hold her hand and say everything was going on as it should. After one of these visits I took him aside and said I would like to call a doctor.

'A doctor,' he says, as though he had never heard of such. 'It says in The Book—'

'I know all about what it says, but I should like to call a doctor. I think he might help.'

'Is her life in danger?' he asks then.

He had an uncomfortable look he gave you with his blue eyes, so that it was not easy to look straight back at him. Well, uncomfortable look he may have had, but nobody ever said yet that Annie Walker was afraid to call a spade a spade.

'There are two lives to be considered, Mr Bartlett,' I said. 'The life of your wife and the life of your child. A doctor might help them both.'

'Are you not confident of your own skill as a midwife, Annie?' At that I lost my temper a little.

'No question of that,' I says sharply. 'I've delivered dozens of children, and nobody can say that I've ever failed in my duty. But no matter what it says in that book you both believe in, there are times when a doctor should be called, and it's my duty to tell you that this is one of them.'

'Is my Adelaide's life in danger? Do you fear for her?'

'No,' I says. 'It's not her I fear for, but the unborn babe.'

At that he sticks out his jaw in a way he had, and with a click, which came from the fact that he had a set of false teeth in the lower jaw and that they were a bad fit, he said, 'Then I would sooner not have any man interfering with my Adelaide. I would sooner you took the case through yourself. That is my answer.'

I accepted the answer, and have been sorry for it since. This was in the morning, and she was lying upstairs exhausted, poor little lady, with the pains still just as bad. We went on all through the day and she tried and tried, but nothing happened except that she was weaker. I would have liked to give her something to ease the pain but she wouldn't have it, saying that The Book was against it. I got the book and showed her a passage where Dr Nichols said in certain cases anaesthetics might be used, but she just shook her head. She gripped my hand when the pains came, so hard that it hurt.

Things went on that way until the evening, when Mr Edwin returned home and went up to see her. He came down looking a little shaken, and asked what I thought. I said there had been no progress, and that he knew my views. The old man was there at the time, and he made some remark about Frenchies not having the toughness of an Englishwoman, at which his son turned on him quite fiercely and said he'd prefer his room to his company if he hadn't a sympathetic word to say. At that the old man went out, and Mr Edwin paced up and down the living-room. Then he pulled out a great turnip watch from his pocket. The time was eight o'clock, and he said we'd give it a little longer, and then if need be he'd send for Dr Woodward in Dulwich Road.

It was three hours later when I could tell that things were reaching a climax and that they were not right, and I told him so. 'I want the doctor here when the baby is born, Mr Bartlett,' I told him. His teeth clicked, and he stuck out his jaw, and hesitated. 'I beg you to send for Dr Woodward,' I said, and I think that word 'beg' was decisive. He said, 'Very well.' But by the time the doctor came, nearly an hour after, it was too late.

She had been delivered of a child, and it was still-born. It would have been what Mr Edwin wanted, a boy.

When Dr Woodward came he was kind, and said it was very likely it would have made no difference if he had been called earlier, but I never believed that. I thought then and think now that if Mr Edwin had agreed to calling a doctor when I first asked, the child might have been saved.

As for Adelaide, she said nothing, but just lay in the big bed, a tiny figure with a face white as paper and only the great eyes staring out of it. She only said to me, 'You won't leave me now, Annie, you won't go, will you?' I said that I'd stay just as long as she and Mr Bartlett wanted me. And in fact I did stay for another three weeks.

It was in those weeks that I truly came to know Adelaide and to love her, and by her own request to call her by that name. Up to then I had always called her Mrs Bartlett. She said that I reminded her of a nurse or nanny she once had named Patty, and that this Patty was the only person who had ever truly loved her. I replied that many people loved her, including of course her husband. Her reply was a little strange.

'Oh yes, Edwin loves me in his own way. But it is not a pure way, it has too much passion in it. At the convent where I was educated we were taught that the way of Christian purity is not the way of human passion. And in The Book it says that such passion should be reserved for the purpose of procreation.'

I could not follow just what she meant, but whatever she had been taught it is my experience both in my life as a married woman, and in what

I have seen of marriage as a midwife, that men have desires which must be satisfied. I have known men very angry because they could not have congress with their wives within a few days of them giving birth, and if they are persistently denied then they go to other women, sometimes of the lowest kind. I said something of this to Adelaide, but she said that Edwin was not like that.

'About one thing I have made up my mind, Annie,' she said on another day. 'I shall have no more children.' I said that her feelings were natural after the painful confinement and the disappointment at losing the child, but that they would not last. She insisted on the opposite. 'My mind is made up, and I shall not change it,' she said.

In those three weeks we talked about many subjects, as freely as I have ever talked with any human being. She spoke of her love for the St Bernard dogs. I do not care for dogs myself, and was a little afraid of these great beasts who stood as high as my shoulder, but they seemed to return her affection. She told me that after her marriage she had gone to the convent to complete her education, and said again that she belonged by birth to one of the greatest families in the land. She said that the old man was her implacable enemy and would do all he could to injure her, and that the rest of the family was against her too. She said—and this I had already seen—that her husband did not appreciate her artistic skills, and that his mind was on nothing but business, although she followed this by saying that he was kind and good to her always. Except, she remarked, in making his will.

'Don't you think it a shame,' she said. 'Edwin

has made a will that his property only comes to
me on the condition that I never marry again.'
Apparently this will had been drawn up at the
time they were married, and she thought it very
unjust. I agreed, although I said that with her opinions about purity of behaviour, perhaps she would
not wish to remarry. I said this with a smile, but
she did not smile in return, and in most matters
she was indeed intensely serious. She said that
the important thing was the injustice done to her,
and to other women, by such a clause, which was
apparently very common. She raised the subject
once in Mr Edwin's presence, but he merely
laughed.

She also mentioned Mrs Nichols, and said how
deeply she was disappointed that what had been
said in The Book about the bearing of children
and the pains of labour was wrong. I answered
that I did not think it wrong but simply too positive, but she said that although she valued much
in the book she would never go to see Mrs Nichols
again.

The days passed by and with each day she was
stronger, better able to take her part in running
the household. She was not neglectful of this, and
was an excellent manager. We went out for daily
walks in the district, and she spent much time
with the dogs. Her spirits improved, and it was
clear that she had no further need of my company
even though she wished me to be there as a companion. Three weeks after the confinement I left.
Mr Edwin thanked me warmly, and gave me a
little extra money.

Before we parted Adelaide asked me for a photograph, and I gave her one in my nurse's uniform.

She said that she would always preserve it, and that I was to call upon them whenever I was anywhere near. Mr Edwin said so also, and spoke very heartily. I learned afterwards that Adelaide kept the photograph in her album.

If I were to express my chief feeling about her, it would be that she had a sort of innocence and unworldliness that I have never known in any other woman. She might do or say something outrageous, but it would not seem so to her. I loved her and also—for no reason, since her husband was as good a man as could be wished—felt sorry for her.

PART THREE
Georgius Rex

CHAPTER 1
THE BARTLETTS AT HOME

'When I first knew them they were living at
Herne Hill, and afterwards at Lordship Lane, East
Dulwich, where I was in the habit of going to
visit them. They afterwards went to Merton Cottage, and I continued to visit them there . . . So
far as I could see, Mr and Mrs Bartlett lived on
very affectionate terms.'

ALICE MATTHEWS, in evidence

When the whole affair was over, George and
Alice Matthews often talked about it, and always
with a sense of wonder that approached disbelief.
Alice, in particular, was amazed. 'But George,
they were our best friends, they really were our
best friends. If you don't know your best friends—'
Her husband generally agreed, for he had found
that life went more smoothly when he agreed with
Alice, but he knew that although they had become
friendly with the Bartletts, there had been a time
when Alice said that Adelaide Bartlett thought
altogether much too much of herself, and was
hoity-toity. That was when the Bartletts lived at
Herne Hill, with old Mr Bartlett. Then there had
been the bad luck of Adelaide losing her child,
and after that she had seemed to seek out Alice
and want to confide in her. Alice confided in
George, from whom she had no secrets. One day

when he returned from the city, where he was a partner in a firm of wholesale silk merchants, to their home in Dulwich, she told him that the Bartletts were going to live over another of the shops, not very far away.

'But do you know what, George?'

'I don't, but I shall when you tell me,' said George, who had the reputation of being a humorist.

'The old man isn't going with them. You know I told you some of the awful things he said about Adelaide. Well, Edwin's agreed that now they're moving he'll have to find somewhere else to live. She's so pleased you'd hardly believe it.'

'Oh, I've got a pretty shrewd idea of the way she feels about him. She doesn't exactly hide her feelings.'

'She never says anything.'

'Doesn't have to. If looks could kill—you know the old saying. I've seen her give some looks, and so have you.'

'Only when he—he expectorates. You must admit that's disgusting, you've said so yourself.'

'I'll agree that the old man's a bit of a rough diamond. So is Edwin, for the matter of that. He knows the defects of his education and doesn't try to hide them, which is to his credit.' Mr Matthews was proud of his own attendance at a good grammar school. 'A sound fellow is Edwin, and he's livened up that business no end since he joined Baxter.'

'But George, do you know where Adelaide says the money came from to expand the business?'

'I don't listen to gossip,' her husband said severely. 'And now, my dear, I've had a hard day and I'm going to read the paper and maybe have forty winks before dinner, so you'll have to excuse me.'

On that occasion Alice had to leave the conversation there. But now that she was a confidante of Adelaide's she became a frequent visitor to the Lordship Lane apartment. Down below there was the bustle of the busy shop, which was called The Exchange. Upstairs Adelaide had furnished the rooms in a way that made them look light and pretty, a way Alice thought was really very French. She had obviously enjoyed doing that, as she enjoyed accompanying herself on the piano, but although she never exactly complained she did not seem to Alice Matthews truly contented. Edwin, she said, did not appreciate her playing, he would prefer it if she sang more like a soubrette at a music hall. And then the furnishings, what was the point of making such a place pretty?

'What is it? Some rooms over a grocer's shop. I think I am stupid to try to give it some feeling, some charm. If Edwin has his breakfast at seven each morning, and his dinner on the table half an hour after he gets home, he cares for nothing else.'

'Husbands,' Alice said. 'They don't appreciate what we do.'

With one of those sudden changes of mood that had come quite to enchant Alice, Adelaide shook her head emphatically and cried, 'No, I am wrong, wrong, wrong. My Edwin is the best of husbands, and I would be a wicked woman if I thought anything else. Am I a wicked woman, Alice, tell me?'

'Of course not.'

'The truth is, you see, that I love Edwin and

know him to be a good man, but he is not romantic. There is nothing romantic about him, do you
agree? He is all business.'

Alice, who thought that Edwin was a clodhop-
ping tradesman, rather coarse but very good-na-
tured, agreed, but asked if that really mattered.

'Oh no, it is not important, I know it is not important. But still, I would like him to be a little
more romantic.'

Alice replied that George too was not romantic,
although she said to herself that George was a
gentleman, while Edwin was—well, what George
called a sound fellow. And then, although George
was a silk salesman and so undoubtedly in trade,
a silk salesman was not on the same level as a
grocer. George did not worry about such social
distinctions, but Alice was strongly aware of them,
and wondered at times whether they should really
be friendly with the Bartletts. But the fascination
of Adelaide, and the mystery surrounding her
birth which she sometimes mentioned in vague
terms, turned the scale. Visits were exchanged
regularly, they occasionally played a rubber or
two of whist in the evenings. At other times Edwin
and George discussed the state of the economy
and the ridiculous notion of Home Rule for Ireland which was being proposed by Mr Gladstone,
and the ladies chatted together. Sometimes Adelaide played and sang, mostly sad songs like Lord
Tennyson's 'Maud' or patriotic ones like Mrs Her-
mans's 'The Stately Homes of England.' George,
who had a fine baritone voice, sang away lustily,
and Edwin would join in too.

Altogether these were jolly evenings, yet Alice
sensed that Adelaide was not fully satisfied by

them, or by life in general. What did she want, after all? She had got rid of Edwin's father, that old curmudgeon; she had a devoted husband. Of course, there was the question of children, but no doubt others would come to replace the little one tragically lost. Alice, who had three and found them rather a handful, secretly thought Adelaide rather lucky to have these years of freedom. The subjects of marriage and children were rarely touched on in their discussions, although Adelaide said once that she thought ideal love, true Christian love, should be absolutely pure. Alice hardly knew what she meant, and did not enquire.

One of the things that Adelaide wanted, however, was made clear when one day Alice went round to Lordship Lane and found her friend looking radiant, as she said they were moving again. They were renting a house near Merton, not quite in the country, but still farther out than Herne Hill or Dulwich.

'Oh, Alice, it is the sweetest, prettiest cottage you can imagine, with a lovely garden. And there will be room for the dogs, we can have them there and look after them properly, and I am sure we shall train a champion.'

Alice expressed the enthusiasm expected of her, and then asked how Edwin would get to the shops, which he liked to visit every day, going from one to another.

'He has it all worked out. He will walk to the station and catch the seven o'clock train to Herne Hill. We shall be up early, but I don't care for that, I don't care for anything if I am away from the shop. Do you know, I could smell bacon all day from the moment I got up in the morning until I went to bed at night? I think I have the best husband in the world, Alice, don't you?'

'I know wild horses wouldn't drag George away from our home,' Alice said, although in truth she too would not have wanted to move from her comfortable house. 'But what about Edwin's father?'

Adelaide made a face. 'We shall have him sometimes for Sunday dinner.'

'But not to live with you?'

'Oh no. He will never live under our roof again, Edwin has agreed to that.'

'She can twist Edwin round her little finger,' George said when she told him the news. 'And she does. I'm not sure you should see so much of her.'

'Why ever not?'

'I don't quite know why not,' George Matthews said. 'There's something—well, unEnglish about her. Something unhealthy.'

This unEnglish quality, if it was that, attracted Alice. She found in Adelaide a mixture of innocence with a sort of worldliness that had perhaps come from her wide reading. There were always books lying about, some of them novels, but mostly works on new religious movements like theosophy, on vegetarianism and other health movements, and on grand society in the past. She knew a lot about social customs and scandals at the court of Louis XV, and she had spent a whole afternoon describing to Alice details of the life of the Russian royal family, which she had got from a book of reminiscences. She did not buy the books, but had a subscription to Mudie's circulating library, and Alice sometimes wished that

she had the time to do some of Adelaide's reading.
Yet with this there went an ignorance of so many
commonplace things that Alice wondered where
her friend could have spent her childhood. It was
clear from the hints she dropped that she had
been brought up in a different social world from
that of the grocery shop, a world from which she
was now mysteriously excluded. Altogether she
was unusual, and Alice was pleased to have her
as a friend.

The cottage at Merton was certainly very
pretty. It was not large, but there was room
enough for a couple and one or two children, if
children should come. There was a little drawing-
room with Adelaide's piano at one end of it, a
dining-room, and three bedrooms upstairs. A daily
woman came in to do the housework, and her
husband tended the garden and helped to build
the kennels made at one end of it for the St Bernards. It was, as Alice said to George, a cosy little
place rather like one of those described in Dick-
ens's novels, even to the roses round the door.
George said that it might suit the Bartletts, but
he would call it poky, and anyway he had no time
for novel-reading.

A little incident that occurred soon after the
Bartletts had moved in confirmed his view about
the unhealthiness of Adelaide. George and Alice
had come over for the evening. Adelaide had
made supper, all kickshaws as George said, with
nothing substantial to eat, and the men had gone
into the tiny study to smoke their pipes, while
Adelaide and Alice talked in the drawing-room.
Adelaide waxed strong as she often did on the
importance of preserving health rather than cur-

ing illness, and on the folly of doctors who only treated diseases rather than trying to prevent them. She continued talking in the same vein when the gentlemen returned, and Alice could see her husband becoming fidgety as he often did when he thought that a woman was laying down the law. At last he interrupted.

'Do you mean to tell me that if I'm ill I shouldn't go to a doctor, is that what you're saying?'

'No, no.' Adelaide waved her hands, a habit she had when she became excited, and which Alice put down to her French origins. 'If you are ill you must have a doctor, but what would happen if nobody was ill? There would be no need for such people. So doctors do not study to preserve health but to cure disease. If they were paid according to the health of the country, and received less money when there was an outbreak of chickenpox or scarlet fever, then they would try harder to keep us healthy. They have an interest in disease, as soldiers have in war.'

'I'm a plain man and maybe that's too clever for me, but it sounds like stuff and nonsense.'

'Adelaide got it from a book,' Edwin said.

'Book reading,' George Matthews said, as though he had expected nothing better.

'You have read the book, Edwin. You thought it was valuable, you agreed with Doctor Nichols's ideas.'

'Had to go to a doctor when I had dyspepsia a couple of months back though, didn't I?' Edwin guffawed and his teeth clicked.

'You must read the book. Do please read it, and then you will understand.'

Adelaide almost ran to the shelves, took down

a small volume and pressed it into George's hand. He took it, warning her that he was not a great reader. On the following day he looked at it in his wife's presence.

'*Esoteric Anthropology.* Funny sort of thing to call a book, what's that when it's at home?'

Alice shook her head. She had read the book, or parts of it, and thought Adelaide had been unwise to lend it to her husband.

George went on reading from the title page. ' "*The Mysteries of Man.* A comprehensive and confidential treatise on the structure, functions, passional attractions, and perversions, true and false physical and social conditions, and the most intimate relations of men and women." H'm.' He went off with it to the room he called his den, and came back an hour later puffing as though he had run a three-mile race, which Alice knew to be a bad sign.

'Alice! Have you looked at this book?' She was ready for the question, and said no. 'I forbid you to do so. It is absolutely disgusting. There are descriptions—and drawings—I would not have believed a printer could be found to print such things, nor a binder to put the pages together. That woman—'

'You mean Adelaide?'

'To read such stuff. And to think that I would read it! I cannot imagine—' Words failed him again.

'You can tell her something of that when you give it back.'

'I could not trust myself to speak of it. You had better give it back.'

'Without looking at it? Oh, George.'

'I will make a parcel, so that you need see nothing offensive. Then just give it back to her. I do not see that you need make any comment. I take it that you wish to continue seeing the Bartletts?'

'Of course I do. Adelaide is my friend. And I thought you liked Edwin.'

'Edwin is a good honest fellow.'

'He thought the book was valuable, if you remember.'

'That is as may be. Edwin is a man. But for a woman to read it, and lend it to a man.' He shook his head. 'Something unhealthy there. I tell you, Alice, Adelaide Bartlett will come to a bad end.'

AFTERWARDS (III)

The body is mere flesh that decays, but the spirit must be iron or steel, whatever substance is durable and turns a brave resisting face to the assaults of the world. This was the face she turned on that terrible New Year's Day, deliberately refusing to flinch from what had to be done. Was it necessary for her to help Mrs Boulter, who had been sent round by the undertaker to lay out the body? Perhaps not, and people were to say that it showed callousness on her part, but the flesh from which the spirit has departed is no more than clay. The laying-out also occupied her mind, so that she did not worry about the unexpected need for a post-mortem. Mrs Boulter, a little Cockney sparrow, chirped away cheerfully.

'My, now, I see the gentleman's legs are tied. Did he have a fit then, was that what killed him?'

'Nothing like that. No, poor dear, he suffered with his head, also with his teeth for some time.'

'His head and his teeth was it now? Dear, dear.'

She had an impulse to talk to the woman, an impulse she indulged although she knew it to be unwise, and it began by her commenting on the strangeness of life. Mrs Boulter, busy with her arrangements, agreed.

'He's young to be took, but you never can tell, can you? And what about you, mum, I pity you to be left a poor widder woman at your age.'

She responded, truthfully but as she knew afterwards foolishly. 'My husband was very good to me. He made a will just a little while before his death.'

'Did he now? Left his money to you, did he?'

'Yes, the will was in my favour. It would not have been right for me to be left penniless. All my money was in his business, and I was married before the Married Women's Property Act. If he had not made the will I should not have received a penny.'

'Is that so now? I'm sure that's right, dear, though if Boulter was to drop dead tomorrow it wouldn't make a ha'porth of difference to me.'

That was the end of the conversation, but because the matter was on her mind she said something of the same thing to Mrs Doggett a little later on, and both women remembered it. She was kept busy. There was the undertaker to take his measurements, and after that telegrams to be sent. She went into the back room and wrote them out, telegrams to the Old Man, to Baxter and to Alice Matthews, saying the same thing to them all. 'Edwin is dead. Come at once.'

Doggett, precise little Doggett, took the telegrams to the post office for her. Then Mrs Doggett came up and said that she had had no breakfast, and must eat something. Adelaide responded by saying that she could not touch a morsel of food, and then in the course of conversation mentioned the will. No unfriendly word was said either by Doggett or his wife, but she could feel a wariness, even hostility, in their attitude. She longed for a friendly face, somebody with whom she need not be on guard. When Alice Matthews appeared, Adelaide truly fell into her arms.

Alice was all she could have wished of a friend, warm and helpful and comforting. There were explanations to be made, for although George and Alice knew of Edwin's illness, the latest news had been that he was recovering, and would be back at work again early in the New Year.

'What was it, then? What did he die of?' Alice asked.

She shook her head. 'We don't know yet. There must be a post-mortem. But Dr Leach is very good and kind. He is arranging it all. He says there will be no trouble.'

'Of course not,' Alice said. 'There can be no need to worry. But I will tell you something that must be done, and should be done today. You must order your mourning.'

'Alice, I don't know if I can. Not today.'

'I will come with you. It will do you good to get away from here. I will be here all day, and tonight you must come to us.'

'Alice, you are very kind. But I must stay here, it is my place to be here.'

Before anything further could be said Edwin's partner Mr Baxter arrived, and soon after him Dr Leach. Where was the Old Man? His absence was explained by Mr Baxter, who said that Mr Bartlett would have left for work before the telegram arrived. Then Baxter went to look at his late partner on the little iron bed, and came back pale and shaking.

'My poor Edwin. I loved him like a son. He was the life and soul of the business.' He stood there for a moment, shaking his head. 'I know where Mr Bartlett is working. I will go and fetch him.'

Almost in the moment of his departure Dr Leach arrived, bringing bad news.

'Dr Green—you remember that I was particularly anxious for him to undertake the post-mortem, he is a man of immense experience—Dr Green has sent a telegram to say that he is too busy to perform it today. He suggests that I should act independently.'

Adelaide put her hands together and said imploringly, 'Oh, Dr Leach, please do that.'

'It is not to be thought of. It would not be in your best interests, Mrs Bartlett.' To Alice Matthews's surprise, the doctor then took Adelaide's hands, and gazed into her eyes. 'It is your interests that I have in mind, Mrs Bartlett. There must be an independent doctor.'

'Can't Dr Green be persuaded to come? Spare no expense. Get any assistance you want. If Dr Green is the best man then you must have him, but I long for all this to be done with, you understand.'

'I do, indeed I do. I greatly fear that nothing will be possible today.'

'If not today it must be tomorrow. But make it as soon as possible.'

'I will send another telegram. If you will excuse me . . .'

Dr Leach relinquished Adelaide's hands, and

bobbed his head to Alice Matthews. Before he could leave the room, however—the conversation had taken place in the drawing-room, with Edwin's body decently screened from view—steps were heard upon the stairs, and the door opened.

The Old Man had arrived at last.

He had been home and changed his clothing, so that he was not wearing his workman's overalls. He ignored Alice, gave a grim nod to Dr Leach, whom he had met before, and said, 'Where is my son?'

'If you will excuse me—' Dr Leach said again. The Old Man turned on him his mottled red bull-dog face.

'I'd be glad if you'd stay, doctor, I'd like a word with you. After I've seen him. Where is he?'

They led him to the body. He knelt and kissed the pale forehead, then lingered with his head bent over the body until Adelaide asked what he was doing.

He stood up. 'I was smelling his mouth. For prussic acid, I know the smell. But I didn't find it.'

Alice looked at her friend in astonishment. Adelaide did not speak, her face was blank. Alice put an arm round her shoulders, but it was shrugged away. The Old Man turned to Dr Leach.

'We must have a post-mortem examination, doctor. This cannot pass.'

'Do not disturb yourself, Mr Bartlett. Come and sit down.' The Old Man shook his head in violent refusal. 'Very well. I am arranging for a post-mortem. I could not give a certificate without one. That does not mean I share your suspicions.'

'Who will conduct it? Is it to be you?'

Dr Leach's head moved upwards in its high collar. 'I have asked Dr Green, of Charing Cross Hospital. He is a physician of the highest repute. You have met Dr Dudley, who will also be present. And Dr Murray from Charing Cross. Also myself. I hope you will agree that is adequate.'

'When is it to be?'

'Probably tomorrow. When the time is fixed, I will see that you are notified, so that you may be present to know the result.'

'I want another doctor. One to act for me, and the rest of the family.'

'Very well. I will get you one.'

'Oh no, you won't. *I* will get *you* one. I want one who's had nothing to do with the case, nor with this neighbourhood.'

Dr Leach flushed, but he kept his temper. 'I make allowances for your distress, Mr Bartlett. Very well, if you come to my surgery, I will give you a list of names and you may take your pick. I am leaving now, I have to send a telegram to Dr Green.'

The Old Man grunted, and began to follow the doctor out of the room. At the door he turned to Adelaide. 'You'll not have him put in the coffin. Not before the post-mortem.'

'That has nothing to do with me or with you. Dr Leach must see to that.'

With that they left, and Adelaide again threw herself into her friend's arms. 'They are all my enemies, all the family. Oh, Alice, I have tried so hard to be friends with that old man. Shall I tell you something about him? He spits. Everywhere he goes he spits.'

Alice had found the scene extraordinary and

distasteful, but she did her best to console her friend. They went out to a shop near Oxford Circus and ordered the mourning. The weather was cold, with a thin driving rain, and Adelaide wore her cloak. She took little interest in the clothes, which was natural enough. When they returned George had arrived, Mrs Doggett brought up tea, and they sat round the fire while Adelaide told the story of the previous night once more, how much better Edwin had been, how he had asked her to hold his toe and she had done so through the bedclothes, how she had fallen asleep and woken to find him dead . . .

George felt himself duty bound to take a last look at his friend. Dr Leach had paid a visit and said that the body might be put in the coffin, and it had been taken to the back room, together with the iron bed, so that the presence of death was not so oppressively near. Nevertheless, George Matthews would not have cared to spend the night in the apartment, and like his wife he urged Adelaide to come back with them. She refused very positively, saying that it was her place to remain beside her dead husband. In the course of the evening Dr Leach came in once more, flushed with success, to say that Dr Green had agreed to carry out the post-mortem tomorrow. It would take place at the house, at two-fifteen in the afternoon. He had arranged for a certain Dr Cheyne to attend it on behalf of Mr Bartlett.

Adelaide thanked him. 'You remember, doctor, how my husband said to you once that his family hated me. You see that he did not exaggerate.'

'You must forgive him. He is an old man, and full of grief.'

'And me, doctor, am I not also to be considered as grieving?'

Dr Leach gulped. 'You, Mrs Bartlett, are full of courage.'

With that he left, and a little later George and Alice left too. On the way home Alice said that Dr Leach was certainly smitten. George, to whom she had told the story of Mr Bartlett's outburst, replied that it was all a deuced rum affair, and she should keep out of it as much as possible.

Left alone, Adelaide took one of the pills Dr Leach had left her, and settled down to sleep on the sofa. She was not dissatisfied with the day. The Old Man had shown himself in his true colours, and surely when the post-mortem was over Dr Leach would issue a certificate. But of course there were other problems still to be dealt with. She had written a letter to Georgius Rex. No doubt he would come tomorrow. She fell asleep thinking of Georgius Rex.

CHAPTER 2
FROM ADELAIDE'S JOURNAL

19 October 1884 I will put down the details of my day, my day which hardly varies except when I visit Alice or she comes here, or my dear Annie pays a visit who was such a help to me in the grievous time. I rise at six and so does Edwin. He takes a cold bath while I prepare breakfast for him, a steak, a chop, or a dish of kidneys. He is partial to these and likes them underdone, so that the blood is running out. I eat only fruit for breakfast. I have not adhered to Dr Nichols's vegetarian principles, but still cannot bear to eat part of a dead animal at breakfast.

In his bath Edwin roars lustily in the winter. 'Oh ho ho, this water is cold, Oh ho ho, I'm very bold, to plunge in this cold water.' Or some similar rhyme he has made up. In the summer he sings 'The British Grenadiers,' 'D'ye ken John Peel,' or another song. At breakfast and other meals he now takes out his teeth unless the food is very tough, saying that they hurt. He leaves before seven to catch the train to Herne Hill, and in the course of the day goes to all the shops. There are now six of them, all doing good business. He specializes in the mixing and tasting of the teas among other things, while Mr Baxter does most of the ordering from suppliers. I do not doubt that he works hard, but never so hard that he fails at some time of the day to see his father, that evil man who hates me. Sometimes they take what Edwin calls a bite of lunch together, sometimes the Old Man goes to one of the shops and awaits Edwin's arrival. Does he ask for money? Edwin says not.

And what of my day? At eight o'clock Mary Jane arrives. She is my daily help, who comes to clean the house, wash up, etcetera. She is willing but stupid. She is paid very little, so what else can be expected? There are orders to be given to the butcher and other tradesmen when they call, and my day's work is done except for looking after the dogs. I love them, especially my wonderful Golden Glory, but they hardly fill a life. What else do I do with my freedom?

I read books from Mudie's library, books the postman brings three times a week. I strive, I *strive* to understand through them the meaning of this world and my place in it, but I am too ignorant. I have attempted to read philosophy, Aristotle and Locke and others, but I do not understand, or where I understand it seems to me that often the philosophers are wicked heathens, who question the Lord and His purposes. I return from them to the Bible and the Lives of the Saints.

I read also tales of the French nobility, remembering that one who gave me a name although he was not my father. Then some historical books for instruction, although they are mostly dry and dull. And medical works—although these do not come from Mudie's, I have to buy them—which tell of the nature of the human body, something of which I was kept ignorant in youth. I rarely read novels, for they offer no story so strange as my own.

And what else? I practise my embroidery and tapestry work, and do some Berlin woolwork. I finished last week a cushion with the head of one of our St Bernards worked in cross stitch and decorated with beads. Edwin said that he would not have known it for a St Bernard, but thought it was a spaniel. When he saw me upset, he kissed me and said that it was a fine piece of work. I think that he meant to be humorous with the first remark.

My great solace is those noble St Bernards. We have six of them, gentle, faithful and true. Are they not the noblest animals in creation? It is said that one St Bernard de Menthon trained them long ago to track and rescue travellers lost in the snow, in faraway Switzerland. I can believe the tale, for my—our—six St Bernards would be capa-

ble of any action to help and protect me. Rightly
are they called the holy breed. Sometimes I spend
the whole afternoon in exercising and talking to
them. I prepare their food, I watch for signs of
the distemper that is inclined to affect them, and
treat it, I give them worm pills when necessary.
They are a true joy to me, and to Edwin too, making a firm link between us.

At six or just after Edwin returns. He likes to
have his dinner ready punctually at seven. This
may be a light meal, but there must always be
meat except on Fridays, and after it a good Stilton.
After dinner I ask if I shall play for him. Sometimes
he says yes, but his inclination is to fall asleep
while I am still at the piano. Often he has papers
to look at, new catalogues and such. In that case
we sit reading together, he perhaps making notes
on goods to be ordered, until ten o'clock when
we retire.

Since that terrible time I have told him there
must be no more children, and he has accepted
this, but sometimes he insists upon what he calls
his rights. He keeps preventatives locked up in
the chest of drawers. This insistence often happens on Fridays. Oysters and eggs are amatory
foods, it says in The Book, and they seem to have
that effect upon Edwin. He is a sober man, drinking nothing except a little beer or wine, but when
amatory can be extremely *coarse*. 'That'll put lead
in my pencil,' he will say when eating oysters. I
did not understand the phrase, which fact made
Edwin laugh, but know now that it refers to the
penis. Dr Nichols says in The Book that 'its shape
is that of a cylinder, with a soft, delicate cushion,
called the glans penis, at the end. This is the most
sensitive part of the organ, and in the sexual or-

gasm is the seat of exquisite pleasure.' It has given
no such pleasure to me. I feel degraded by contact
with it.

Such is my life. Each day the same round is
repeated.

December 6 I have not written here now for
more than six weeks. Reading my last outburst
(I have to call it such) I feel ashamed. Edwin is
my good kind husband. If we meet few people,
that is my fault. What have I in common with
the likes of Mr Baxter, estimable though he may
be? Or Edwin's other business acquaintances?

December 7 Something more about Edwin. In
one of the medical books there is a chapter given
to hypochondria—that is, imaginary illness—and
I find that Edwin is a hypochondriac. His health
is very good, but he does not think that is so. He
often says he has pains, mostly in the abdomen.
Then he says there is a nerve in his leg that is
making his foot twitch, or at another time that
he has pains in his arm. But mostly it is the abdomen, which he feels blown out. No doubt that is
from indigestion, which is not surprising with the
amount of meat he eats, but he does not put it
down to that, but to fruit or vegetables that have
disagreed with him. Today he has given up brussels sprouts, saying that they give him dyspepsia.
Next week it will be cabbage or another green
vegetable, and then a few days later he forgets,
and starts to eat them again.

December 8 The Old Man to dinner. Edwin ate
half a dozen slices of beef, and put pickle on it,
but hardly touched his cabbage saying it was not

well cooked. The Old Man just the same as ever.
Called him 'Father', he called me his dear Adelaide. Hypocrisy.

December 15 The sexual relation, Dr Nichols
says, should only be indulged for the purpose of
reproduction. He says also: 'a woman who wishes
to guard the health and life of her husband, must
induce him to entirely refrain from amative indulgence.' Said this to Edwin who has read The Book,
or read in it. He merely laughed.

December 17 Have from the library two *very
interesting* books, one called *Psychology and Human Understanding*, the other on the subject of
mesmerism. The book about psychology, which
is by a professor at Aberdeen, says that all human
beings are dominant or dependent, and tells how
to recognize these dispositions. The dependent
person is childish, likes playing jokes, often seems
younger than he is. He can be violent in temper,
but secretly wishes to have his mind made up
for him, and always gives way over important matters to avoid responsibility. There are other char-
acteristics given, and they *all* (except the temper)
apply to Edwin. He wishes to be dominated. When
there is any real problem—outside his business—
he asks my advice, wishes me to decide. Now that
I understand this, understand him better, I shall
be ready to make decisions when he consults me.

The other book is on the practice of mesmerism,
about which Mrs Nichols talked to me long ago.
It seems that this is now named hypnotism, and
the book is *Hypnotism, or Animal Magnetism*. It
seems also that almost anybody can be hypnotized, and there are all kinds of methods, from

fixing the attention with the eyes or making passes with the hands (Mesmer used these), to the use of magnets, ticking watches held to the ear, etc. And the person hypnotized is not always sent to sleep, but sometimes talks quite normally.

Shall try this on Edwin one day. I am still reading the book.

December 18 Christmas near. The family will come for Christmas dinner. I shall endure it, and smile. My greatest wish in life is for one pure and perfect friendship, unmarked by sensuality. Is that hope unattainable?

December 26 All came for Christmas. The Old Man, Charles and his silly wife, the sister Elsie, some cousins. They are unutterably coarse and vulgar. After the Christmas turkey, when the pudding and mince pies are on the table, they have a practice which I do not understand, and in any case detest. With the appearance of the mince pies they sing: 'Oh, I don't like lamb, ham or jam, and I don't like roly-poly. But I do like a nice mince pie, and then I have a helping twice.' At 'twice' each makes a frenzied attempt to squash with his fist the mince pies on the plate of his neighbour, shouting and laughing as they do so. This year it was too much for me. I pushed my broken mince pie away from me and said I was not hungry. The Old Man told me I was a spoilsport.

December 27 Made my attempt to hypnotize Edwin. It was a success, or at least I think so. I cannot yet be sure.

He sometimes has bad headaches, especially after he has drunk more than a glass of wine. He had one today, after the family visit. I told him that I might be able to cure it by an old remedy I knew, if he would co-operate. He agreed, and we sat in chairs opposite each other. I asked him to look for two minutes at a silver bracelet which I held in front of and just above his eyes. (This is called Braid's method.) He did so. Then we had a conversation. I will put down a little of it.

'Edwin, you have a headache. But when we finish talking it will be better. Do you understand?'

'Yes.'

'Repeat what I said.'

'When we have finished talking my headache will be better.'

'You are not asleep.'

'No, I am not asleep.'

'But when we have finished talking you will not remember what we have said.'

'No, I will not remember.'

Except that there was something mechanical about the way Edwin spoke he seemed normal. I was going to end the session by giving him a tap on the arm (recommended if Braid's method is being used) when I remembered that unbearable Christmas Day. I suggested to Edwin that his family should never come again at Christmas. He agreed. Then I said this should be the first thing he said to me tomorrow morning.

I tapped him on the arm. He blinked, smiled, and said his headache had gone. But was it just an accident? Tomorrow we shall see.

December 28 He said it. Those were his *first words* spoken to me on waking. Mrs Nichols was right, I have the gift!

January 1, 1885 Today, today, another sad New Year. What poet wrote those lines, why do I put them down? Was the New Year sad? Not especially. George and Alice came here, we sang songs and ate cake, and at midnight joined hands to sing 'Auld lang syne,' then stood in the garden and listened to the bells. In the garden all was crisply cold and beautiful, with frost silvering the trees. Edwin kissed me and said that he loved me. Yet it was as though a deep cloud rested on my spirit, blanketing all chance of happiness. Does the future hold anything better than the past? And what has the past given me? Is it ungrateful to say—nothing that I wished? I fear it is, yet that is my answer.

January 3 Much disturbed in mind, able to take pleasure in nothing, not this cottage nor my life in it, nor even in the dogs. Spent all the afternoon preparing Golden Hero for the Southern Counties show in which he is entered next week, and for which Edwin says he has a chance of getting a rosette. Washed and brushed him, gave him words of command, all of which he obeyed instantly. His noble head! Looking at him I could weep for the lack of dignity in man.

January 7 Continued depression. Edwin observed it, tried his best to comfort me, but in vain. He spoke of another child. Impossible.

January 11 The Old Man to Sunday dinner. Moaning about the discomfort of his lodgings, trying to suggest that he should live with us again, although not positively asking it. E. did not give way, but afterwards said it was hard on his father.

At dinner they equalled each other in their disgusting habits. They sucked bones, made squelching noises. The Old Man spat. Edwin's teeth hurt him, and he took them out. The stumps beneath are black and look rotten, but he will not see a dentist, said he had enough pain in the past to last a lifetime. Tried to persuade him, without success. This is one subject on which he is not dependent!

January 13 Took Golden Hero to show. Edwin had to go to City warehouse, did not attend. G.H. was not placed in first three.

This evening E. had another headache, asked me to try to cure it as I had done before. Did so. Said two other things. First that the Old Man must never come to live with us again. Next, that he should go to the dentist. Asked him to repeat both later. He repeated the first, but not the second. Looked up the book. It says that a subject cannot be persuaded to do something entirely against his will. Suppose that is the explanation.

January 18 To church today, our parish church. A poor sermon, the vicar a man who does not preach but brays. He brayed about charity. 'The greatest of these is charity.' I agree, I agree. But what if in return for our charity we are met with malice, envy and lies, as I have been by the Old Man? Must we still extend charity, offer the other cheek for him to spit at? Sister Ursula at the Convent would say yes. How long ago that seems, before I knew what it meant to be a wife.

January 19 Edwin has given up carrots. Says he thinks that because they come from the ground they have dirt in them which gets into his stomach. Yet he still eats onions.

January 25 Went today with Edwin to first service held at Wesleyan chapel in Merton High Street. The chapel is new, and smells of bricks and mortar, also very bare. None of the beautiful ceremony associated with the Mass, which I have attended rarely but have always been extremely moved. Edwin's family, however, have always been Dissenters—Methodists—Wesleyans—I do not understand these differences, for surely there is but one God. They seem to wish to do away with all the colour and beauty of the religious service. In any case, Edwin was curious about the new chapel and about the preacher.

This was a gentleman named the Reverend George Dyson, whom Edwin said had some reputation. He is a fine upstanding man, with the high forehead that denotes intellect. The place was almost full, and the Rev. Dyson spoke well and with passion. Greeted us afterwards as we left the chapel, said he was pleased to see us. We gave our address, said we hoped he would call.

CHAPTER 3

THE WESLEYAN MINISTER

'It is not a pleasant spectacle, that of a Christian minister entering into this unwholesome discussion about the two wives, one for companionship and one for service—joining in it apparently with little touch of those sentiments which you would naturally expect such matters to arouse in the

breast of a Christian minister—gradually becoming the intimate friend of both husband and wife;
according to his own account, before there had
been a shadow of a justification for it or a hint
by the husband that it was welcome, addressing
to the wife the words of unhallowed and unChris-
tian admiration; steadily taking advantage of the
husband's weakness, increasing the frequency of
his visits, and kissing, according to himself, in the
presence, and according to himself also, in the
absence of the husband, the wife.'

MR JUSTICE WILLS, summing up

At this time George Dyson was twenty-six years
old, nearly three years younger than Adelaide and
fourteen years Edwin's junior. He was a tall,
broad-shouldered young man, with a bushy moustache, and hair cut short to conceal the fact that
it was already a little thin in front. He was a fluent
orator, and the effect of his sermons was enhanced
by eloquent gestures and by the rich creamy tone
of his voice. In the Wesleyan ministry they did
not pay their servants highly, and George Dyson
subsisted on a stipend of £100 a year. Nevertheless, he was happy in the consciousness of his tal-
ents, and in the awareness that he was marked
out for early promotion.

He was a bachelor, but had an eye for an attractive woman. The Bartletts came regularly to chapel, the man red-faced and stocky, the wife small
and fragile in appearance, and he felt it to be
his duty to call on them. He did so, took tea, was
a little disturbed by his feelings in the presence
of Mrs Bartlett, and let a while elapse before he
called again. On a fine Sunday in June, however,
he did so, and again took tea.

It was a pleasant occasion. Edwin Bartlett, he learned, was a grocer, evidently one of those worthy members of the artisan class who had improved their position in the world. Adelaide was— what was she? Her appearance had about it nothing of the pink-and-white prettiness that Dyson generally admired, and she said little, but still there was some emotional current flowing from her to which he was susceptible. When he mentioned that he was going to Dublin in the following week to take his Bachelor of Arts degree, Edwin Bartlett was much impressed.

'I've always wished I had education, Mr Dyson, and that's a fact. It's a great disadvantage in life, the lack of it.'

'Edwin, you should not say that. You know it has been no disadvantage in your business,' his wife said in a low, gentle voice.

'Maybe not, my dear, but I wish I had more book learning. Mrs Bartlett, now, is always reading, has what I may call a true thirst for knowledge. She studied when she was younger, and I know is anxious to take up her studies again. I don't suppose it would be possible that you could spare the time—' He stopped in slight confusion, and Mrs Bartlett spoke.

'What Edwin wishes to know is whether you could spare time, on your return from Dublin, to give me some tuition in subjects of which I am ignorant, especially in Latin and history.'

'With a suitable remuneration, of course,' her husband added.

George Dyson thought afterwards, but too late, that he should have been warned by the attraction he felt towards Mrs Bartlett. He could have said he had no time, or made another excuse, but he did neither.

Instead he said in his orator's voice, with its faint underlying lilt, 'Why, I am honoured that you should ask me. I shall be delighted to instruct Mrs Bartlett in any subject where my knowledge may be useful. There are calls on my services from religious bodies, but apart from those I can call my time my own when I return from Ireland. There is only one thing upon which I must insist, Mr Bartlett. You have asked me as a friend, and I have replied as a friend. There can be no question of remuneration.'

'I call that downright handsome,' Edwin Bartlett said. 'I'd like to shake you by the hand and say thank you.' His hand gripped George Dyson's with a heartiness that was almost painful.

Mrs Bartlett gave thanks too, in her low voice. That was how it began.

'Do you think, Mr Dyson,' she asked him one day as they sat in the little drawing-room, 'that there can be such a thing as perfect love?'

He put down the Latin primer. 'Perfect love casteth out fear. First epistle of St John.'

'Yes, but that is the Bible. People do not seem in those days to have felt as we feel now. I meant human love, modern love. Can that be perfect?'

She sat almost at his feet, on a stool that she had embroidered herself, and her great eyes gazed up at him. 'Perfection is in the Lord. We poor humans can only strive towards it.'

'But that perfection, if we could achieve it, would not be fleshly, would it? I have read only a little philosophy, but it would be the kind of love they call platonic, is that not true?'

He said a little uneasily, 'I have not read Plato's works, but I know that he is a great philosopher.' And then, with a touch of whimsicality, 'Perhaps that is a subject in which *you* should instruct *me*. And perhaps we should return to our Latin.'

'Mr Dyson, you are so kind to me, so kind and gentle.'

'I wish you could bring yourself to call me George. Perhaps not in public, but when we are together.'

'Would that be proper?'

'I do not see why not. And if you will permit me to call you Adelaide—'

'Oh, I should like that. Mr Dyson—George—I look on you as my mentor in all things, not only history and Latin. Edwin is the best of husbands, but I could wish that he was gentle, as you are. And I could wish also that he was a gentleman. Again, as you are.'

He placed a finger over her lips. They quivered beneath his touch, as the body of a bird quivers in the human hand. 'It is not right that you should speak to me like that of Edwin.' He added softly, almost in a whisper, 'My birdie.'

'Why do you call me that?'

'Because your lips tremble like the body of a baby bird.'

'You are a poet, George. Do you know what Edwin and I call you when we speak to each other about you? Georgius Rex.'

'And why is that, pray?'

She clapped her hands, childlike. 'Because you look like a king.'

He went home that afternoon and on later afternoons in a dream that, as he assured himself, was

not sensual but embodied the perfect love of
which she had spoken. At home, in his apartment,
he was moved to write a poem for her, something
he had never done before:

> Who is it that the Lord above
>   Hath given pure and perfect love,
>   And hath embodied human grace
>   In her small figure and her face?—My Birdie.

> Who is it that hath burst the door
>   Unclosed the heart that shut before
>   And set her queenlike on its throne
>   And made its homage all her own?—My Birdie.

There were six more verses, and the whole
seemed to him extremely beautiful. She thought
so too, when he gave her the poem, which she
called the most wonderful gift she had ever received. When he expressed doubt about her suggestion that she should show it to Edwin, she
agreed and said that it would be their secret.

Apart from this, however, everything was told
to Edwin. On the days that George Dyson came
to the cottage, he often ate his midday dinner
with Adelaide, and then stayed until six o'clock
when Edwin returned. Edwin would say how delighted he was that his little wife was being educated so that she would be truly cultured, and
able to instruct her ignorant husband in many
matters.

At that Adelaide would run to him, and kiss
his cheek. 'Edwin, you are not to say such things.
You know that you have a thousand times more
knowledge than I of what goes on in the world.
I shall just be a little less ignorant, that is all.'

'No, by Jove, that isn't all by any means.' And

then, more than once, he launched into what George Dyson chose to regard as a very whimsical way of talking.

'What do you say, as a preacher and a man of learning now, about the teaching of the Bible in relation to a wife's duties, eh?'

The first time this was said, Dyson had asked just what was meant, and Edwin explained. The sweat stood out on his forehead as he spoke. He was a very sweaty man, whose palms were always slightly moist.

'My view is, and I've often maintained it, that a man should have two wives, one for companionship, the other for service. What I mean by service, now, is generally running the household, cooking, that sort of thing. 'Tisn't fitting Adelaide should do all that, she's fine-bred and delicate as you can see for yourself. She should be the companion wife, educated and intelligent, able to discuss any subject under the sun with her husband. What do you think?'

Was he serious? He had a kind of smile on his face, but then that was often so. He seemed perfectly serious. George Dyson said cautiously, 'That sounds more like Mohammedanism than Christianity to me.'

'I dare say. But the point is, I've read my Bible and there's nothing in it against polygamy.'

'I could not possibly accept that.'

'Very well, you're an educated man and a minister. You just show me where it says in the Bible a man shouldn't have two wives.'

'What I would say to you is that the whole tenor of the Bible is quite contrary to the idea.'

'You see, my dear, he can't show me because

it ain't there. Ask me, it's a matter of plain common sense. You'll stay to supper?'

The subject dropped. It recurred, and George Dyson could not be sure what Edwin meant in advancing such views. Did they spring from opposition to George himself? Apparently not, for when Dyson asked whether he might take Adelaide to look at his apartment one day, Edwin agreed in the heartiest terms.

'Of course Adelaide may go with you. I believe in trust between human beings. I said to Baxter the other day, when he was on about a customer who'd let his account run on for months, Edward, I said, a gentleman's a gentleman, he doesn't reckon to settle his accounts like you and me, and you've got to trust him. So I trust everybody, and it's coming to something if I can't trust a man like you, Mr Dyson.' This was said with a sincerity so evident that it touched George Dyson's heart. He too felt that there was nothing wrong in Adelaide paying a visit to his Merton rooms.

The two of them spent an enchanted afternoon there. She exclaimed over his old school photographs, saying that he was so much more handsome now than he had been then, and she looked at the two shelves of books that made up his library and was pleased that most of them were books of poems. In his rooms also he kissed her for the first time. That was, as he recalled, the right way to put it. He had kissed her on the lips. She, although she made no resistance, had not kissed him. Afterwards he felt that the kiss was a betrayal of trust, and said that Edwin must be told. To this she assented, although her words seemed to him strange.

'You must do what you think right. We should all do what is necessary to our natures, do you not agree? Our kiss was platonic.' He stammered a little as he said that of course it had been. 'It could not have been anything else,' she said almost fiercely.

There was about her something tantalizing, remote, other-worldly. On that afternoon he decided he would have wished her to be his wife, were she not already married to Edwin Bartlett. When the matter of the kiss was mentioned to Edwin, he clapped George on the shoulder.

'So you have kissed Adelaide. And you want to know whether I approve. Certainly I do, are we not all friends? I shall put it to the test by saying that you must kiss her again. Now, this minute. I command you to kiss my wife. Come along.' He positively pulled the two of them together until the embarrassed George bent and touched Adelaide's cheek. Then Edwin put an arm round his wife's waist and kissed her himself, firmly on the lips. Adelaide stood with unchanged expression throughout this, her eyes appearing to look at some distant prospect.

'Now we all love each other as good Christians should, is that not so? Adelaide will play for us, and we can be jolly together.' Later that evening, when Adelaide was out of the room, he said, 'She has been so much happier since you were good enough to give up some of your valuable time to her. You know she is a lady. It is right that she should be educated.'

'All are equal in God's sight.'

'That may be, but she's a lady and I ain't a gentleman, as I don't need to tell you.' And indeed

nobody could have mistaken Edwin Bartlett for
anything but a good honest tradesman. 'I dare
say you wonder why we live out here at Merton,
away from people. The reason is—she's a foreigner, you know that?'

'I knew that she was of French extraction.'

'Right. And being a foreigner, and a lady too,
her ways ain't the way of my family nor my
friends. They think she's stuck-up, putting on side,
when as I've told them it's only that she's shy.
And there was trouble with my father. Take it
all in all, I thought it was best to up sticks and
come and live quietly out here. Then there's another thing. She's of a delicate constitution, physically I mean. Do you think they're a different
structure from each other, women? Some strong,
some weak, would you say that was right?'

'All of God's creatures differ. But I am afraid
I have no knowledge of such things.'

'No, s'pose not. Anyway, that seems to be so.
She had a child but it died. Stillborn. She was
very upset.'

George Dyson's instinct was always to take refuge in a Biblical quotation when embarrassed, but
he felt it might be inappropriate to say that the
Lord giveth and the Lord taketh away. 'No doubt
you will be blessed with others.'

'That's just the thing you see, she don't want
any more. In fact she don't want—' He whispered
in George's ear. 'But a man has his needs, ain't
that so? Though I suppose, Mr Dyson, you being
a minister wouldn't know about that. After a fish
supper, oysters especially, I can tell you—'

At that point Adelaide returned and the conversation ceased, to George Dyson's relief.

She was happier because of his company, and
for much of the time he was able to persuade
himself that this justified his visits. There were
other occasions, however, when he was conscious
of feelings that he knew to be improper for any
man, let alone a minister, to have about another
man's wife. He continued to be fascinated by her
changes of mood. On some days she would settle
down immediately to study, or would ask if he
cared for her to play to him. On others she would
greet him sullenly, and her face then would be
doughy and plain. She surprised him by her effi-
ciency in running the household, dealing with
the servant and gardener, and handling the
dogs. He did not care for these great beasts, although they seemed friendly enough, but she
tended them with love, putting fresh straw in
their kennels, giving them physic when they were
sick. When she was mixing medicine one day for a
dog with a persistent cough, he wondered at her
skill.

'I know something about medicines.' She measured carefully a liquid which she mixed into a
bowl of minced meat.

'For dogs, you mean?'

'Oh, more than that. I think it is right that a
woman should know such things. I have a medicine chest, and know what drugs to give for all
sorts of aches and pains.'

'And how does my little Birdie come to know
such complicated things?' he asked playfully.

'Why, by studying books about medicine. Edwin
has a good deal of pain with his teeth, and I am
able to give him something to relieve the pain.
And then he has dyspepsia quite often, and I pre-

scribe for that. He does not like visiting a doctor, it makes him uneasy. But mostly the trouble is with his teeth. You must have noticed. He was badly treated by a dentist some years ago, and absolutely refuses to see one now.'

George Dyson, whose own teeth were splendidly white and in perfect condition, had observed that Edwin took out his lower denture when he ate, and had also noticed the foulness of his breath. He said only, however, 'What a clever little Birdie it is.'

'Such things are part of a wife's duties. Come along, Glory, this will help your cough.' The dog, Golden Glory, obediently came across. She stroked his ears, and he began to eat the bowl of food. She looked at George Dyson with her great eyes. 'I love the dogs, but that is not perfect love. That can only be the love of God, is not that true, Mr Dyson?'

He returned some equivocal answer, and when he returned to the house he thought the time had come to break his news to her. He was soon to be transferred and in a sense promoted, although there would be no immediate increase in his stipend of £100 a year. He was to take charge of a larger chapel in Putney. He would be busier there, would be bound to live at Putney, and although it was only a few miles away would certainly not be able to visit her regularly at Merton.

He did not know what he had expected, tears or anger, when he told her. For a few moments her face became whiter than usual. Then she said, 'I think it possible that before very long we shall leave here ourselves.'

CHAPTER 4
FROM ADELAIDE'S JOURNAL

August 5, 1885 Today Georgius Rex gave me his grievous news. He is to be moved from here, and we shall not see him again. Those were not the words he used, but it was their meaning. My reply seemed to be spoken automatically, as though by somebody else. I said that we should leave. There was no reason to say this, we had not talked of it, Edwin and I. Oh, I am desperate, desperate.

August 6 Sought solace in the holy poems of Vaughan and Traherne, but found none. Tried to reason out my feelings for Georgius Rex, what are they? I worship the nobility of his bearing, the purity of his brow. I love his tenderness, his delicacy of feeling, his learning. Yet I insist that there is *nothing fleshly, nothing evil,* in my love. I do not desire the fleshly embrace. I feel perfect love. I wish to see him, I must see him. Nothing more.

Yet what of Edwin? Whatever the crudeness of his manners, no woman could have a better husband. And I care for him, make a good home for him, converse with him, play for him. And now that I know the secret of his psychology, his desire to be dominated, I make decisions about everything that affects our personal lives. He is happy that I should do so, happy that I see G.R. Yet this is not true of all things. Last night he was importunate. I resisted. He abandoned the attempt. Degrading.

I have tried to exercise my *gift* to free myself
of this torment, but in vain. I do not now always
use Braid's method, but find that I can put Edwin
into his condition of waking sleep (I do not know
what else to call it) by asking him to look directly
into my eyes. I have then told him he will no
longer wish for the contact of the flesh. He repeats
my words, but to no avail. My hypnotical guide
says that nothing can be achieved against the subject's own deepest wish, and it seems that in Edwin the sensual passion is too strong. A day or
two after one of these sessions he becomes importunate again. This is true especially after a fish
supper.

August 7 Today wrote to Mr Casumain, the Evil
One, from whom I have not heard in years. Told
him of my plight, appealed to him for help. I must
leave here, I must leave Edwin. I can no longer
endure the wifely relationship. That relationship
is condemned by the fact that it produced my
dead son.

August 8 G. R. here today, but for how much
longer? Left before Edwin's return. After Edwin
had his evening meal spoke to him and said I must
leave here, it was too isolated. Now that G. R.
was departing I should see nobody.

Edwin was considerate as always. Said he was
not attached to the cottage, that it was I who had
wished to leave our other homes (true, but it was
to avoid the jeers and sneers of his family and
friends). The cottage rental comes up for renewal
at the end of this month, and we could leave then
if I wished. Said he would be content to live any-

where I pleased, provided he could get easily to
the shops. Said also that he knew I had derived
comfort and profit from our friendship with Georgius Rex—which is what we call him to each other,
although not to his face—and that he wished it
to continue. So it is settled. The dogs must return
to Herne Hill, which I regret. But we shall leave
here.

August 9 A reply from the Evil One. He rejects
my plea totally. He says: 'You are married to a
good and respectable man, and must content
yourself in your present condition of life which,
so far as I understand your letter, presents no
hardship of any kind.' What else did I expect?

Importunacy again tonight, and my rejection.
An unhappy scene, Edwin wept, I refused to stay
in his bed. He asked if I would sit outside it, holding and stroking his toes. I did so for a time. Then
slept on a sofa.

Today Edwin was up, had his cold bath, went
to business as though nothing had happened. This
evening he complained of dyspepsia, acute stomach pains. He said that he thought raw fruit was
bad for him, apples especially, and would eat no
more of them. Two weeks ago he said the same
about tomatoes, blamed the pips. Now he has forgotten, eats tomatoes again.

Tonight also he had a headache, asked me to
try to cure it as I have done before. Used the
gift, and while he was under the influence suggested to him that on leaving the cottage we
should have a holiday. We have not taken one
in the whole of our married life. Suggested also
that G. R. should join us for part of the time. Later

he repeated this to me as his own idea. He desires
the company of G. R. almost as much as I do, is
flattered that a man of culture should treat us as
friends. We spoke of various places, and decided
on Dover. Edwin must still attend to business,
although Mr Baxter will take most of the burden.
Dover will be convenient for reaching Victoria.
He will not need to leave until nine in the morning, and will return by an early train. Edwin tries
to do what I wish. He is a good, kind man.

August 12   We talked in such a friendly way of
our plans. We leave here at the end of the month,
stay in Dover until the end of September. Then
furnished lodgings for a time, until we find another home. Where will that be? Nowhere near
Herne Hill and the Old Man will have no place
in it, that is certain.

G. R. today. He will join us at Dover for part
of the time we are there. Edwin will pay his fare,
at which he protested but not strongly. He stayed
until Edwin's return, then kissed me goodbye. I
do not care for such kissing, but his is less objectionable than Edwin's.

August 15   Made the journey to Dover, inviting
my faithful Annie to go with me. Paid her fare.
Took the first floor of a lodging house, sitting-room
facing the sea and two bedrooms, one for G. R.

Annie asked if I had spoken to Edwin about
making a better, more just will. I had not, but
did so on my return. Edwin agreeable. Says he
intends to make a simple will leaving everything
to me, nothing about losing it if I get married
again. Asked: 'If I were dead, would you marry

Georgius Rex?' Said I had never thought of such a thing.

August 22   Packing up.

August 29   The dogs have gone to Herne Hill. I shall miss them.

August 31   Our last day here. I write in the morning, awaiting the arrival of G. R., who is to dine with us tonight. Tomorrow to Dover.

CHAPTER 5
THE MONTH AT DOVER

'They go to Dover, and they spend a month at Dover, and during that month at Dover Mr Bartlett must have very severely taxed his physical energy. You hear how he used to start at three o'clock in the morning, take the boat train, and come back at nine or ten at night. Flesh and blood won't stand that.'

MR JUSTICE WILLS to the jury

Was it right, could it be right for him to go down with the Bartletts to Dover? The question perturbed George Dyson considerably. Upon the one hand it could not be denied that for a third man, even a man of the cloth, to accompany a husband and wife on holiday, and to occupy a room in their set of apartments, was extremely unusual. Was it also undesirable? He asked himself this question, and found the answer that no doubt it was in many cases, but not if the husband and wife approved and even wished it. But then further, was it proper that Edwin Bartlett should pay his train fare? Well, it was necessary since he could not afford such things, so what was the use in worrying about it?

Upon the other hand—what was there upon the other hand? Why, the fact that he had Edwin's assurance that his presence was good for Adelaide, and that his absence for a period of time depressed her spirits. Edwin admired and trusted him, there could be no doubt of that. Was the trust misplaced? Did he wish for carnal knowledge of her? He put aside the question as unthinkable, one that he must not contemplate. Would he wish to make her Mrs Dyson, if Edwin did not exist? He was under the impression that he would have to wait two years after declaring such an intention, according to Wesleyan rules—but of course the matter did not arise.

He stayed three days and then returned to London, to prepare for his new post and to regard with pleasure his name on the notice board outside the Putney chapel, but at times in those three days he did wonder what Edwin Bartlett was about, to leave him so much in Adelaide's company. Edwin left by the nine o'clock train in the morning and returned about six, so it seemed hardly worth his coming on holiday. When George mentioned this, Edwin said that he had a lot to do with the shops, and that in any case Adelaide greatly enjoyed the company of somebody who knew so much of literature, and was such a fine scholar. That she enjoyed his company was undoubtedly true. They wandered round the town, went to the castle, looked at the shops, went down to the docks and saw the ships.

'I wish I were on one of them, sailing to France.'

'For another holiday?'

'For ever.' Her hand on his arm tightened. 'I hate this life.'

'You must not say such things.'

'But I *do* say them. And I mean them,' she said fiercely. When they returned to the apartment he felt the unmistakable quiver of desire, and took her in his arms. She stayed in them a moment, but when he placed a hand on her breast broke away, crying 'No, no.'

He dropped immediately to his knees. 'My Birdie, I have been tempted. Lead us not into temptation, saith the Lord. I have been tempted and I have sinned in thought, although not in deed.'

'That is nonsense. I did not tempt you. You simply showed yourself to be like all men.'

'It is true,' he said humbly.

'To wish for that kind of sensuality cannot be perfect love.'

'Indeed it is not.'

'And we should surely look for perfect love, beyond human desire.'

'I must return to London. I shall leave tomorrow. We must not meet again.'

'If you are so little able to control your sensual feelings, that will be best. I look for perfection and am prepared to worship it. I can accept nothing less.'

He left the house, and took the first train to London. Back in his Putney rooms he reflected upon it all. He knew that if she had given him encouragement he would have attempted the act itself, an act that would have been a sin for any man, but a much greater sin for a minister. He spent much time on his knees in prayer, and much more in making the necessary preparations for his new ministry, which would be altogether bigger and better. It was gratifying to see *The Rev. George Dyson, B.A.* upon the board outside the chapel. Yet every day he looked to see if there was a letter from her, and felt disappointed not to receive one. And although he took many cold baths, he was unable to extinguish that spark of desire which might, he knew, become a burning flame in her presence.

Two weeks passed, and he had begun to think that he would hear nothing more of the Bartletts, when on a Saturday afternoon he received a visit from Edwin. He was shocked by the man's appearance. Bartlett's usually ruddy cheeks were pale, there were marks on his face where he had cut himself while shaving, and when he sat down his hands moved again and again over the nap of his hat. Dyson's slight perturbation was dispelled by his first words.

'I consider you as a friend of the family, Mr Dyson. I have come to give you some information. And for help.'

'As I am a friend, I hope that you will call me George.'

'Thank you. I am honoured.' He paused for a moment, then continued. 'I have made a new will. The old one, in which my property would have come to Adelaide only if she remained a widow, was unjust. It is now left to her without qualification. And I must tell you that I have named you as one of my executors with my solicitor, Mr Wood, as the other. I hope there is nothing objectionable in that.'

'On the contrary. Let me now say that *I* am honoured by your trust, Edwin. But this will is a mere precaution, of course. You have many years of health and happiness before you. And before you continue, there is something I must say to you.' Now that he knew he was not to be accused, something impelled George Dyson to make a confession of his feelings. 'You have trusted me with your friendship, and you have permitted—nay, encouraged—me to be friendly towards Adelaide. I must tell you that I have grown very much attached to her, and it is right to let you know it. This attachment has been disturbing to me in my work, and it was for this reason that I left Dover so abruptly. I ask you to tell me frankly, should I discontinue my friendship with you both?'

It did not occur to him that the question was one that he might more suitably have answered himself. He heard the reply, the inevitable reply, with what seemed a quickening of the pulse, a surge of blood in his veins.

'Why should you discontinue it? Your preaching has been a great and undoubted benefit to Adelaide.'

'I am glad of it. But I was not talking about my preaching.'

'Then let me say that we value your friendship, the friendship of a man of true culture, very highly. Both of us. It was partly to ask for an act of friendship that I came to see you.'

Dyson inclined his head benignly, saw his reflection in a glass across the room, and admired his expression. He was still looking at himself in the glass and reflecting that he looked his best with chin raised a little assertively as became a servant of the Lord, while he heard Edwin Bartlett telling him that Adelaide had been greatly out of sorts since his departure, so much so that at times she would hardly utter a word. She had said once that she could not bear Edwin in her sight, and for the last few days he had tried to remove himself from her presence as much as possible. He had taken the boat express up from Dover at three in the morning, and instead of returning by the four o'clock afternoon train had taken an evening train at eight o'clock. George Dyson exlaimed in distress at this.

'But you hardly see her.'

'That seems to be her wish. It will not do, Mr Dyson.'

'George.'

'A husband has his rights. A man his needs.'

'For two wives,' he said, trying to make a little joke of it.

'Mr Dyson—George—for a time now I have had *no* wife. You understand me. And a man has his needs, which must be satisfied if he is to remain healthy.' The loose denture in his lower jaw clattered. He looked ghastly ill, as though about to faint.

'Are you telling me that on these days when you left very early and returned very late—'

'I relieved my needs, yes, yes, that is so. But it is not right. A man has needs and his wife should satisfy them, does not the Bible say so?'

'Calm yourself, Edwin. I am not sure that what you say can be justified in the Bible.'

'It says in *Genesis*, "A man shall cleave unto his wife, and they shall be one flesh."'

'But also in the epistle of St Peter that a man

should give honour to his wife as the weaker vessel.'

'If she is the weaker vessel, then she must obey her husband. It is not right for her to deny him.'

'Mr Bartlett—Edwin—I must not intervene between you, that would not be proper. But I must say something of these habits at which you are hinting. You must know that they are a sin in the eyes of the Lord, and also that you run grave risks of disease by indulging such practices.' The other seemed about to speak, but said nothing. 'I do not understand in what way you think I can be helpful.'

'Write to her. Will you do that for me? Write, and show her the error of her ways. Look here, look at this. It is a letter that she sent me years ago when she was at a convent in Belgium, where she went to be educated. You can see how she writes of wishing to be nothing more than a good and obedient wife. Remind her of that. Tell her that during my lifetime this is her duty.'

Dyson read the letter, which was couched in the simple devotional language of a schoolgirl, and handed it back. Then he spoke.

'I am grieved by what you say, Edwin. I am anxious to help in any way I can but it would not be proper for me, or any other man, to discuss the secrets of the bedchamber. What I can do, and I will do it, is to write a letter to Adelaide, reminding her that she is your wife and should remember the duties of a wife towards her husband. And if you think it might be helpful, I will suggest that I pay another visit to Dover. But only if you wish it.'

'Indeed I do. Have I not said that I wish our

friendship to continue, and that I have the fullest trust in you?'

So it was settled. The letter was written, in the terms he had spoken of, and it mentioned his impending visit. He could not have said, he hardly knew himself, what motives moved him, but among them was a longing to see Adelaide again. A reply came from Edwin by return of post. It began:

Dear George,
Permit me to say that I feel great pleasure in thus addressing you for the first time. To me it is a privilege to think that I am allowed to feel towards you as a brother and I hope our friendship will ripen as time goes on without anything to mar its future brightness. Would that I could find words to express my thankfulness to you for the very loving letter you sent Adelaide today. It would have done anybody good to see her overflowing with joy as she read it whilst walking along the street . . .

The letter ended: 'Looking forward to the future with joyfulness, I am, Yours affectionately, Edwin.' It was followed by a telegram to say that a cheque was in the post to cover his fare when he came down again to Dover. As he wrote in reply, saying that he responded to the wish that their friendship would ripen with the lapse of time, and that he did so confidently because of the trust and esteem on which it was based, it seemed to him that fate was driving him irresistibly into the arms—or if not into the arms, at least into the presence—of Adelaide. He had done his best to avoid such a conclusion, but Edwin had encouraged it, had suggested almost that his presence at Dover was indispensable to the Bartletts' happiness. He ended with what seemed to him just the right affection-

ate note. 'Dear old Dover! It will ever possess a
pleasant memory for me in my mind and a warm
place in my heart,' and signed himself, Yours affectionately, George.

He went down again to dear old Dover, and
stayed there for the last days of the holiday. Edwin
received him warmly, and seemed to have over-
come that difficulty in using his Christian name.
He still went up to London on the boat train,
but returned about six in the evening, and seemed
more cheerful than when they had talked at Putney. Adelaide was simply Adelaide. What more
could he say, but that she bewitched him? When
they met she offered her cheek to be kissed, but
did not show the delight in his presence that he
had hoped. They were together during the day,
and there were times when he thought that she
was using him as a means to execute some object
she had in mind, rather than taking pleasure in
his company as he did in hers. At other times
she would be gay, kittenish, deeply respectful of
his scholarship and ready to sit quite literally at
his feet while he read aloud poems, or the *Lives
of the Saints*. He greatly admired the work of
Lord Byron, while deploring the poet's scandalous
life, but although she enjoyed 'The Prisoner of
Chillon' and 'Mazeppa,' she did not care for the
love poems.

> 'When we two parted
> In silence and tears,
> Half broken-hearted
> To suffer for years,'

he read, but she listened coldly, and said that if
the poet's heart had been only *half* broken, he
could not have suffered greatly.

'As for me, my heart was broken when I was
very young, and was denied my proper place in
the world.'

'And what was that? A place at Court?' He had
meant it as a joke, but her eyes flashed fire.

'Do not joke about things of which you are ignorant. Yes, perhaps a place at Court. Certainly not
a place as a grocer's wife. Sometimes I think that
I shall go mad, the life I lead is so tedious, so
lacking in beauty. I cannot bear it. Is it not beauty
that we should look for in our lives? Do you know
why I like to be with you, why I named you Georgius Rex? Because you are kingly, you are noble,
you are beautiful.'

Such words were not altogether distasteful, but
still he felt bound to deprecate them, to say that
worship of the Lord should rule our lives, that
we should desire goodness and if we did so would
discover beauty. At that she went on her knees,
asked him to pray with her, and said that she was
a wicked woman who often sinned in thought.

On the last day of the holiday Edwin took him
aside, and expressed gratitude for his help.

'Your presence has been of much benefit to Adelaide.'

'And to you also, I hope.'

'Yes. I consider you as one of the family, George.
I have not forgotten your affection for Adelaide.
Indulge it, by all means, it may be the means of
getting her into a better frame of mind.'

It was evident that Edwin considered ministers
to be made of something other than flesh and
blood, but Dyson did not say so. Instead, he asked
if Edwin's difficulties were now resolved.

'By no means. She says she likes me, but doesn't
care for that sort of thing. Did you ever hear such

rubbish? But just at present—' He paused so long that Dyson asked what he had been about to say.

'Nothing. But just at present it's not a problem, that's all.' His blue eyes looked hard at Dyson, who did not care to question him further. 'Here's what it is, what I was going to say. You won't give us up now, when we go back to London, will you? You'll come and see us. I'm a plain man, don't know how these things are rightly put and you'll have to excuse me for that, but I want to say this. If money's a consideration, and I know it is, then that's something you've no need to worry about. Baxter and Bartlett is in a good way of business.' He smacked his jacket, within which a wallet gave off a satisfyingly solid sound.

Was ever man so tried, so tempted? He made a grateful reply, saying that he would have to see how much of his time was taken by duties at the new chapel, but he knew that the decision was his alone. Edwin gripped his hand, and with teeth clicking said that his friendship was a standby to them both.

On the last day Edwin took the train to Herne Hill. Later in the day Dyson escorted Adelaide to an hotel in the Strand, and saw her settled in. Edwin was to join her in the evening. When they said goodbye he took her in his arms and was surprised again by her slightness and smallness.

'My Birdie.'

She disengaged herself. 'Tomorrow I shall find rooms. Then I hope we shall see you.'

'It is wrong to do it. I ought not to see you.'

'You must decide that for yourself.' She turned her back on him, looked into a wall mirror, patted her thick black hair.

'Edwin has said he wishes our friendship to continue. As I told you, he knows of my affection for you. And for him also, of course.'

'Of course.'

CHAPTER 6
FROM ADELAIDE'S JOURNAL

September 3, 1885 Have brought down to Dover the *Lives of the Saints*, read them constantly. In their lives was perfection, a love not mortal but heavenly. Tried to say something of this to G. R., with little success. If he loves me, and I must now say *if*, that love is impure, not heavenly.

September 5 G. R. departed. The sun sinks in the sky.

September 12 Edwin's behaviour unaccountable. He leaves by the boat train, returns late at night. Yet he told me that September is not a busy time in the shops. What does he do in London? I do not care to know, but note that his importunacy has ceased.

September 17 Deep, deep depression in these last days. I long for G. R.'s presence, yet when he is here the sensuality of his nature distresses me. What does love mean if it is not the love of God?

September 19 Edwin returned at 11 last night. Went to bed. He asked me to perform an act which The Book says is weakening, debilitating, can lead to madness and imbecility. He has read

The Book, knows what Dr Nichols said, but still persisted. Refused, left his bed, read in the sitting-room. Edwin left at 2:30 A.M. to catch the boat train.

I cannot endure this life.

September 21 A letter from G. R.! Edwin had been to see him, and he sent a letter so good, so loving, that I read it again and again. No trace of sensuality in it, nothing but purest love. He says that I must do my duty to Edwin, but when did I fail to care for him? Edwin almost as delighted as I by the letter, has written to G. R. a reply which he showed me, very fine and manly. Am I not lucky, to be loved by two such men?

September 24 Edwin now leaving and returning at usual times. Found bottle of tablets in bathroom cupboard today. He seemed confused when I asked their purpose, said something about dyspepsia. I do not believe him. Tasted one of the tablets, spat it out. Not bismuth or milk of magnesia. I believe that he has a disgusting disease.

September 25 Dr Nichols tells of the progress of the disease, primary, secondary, tertiary. The details are horrifying. I cannot bring myself to ask a direct question, but shall keep careful watch. I read in The Book: 'A person simply sleeping with another, or even in the same bed—possibly by bathing in the same water—may take the disease.'

September 27 Return of G. R. His manly form, his glowing face, his noble head. I am ready to worship him as a man of feeling, a man of God.

*   *

September 30 But not, *not* the sensualist who
fumbles at my clothing. I too am guilty of human
weakness. I wish to be in G. R.'s company. Edwin
has the disease. There can be no doubt. He is
taking all sorts of pills, and they are not those
he takes for dyspepsia and his other often imaginary troubles. If I were infected—what a terrible
thought, it must not happen.

Supposing Edwin died from his disease, I would
accept G. R. as my life companion. But it should
be a marriage of true minds, as Shakespeare says,
nothing more. Does G. R. understand this? He
must understand it. I am only a feeble woman,
but I feel in myself a power of mind and a strength
of spirit that can conquer all obstacles. And then
I have the gift, surely the gift must help me.

Today I reminded myself of my origins, repeated the name I was given at birth. It is not
my own name, but it is a noble one.

PART FOUR
Claverton Street

CHAPTER 1
A SINGLE BED

MR POLAND (prosecuting counsel): Have you seen, when Mrs Bartlett and Mr Dyson have been there, anything to attract your attention when you went in?

ALICE FULCHER: I have seen them sitting on the sofa together.

MR POLAND: Yes, and—?

ALICE FULCHER: And I have seen them sitting on the floor, with her head on Mr Dyson's knee. Mr Dyson was sitting on a low chair.

Evidence at trial

Claverton Street was wide, pleasant and quiet. One end led down to the Thames embankment, the other to a maze of Pimlico streets. No. 85 was near the river, a house similar to the rest of them, flat-fronted and with long, narrow, first-floor windows, built in the 'sixties, twenty years ago. The brass knocker and letter-plate were well polished, the house like the street had the air of a social class distinctly higher than anything in suburban Herne Hill or Merton. It would do very well, Adelaide thought. As she rang the bell she noticed that a plate outside the door said that F. H. Doggett, Registrar of Births and Deaths for the Pimlico district, lived here.

Mrs Doggett had the drawing-room floor to let, and took Mrs Bartlett up to see it. They were

two fine rooms, the front one with long sash windows looking out to the street. The room had been
cleverly divided to serve as sitting- and dining-
room, with a sofa and armchairs at one end, din-
ing-table and sideboard at the other. There was
a piano. Mrs Bartlett clapped her hands when she
saw it, sat down and played a few bars.

'I love playing. You will not object to it?'

'It's what the piano is there for. But *not* after
eleven o'clock, if you please.'

'Oh, there is no question of that. Mr Bartlett
and I are always asleep before then. Sometimes
he falls asleep when I am playing. He says that
the sound soothes him.' Mrs Doggett sniffed.
There was something foreign about her visitor's
looks and way of talking, and she did not approve
of foreigners. 'But he does not have the best of
health.'

'Not an invalid, I hope. I couldn't let to an invalid.'

'No, no,' Mrs Bartlett laughed at the idea. 'But
he has a little internal difficulty that troubles him
now and then. A kind of dyspepsia.'

'And this is the bedroom.' Mrs Doggett pulled
aside the folding doors separating the rooms to
reveal a double bed, a washstand and basin, a large
clothes cupboard, and an ordinary sash window
looking out to the back. Mrs Bartlett nodded her
approval, then hesitated.

'One little problem. Mr Bartlett's internal difficulty makes him restless at night, so that it is more
convenient to have single beds. I am sure you
will not mind making the change.'

'Single beds.' In a way Mrs Doggett was slightly
relieved, for the request seemed to suggest that

the immorality associated in her mind with foreigners was not in question. On principle, however, she felt bound to oppose it. 'I don't know, I'm sure. I haven't two singles I could put in. I should have to buy something.'

'There is no hurry. It will be at your convenience, of course. But perhaps after a little while you can find something.'

Her tone was so mild that Mrs Doggett agreed to provide a single bed as soon as possible, although there was something about this funny-looking foreigner that she didn't quite fancy. She said with a touch of sharpness that no doubt Mr Bartlett would want to look at the apartment himself, and made a mental note that if there seemed anything shady about him she would make an excuse and say the apartment was let. When she saw Edwin Bartlett, however, her doubts vanished. He was short and stocky, blue-eyed and ruddy-cheeked, very plainly an Englishman. Mrs Doggett gathered from a few well-phrased questions that he was in trade, but who paid any attention to that in these days? From what he said, he was in a good way of business, and that was what mattered.

She noticed also that he was most considerate to his wife, and deferred to her in everything. When Mrs Doggett said that it was a bit of a journey from Claverton Street to his shops in South London, Mr Bartlett replied that they had tried living over the shop, but that didn't suit. 'If Mrs Bartlett is pleased to live here in Pimlico, then I am pleased too, Mrs Doggett. You may take that for a fact.'

As she said afterwards to her Horace, it was

easy to see who wore the trousers in that family, although it seemed that butter wouldn't melt in her mouth. They got down to details, and it appeared that he liked water brought up for a cold bath every morning, a good breakfast at seven-thirty sharp, and dinner when he returned in the evening. Mrs Doggett would be doing the cooking. What about ordering? Mrs Bartlett would like her to do that too.

'Very well,' Mrs Doggett said. 'Now, are there likely to be visitors for evening dinner, because where visitors are concerned I have to charge extra.'

'A gentleman friend of ours will be dining perhaps once a week.'

'Then I shall be pleased to be informed in the morning so that I can order according.'

'Of course,' Mrs Bartlett said. 'It is only a clergyman.'

'Mrs Bartlett is a great student,' her husband said proudly. 'The Reverend Dyson is kindly helping her with her studies.'

Only a clergyman indeed. As Alice said, the man was there morning, noon and night. That might be a little bit of an exaggeration, but he came twice a week, sometimes three times, and there were days when he arrived as early as half past nine and stayed all day. As for reading books, Alice had seen books about in the room when she tidied, but she had never noticed the reverend gentleman with them under his arm, or seen them being studied. If they were studying books, why were the curtains sometimes pulled together and then pinned, so that nobody could see in, and what was she doing with her head on the reverend gentleman's knee, bold as brass, not even bother-

ing to move when Alice went in? I am not one
to listen to tittle-tattle, as Mrs Doggett said to her
husband, but something as shouldn't be is going
on there.

'And how many times has Alice seen this, then?'

'Just the once,' Mrs Doggett said reluctantly.

'There you are. He's a man of the cloth, remember, and an educated man too, you say. He's giving
Mrs Bartlett instruction.'

'Instruction!' Mrs Doggett snorted. 'I'll tell you
something else, Horace. He's keeping his old
lounge coat here, and his slippers. Gets them out,
calm as you please, and when Alice goes in he's
sitting back, quite at home. I never heard the
like.'

'Well, there's no secret in the visits, her husband
knows. And sometimes he stays until Mr Bartlett
comes back, you told me so yourself. It's none
of our affair, I don't know why you're bothering
your head with it.'

'And another thing. She said Mr Bartlett was
dyspeptic. You know what he ate for breakfast
today? Eggs, sausages, bacon, fried bread, and
then toast and marmalade. Tonight it's going to
be pork chops. Funny kind of dyspepsia. And then
he brings home fancy bits of things from his shops,
it seems he's a grocer. Mind you, he's always taking pills. Alice tells me she's seen a whole row
of bottles. Shouldn't wonder if he's one of those
who thinks he's ill when he isn't.'

'Perhaps that's so, my dear, perhaps that's so.
As long as they pay their rent, that's the main
thing.' Mr Doggett, who had never spoken to the
Bartletts, was determined not to get involved in
their affairs.

*   *

'My text today comes from the epistle of St John. "Perfect love casteth out fear." You may have noticed that I did not say "The text for my sermon," and I do not want you to think of this as a sermon, a lecture, given by somebody who knows better than you how men and women should behave to each other. We are all the vessels of the Lord, all subject to temptation. All of us sometimes do acts, petty and mean, of which afterwards we are ashamed. These actions are prompted by jealousy, envy, and above all by fear, that fear which comes from the absence of love.' The Reverend George Dyson flung his arms wide, and his voice rose in the scale to become sonorous as a bell. 'Oh, brothers and sisters, I say to you, love one another, for perfect love casteth out fear. If love is our motive, if our actions in life spring from the love of Christ and the love of man, then we shall put away all malice and uncharitableness. Every one of our actions will be virtuous, no matter how slight those actions may be, because they are born in love of the Lord . . .'

The chapel at Putney was well filled, and those who listened had their faces turned towards the speaker, a little as if he were that God whose name is love. The place seemed to Adelaide bare and crude like all Wesleyan places of worship. It lacked the colour and feeling of the Catholic faith for which she still yearned, although Edwin's dislike of what he called the Scarlet Woman was such that she had not been in a Catholic church for years, but the eloquence of the speaker more than compensated for anything missing in the place of worship. She concentrated intensely on the words, trying to find in them a meaning attached particularly to her own life. For those who loved

perfectly and had trust in the Lord all things were
possible, was that not the message? If through perfect love you had expelled carnality, you were
surely a superior being, one who could not be
judged by common standards. Beside her Edwin
sat with eyes tightly closed, as always in church
or chapel. He breathed a little stertorously, yet
he was not asleep but paying particular attention
to the underlying meaning of the talk.

Afterwards, as they filed out, the young clergyman had a word and a smile for everybody, a
particular smile and pressure of the hand for Edwin and Adelaide. Edwin said that it had been
very fine.

'My dear, dear friends. Thank you.'

'Shall we see you tomorrow?' Adelaide asked.

'Not tomorrow, alas. I shall call on Tuesday, if
that is permitted.'

'Permitted! I should say so.' That was Edwin.
'And stay to dinner. I shall try to be back early.'

The Reverend George Dyson gave them a smile
full of sweetness as they passed on.

A week after they moved into the Claverton
Street rooms, an iron bed was brought up and
put into the back bedroom, under Mrs Doggett's
supervision.

'There you are, then,' she said to Mrs Bartlett.
'I hope that will suit. I've been to the expense
of buying it.'

'Thank you, that will be excellent.'

'Has Mr Bartlett had bad nights, then?'

'Mr Bartlett always sleeps poorly because of his
digestive troubles. He is very kind, and does not
wish to disturb me.'

So there was no further risk of infection through

sleeping in the same bed. Edwin made no objection to using the small bed when she said that he kept her awake, but he was occasionally importunate, especially after a fish supper. He seemed now resigned to her refusal, although he would sometimes ask her to stroke his foot, and especially his big toe. She complied with the request, although she closed her eyes or kept them averted while she performed the action, so that she could not see the expression on his face. She looked in the drawers to see what new medicines he was taking. There was a different one each week, and all had in them tinctures of some kind of metal, lead, zinc or mercury. He presumably thought they were remedies for his dreadful disease.

She said nothing to Edwin or anybody else of her knowledge about his illness. She had lately acquired *Squire's Companion to the British Pharmacopoeia*, and the information it contained gave her all sorts of ideas. She had made a decision as to what must be done, although not as to the way of doing it. She broke into one of George's poetry readings one day to ask: 'Have you wondered why it is that Edwin throws us so much into each other's company?'

'He has perfect trust and faith in the purity of our love.'

'There is something else. Edwin knows that his life is not likely to be a long one. He would like you to be my friend when he is gone.'

'I would wish to be something more than that.'

She fixed him with those great eyes whose intensity he found so disturbing. 'I may need help. Will you give it when I ask?'

Her meaning was not clear to him, but he had

a vision of Edwin being placed in the ground,
and of her pleading face upturned towards him.
He said that he would help her always, and then
asked what was the matter with Edwin.

'He has internal trouble. He does not like it
spoken of, and will not go to a doctor. He is afraid
of doctors, as he is of dentists, so I have to nurse
and doctor him myself. You know I have some
skill in medicine, and I took advice from Dr
Nichols.'

He had heard something already of Dr Nichols's
strange and interesting ideas. No more was said,
except that she asked him not to speak to Edwin,
because he was upset by mention of illness. From
that time onwards, however, George Dyson was
intent to notice any sign of the illness she had
mentioned. Nothing was apparent, except some
weariness when Edwin came home at night, natural enough in such a hard-working man. It was
true that he sometimes complained of dyspeptic
pains, caused no doubt by his unwise eating habits,
the consumption of large quantities of meat and
pastry, and avoidance of all vegetables except potatoes. He and Edwin had no further private conversation such as had taken place at Putney, but
the implication of Adelaide's words remained with
him. If Edwin had some disease of a mortal kind,
would he wish to marry Adelaide after an appro-
priate passage of time?

There was a sense in which he was almost married to her now. When he came to Claverton
Street he put on his old coat and slippers, he had
meals there, was like a member of the family.
Yet there was a wide gap between that, and what
he understood as marriage. Those sensual long-

ings, that desire to touch and hold Adelaide, to lie with her in the double bed from which they were separated only by a door, all these things were a torment to him. He prayed to be released from such desires, but they did not go away. Nor could he break himself of the custom of paying two or three visits a week, although he was aware of neglecting his flock at Putney. Edwin and Adelaide came every Sunday to hear him speak, and their presence seemed to give special force and persuasiveness to his words. Adelaide referred once or twice to the illness, but there seemed no sign of any trouble more serious than bad teeth.

And then one evening, when the three of them sat round the drawing-room fire after dinner, Edwin spoke, using—as he rarely brought himself to do even now—George Dyson's Christian name.

'I want you to know, George, how grateful I am for the friendship you've given us. You are an educated man, a Bachelor of Arts and a scholar, and it's an honour for us to have you as a friend.' Adelaide made a movement, and he corrected himself. 'An honour for me. Adelaide's different, as I think you know, and she's educated too, she's got book learning. So what I have to say is that I hope you'll be a friend to her when I am gone. She'll need friends then.'

He did not know what to say, and took refuge in playfulness as usual. 'Come, come now, Edwin, no morbidity. You'll be with us for many a year.'

'That's as may be. But I hope you'll look after my Adelaide.'

Edwin put an arm round her neck, and she placed an arm round him. 'And I love my Edwin. And we both have a true Christian love for you, isn't that true, Edwin?'

Edwin laughed heartily, and said it was perfectly true. He kissed Adelaide, and invited George to kiss her as well. There was a good deal of laughter. Adelaide played 'The Lost Chord' on the piano.

So October and November passed.

CHAPTER 2
AN AFTERNOON WITH MADAME BLAVATSKY

'As pure water poured into the scavenger's bucket is befouled and unfit for use, so is divine truth when poured into the consciousness of a sensualist. Observe, that the first of the steps of gold which mount towards the Temple of Truth is— A CLEAN LIFE. This means a purity of body, and a still greater purity of mind, heart and spirit.'
Letter to H. P. Blavatsky from her Master

It was in November that Adelaide had the experience which she thought of afterwards as the most important event of her life. It was a single meeting only, a meeting followed by a letter, but the memory of that afternoon remained with her always.

She was looking at dresses one day in Gorringe's, the big store near Victoria, when somebody spoke her name. On turning, she saw a lady whom she had met during her attendance at Mrs Nichols's classes. The memory of those days carried more pain than pleasure, but she allowed herself to be borne away to Stewart's teashop nearby, and there over China tea with very thin bread and butter and scones, listened to Mrs Win-

stone (after a few minutes she recalled the name)
recounting the latest news. The news, that is, of
what might be called the Nichols world, for Mrs
Winstone was a profound believer in hydropathy,
and a subscriber to the *Herald of Health*. She was
tall and thin, wore clothes that seemed to have
been loosely draped over her frame, and had rings
upon six of her fingers. Mrs Nichols, Adelaide
learned, had passed on more than a year ago, but
the doctor continued his editing and his writing
from the house in Earls Court.

'I miss the classes greatly,' Mrs Winstone said.
'Mary Nichols was a true healer. But I am now
a theosophist. Have you joined the movement?'

Adelaide said she knew little of it, and asked
what a theosophist believed.

'They are concerned with higher things, another world.' Mrs Winstone's hands glittered as
she gestured upwards. She went on to talk of the
Theosophical Society, and the meetings held each
month at which discussion was altogether free.
And the greatest figure in the Society was in London for a visit. Adelaide's wandering attention was
caught by a single sentence.

'She is a holy woman, she believes in total purity
of mind and body, she has abandoned the sensual
life.'

The rest of the conversation passed her by, but
the holy woman's views coincided so much with
her own that she felt compelled to write a letter.
In it she said that she was striving towards a life
that moved away from sensual things, and would
be grateful for any advice that Madame Blavatsky
could give her. The reply was written in a bold
hand, enclosed in a thick envelope on the back

of which was printed: 'There is no religion higher than the truth.' The letter was no more than a couple of lines. It said: 'Dear Friend, I welcome all seekers after truth. I shall be at home on Friday at four-thirty. Come!' It was signed H. P. Blavatsky.

The house was in Holland Park, not far from the place where she had visited Mrs Nichols in days that seemed very long ago. The door was opened by a young Hindu, who with a slight bow but no words led her to a large room at the back of the house, overlooking the park. All around were souvenirs of India, where the sage had spent much of her life, Benares bronzes, Palghat mats, Adoni carpets, Moradabad platters, Kashmir plaques. Bookshelves were all around the room, and more books were piled on tables. All these Adelaide noticed later. She had eyes now only for the extraordinary figure who rose from a chair beside a desk to greet her.

She was tall, and tremendously fat, with a great head covered with bright frizzy hair that was barely touched by grey. Her face was the colour of earth, with thick, coarse features. The nose was big and blunt, the mouth huge, the chin blended with the mass of flesh beneath. Her hands and feet were surprisingly small and delicate. She wore a kind of black sack with no ornament of any kind, and her feet were encased in old leather slippers. The effect might have been repulsive, but was not. Adelaide accepted and felt warmed by her embrace. Her English was strongly accented, but perfectly grammatical.

'I am Helena Petrovna Blavatsky, and I am a Russian as you can tell from my name. I seek always and everywhere for truth. And you, little one, you also are a seeker after truth. It is a pleasure to meet you on my visit to London.'

'How long do you stay here?'

'I do not know myself. My master will tell me.' She laughed, a laugh that seemed to shake her whole body. 'Do not look so surprised. My master is my teacher, my guru. His name is Gulab Lal Singh, and you may read about him in my books. Whatever I say you may believe, because it is not I who say it but my master. Do you wish to know about the Theosophical Society?

'First you must know that it is in no way political, and in no way interferes with any religious convictions you or any other member may have. Our approach is purely scientific, we bring back out of darkness and oblivion the mighty and ancient doctrines of the East which leave behind all that modern science knows, and of which it is so proud. We reject the materialism of science, we offer the immortality of the soul through the purification and education of the inner self.' She suddenly called: 'Mohini.'

The young Indian reappeared. 'Mohini is a young Brahmin who has come here with me. He is a chela and he too has a master, a Mahatma named Koot Hoomi. Come, Mohini, receive my blessing.'

The young man went on to his knees and bowed his head so that it touched the carpet. She laid her hand upon it. He rose, with head still bowed.

'What is a chela?'

'It is the same as a monk, an ascetic. He rejects all earthly influences, and must not touch or be touched by a woman. I touched him, you may say, but it was not I but my master. He feels too much the influence of human magnetism, which can be transmitted by the touch of a hand, or a kiss. So he refrains from touching, to keep himself perfectly pure. Do you wish to question Mohini?' She shook her head. The young man bowed again, and retired.

'I should like to live such a life as his. Away from all sensual influence.'

'Yes, you said something like that. Where is your letter? I have so many, people write to me from all over the world.' She began to look through the papers on her desk. 'Here it is, yes, sensual things, yes. How can I help you, little one? I am not a saint, you know, Blavatsky is not a saint.' Again the gust of laughter agitated her body, the sound rich and deep as if she were a man. 'Everybody has a story to tell. What is your story, my child?'

She told her story, or told more of it than she had revealed to anybody. She spoke of her noble origin, her marriage, of the clergyman whose love for her she feared was sensual, of Edwin's importunacy, and of her desire for a love that should be wholly pure. At the end of her narrative a silver tinkling sound could be heard, which seemed to come from immediately above their heads.

'Did you hear that? It means that my master is here, although you and I cannot see him. He says that I may trust you, and should do for you whatever I can. It is the master's wish that I should tell you about myself. Have you read my book, *Isis Unveiled?*' Adelaide shook her head. There was something about Madame Blavatsky, the bulk, the utter self-confidence, the young Indian chela, the atmosphere of a world altogether unlike anything she had known, that overwhelmed her. 'It does not matter. When you are ready for the book you will read it. But here is a mystery. The great goddess Isis reveals her secrets only to a being virginally pure. That is why Mohini may in time become as great an adept as his master Koot Hoomi. He is a virgin, an ascetic who never looks on women. Yet you saw Mohini kneel to me, and that is because he knows I am a priestess, and through my master can direct the forces of nature. But—this is what the sceptics ask—how is it possible for old Blavatsky to be an adept? She is madame, not mademoiselle, in her youth she had all sorts of romantic adventures. How can she be an adept?'

Madame Blavatsky leaned back in her chair, and vented another of those gusty laughs. The great earth-coloured face shone with sweat, the pores on the nose were clearly visible. It seemed plain that she was ready to answer her own question, and she did so.

'I will tell you how. I am not capable of loving passionately, such a thing is beyond me, it has been all my life. My family was noble like yours, but they were miserably narrow beings. I married Blavatsky to get away from them, but he never was a husband to me, and I soon ran away from him. I have wandered all my life from land to land, everywhere I have studied the hidden secrets of the universe, in a dozen countries there are disciples who honour my name. Now I am an old woman, I am called Madame Blavatsky, but still I remain an untainted virgin with the heart of a young girl. You have heard other things

perhaps, you have heard of my child?' Adelaide
shook her head. She was incapable of speech.
'They say, those enemies who think it worth
spreading lies about old Blavatsky, that a child
was born to her. I will tell you the truth of that.
This was something done to save the honour of
a friend, you understand? The boy was not my
own, but I adopted him, educated him, called him
son in the face of the world. Yet Blavatsky remained a virgin. She did so by an act of the will.'

There was more, much more, as the afternoon
uncoiled. Tea was brought in by another Indian,
together with very tiny cakes. The tea was strong,
and like the cakes had a curious scent. Madame
Blavatsky urged the food on her visitor, but
touched nothing herself. Colonel Olcott, who was
introduced as the president of the Theosophical
Society, came in and sat with them for a few minutes. The Colonel was an American, a tall handsome man whose appearance was marred only
by one wandering eye, which at times looked in
a corner of the room when the other eye was
looking straight forwards. But everything else was
submerged beneath Madame Blavatsky's personality, and beneath what she had said. It was possible to have been married, to have brought up a
child regarded as a son, yet to remain a virgin
by an act of the will. Was not she herself also a
virgin by an act of the will?

Adelaide said nothing of the visit to Edwin or
to Georgius Rex. She felt she had been granted
a vision which they could not share. She thought
of joining the Society, but her interest was in its
founder rather than in the doctrine. She longed
to see Madame Blavatsky again, and wrote asking
for permission to pay another visit, and asking

also whether one could will oneself to become a virgin even after unwilling participation in sensual acts. The reply came with that message about religion and the truth printed on the back. The letter said:

My dear Little One,

Your letter pleased me much, but it is not fated that we should meet again here. My right hand is so swollen that my fingers are numb and I can hardly write. This country does not suit me. I leave tomorrow, to settle for the winter at Würzburg, a few hours from Munich. I shall see if the waters at Kissingen help my gout. Mohini goes with me, and Olcott. Others promise to come. Why not you?

In answer to your question: with faith all things are possible. Everything we *imagine* may become *real*.

My cordial bow to you, and eternal, unceasing love and friendship. Farewell, till we meet again.

H. P. Blavatsky

This, then, was her single meeting with the priestess of Isis. Afterwards she heard much hostile talk about Madame Blavatsky, of the childish tricks she played like the one with the silver bell, of the way she set one follower against another, of allegations that much in her books and her talk was quoted or copied from ancient writers, that she was concerned only to impose herself upon a credulous world. She heard such things, but did not believe them. For her Madame Blavatsky remained a great seer, a guide possessed of infinite wisdom. The message contained in the letter, that everything we imagine may become real, was one upon which she acted—rashly perhaps, as she thought afterwards—in the desperate days ahead.

CHAPTER 3
EVENTS RELATING TO
A DOG SHOW

'The dogs are benched by Spratts Company at the western end of the building, and the two rings for judging are immediately in front of the organ and orchestra. There is ample space and light, so that the dogs can be seen without difficulty.'

The Times 9 December 1885

'Worms,' said Mr Halls the vet. 'The young feller's got worms. Been giving him raw meat, have you? No. How about his milk then, made sure to heat it? Ah hah, Mr Bartlett, you're looking just a wee bit guilty. *Must* heat the milk for puppies.'

'I think it was my fault,' Adelaide said. 'I forgot.'

'Ladies' privilege,' Mr Halls said. 'Never mind, though. Two or three doses of this, and he'll be right as rain. Come along, my lad, open up.' The puppy, which lay listlessly on its bed, obediently drank the spoonful of liquid.

'That's a good little feller. Now then. Give this half an hour before the morning meal. Who'll be doing that?'

'I shall.' That was Edwin.

'Repeat twice a week. Get that bed cleaned out, keep him away from the others, he'll be right again in a few days.'

Adelaide asked the nature of the mixture. 'Ounce of senna, half of glycerine, scruple of santonine, fill up with aniseed syrup so that the dog

237

doesn't taste the santonine. Never known it to fail. Now, where's the other patient? Is he any better?'

They were in the big yard at the back of the Station Road shop where the five St Bernards each had its separate kennel, the three puppies being housed separately.

'No better at all.' Edwin's lower lip trembled. 'He seems to me weaker. And he was our best hope for the show. Poor Golden Hero.'

Adelaide echoed the words. The animal got up as they approached, wagged his tail a couple of times, and then lay down again as though exhausted. A part of the yard adjacent to the kennel had been wired off, so that he could take exercise without having contact with the other dogs.

'Man proposes, God disposes,' the vet said sententiously. 'With distemper he's bound to be worse before he's better. You'd better stay outside, don't want to run unnecessary risks of spreading infection.' He himself was wearing overalls, galoshes and gloves, the last of which he removed as he began to examine Golden Hero, talking to the dog encouragingly while he did so. Then he straightened up and shook his head.

'He is weaker, as you say. Has he taken any food at all?'

'Hardly anything,' Edwin replied.

'Then it means a clyster. I shall want your assistance, Mr Bartlett, and also a pail. Perhaps you'd like to take a short walk, Mrs Bartlett. This is no sight for ladies.'

'If you wish to be a lady you don't go into a kennels, Mr Halls,' Adelaide said tartly.

Mr Halls shrugged. He tilted his bowler so that

it was almost at the back of his head, and produced
from his bag an old coffee can with holes punc-
tured in it. The bottom of the can had elasticized
straps on it, and he fitted these over Golden Hero's
head while Edwin held the dog. Then he took
from the bag a small blue bottle and, using a dip-
per, put some twenty drops through the holes in
the can, talking cheerfully while he did so.

'The Halls patented tin can chloroform dropper,
guaranteed more effective for dogs than that old
folded napkin. No you don't, boy.' Golden Hero
had staggered protestingly to his feet, but now
he sank back and flopped over on his side. 'They
don't like the stuff, but it does the trick. Now then,
old feller, it's just as well you don't know about
this.'

'What is that?' Adelaide asked, as the vet took
from his bag a length of rubber tubing and a glass
funnel.

'That, madam, is a tube for rectal lavage,' Mr
Halls said with a tartness equal to her own. She
watched as the tube was inserted into the rectum,
the water poured in, and the contents of the rectum siphoned into the pail. The smell was unpleasant.

'Now we wait ten minutes. In the meantime,
Mrs Bartlett, perhaps you would be good enough
to warm this broth I have brought ready for such
an emergency.'

Ten minutes later, while Edwin held Golden
Hero's legs in the right position, the broth was
poured in slowly, with a rubber catheter replacing
the rectal tube. When it was over Mr Halls said
briskly, 'Very good. I'll be back tomorrow to repeat the dose. I shall need a bit of assistance.'

Adelaide said, before Edwin could speak, 'Mr Bartlett is busy. I will help.'

Mr Halls nodded. 'Right, then. Same time tomorrow. Four o'clock on the dot. He'll soon come round from the chloroform.'

When Mr Halls had gone Edwin said, in a voice that quavered slightly, 'And only two days ago I washed him, hoping he would be fit for the show.'

'Never mind. We still have The Saint and Golden Girl.'

'But Golden Hero was our prize-winner. He would have won a prize, Adelaide, I know it.'

'Don't worry. We'll have a dog at the show anyway.'

'Addy, I swear you are the best little wife a man ever had.'

'Thank you, Edwin. But you know I do not care to be called Addy.'

That was on Sunday. On Monday Edwin was busy up at the City warehouse, and Adelaide went over to Herne Hill on her own. Golden Hero seemed a little stronger, and Mr Halls said that another couple of days should see him really on the mend, to the point that normal feeding might be resumed. That evening Edwin said that she need not bother to go on Tuesday, because he would be at Herne Hill. During the process of administering the clyster, however, he became violently sick. Mr Halls, bowler pushed right back, viewed him with a cynical eye.

'Trouble with all you animal lovers is you're lily-livered. Little bit of nastiness, you don't have the nerve for it.'

'Not that,' Edwin said. He was very white, with only one or two blotches suggesting his usually

ruddy complexion. 'I was all right on Sunday. Felt
bad ever since lunch. Trouble at both ends.'

'You're looking queer, I must say. Better get
off home.'

'Can't understand it. Do you think I might have
caught something from the dogs?'

'Wouldn't say it was out of the question, not
by any means. Something like distemper, you've
got to take precautions, no knowing what can happen if you don't.'

Edwin reached home in a state approaching
collapse, but refused to go to bed. He lay on a
sofa before the fire, wearing a dressing-gown and
lamenting that he would not be fit for tomorrow's
dog show. He did not touch his dinner, but scouted
Adelaide's suggestion of calling a doctor.

'Halls says I might have caught something from
the dogs. Don't know why, I've been careful
enough.'

'Perhaps. But, Edwin—'

'Yes, my dear?'

'You have some new pills, I saw a bottle in the
drawer. What are you taking them for? I am afraid
they may be responsible.'

'No, no, rubbish.'

'Why are you taking them?'

Edwin made no reply, but closed his eyes,
rested his head on the back of the sofa, and within
a minute or two began to snore. Adelaide contemplated him as she wrapped a blanket round his
knees. She had no idea what had caused his illness,
unless it was the pills, but she had always in mind
those words of Madame Blavatsky's, that everything we imagine may become real if the power
of our imagination is strong enough. Could the

mystical reality in nature that was unknown to science be exerting itself so that Edwin, knowing her wish to be free of him, had in consequence become ill? Perhaps he would die, as it were expelled by nature from a world in which his presence was no longer necessary. Such speculations fascinated her.

In the morning he seemed better, ate a little of the large breakfast brought up by Mrs Doggett, and said that he was quite well enough to go to the show. It was to be a day out for the three of them, and just after nine o'clock George Dyson appeared. He commented on Edwin's pallor, but was told that he felt perfectly well.

The St Bernard Dog Club Show was being held that year at the Albert Palace in Battersea, London's latest place of entertainment. The Palace, which was constructed like the Crystal Palace almost entirely of iron and glass, was situated just outside Battersea Park, separated from it only by the road leading to Albert Bridge. It consisted of a central transept with a nave at one end, the whole being nearly five hundred feet long, all divided by iron columns and lattice girders. The enthusiasm of the late Prince Consort had been chiefly responsible for the Palace being built in working-class Battersea, but as *The Times* had forecast, the upper classes were reluctant to cross to the unfashionable side of the river even to see the collection of paintings showing the winning of the Victoria Cross that were permanently on show, and attendance at the Dog Show was poor. It was being held in the nave, one end of which was filled by the great Holmes organ. The place was filled with St Bernards, and Adelaide ex-

claimed with pleasure at the perfection of many
of the dogs. They found The Saint and Golden
Girl, who had been brought to the show separately, and were being looked after by dog-han-
dlers.

'They are *beautiful,*' Adelaide said. 'Look at The
Saint, George, does he not have a truly fine head?'

Dyson nodded. He preferred small dogs to these
huge St Bernards. Edwin sat down, with his chin
resting almost on his chest.

There were twenty different classes, for rough
and smooth-coated dogs. The Saint and Golden
Girl were entered for classes to be judged in the
morning, The Saint in the class for rough or long-
coated dogs over eighteen months old, Golden
Girl in a similar class for bitches. When Edwin
was asked if he would lead The Saint to the judging ring he shook his head, and the dog-handler
took him along. The judges walked round the
entries, examining the shape of the head, paying
particular attention to the width and depth of the
chest, looking closely at the straightness of the
legs, consulting with each other and marking their
books. As one group of dogs was led away, another
entered the ring. Adelaide's excitement was intense. She stood beside the ring, her hands grip-
ping the ropes. When Dyson spoke to her, she
did not hear what he said.

The judges conferred endlessly as it seemed,
but at last the announcement came. The class had
been won by Prince Battenberg. There were
three other prizes, and nine dogs were highly
commended, but The Saint was not among them.
She looked round to find herself alone, and made
her way back to the place where she had left Ed-

win. He was on a chair, head down, with Dyson standing beside him.

'You did not answer when I spoke to you. I said that Edwin was unwell.'

Edwin's eyes were closed. He asked faintly, 'What happened?'

'We did not win,' she said shortly. 'I think we should go home. George, will you try to find a cab?'

When he had gone Edwin asked her to stay to watch Golden Girl.

'She has no more chance of winning than The Saint. What is the matter?'

'Pains. Sickness. Must have caught it from the dogs.'

Upon reaching Claverton Street the two of them helped Edwin upstairs, and then Adelaide took him into the bedroom. When she came out she said that he was a little easier.

'I think you should call a doctor.'

'Edwin does not wish it, but I shall get one to-morrow. But I do not think he will live long.' She had been bending over the fire. When she looked up at him, her expression was so strange that he was almost frightened of her. 'When he is dead I shall be free.'

'You must not say such things. It is as though you wished for his death.'

She stood up and faced him calmly. Her head reached only to his shoulder. 'I wish for nothing, but there are things that I know. Edwin's death is something I have imagined or foreseen.'

AFTERWARDS (IV)

In Mrs Doggett's smoking-room on the ground
floor the three of them sat and waited, Adelaide
and the solicitor Mr Wood, and George Dyson.
Mr Wood, a cheerful man by nature, had tried
to make conversation about the wretchedness of
the weather, saying that the New Year had come
in like a lion, but he found his companions unre-
sponsive. Mr Dyson, Mr Wood's fellow-executor
under the will, whom he was meeting for the first
time, sat straight-backed in an uncomfortable
chair. The widow herself sat and stood, walked
about the little room, looked out of the window
at the snowflakes flickering down, then sat again.
Mr Dyson asked permission to light his pipe, something which the solicitor did not care to see done
in a lady's presence, not even in a smoking-
room.

'What can be keeping them? It is a very long
time,' Mrs Bartlett exclaimed.

Mr Wood consulted his watch. 'Half past three.
A post-mortem takes a little time, especially in
the unusual circumstances.' At that Mr Dyson
spoke. 'What unusual circumstances? I understood
that some blood vessel had broken in or around
the heart.'

'I said only that that was Dr Leach's opinion,'
Mrs Bartlett said, and Mr Wood observed that the
post-mortem was being held just for the purpose
of determining the exact cause of death. Neither
the widow nor Mr Dyson commented on this re-

mark, but she resumed her pacing. She looked out of the window again.

'There is Mr Bartlett, Edwin's father. Standing outside.'

Mr Wood had noticed Mr Bartlett on his arrival, and remembering that day in his office when the old fellow had reluctantly signed a humiliating apology to his son's wife, had not been surprised that he should stay outside rather than be reminded of that occasion. Mrs Bartlett said that he must come in and turned to Mr Dyson, but before he could get out of his chair the front door closed and Dr Green, an elderly figure with mutton-chop whiskers, got into his waiting brougham and was driven away. A moment or two later Mr Bartlett came in. He nodded to Mr Wood, ignored Mr Dyson, and muttered some inaudible words to Adelaide.

'You were waiting outside, Father. You should not have done that.' Mr Bartlett grunted in reply. 'One of the doctors has left—'

'Dr Green,' the old man said. 'Wouldn't say anything.'

'That means we shouldn't be long now,' Mr Wood said cheerfully, but in fact it was twenty minutes before Dr Leach entered the room and asked them all to come upstairs. His round face was solemn, and his fingers pulled at his collar. They went into the drawing-room, and there the four of them confronted the four doctors. The doctors stood together in front of the folding doors that led to the back room where the body lay, a little as though they were protecting a sacred relic. All looked severe, Dr Murray who was Dr Green's assistant, lantern-jawed Dr Chaney, and

grizzled Dr Dudley, who gave a brief sympathetic
nod to Mr Bartlett. Dr Leach, his head pushed
upwards, stood a fraction in front of the others,
their spokesman.

'Ahem. These gentlemen wish me to state that
we have very carefully examined the body of the
deceased under the—ah—supervision of Dr
Green.' At this point his voice cracked slightly
and moved into a higher key. He coughed and
recovered. 'We are unable to discover any patho-
logical legal cause—that is to say, any natural or
obvious cause—of death. The contents of the
stomach are suspicious, and we have preserved
them.' He paused as though about to say more,
then ended lamely, 'That is the statement.'

From behind him Dr Dudley said, 'Something
more, Dr Leach.'

'Yes.' Dr Leach spoke with conscious effort. 'In
the circumstances these rooms must be locked
and sealed, under the jurisdiction of the coroner.
Nobody must enter them. Nothing must be removed.' Adelaide's bag stood near the door and
beside it was her black cloak, over a chair. 'Mrs
Bartlett, you must not remove your bag or your
cloak. Everything must be left.'

There was silence for a moment. Then old Bartlett picked up the cloak. 'Adelaide may take her
cloak.'

'I do not want my cloak.' In this moment of
strain her accent was noticeable. 'I want nothing,
I will take nothing.'

He went on as though she had not spoken. 'She
may have her cloak, I will be answerable, there
are no pockets in it.' He handed her the cloak,
and she took it with a shrug.

'That—ah—concludes the proceedings.' Dr Leach thanked his fellow doctors. Dr Dudley went across to Mr Bartlett and put a hand on his shoulder. His voice was penetrating.

'Your son has no business to be lying in there, a strong man like that.'

The old man merely shook his head. Adelaide seemed not to hear the words. She was already on her way down the stairs, accompanied by the solicitor and Dyson. Mr Wood said that he was sure all this would be cleared up very soon, and that he would keep in touch with them both. Then he raised his hat and left. Old Bartlett left too, kissing her on the cheek when he said goodbye. The doctors lingered a little up above. Then they came down, giving a grave farewell to Adelaide as she stood with Dyson at the bottom of the stairs. Dr Leach came last, and she drew him into the smoking-room.

'Doctor, you have met Mr Dyson, who is a friend of mine and of Edwin's. Can you not tell us, tell me, anything at all about the cause of poor Edwin's death?'

'Mrs Bartlett, I understand your anxiety. Believe me, I am deeply sorry, but Dr Green was very positive, *very* positive, about his findings.' The doctor looked a little disapproving, as though to convey that such positiveness was by no means a virtue.

'It is not right that I should be kept in ignorance.' She placed her hand on the doctor's, and he responded by a slight rolling of the eyes, which were like raisins in the plump suet pudding of his face.

'There was undoubtedly, when we opened the

stomach, a pungent odour. Dr Green suggested chloroform.'

'And what do you think? Could it possibly be chloroform?'

'I think not. Oh no, decidedly not, I don't see that as a real possibility. You remember the chlorodyne you showed me? In my view the smell is probably attributable to that.'

'And what will happen now?'

'There will be a further examination of the— ah—relevant parts by a Home Office analyst.'

'I told you that he did not drink the chlorodyne.'

'Indeed you did. There is no cause for worry, my dear Mrs Bartlett, believe me.' The doctor's back was to George Dyson, or he would have noticed that at the mention of chloroform the tall clergyman's face became white as paper, and that he sat down, feeling uncertainly for the chair back behind him. 'But it is most distressing for you. May I ask where you will spend the night?'

'I shall go to Mr and Mrs Matthews, whom you met. They are my friends, almost my only friends. Doctor, I should like to beg a favour. All my clothes are locked up, and that is unimportant, but I cannot go without a hat.' She took a bunch of keys from her handbag. 'Here are my keys. I shall not want them again, indeed I must not have them since the rooms are to be locked. But I need my hat. It is in a drawer of the room where Edwin—' She faltered, and said, 'Will you be very kind and get my hat, doctor?'

Dr Leach admired her dignity, her poise, the whole style with which she said those words. He insisted that she should go up with him. Then he went into the back room and brought to her the whole drawer, so that she might choose whatever hat she wished. She selected a black hat, and then Dr Leach locked up the apartment.

Dyson took her away in a hansom. She did not look at him nor he at her, and they sat apart in the carriage as though their former intimacy had ended, as though indeed they were strangers. He kept silent for some minutes, but when they had crossed Vauxhall Bridge and were driving down the South Lambeth Road he spoke. It was dark in the hansom, and he could see her face only when it was revealed momentarily by the passing gas lamps. His voice lacked its usual richness and firmness, was almost timid.

'Adelaide, I must say something.'

'What is it?'

'The chloroform. Dr Green mentioned chloroform.'

'And Dr Leach did not agree with him.'

'The chloroform I bought at your request. What has happened to it?'

The words went out in darkness, and she did not answer them immediately. 'I did not expect—' she said, and then stopped. They turned into Clapham Road, and for a moment the lights were bright. They showed George Dyson her face turned towards him, the features as it seemed heavy with anger and scorn. He flinched from that terrible face, but then it was dark again and he thought he must have been mistaken, for her voice was quiet.

'The bottle is there just as you gave it to me. I have had no occasion to use it.'

'If questions should be asked—'

'This is a very critical time for me. I should

have thought you would understand that. Do not question me.'

He was conscious of a power emanating from her, of a struggle between her will and his own which he knew that he must not lose. It was difficult to speak, but he forced himself to do so.

'I shall see Dr Leach. I must know more about the results of the post-mortem.'

'Oh, do what you wish, but don't bother me about it,' she cried. This time the note of scorn in her voice was unmistakable. Nothing more was said until they reached Herne Hill.

CHAPTER 4
THE SUSCEPTIBILITIES
OF DR LEACH

'We now come to the story of the illness beginning on 10th December. What was that illness? . . . What is the worst that has been said of it? He was found to be suffering from sub-acute gastritis. Well, gentlemen, that sounds very formidable, just as ecchymosis of the visual organ sounds appalling; but just as the one means a black eye, so does the other mean an attack of indigestion.'
ATTORNEY-GENERAL, closing speech

'You must have seen something very much more than would be accounted for by an overdose of blue pill?'
MR JUSTICE WILLS to Dr Leach

To the outer view Dr Alfred Leach presented a solemn and self-satisfied appearance. His frock coat and trousers were immaculate, his high wing collar pushed up his head, concealing the beginnings of a double chin. His voice was full, round and smooth like his face, and he spoke always as though he were not merely offering a medical opinion but handing down a final judgement from on high. He had gone to Aberdeen University, taken his LRCS at Edinburgh, worked as assistant house surgeon in one hospital and house physician in another, and had then put out his plate in Charlwood Street, less than a quarter of a mile from Claverton Street, rather more than a year ago. The plate said not only LRCS, but also LSA and LM, meaning that he was a Licentiate of the Society of Apothecaries and a Licentiate of Midwifery.

His practice, indifferent at first, had been growing. Behind the wing collar and the frock coat his patients discovered a genuine kindliness, behind the pompous language a real concern for their welfare. And something else was concealed by the formal clothing, the doctor's susceptibility to what he had sometimes been known to call feminine pulchritude. He had an eye for a neat foot, and admired a well-turned ankle and a tiny waist, although of course such admiration stayed always within the limits of propriety. 'She made a *deep* impression on me,' he was accustomed to say to friends of any lady who engaged his interest, and Adelaide Bartlett made a deep impression on him at first sight.

She wore a plain dress in some pale colour, with no ornament—Dr Leach did not care for ladies to be hung about with jewels—and he was struck especially by the combination of frailty and power she conveyed. Her features were large rather than small, she had thicker lips and a firmer chin than

he cared to see in a woman, yet the impression
she made upon the doctor was one of extreme
delicacy. And her eyes were remarkable in their
intensity and earnestness, they were eyes that,
as he said in talking about the case afterwards,
would draw the heart out of a man. She told him,
in a low voice with a faint but pleasant foreign
accent, of her husband being taken ill two or three
days earlier. The symptoms were sickness and di-
arrhoea, with a good deal of pain. She added, after
a moment's hesitation, that she had kept some
of the motions and that they showed traces of
blood.

Dr Leach shook his head and said gravely, 'This
appears to be a very peculiar case. I will come
as soon as I can.'

In truth he was not busy that morning, and he
was round within the hour. The phrase 'a very
peculiar case' was one he liked the sound of, and
he had used it often. He found the patient sitting
up on the sofa in the drawing-room, a short muscular man who looked younger than his forty years.
The man was a little shaky in his movements and
not inclined to speak much, but still far from totally prostrate. The pulse was rather weak, and
he complained of pains in the abdomen. The doctor, tapping away with his stethoscope, found a
certain dullness there on percussion. He looked
at the motions, but they told him nothing in particular. It did not seem to him a peculiar case, but
rather a simple matter of gastritis caused probably
by too many of those blue pills containing mercury, which many people used to cure constipation. No doubt that was the cause, but as he had
learned during his short time as a doctor, patients

liked to air their views on whàt they believed to
be the cause of their troubles. He pulled up a
chair near to the patient, and asked what Mr Bartlett thought. He said in a low voice that it was
probably overwork.

'Indeed?'

Mrs Bartlett chimed in to say that her husband
left home at eight o'clock each morning, and did
not return until six or later. That did not seem
to the doctor an exceptionally long day, but still
something must be said. What could one prescribe
for overwork? He said in his richest, plummiest
voice, 'My advice is, Mr Bartlett, that you should
see nobody connected with business until you are
feeling better.'

'Nobody, doctor?'

'Nobody at all,' Dr Leach said firmly.

He wrote out a prescription for a standard stomach mixture containing bismuth, with a tonic in
it as well, and then became aware of a curious,
unpleasant smell emanating from the patient.
Why had he failed to notice it before? He asked
Bartlett to open his mouth, and was shocked by
what he saw. Many of the teeth were evidently
decayed and the gums round them were red and
spongy, but what disturbed him was the blue line
at the edges of the gums which suggested a much
larger dose of mercury than he had expected. Perhaps there was something peculiar about the case,
after all. He felt the need to go back and consult
the authorities in the textbooks.

Mrs Bartlett asked him to come into the bedroom, where he noticed the presence of a small
iron bed as well as the usual double bed. She said
eagerly, 'What do you think, doctor?'

'My dear Mrs Bartlett, there is no cause for concern. My diagnosis is sub-acute gastritis, although I must add that it is only tentative. We shall see how he reacts to the medicine I have prescribed, which should be made up immediately. I am bound to say that there is a suggestion of mercurialism.'

Her eyes were wide. 'That would be more serious?'

'More serious, yes, but we shall be able to treat it, never fear.' He patted her hand, and she gave him a faint worried smile. 'I shall think over the case, and will look in again later today.'

He consulted the authorities and returned in the afternoon, wearing his most serious look. When Adelaide met him at the door and asked if it was mercurialism, he said only, 'We shall see.'

Edwin Bartlett still lay on the sofa. A good fire burned in the grate and, looking round the room with the photographs on the mantelpiece, the piano in one corner, and the knitting Adelaide had just laid down, the doctor thought that for furnished rooms these were comfortable and homelike. The patient said that he had taken a dose of medicine, but had vomited again, and felt no better. He had also sent a note to his partner to say that he would not be in to business today or tomorrow.

'What do you think about the next day, doctor?'

'It is impossible to say at present. I must conduct a further examination. Mrs Bartlett, perhaps you would care to leave us for a little.'

'Why should I do that?' She had picked up her knitting.

'The examination is of a delicate nature.'

'I think Edwin would prefer me to be here. And I shall not be shocked. Do you wish me to go out, Edwin?' He shook his head.

'Very well. You must remove those trousers, Mr Bartlett.'

What the authorities had told him was that mercury was often prescribed in large quantities by quacks as a cure for venereal disease. He was looking for the characteristic ulcers and chancres of syphilis, or the signs of discharge that mark gonorrhea. A doctor should not be embarrassed by such an examination, but Dr Leach felt a certain unwillingness to look as closely as he would otherwise have done in Mrs Bartlett's presence. He heard the click of the needles behind him, and he unconsciously tried to shift his position to conceal those private parts from Mrs Bartlett. He saw no signs of the tell-tale syphilitic ulceration, but his examination was a little hurried, and he did not look to see if there was a discharge on the clothing. He had questions to ask, questions which he did not feel capable of putting with Mrs Bartlett in the room. But before he could formulate a means of getting her away the invalid spoke.

'You have examined me, doctor. Can you say what is wrong?'

Let him have it straight from the shoulder, Dr Leach thought. 'Mercurial poisoning.'

A short pause. Then: 'And how could that come about?'

Not sharply, for sharpness was not in his nature, but with ponderous heaviness the doctor said, 'From taking mercury, how else?'

'I have not taken any.'

A clear enough answer, but the man was lying.

'Think it over,' Dr Leach said, and then: 'Mrs Bartlett, would you fetch the bottle with the medicine
I prescribed? I should like to look at it.'

She went into the bedroom. As soon as she had
gone he said, 'Come now, Mr Bartlett, you have
been taking medicines, isn't that so?' The patient's
eyes were half-closed, but he murmured something. 'What's that?'

'I have not taken any. Doctor, I feel sick.'

The sound of his vomiting brought Adelaide
back. She gave the doctor the bottle, then went
to her husband, held the pot for him, gently
helped him back on to the sofa, wiped his forehead
with a cloth. Dr Leach warned them both that
the patient should take no patent medicines, nothing except what he had prescribed, and left.

Back in his surgery he wrote up his notes. It
seemed clear that Bartlett had suffered from
syphilis in the recent past. Or perhaps—for Dr
Leach had a number of theories about medicine,
one of which was that patients were often hysterical and imagined ailments from which they did
not suffer—perhaps he was suffering from syphilo-
phobia, which was the name he gave to a case
of imaginary syphilis. He had gone to a quack,
the quack had filled him up with some medicine
containing mercury, and this was the result. But
how could one say such things to a delicately nur-
tured woman like Mrs Bartlett?

He paid another visit on the following day. Bartlett again lay on the sofa, wearing trousers and
shirt, with a dressing-gown over them. His pulse
was stronger, and he said that the vomiting had
almost ceased, but the blue line round his gums
was still there. He was, however, eager to speak,

although his voice was not much above a whisper.

'Doctor, I think I know what has caused this illness.'

'You do? Tell me, by all means.'

'It was a pill which I took when I was at my place of business.'

'Indeed? What kind of pill?'

'That's the trouble, I'm not sure. We sell—at my place of business—all sorts of things . . .' He closed his eyes, and Adelaide elaborated.

'Edwin's shops are groceries, but they also sell many patent medicines. Samples are sent in to them and Edwin took one of them, isn't that so?'

'That's right.' Bartlett opened his eyes. 'I took a pill, two pills I think, from one of the samples.'

'Good Heavens! Are you in the habit of taking pills at random in this way? And what was the pill?'

'I have done it before. And about the pill, I am afraid I have no idea what it was. There are so many.'

'Then what made you think it would do you good?'

To this unanswerable question the patient made no reply, but closed his eyes.

'Do you think the pill has caused this mercury poisoning, doctor?' his wife asked.

Dr Leach believed himself to be a quick-thinking man, as every doctor had to be to deal with the fads and worries of patients. Now, as he stood teetering on his heels in front of the fire, he thought that although this was an obvious fabrication it would not do for him to say so. The man had been in a quack's hands and refused to admit it. He had taken an overdose of some pseudo-remedy containing mercury, and poisoned himself. Mrs Bartlett must be preserved from knowledge of this. The more he saw of Mrs Bartlett, the more he was impressed by her care for the patient. She suggested that her husband should be moved into the drawing-room. The iron bed on which he slept was brought in there, put near the window, and the furniture rearranged to make a kind of screen. This was certainly more cheerful for him than staying in the bedroom, but was it not inconvenient? She said that was of no importance. She would no longer sleep in the bedroom, but in a chair beside the bed. She arranged with Mrs Doggett that she would use the smoking-room downstairs to see visitors, and she talked to Dr Leach down there each day before taking him up to the patient, to tell him of Edwin's progress.

The doctor had paid his first visit on Thursday, December 10th, and thereafter he called sometimes twice, sometimes three times a day. Mrs Bartlett said that Mr Baxter had seen her husband. Mr Baxter, now, who was that?

'My husband's partner. You said that he was to see nobody connected with business, but Mr Baxter was very pressing. It was difficult for me to refuse.'

'Of course, I quite understand.'

'But Edwin was restless afterwards. And old Mr Bartlett called, Edwin's father. He asked what was the matter, and Edwin said mercurial poisoning. I must tell you, doctor, that Mr Bartlett does not like me.' Not like little Mrs Bartlett! Dr Leach made a clucking noise indicating disbelief. 'I wrote to him last night saying that I would send a note each day to tell him of Edwin's progress, but that nobody was to see him unless you gave permission.'

'That was all for the best,' Dr Leach said heartily. 'The fewer visitors, the better. Now let us have a look at the patient.'

The patient rather baffled Dr Leach. His pulse was stronger, the blue line round the gums was disappearing, he no longer vomited, his bowels were open, but he seemed very low-spirited and complained that he could not sleep. Mrs Bartlett had already spoken about this downstairs.

'He *does* sleep, doctor, but not unless I sit and hold his foot through the bedclothes.'

'Hold his foot?'

'Yes, especially his toe.'

'Goodness gracious.' Dr Leach rarely laughed, but he did so now. 'Upon my soul, that's very droll. I never heard of such a thing.'

'I assure you it is so.'

'I am beginning to think, Mrs Bartlett, that your husband is a very uncommon patient. I think he is an hysteric.'

'They are subject to fits of weeping and laughter, are they not? Edwin sometimes weeps, especially lately.'

'Upon my word, you are a very knowledgeable lady, to know such a medical term.'

'I read medical books, doctor. I like to know something about practical things.'

Hysterical or not, Edwin Bartlett complained of sleeplessness. Dr Leach gave him a morphia pill, together with a mouthwash. He changed the medicines constantly, trying to find something that would suit the patient. One day there was bismuth suspended in bicarbonate of soda, with bromide of ammonium to act as a mild sedative, and just a couple of drops of chloroform. When this seemed to do no good he prescribed a tonic of gentian and nux vomica, and then a morphia injection. Certainly the patient had medicine in variety, and nothing much seemed to be physically wrong with him, but still he complained. Only one thing was left, and it was something Dr Leach had remarked at the beginning: those dreadful teeth. When he told Mrs Bartlett this, at one of their sessions in the smoking-room (it proved convenient and pleasant to call in the afternoon, when Mrs Doggett provided a good tea), she expressed dismay.

'Edwin had an awful experience with the dentist some years ago. He will never visit one.'

'Yet I believe the teeth are the source of the trouble. You must have noticed that his mouth is unhealthy.' She nodded. 'If he will not go to the dentist, there is nothing for it but that a dentist must come to him. I know a very good man nearby. I will arrange an appointment.'

'And, doctor, you will give Edwin the news, won't you? I'm afraid he will be upset.'

Dr Leach told the patient that he thought the basic trouble lay with his teeth. It was absurd, he thought, that a grown man should be afraid of a little dentistry, but Edwin gave unmistakable signs of fear. He shivered, and then wept a little, but he agreed that his gums were very painful, and made no further protest. Dr Leach prescribed a different tonic and another morphia injection, and told Mrs Bartlett that he felt sure her husband would be up and about once the teeth had been attended to. He was becoming concerned about

Mrs Bartlett. She would not hear of a nurse being called in, nor of going to sleep in the bedroom.

'What is the use of my going to bed, doctor? He will walk about the room like a ghost. He will not sleep unless I sit and hold his toe.'

Hold his toe, indeed. This peculiar case certainly had some droll aspects.

CHAPTER 5
THE DENTIST'S VIEW

MR MOLONEY: What was the condition of his
   teeth? I do not want details.
MR ROBERTS: Loose.

Evidence at trial

Thomas Roberts was a dental surgeon, and one who prided himself on being up to date. He took the unusual view that the object of dentistry was to keep healthy teeth in the head as long as possible, and to remove unhealthy ones with the minimum of pain. He had been involved in arguments with some of his more robust colleagues about this. 'If you don't make 'em holler they'll think there was nothing wrong, and after that they don't trust you,' as one of his rivals crudely put it. But perhaps Mr Roberts's views were gaining ground, for certainly his practice was increasing, and what others derisively called his bedside manner seemed to be liked. He lived only four doors away from Dr Leach, and knew the doctor slightly. Now he listened with judicious interest to an account of the case, and heard with surprise the request that he should visit Mr Bartlett in Claverton Street.

'Is it not possible for him to come here? I have the very best and most modern equipment in my surgery.'

'*Physically* it would be possible,' Dr Leach said. 'But *mentally* it is beyond him. Of course, if you feel that there is an ethical objection I should entirely respect your feelings.'

'Ethics don't come into it, just a matter of convenience for me and comfort for the patient.' Privately the dentist thought the doctor a pompous young booby. 'You say he's taken mercury in some form or another.'

'That is my tentative diagnosis. But he also shows marked signs of being an hysteric. It is a peculiar case, and he is a strange man. He is fortunate in his wife. Mrs Bartlett is an angel of goodness and patience.'

That afternoon Mr Roberts met the angel of goodness and patience, on the landing outside the apartment. She seemed to him an insignificant-looking little woman. Since they were alone, he asked whether her husband was in the habit of taking mercury. She spread her arms wide.

'Dr Leach has asked that already. I do not know. But he takes pills, he is always taking pills.' She put a hand on his arm. 'He is afraid of dentists, please be gentle with him.'

He nodded, and went in. Dr Leach was already there, standing beside the fire. The room had the close smell of a place that is being used by an invalid and it was kept unduly warm, or so the dentist felt. If he had been in charge he would have had the windows open, even though it was a vile day, with an east wind blowing. Edwin Bartlett lay on a sofa, wearing a dressing-gown over his trousers. He seemed listless, and a little fearful when asked to open his mouth.

The dentist was shocked both by the rottenness of the teeth, and by the state of the gums, which seemed to him entirely consistent with the man having taken a large dose of mercury. Most of the upper teeth were loose, the stumps of the lower ones were decayed, and it was obvious that many of them would have to come out. When he began to say this, Bartlett cried out that his wife must be there, he would agree to nothing unless she was there. Dr Leach went downstairs to fetch her. As soon as she entered, Bartlett said piteously, 'He says I must have my teeth out. Adelaide, don't let them hurt me, you know how it hurt me before.'

She sat beside him. 'Now, Edwin, don't be foolish. If it must be done, then it must be done. I am sure Mr Roberts will be gentle.'

From the fireplace Dr Leach orated: 'In my view the greater part of the trouble is connected with the teeth and gums.'

Mr Roberts had been taking instruments from his case. He removed also a small bottle containing a colourless liquid, which he held up so that Bartlett could see it. 'This bottle contains a solution of cocaine, a new drug that has only recently been used. I shall paint it on your gums, and that will freeze them for a short time with the result that you will feel nothing.

'No pain?' The question was asked incredulously.

'I assure you that is so. What I propose, Mr Bartlett, is this. I shall remove only two teeth today. Tomorrow, when you are convinced that the operation is painless, I shall proceed to extract some of those stumps. Mrs Bartlett, will you be good enough to bring me a jug of water?'

She brought the water, and then watched attentively as he painted the upper gums with a tiny brush, keeping up a flow of conversation in the meantime.

'In a few moments the gums will be numb, and you will have no sensation in them. There is no need to look at the instruments. In the case of patients who feel a little nervous I recommend that they should close their eyes. Open your mouth and close your eyes, as the rhyme says. Good, very good. Did you feel anything then? I thought not. Very soon we shall be ready to proceed. Mouth wide open, please.' The two loose teeth at the top came out without any trouble at all. The dentist kept up his flow of patter, and then said, 'Open your eyes now, Mr Bartlett, and rinse. It is all over.'

Bartlett opened his eyes, rinsed his mouth into a bowl, and then said, 'What do you mean, all over?'

'The teeth are out. And you felt nothing.'

'Nothing at all. It is wonderful.'

'You will feel better when the others are removed. Now, my surgery is nearby, and I should like you to come there.' At this, however, the patient became upset, saying that he could not leave the house, and Mrs Bartlett asked whether Mr Roberts would be kind enough to visit them again. He consented, although when he was leaving he saw Dr Leach in private for a moment, and said he agreed that Bartlett showed signs of hysteria.

On the following day the process was repeated. This time he removed eleven decayed roots of teeth, those that had been sawn off years before to accommodate the lower plate. Bartlett seemed a little more relaxed, and showed no fear of the operation. On the next day Roberts paid a call to examine the state of the mouth, which had improved. The patient asked when he would be finished.

'There are at least four more that should come out. But we will leave that until next week. Removal of so many teeth is a shock to the nervous system. But you trust me now, do you not?'

'Oh yes. It was wonderful that there was no pain. When you are finished, however, I shall have no teeth left, it seems to me.'

'You may have a few, but you will be better without the rest. Then, if you agree, I shall make you a new and better-fitting plate.'

'The sooner the better. Adelaide says I should trust you, and do whatever you say.'

That was an extraordinary way to put it, the dentist thought. He was a married man himself, and paid due attention to his wife's opinion, but it would never have occurred to him to ask her view about whether somebody should be trusted or not. On all such matters it was surely obvious that men knew much more of the world, and were therefore better judges than women. He said something like this to the doctor, at one of their conferences about the case. Dr Leach was not less ponderous than usual.

'In the ordinary course of things I should agree, but Mr and Mrs Bartlett are not an ordinary couple, and this is a strange case. She is a wonderfully devoted wife. Do you know that she sits every night in the chair beside his bed, and that he will not go to sleep unless she holds his foot?' He coughed, feeling perhaps that he had said too much.

'I am sure she is a splendid nurse. But he seems to take no decisions of his own.'

'Exactly. Mrs Bartlett does everything, she is too good, if that were possible. I think of recommending that he should take a holiday in a few days, entirely on his own. What do you think of that?'

'An excellent idea. These extractions can be lowering to the spirits.'

Early in the following week, five days after his first visit, Mr Roberts removed four lower incisors, again with the help of cocaine. The gum condition was much better, the breath less noxious, Bartlett more cheerful. He now had few teeth left, but one of them showed signs of decay. It would have to come out, but gas would be necessary, and that involved a visit to the surgery. Bartlett said he still did not feel up to going out. The dentist said that there was no urgency, they would wait until he felt stronger.

He saw Edwin Bartlett once more, on the day before his death.

CHAPTER 6
RECOVERY

MR CLARKE: You said that, in your view, he had little to recover from; but did you promise then, on his agreeing to go to Torquay after Christmas, to take him down and put him under the care of a medical man down there, Dr Dalby?

DR LEACH: Yes. I said I would accompany him, and I mentioned Dr Dalby because I thought

> it would give him confidence that he would
> be looked after. He required no looking after
> practically.
>
> Evidence at trial

One of the things that Dr Leach most admired
about Mrs Bartlett was the calm and composure
she displayed in the face of her husband's inveter-
ate low spirits, but three days before the dentist
removed those lower incisors she met him in the
smoking-room with red-rimmed eyes and a look
of dejection when he paid his evening visit. When
he asked whether her husband was worse she
shook her head.

'It is just that—I said something of my differences with Mr Bartlett's family? And you remember that you agreed he should be quiet and have
few visitors. I have done as you said, and I have
written almost every day to Edwin's father and
to his partner, little notes to say that he is making
progress and the tooth-drawing has gone well. I
truly have no time to write more.'

'Of course not. With your sick-room duties it
is wonderful that you can spare the time to write
at all.'

'But they are not satisfied, or at least his father
is not satisfied.' She wore an old grey dress that
evening, and had taken little trouble with her hair,
so that she really looked quite plain. Yet some
distinct attraction emanated from her so that the
doctor felt an inclination, which of course he resisted, to take the woebegone little lady into his
arms. 'He has asked—but it is not right that I
should speak of this without Edwin. He must tell
you what he thinks.'

The smoking-room was chilly, but upstairs a

good fire blazed and the room seemed to the doctor cheerful and homelike. He examined the patient, who was in bed, and found his pulse and heart normal, and his mouth looking much healthier than it had been a day or two ago. He had no pains now, but complained of difficulty in eating, which was natural enough after his dental operation. He said also that he could not sleep.

'I will give you something for that. But it is not right that you should be in bed at this hour. You ought to be up and about.'

'He was up this afternoon,' Adelaide said. 'But about five o'clock he felt weak and went back to bed. But now, doctor, I have something unpleasant to say. I hope you won't be offended. My husband's relations, who are never content with anything I do, want to send for another physician, one of their own choosing.'

Dr Leach sometimes blushed at awkward moments, and felt himself blushing now. He was annoyed, for his interest in the case was great and he felt his handling of it to have been impeccable, yet it was a request that he could hardly refuse.

'Very well, let them send him one. I have almost done with you, Mr Bartlett.'

'Done with him?' Adelaide echoed in surprise.

'Yes indeed. He is much better, the only trouble now is the teeth. You should take an outing or two, then a holiday on the south coast. After that you'll be right as rain.'

Edwin, who had been lying back on his pillow, sat up. 'You won't desert us? We have every faith in you, we want nobody else.'

'That is most gratifying. Thank you.' Dr Leach felt the blush subsiding.

'It is true, and I am sorry to say it, but my family

are not friends to my wife.' Then, with more energy than he had shown during the whole time
the doctor had seen him, he went on. 'We are
determined that in future we shall manage our
own affairs, with no interference from other people.'

The doctor was sitting on the chair by the bed
that Adelaide occupied at night, and she was beside the fire. She said now, 'Do you know, doctor,
if he should get worse or die, Mr Bartlett's friends
would accuse me of poisoning him?' Dr Leach
remembered the sentence afterwards because it
was the first time that the word *poison* had been
used in such a sense, but at the time he thought
nothing of it.

'Oh, that is all nonsense,' he said. 'At my first
visit you were suffering from an overdose of mercury. I called it mercurial poisoning, and Mr Roberts agreed with me, but that is better now. I
shall be delighted for you to see any doctor your
friends or family choose.'

'I will not see anyone *they* choose,' Edwin said.
'It shall be any gentleman *you* choose to bring.
I will see him, not because I lack faith in you,
doctor, but for my wife's protection.'

The doctor made a little speech, in phrases that
he thought rather well-turned, about appreciating
their faith in him. He returned on the following
day with a doctor who had been in practice for
as many years as Dr Leach had been alive.

This was Dr John Gardner Dudley, a bluff forth-
right man with close-cropped grey hair and a
bruiser's face, whose practice was in Belgrave
Road, a few minutes' walk from Claverton Street.
He had listened to the younger doctor's account

of the case, of the suspected mercurial poisoning, the blue line around the gums, and the various details that Dr Leach had put down in his notebook, with secret amusement. As a man of experience he knew that there was no need for all this fandango of putting down an impression of what had happened after every visit. Nine times out of ten there was nothing much wrong with patients who had so-called gastric trouble. They'd eaten too much, drunk too much, and just needed an indigestion mixture. Get them out and about, taking exercise, enjoying life, and they forgot all about their gastritis.

Mind you, an examination was necessary and he carried it out, listened to the heart, tested the reflexes, pressed the abdomen. Everything in perfect order. Only thing wrong was the man's gums, which were certainly spongy and inflamed, but that was to be expected after the extractions. Blue line round the gums? Either it had disappeared or Leach had imagined it. At the same time, Bartlett was certainly in low spirits and uncommonly lethargic. Such lethargy irritated Dr Dudley, who was active by nature.

'What's wrong then, eh? What do you complain of?'

'I suppose I have been overworking. Mentally and physically. I need rest.'

Dr Dudley turned to Mrs Bartlett, who had been watching the examination with interest. 'What about health in general?'

'It has always been very good, except for occasional dyspepsia. Isn't that so, Edwin?'

'Good, yes. I have had mercurial poisoning and I need rest, that is all.' He said this with eyes al-

most closed. Now he opened them—clear blue
eyes, Dr Dudley noted, not at all bloodshot. 'I
have slept badly for some time, hardly at all in
the last few nights.'

'Habits, what about those? Temperate, would
you say?' This again was addressed to Mrs Bartlett.

'Edwin likes a glass of wine at dinner, and so
do I, but nothing more. He has always been a
hearty eater. He lost his appetite, but it is returning.'

Dr Dudley took Dr Leach by the arm and led
him out of the room. They returned after a couple
of minutes, Dr Leach with a look of satisfaction
that he was unable to repress. Dr Dudley had
when necessary a stentorian voice, and he used
it now at something like three-quarters volume.

'Dr Leach and I are agreed. You are a sound
man, Mr Bartlett. You have had dyspepsia, I don't
doubt, and trouble with your teeth, but that is
almost over. I will tell you what I prescribe for
you. No more lying in bed. Sit up, get up, go out
for a walk, take a drive. Go on holiday as Dr Leach
suggests. There is no reason in the world why
you shouldn't. Do you hear me, Mr Bartlett?'

Edwin Bartlett opened his half-closed eyes. 'Yes.
But I am really very tired. I think it would kill
me to go out. Perhaps I shall feel stronger tomorrow.'

Dr Dudley felt his irritation growing, and
turned to Mrs Bartlett, who said, 'I shall do what
I can.'

'And we have agreed on a prescription for the
sleeplessness.' He was surprised when Mrs Bartlett
asked what it would be. 'Fifteen grains of bromide
of ammonium and twenty grains solution of hy-

drochloride of morphia. Are you any wiser, Mrs Bartlett?'

'A little. You see, I have *Squire's Companion to the Pharmacopoeia*, I can read a prescription. Dr Leach has been giving morphia injections.'

Dr Dudley said shortly that he was aware of it. He disapproved of women taking an interest in medicine. After prescribing a new tonic containing nux vomica and taxecum, and again exhorting the patient to be up and about, Dr Dudley left. He did not enter the house again until the post-mortem.

Afterwards Dr Leach saw Mrs Bartlett downstairs in the smoking-room. He had expected her to share his own pleasure at the confirmation of his diagnosis, but she was upset.

'I am very worried. Today Edwin talked again about dying.' He had done so in the doctor's presence in the first days, when no doubt he really did feel ill, but that he should do so now was ridiculous.

'He heard Dr Dudley. He is a sound man.'

'Edwin will not believe that. He says he will die. When we are alone he is always speaking of death.'

'It is in the mind, Mrs Bartlett, all in the mind. Let him take a holiday down at Torquay. I will go with him and put him in the care of a medical man there.'

'I shall go too.'

'You will *not* go, Mrs Bartlett. Come now, don't be upset, let me explain. You are a wonderful nurse, a man could hope for nobody better, but I will be frank and say that you pet and mollycoddle your husband too much. Let him go away for

a couple of weeks on his own, and I guarantee
he will be his own man again when he returns.'

For Adelaide these were days in which she
seemed to be possessed by two distinct personali-
ties. There was the Adelaide who tended and
nursed Edwin with care and patience. She did
not dislike this nursing, and Edwin enfeebled was
in some ways more congenial to her than Edwin
in full health. His dependence on her and the
ending of his importunacy made their relationship
something nearer to the perfect marriage of
which she dreamed. But she knew that this perfection would be marred if Edwin recovered his full
health, and that the degrading abandonment to
his sensual impulses that had caused his illness
(she had no doubt of this, whatever the doctor
might say) would be resumed. With total faith,
what is imagined may become real. She had total
faith, but what was it she imagined, what did she
desire? She was unsure.

In the meantime there was the gift. She had
practised this three times since Edwin's illness,
but not with great effect. When she told him that
he would fall asleep in half an hour he did so,
but he woke quickly, and seemed afterwards to
feel that he had not slept at all. She told him that
on waking the pain in his gums would have gone,
but within an hour he was complaining of it as
much as ever. And he had begun to think that
there was something strange about that intent
looking into her eyes, asking outright whether she
was mesmerizing him. She asked why he thought
so.

'I don't know, I feel strange at times, that is

all. Perhaps it is Mr Dyson—George.' She echoed
the name in surprise. 'Do you remember that in
the summer I asked whether it was not mesmeric
power that gave force to his sermons?'

'But he said no, that was not the case.'

'He denied it, certainly, but when he speaks
in public we are all gripped and held in a way
that cannot be natural.'

'He is a very fine preacher.'

'It is something more than that. I asked him a
second time, when you were not present. He
laughed and said that any powers he possessed
had been given him by God, and he could not
make worthier use of them than in his sermons.'

She said sharply that he was talking nonsense,
although it amused her that he should attribute
the gift to Georgius Rex, who had no trace of it.
The illness had certainly changed him, so that he
who had always been such a busy bustling man
was now unwilling to get dressed, and positively
refused to go out. Was it weakness, caused by the
dysentery which had now left him, or the progress
of the disease, or simply the effect of all the drugs
prescribed by Dr Leach?

Georgius Rex still came to Claverton Street two
or three times a week, but of course there were
no more *tête-à-têtes* in the drawing-room. The
clergyman would visit the invalid, and then he
and Adelaide talked in the smoking-room. He was
ill at ease in the sick-room, and confided to Adelaide that he did not know what to say to those
who were ill.

'You are meant to comfort them. You especially,
a man of the cloth.'

'You are right. It is a weakness in me, but I

cannot endure the presence of the sick. It is only by making a great effort that I have been able to bring myself to visit friends in hospital. Edwin seems a little better.'

'He does not think so himself. Supposing that he should not get better—'

'We must not contemplate such a possibility,' he said before she could complete the sentence. 'We must pray for his complete and early recovery.'

On the day of Dr Dudley's visit he told her that he must go away for Christmas, to stay with his family at Poole in Dorset. 'I do not like to leave you, especially when Edwin is ill, but I have always spent Christmas at home, and I am expected.'

'Then of course you must go,' she said coldly. 'Edwin seems better.'

'You say that always. He is no better. But I understand that you cannot endure a sick-room. By all means enjoy your Christmas. Do not think of how it will be spent here.'

'Adelaide, do not be cold to me.' He got up from the sofa in the smoking-room, tried to embrace her. 'You know that I love you.'

She pushed him away. 'If that were true, you would try to help me.'

'If I could—but there is nothing I can do. I adore you. Oh, I am ashamed of what I am saying.'

'I must return to Edwin. You had better go.'

After each visit George Dyson swore to himself that he would cease going to Claverton Street. He was ashamed of his conduct, yet once in Adelaide's presence he was in thrall to her, and hardly capable of any thought except how desirable it would be to possess her.

He went down to Poole, and stayed there for six days. He hoped that on his return everything might somehow have changed. Did he wish for Edwin Bartlett's death so that he might eventually marry Adelaide? The thought entered his mind, but he prayed every night to be free of it.

Now it was Christmas week, but in the Bartletts' apartment there was no thought of celebrating the season. Nor was there any question of the family paying a visit, for Edwin agreed with his wife that their presence would only be a disturbing influence which might delay his recovery. Old Bartlett had to content himself with the daily letter from Adelaide, which gave news of Dr Dudley's visit and said that Edwin was making good progress.

And Edwin improved, he undoubtedly improved. He got up and dressed in the late morning, and his appetite returned. He had a joking exchange with Mrs Doggett, when she asked whether he would be able to eat a slice of turkey for his Christmas dinner.

'Two slices off the breast, Mrs Doggett, and one off the leg. Then you could add a couple of your excellent sausages, a good spoonful of stuffing, a slice or two of ham—'

'Goodness me, Mr Bartlett, I can see you're feeling better.'

'I am, Mrs Doggett, indeed I am. Not that I'm myself yet, mind, I'm far from that.'

Nevertheless he cleared up a plateful of liver and bacon that evening, and Mrs Doggett confided to her husband that she believed his troubles were three-quarters imagination.

Dr Leach had come to a similar conclusion. He still paid two or three visits a day, for he was fascinated both by the case and by the Bartletts, and was considering writing an article for one of the medical journals about its strange features. There was the matter of going out, for instance. It was all very well for Dr Dudley to say that Bartlett should walk or drive daily, but the man positively refused to set foot out of doors.

'I cannot do it, doctor,' he said pleadingly. 'Truly I cannot. It would kill me.'

'Nonsense. Come along now, Mrs Bartlett and I will see you downstairs, and in the street you can take my arm.'

'It would do me no good. Look at the weather out there.' It was certainly an unpleasant day. Horses sloshed through the puddles, and in spite of the rain there was a wind so high that men were clinging to their hats. 'It would be dangerous for me. I might catch cold.'

'Wrap up and you won't catch cold, I'll guarantee it.'

But nothing could stir the man. Downstairs later on, he said to Mrs Bartlett that he had never known a patient so obstinate.

'He does not believe he is getting better. He thinks he is going to die.'

'That is so ridiculous.'

'Then he says he does not sleep, although I can assure you that he does.'

Dr Leach shook his head. 'I am afraid it all indicates hysteria.'

He increased the chloral hydrate without effect, for Bartlett still said he did not sleep. And now suddenly a new complication appeared. In one of the motions kept for him by Mrs Bartlett there was, quite distinctly, a lumbricoid worm. Well, worms were not uncommon. In fact Dr Leach had had one himself a few months back, and had taken a vermifuge which had been totally effective. The only trouble with this powerful vermifuge, which was based on santonine, was that it had to be expelled from the system after doing its work. The doctor had ignored this precaution in his own case, and had found his ears buzzing, his head swimming, and everything looking green. He therefore gave a purgative after the vermifuge but neither had any result, for Edwin Bartlett was now totally constipated. He did not see everything looking green, nor did his ears buzz, but he became very depressed, saying that he was sure worms were wriggling around in him and even crawling up his throat. Was there ever a more infuriating patient?

The doctor, with what he felt to be considerable cunning, prescribed a placebo, saying that no more than ten drops should be given in wine, and that although a second dose was permitted, a third must at all accounts be avoided. The device had no result. Edwin Bartlett remained constipated, and presumably worm-ridden. Dr Leach now changed his tactics drastically, giving the patient Epsom salts and then two globules containing a powerful and rapidly-operating aperient, croton oil. The patient said the oil was rather stimulating, but he remained constipated. He was denied Christmas dinner, for the doctor felt that a large meal must be bad for so thoroughly constipated a man. And then quite suddenly the battle, for it really had been nothing less, was won when

Edwin Bartlett produced a respectable motion, without any sign of a worm. It was a battle, however, that Dr Leach felt to be wearing him out. The way in which imaginary and real troubles succeeded each other was fascinating, but there could be no doubt that the essential thing was for Edwin Bartlett to get away to Torquay. The idea of the visit to Torquay was one that he now brought into every conversation. The patient either evaded it or took no notice.

And then on the evening of Boxing Day, with the worm expelled and no trace of another, he mentioned Torquay again and got a different response. Bartlett said that he knew he was better, but felt himself not yet fit for travel. He spoke of going next week, which delighted the doctor. During this conversation he seemed perfectly reasonable, but what ensued was so remarkable that it remained fixed in Dr Leach's memory. Was Edwin Bartlett out of his mind? The possibility had occurred to him more than once, and now did so again. On the other hand he prided himself on being always up to date, and recent developments in medicine had been so remarkable that, as he was already to acknowledge, *anything* was possible. He was fond of quoting that passage in *Hamlet* about there being more things in heaven and earth than were dreamed of in Horatio's philosophy.

At about ten o'clock on that evening—it was late, but the doctor did not grudge the hours spent in the Bartletts' company—he was sitting by the fire drinking a glass of ruby port from a bottle sent along by Mr Baxter, and chatting casually with the patient, who had his feet up on the sofa, and with Mrs Bartlett who was in an easy chair opposite, and was sipping at her own glass of port. It was quite as though he were a member of the family, which he found agreeable. He expanded on his own medical experiences, as he was inclined to do, and mentioned that a particular patient had behaved as though he had been mesmerized. Edwin was at once alert.

'Do you believe in mesmerism, doctor?'

Dr Leach replied with his quotation, and continued, 'You must not assume that I am an expert, however, nor a true scholar in the subject. I have not read *Braid on Magnetism*.' At that point Mrs Bartlett asked whether that was one of the standard works. He replied that it was, but that there were others. Edwin interrupted impatiently.

'Could you mesmerize me? Will you make the experiment?'

'Certainly not. It is my opinion that no medical man should attempt to use the mesmeric power.'

'But you could do it if you wished? Do you understand the method?'

Dr Leach had attended only one not very successful experiment in mesmerism, but he was always reluctant to admit ignorance. 'I have watched the effects obtained by a skilled mesmerist, and of course I am interested in the psychology of it. If we could understand psychology, Mr Bartlett, we should have the key to most human problems.' A good phrase that, he thought, one that he might use again. Edwin Bartlett had swung his legs off the sofa, and was more lively than the doctor had seen him.

'Can you tell me, doctor, am I under mesmeric control now?'

The doctor gave one of his collar-tightening chuckles. 'Do you think you are?'

'Yes, I do. We have a friend whom I believe to be a mesmerist. We saw a great deal of him in the summer. I believe he has mesmerized me through my wife.'

'This is all most amusing.' Perhaps by leading the man on he would obtain a key to his strange psychology. 'Do tell me how you came to such a strange belief.'

'I don't know.' Bartlett passed a hand over his forehead. 'I do such silly things.'

'What things?'

'That's just the question, isn't it? Things I wouldn't do if I hadn't been mesmerized.'

That, the doctor felt inclined to say, is a circular argument which does not make sense. He refrained, because the thing to do was to draw the patient out, and he was a little annoyed when Mrs Bartlett tried to turn the conversation by saying it was all ridiculous nonsense. However, as he put it afterwards in evidence, he obtained her permission to continue the conversation *au grand sérieux*, because he felt that only by doing so could he discover the basis of the patient's delusion. Did he hear the voice of this mesmerist telling him to do this or that? Had the mysterious friend implanted in him a fixed notion to sign a cheque or a draft bill? Was he perhaps not truly a friend, but somebody trying to use Mr Bartlett for his own purposes? These questions were answered in the negative rather impatiently, and the doctor began to feel a little impatient himself with this rigmarole.

'Mr Bartlett, believe me, I am sympathetic—'

'I do believe that, doctor, I do indeed.' Now there were tears in his eyes, which Dr Leach valued as a sign of generous feeling.

'I do not despise ideas because they are outside everyday experience, but I am bound to say that if some of my fellow medicos heard this conversation, they would think Mrs Bartlett the only sane person among us three.' At this Edwin shrugged helplessly, while Mrs Bartlett gave a small smile. 'But come now, tell me some of these things you would not do unless you were mesmerized. Do they happen while you sleep?'

'No, no, I cannot sleep.' At this Mrs Bartlett, who could not be seen by her husband, put her hands together and closed her eyes to indicate that he *did* sleep. This was done in the sweetest, prettiest way. 'But I can tell you something, something I did.' He was more excited now than the doctor had ever seen him. 'Two nights ago I could not sleep. I was nervous and restless, and my wife was asleep in the easy chair. I got up, and went and stood over her like this.' He got off the sofa, went across to her, and stood above her with fingers held out stiffly. 'I stood there for two hours.'

Mrs Bartlett began to say something, but Dr Leach shushed her. Surely this must be the basis of an article on delusions? 'And then?'

'All the time I felt the vital force being drawn from her to me. I felt it going in through my fingertips. Then I lay down and slept.'

Mrs Bartlett burst out laughing. 'Doctor, can you imagine such a thing?'

Dr Leach could not, but what he did see clearly was the article headed 'A Study in Hysterical Delusion,' by Alfred Leach, LRCS. He asked further questions, but was given no other examples of the patient's delusions. He left just before midnight, and as he got up to go noticed on the mantelpiece a photograph of the clerical gentleman who had been in the room two or three times when he paid his visits. It crossed his mind that this might be the mysterious friend referred to by Mr Bartlett, but he put the thought aside as absurd.

He returned at midday on the next day, which was a Sunday, and now—the turns in this case were astonishing, it was by a long chalk the most fascinating affair Dr Leach had come across in his medical experience—Edwin Bartlett was much better. Indeed, it would not have been too much to say that he looked a different man. He was up and dressed, there was a sparkle in his eye. When enquiries were made about the bowels, he said breezily that they had moved, everything was in order. Adelaide had preserved the motion, and when Dr Leach inspected it he saw nothing abnormal. More than this, Edwin Bartlett had felt very hungry that morning, and had breakfasted on sausages, eggs and bacon.

It was all strange, but gratifying. What about their extraordinary conversation of the previous night, had the patient perhaps forgotten it altogether? The doctor mentioned it in a casual manner, and was rewarded by a laugh.

'I talked a lot of nonsense. It was good of you to listen to me.'

Perhaps he might be pressed a little. 'So you no longer believe that you are in a mesmeric state?'

'No, no. As I say, you were kind to let me go on with it. But then you have been kind, more than kind, during this whole time. I want you to know how much my wife and I appreciate it.' Adelaide murmured her agreement.

'I have only done my duty as a physician. It is obvious that you are very much better. I do not think I need come again until tomorrow. Then next week you must be off to Torquay.'

'And after that, back to work, I hope.'

'I see no reason why not.'

Mrs Bartlett had been almost silent that morning, and the doctor had noticed an unusual flush on her cheeks. When they were down in the smoking-room, he said that there was now no excuse for her not going to bed and having a good night's sleep.

'I know you are afraid of leaving him, but he is now so much better that there is no reason why you should not be together in your double bed in the back room.'

She recoiled as though he had said something terrible. 'I could not do that. I beg your pardon, doctor, but my nerves are bad. I don't know how much longer I can bear it all.'

This was just what he had feared. He told her that she would break down if she had no rest, and repeated what he had said before, that she should engage a nurse. At this she became what in a woman he admired less he might have called violent.

'It is *useless* to say that. Edwin will not have it. He will have nobody but me.'

'And he could have nobody better, but at the same time I must take care not to exchange one invalid for another. Even such a charming one,' he added gallantly, and was rewarded with a smile. 'I thought it better not to mention it this morning, but it would be excellent if you could persuade your husband to go out for a drive.'

She made a gesture of hopelessness. He noticed her accent, as he had done before when she was excited. 'I have tried, but it is impossible. You

say he is better, but I tell you he still talks about
dying. I have tried, but he says it would kill him
to go out.'

'Well.' Dr Leach was a little taken aback. She
seemed distraught rather than delighted by her
husband's recovery, but no doubt this was a matter
of nerves. He wondered whether he should prescribe a sedative for her, but decided against it.
He would pay a visit when Adelaide was out, as
she sometimes was in the mornings, and take Mr
Bartlett out himself. Doctor's orders, he would
say. With a word to assure her that she need have
no further anxiety, he took his leave.

When he had gone, Adelaide walked up and
down the smoking-room in frustration. Edwin was
better, in a few days he would be well, and it
was plain that her ideas about his absenting himself voluntarily from a world in which his presence
was no longer necessary, were illusions. He
seemed to have been much enlivened by that discussion about mesmerism, as though his mind had
been cleared by it. Later there had been importunacy, which of course she had resisted, but what
would happen when he was fully recovered? She
had persuaded herself that importunacy was a
thing of the past, but evidently she had been
wrong. And then, in this time when he was most
needed, she had been deserted by Georgius Rex.
What kind of love was it that flinched from giving
help when it was most needed? When he returned
he should be *made* to help, no matter what his
feelings might be. To help in what? Even to herself she did not define the kind of help, or admit
that its end was the death of Edwin Bartlett.

At this moment everything irritated her almost

beyond endurance, the man upstairs who was rapidly becoming his former boisterous self, the sensual but timid clergyman who called himself her lover, above all the Old Man who called to see his son, unsatisfied with the note she wrote every day with news of his progress. Little Mr Baxter had called today, and had expressed delight at seeing his partner so much better. He had also taken Adelaide aside and told her that Mr Bartlett senior was not satisfied, had said that he was being kept from seeing his son, and thought that he should have a professional nurse. The rage and frustration she felt must be vented in some way. She prided herself upon her self-restraint, but had Georgius Rex been there she would have reproached him for cowardice, if Edwin had been in the room she might have said that she was disgusted by his diseased and almost toothless person. Instead, she wrote a letter to that equally disgusting Old Man, who she felt had done his best to wreck her life.

Dear Mr Bartlett [she wrote:] I hear you are a little disturbed because Edwin has been too ill to see you I wish, if possible, to be friends with you, but you must place yourself on the same footing as other persons— that is to say, you are welcome here when I invite you, and at no other time. You seem to forget that I have not been in bed for thirteen days, and consequently am too tired to speak to visitors. I am sorry to speak so plainly, but I wish you to understand that I have neither forgotten nor forgiven the past. Edwin will be pleased to see you tomorrow, Monday evening, any time after six.

She signed it *Adelaide,* went upstairs to get her cloak and to tell Edwin that she was going to the post, and then put the letter in the box before she could have second thoughts about it. Afterwards she felt easier, and was able to appear her usual equable self, playing the piano for Edwin, coaxing him into taking the most recent medicines prescribed by Dr Leach, one of which he said tasted horrid, tucking him up in bed. Indeed, the word *appear* is wrong, for this delightful companion and nurse was Adelaide Bartlett, just as the letter-writer was Adelaide Bartlett.

That night there was no importunacy.

George Dyson had spent an uneasy Christmas. He had hoped that the stay at Poole with his parents would somehow change both the situation and his feelings, but nothing of the kind happened. He was so much distracted that he was unable to join in the sober jollity with which Christmas was celebrated in the Wesleyan household. On Christmas Eve his father took him aside to ask whether there was any spiritual problem he wanted to discuss. He said there was not, and that he was concerned by a friend's illness, which was true but also a kind of deceit. How could he tell his father or anybody else the truth, that he was hopelessly in thrall to Adelaide? He spent much time in writing a poem about this thraldom, on the lines of Keats's 'La Belle Dame Sans Merci,' but was not satisfied with the result.

Adelaide seemed to him at times a woman whose life was ruled by a desire to achieve some end that was beyond his understanding. He was aware of the way in which he could use voice and gestures to sway a congregation, and he had known from their second meeting that she was drawn to his physical presence as he was to hers,

yet below her delicacy, her charm, and the flattery
that her ignorance afforded to his superior knowledge, he sensed a seam of iron that frightened
him because he knew that it was not in his own
nature. He had longed to get away from her, but
the days at Poole seemed everlasting. In the end
he cut short his holiday, making the excuse to
his father that he was needed in Putney, although
in fact another minister had temporary care of
the chapel. He went to his lodgings, and then on
Sunday the twenty-seventh paid a visit to Claverton Street.

He did not know what he hoped to find there,
except that he longed for some resolution of his
continuing agony. Such a resolution would have
been reached if he had found that the Bartletts
had left the apartment and given no address at
which they could be reached, or if he had received
word that they refused to see him. Had he not
tried to achieve this end by telling Edwin that
he was becoming too fond of Adelaide? Or, of
course, there would have been a resolution of a
different kind if he had found Edwin Bartlett in
a coffin, and the sorrowing widow had said that
when it was possible she would become Mrs Dyson. This last prospect attracted and terrified him.

What he disliked above all was a sick-room, and
this he was spared. The small iron bed remained
in its corner of the drawing-room, but Edwin Bartlett was not in it. He was sitting at the central
table in front of a big jigsaw puzzle showing the
death of General Gordon at Khartoum, which he
said Adelaide had bought him on his recovery,
as an after-Christmas present. He took the clergyman's hand in both his own, and expressed delight
at seeing him again.

'I want to thank you, Mr Dyson, for your companionship in the past, and to say how much we have missed you. Both of us. Isn't that so, my dear?'

Adelaide, who was reading a book, did not reply.

'Come now, I thought it was George and Edwin. I am truly delighted to find you so much better, Edwin. You have been much in my thoughts.'

'Yes, I'm quite my own man again, Addy will testify to that.'

'Edwin, I have asked you not to call me Addy.'

'Sorry, my dear, it just slipped out. She's been a wonderful nurse, nobody could have wanted a better. I'm afraid it's been getting her down though, she's not had a decent night's sleep. Now, tell us all about Poole, and how you found your family.'

He made conversation about his days down there, all the while with an eye on Adelaide. After a time she closed her book and listened, but still hardly spoke. Her face was heavy and sullen, as he had sometimes seen it. Alice came in to lay the central table for supper, and then brought a dish of lamb chops, of which Edwin ate heartily, in spite of the lack of teeth which made him suck noisily on the bone. Adelaide barely touched her food.

After supper she said that she had a letter to post. Dyson remarked that it was time for him to be leaving, and said good night to Edwin. They went out into the night, which was bitterly cold. They had gone a hundred yards in silence, when he halted and said that there was no pillar-box this way.

'I have nothing to post. I wanted to speak to

you, that is all. Let us go down to the river.'

They crossed the road to the embankment, and stood looking down at the Thames. To the left the Houses of Parliament were visible. Moonlight glinted on the river, which was full. In the distance some boat gave a solitary hoot. He wanted to put his arm round her, and at length did so, but she shrugged away and said that he should not touch her.

'What is the matter, why are you angry?'

She did not look at him, but down to the water. Her words, however, were clear enough.

'You deserted me when I needed you.'

'But I explained. I did not wish to go, but my family—I had to see my family.'

'I needed you. I need your help now, for . . .' Her voice dropped, and he did not hear the words. He hardly dared to ask her to repeat what she had said.

'Chloroform. I need some chloroform.'

The request was so unexpected that he lost his usual fluency, and almost stammered. 'But—what for?'

Her voice dropped again, but he heard the words this time. 'Edwin is better. He has been making requests of me, do you understand? *I will not do it!*' She said this with such force that he flinched momentarily, as though burned.

'Could you not ask Dr Leach?'

'Do you expect me to talk of such things to him? It is you I come to when I need help, do you not understand that?'

They stood with their arms on the parapet, a foot apart.

The force emanating from her was such that he would have liked to move away, but could not do so. He had difficulty in uttering his next words, but in the end managed it.

'What do you need it for?'

'If you loved me with anything more than sensual love, you would not ask that. I know about chloroform and about medical matters, that should be enough. Love is trust. Do you not trust me?'

In a voice that might have been a cry for help, he said, 'I must know.'

'Very well. When he makes these requests I shall tell him that chloroform will please and soothe him. Then I shall sprinkle it on a handkerchief. He will inhale it and go to sleep.'

Did he believe her? He refused to ask himself the question. Despairingly he said, 'I know nothing about chloroform.'

'What does that matter?'

'I mean, I do not know what I should ask for.'

'Chloroform evaporates quickly. I shall need a medicine draught bottle. This is the first time I have asked you for anything. Are you going to refuse me?'

He said that he would do it. When he left her he stumbled away like a drunken man.

Did she really need the chloroform for the reason she had given? What other possible use could she have for it? In part because he so much disliked illness, he knew nothing of medicine. He was aware that chloroform was called a poison, and had heard of its use for anaesthetic purposes. He had also seen his mother use it once to remove grease from a jacket. Apart from that he knew nothing. He did not even know the size of a medicine draught bottle.

Although he passed a sleepless night, it never

occurred to him that he might refuse the request. On Monday morning he went to Humble's, a chemist fifty yards away from his chapel. Mr Humble knew the tall clergyman who had recently taken charge of the chapel, and greeted him by name.

'Chloroform, yes, Mr Dyson. Would it be camphorated chloroform you need?'

'Camphorated?'

'Sometimes used for the mouth.'

'Oh no, not camphorated. Do you have chloroform that will take out grease stains?'

'Ah, that would be pure chloroform. This size, Mr Dyson?' He held up a two drachm-bottle, then a half-ounce one, but the clergyman said that they were too small. In the end he bought an ounce bottle for a shilling and threepence. His manner seemed to Mr Humble, reflecting on it afterwards, to be rather wild.

An ounce, he could see, would be nothing like enough. He visited two other chemists, both known to him and one a member of his congregation, and bought two ounces from each of them. Why had he mentioned grease stains, he was asked afterwards? Well, he could hardly name the reason Adelaide had given him. Back at his lodgings he got an empty bottle from his landlady, one that he supposed would be about the size of a medicine bottle, and poured the chloroform into it. Then he soaked the label off one of the bottles he had bought, and stuck it on the new one. The label said: 'Chloroform, Poison.' The bold lettering filled him with unease.

With the purchases made, the act done, he found himself quite unable to return to Claverton Street that day. There was enough to occupy him with affairs at the chapel, but even if this had not been so he felt a revulsion that would have kept him away. By Tuesday morning this revulsion or anxiety had eased, and he was able to persuade himself that he was doing nothing wrong.

On that Monday also Dr Leach fulfilled the promise he had made to himself by paying an unexpected call in the morning. Mrs Bartlett was out shopping, as he had hoped. Her husband was up, but showed the utmost reluctance to come out.

'Come along now. My carriage is outside, I am on my rounds.'

'I cannot do it, doctor. I might catch cold, I do not want to be ill again. If Adelaide were here she would tell you that I might catch cold.'

'But Mrs Bartlett is not here. I am in charge. Come now, it is doctor's orders.'

'Truly I cannot go. It would kill me.'

To get him out Dr Leach had to play his trump card, and say that if his orders were disobeyed he would have to discontinue his visits. After that he had to help Edwin on with his overcoat, and to muffle him up like a mummy. Once in the doctor's brougham, however, he slowly recovered his spirits, and even acknowledged that it did him good to be in the air, although to tell the truth one did not get much air in the enclosed carriage. By the end of the round he had become quite chatty, and was asking questions about other patients. Dr Leach was amused to see that, while Mrs Doggett had given him a hand downstairs, he ran up them again quite lightly.

Mrs Bartlett was at home when they returned, and expressed herself delighted that her husband had been persuaded to go out. 'You will come for a drive with me tomorrow, will you not?'

'Certainly, my dear. It really did me good.'

That evening the Old Man came. He greeted Adelaide and parted from her with a kiss, and nothing was said about the letter. The Old Man was pleased to see his son so much better.

'Soon be back at business,' he said.

'Not quite yet. I am still weak, you know, I had worms. And then I was poisoned, did I tell you that?'

'Poisoned?' Old Bartlett looked from one to the other of them. Adelaide answered. 'Mercurial poisoning. Dr Leach said it was very slight. Edwin had been taking pills containing mercury.'

'Or it might have been lead poisoning,' Edwin added. 'I might have got it from opening the tea chests.'

'What about the other doctor, Dr Dudley was it? What did he say?'

'He fully agreed with Dr Leach,' Adelaide replied. 'Edwin will go for a holiday before returning to business. He will go next week, probably on Tuesday.'

'Poisoning,' the Old Man said, and shook his head. He looked round for a spittoon, did not see one, and spat into the fire. Adelaide turned away her head.

When he had gone they worked together on the General Gordon jigsaw, and found the spear which had stabbed the General. Then Edwin said they should ask Baxter to send some goodies for New Year's Eve, he felt so much better. What should they have? After half an hour's talk she wrote to Baxter:

Will you please send a bottle of the brandy called Lord's Extra; a bottle of Colonel Skinner's Mango Chutney; a bottle of walnuts, and a nice fruit cake? I know these things are not fit for Edwin to eat, but he fancies them.

Tuesday. A cold day, but fine. Adelaide ordered a hansom, and they went for a drive around Green Park. Then Dyson came, Georgius Rex. He was pale, and kept shifting uncomfortably in his chair, until Edwin burst out laughing.

'You must excuse me, but I had a funny thought. I was thinking it was as if you had worms rather than me. You know I had them? I can still feel them in my throat.'

'Edwin, do not say such things, you know it is nonsense. I think it is a joke of his, but not a good one.' The clergyman managed a ghastly smile. 'I think you are not well.'

'It is very warm in here. If you will forgive me, I shall take a short walk.' The return to Claverton Street had turned his feeling of unease to dread. The bottle was in his overcoat pocket, and at that moment he meant to throw it into the Thames.

'I will come with you. We shall not be more than a few minutes, Edwin.'

'Half an hour, an hour, it doesn't matter. The wind will blow away all your troubles, that's what it did for me. You know we took a drive this morning?' Dyson did know, for he had mentioned it three times.

They walked down to the river in silence as they had done before, except that now it was twilight instead of darkness. She said, 'Well?'

Without a word he took out the bottle and handed it to her. With the action the sick dread vanished, and he was his confident self again.

'It is chloroform?' He nodded. She placed her hand on his, and even though that hand was gloved he felt something like an electric current moving between them. 'This is something you have done for me, an act of love. Of pure, not sensual love. It joins us.'

'You know I love you, I have told you so. I want to know nothing more about—about your relationship with Edwin.'

'You shall hear nothing more. Not today or ever.'

She put the bottle in her bag. They walked back to Claverton Street.

Wednesday. On that day Dr Leach deliberately avoided a visit, a move in the strategy of weaning away the patient from undue dependence on him. Edwin remained cheerful, doing full justice to his dinner of roast beef and baked potatoes, followed by junket. In the evening Baxter paid a visit, and was delighted to find his partner practically his old self. He had brought along the box of goodies in person, and Edwin rubbed his hands as they were put out on the table.

'Pickled walnuts, nothing like them. And that chutney. They say you should keep it for cold meat, but I find it goes with everything. And the fruit cake, we shall eat a slice of that before the New Year, I can tell you.'

'He's like a child, is he not, Mr Baxter?' Adelaide said, laughing. 'Now, will you tell him that he can go to Torquay next week without worrying about the business?'

'Devil a bit need you worry. Everything's going smooth as silk. Mind, I don't say we could do without you for ever. I haven't got his palate, Mrs Bartlett, when it comes to tasting and mixing teas. But I mustn't tire you. I'll say good night, and a Happy New Year to you both.'

That night, again, there was no importunacy.

CHAPTER 7
THE LAST DAY OF
THE OLD YEAR

'Although he was sleepless, wretched, morbid, hypochondriacal, presenting the symptoms of a nervous breakdown, the illness had run its course . . . Very likely he talked of his death, but not as a man does who is, or feels himself, in real danger. Dr Leach said, "I always ridiculed the idea," and the last three or four days of his life it is scarcely possible he can have supposed that there was any danger of any sort or kind to his life. . . . He does not seem to have thought so on the last day of his existence.'

MR JUSTICE WILLS, summing up

The last day of the old year was fine, the barometer shot up, and at midday the temperature recorded at Kew was twelve degrees higher than that shown on the day before. Edwin Bartlett woke in good spirits, saying that he had slept well. He exclaimed on the change in the weather, saying that it made you feel good to see it. When Mrs Doggett came up as usual to see what he felt like eating later on, and mentioned that she had seen some fresh plump oysters in the market, he rubbed his hands and said that they were exactly what he would like for lunch, they would slip down a treat. Mrs Bartlett demurred a little, wondering whether oysters were wise when he had felt ill so recently.

'Don't worry. I'm tip-top this morning, absolutely tip-top. A few oysters never did a man any harm.'

The doctor, who came round at eleven, was pleased to find his patient in such good spirits. He made his usual soundings, asked about bowel movements (Edwin had done his duty, no sign of any worm), looked at the mouth. What he saw there disturbed him, but he did not speak of this to the patient. Instead he saw Mrs Bartlett alone down in the smoking-room.

'I speak to you because you know, we both know, you and I, how much Mr Bartlett fears the dentist. And I am bound to say that Mr Roberts must see him again. I don't wish to alarm you, but there are signs of necrosis.'

She looked quite sparkling this morning, he thought, her eyes blazing with enthusiasm, no doubt because of her husband's recovery. She never wore bright colours, but today her blue dress (or perhaps it was a shade of green, he could not be sure) perfectly complemented those strange dark eyes. Her reply now had the kind of tartness she sometimes showed, a quality appreciated by the doctor, who did not care for what he called sugary ladies.

'Perhaps I should be more alarmed if I knew the meaning of the word.'

'My dear Mrs Bartlett, forgive me. You show so much interest in medicine that at times I almost imagine you to be a fellow practitioner.' He laughed into his high collar to show that this was a joke. 'Necrosis is the name we give to some damage or disease affecting the jawbone. Damage may, for example, be caused by a blow.'

'Edwin has suffered no blow.'

'That was merely an example. In his case, no doubt the cause was the mercurial poisoning.' He did not add, for fear of shocking her, that syphilis was the most common cause of necrosis.

'And is this necrosis serious?'

Dr Leach was not inclined to underestimate the seriousness of any illness. 'If left unattended it may indeed be very serious. But we have caught it in an early stage, and it is my sincere hope—I will go further and say expectation—that Mr Roberts will be able to treat it successfully. A thorough examination will be much easier if Mr Bartlett can be persuaded to pay a visit to Mr Roberts's surgery.'

'I will do my best.' She gave him one of her delightful smiles. 'If you make the appointment I will try to make sure that Edwin keeps it.'

She broke the news to Edwin after he had taken a light lunch of half a dozen oysters, brown bread and butter, tea and cake. In the last two of these she joined him, and it was when the oyster shells had been pushed aside and they were drinking a dish of tea that she told him Dr Leach thought Mr Roberts should make a further examination. Edwin's spirits were not depressed. He consented readily enough to go round to the surgery. He told Mrs Doggett that the oysters were the best he had tasted that year, but that they left him feeling hungry.

This hunger was assuaged at three o'clock, when Alice brought up dinner. This was jugged hare with redcurrant jelly, mashed potatoes and plenty of gravy. The meat came off the bone easily, something which was important because he lacked so many teeth. After dinner he had an hour's doze on the bed, but when Dr Leach returned at five o'clock he was delighted to find that Mr Bartlett showed no morbid fear of the dentist. He covered up his mouth, but that was a sensible precaution. In the brougham Mrs Bartlett talked a good deal, no doubt with the intention of keeping up her husband's spirits. The doctor, playing his part, described amusing incidents at a couple of weddings in the neighbourhood, weddings to which he had been invited. Afterwards he remembered what Mrs Bartlett had said.

'This morning, doctor, Edwin and I were saying that we almost wished we were unmarried, so that we might have the pleasure of marrying each other again.'

Dr Leach gave his collar-strangled laugh. 'Very flattering to you, Mr Bartlett, after being married so long.'

Through the scarf that muffled his mouth Edwin Bartlett said, 'Yes, we suit one another very well.'

Then they were at the dentist's. All three went into the surgery, and at sight of the chair and the instruments Edwin began to tremble. However, he sat in the chair, and the dentist placed a hand on his shoulder.

'You are a little nervous. But I have not hurt you before, have I? And you will not feel pain this time, I give you my word. Now, open wide.'

The examination took a minute or two. Then the dentist said to the doctor, 'You were right, necrosis is setting in.'

Dr Leach looked regretful, but pleased at the same time. Mr Roberts's voice was rather loud, and Edwin turned his head. He looked, with the white tunic tied round his neck, like an overgrown baby.

'What is that, necrosis? What is the matter?'

Now both doctor and dentist came forward with hands raised soothingly. The dentist spoke.

'Nothing to worry about, Mr Bartlett. It is a condition arising from the bad state of your teeth, but we shall be able to treat it. Now, there is just one more tooth I should extract.'

'Will it hurt?'

'Not at all. I think, to make quite sure of that, we will use nitrous oxide gas. Dr Leach, may I ask you to administer it?'

When the rubber mask was put over his head, Edwin Bartlett proved not to be the most tractable of patients. He made gestures to indicate that he was still awake, and his open eyes looked up with alarm at the dentist, who stood with forceps poised. Then the eyes closed suddenly, the mask was lifted, and the extraction took only a few seconds. When Edwin came to, he found it hard to believe that the tooth was out. The dentist was brisk about his recommended treatment.

'Just a mouthwash. One containing Condy's fluid will do very well. Then come back and see me in a week.' When Edwin said that he would be at Torquay in a week, Mr Roberts said that he should pay a visit on his return. The gums would have settled by then, and they could make arrangements for a new set of teeth.

So that was well over, and Dr Leach felt he could congratulate himself on a successful outcome. He was going himself to a New Year's party, and warned Edwin against over-indulgence. This was by way of being a joke, and it was taken in good part, with a hearty laugh. Dr Leach dropped them outside their door, and waved good-bye.

They had not been back more than a few minutes when Mrs Doggett came up to ask how Mr Bartlett had got on at the dentist. 'A tooth out. But no pain, not a touch of it. The worst is over, Mrs Doggett.'

'I'm pleased to see you so much better.'

'Yes, and I'm off to the seaside next week. Doctor's orders.'

'That's nice. Did you have that freezing stuff again for the tooth, what's it called now?'

'Cocaine. No, I had gas today. Don't mind what they give me as long as it don't hurt.'

Now Mrs Bartlett spoke. 'Tell me, Mrs Doggett, have you ever taken chloroform?'

'Oh yes. When I had my appendicitis operation, years ago.'

'And it was a pleasant feeling, isn't that true?'

'I couldn't say.' Mrs Doggett had never quite trusted this Frenchified piece, and was not going to admit anything to her, about chloroform or anything else. 'No, couldn't say, I'm sure.'

'Because, you see, I have these sleeping drops.' She held up a blue bottle. 'If Mr Bartlett can't sleep I shall give them to him. They say ten drops is a strong dose, but I might give him twelve.'

That remark about not sleeping put Mrs Doggett in mind of something. 'One thing I came up to mention. Seeing as it's New Year's Eve, Mr Doggett and I will be having some friends here for a little jollification. We won't be late, not really late, but we shall see the New Year in. I hope that won't disturb you.'

'Lord love us, don't you worry. I'll have my head down before then,' Mr Bartlett said.

'Much obliged. Now, seeing you made such a good dinner I thought—'

'I should think I did. I tell you, Mrs Doggett, I ate up every scrap. I could eat three dinners like that a day.'

'My, he *is* better, isn't he?' Mrs Bartlett merely smiled, in what Mrs Doggett thought a sly foreign manner. 'I wonder if there's anything you fancy for supper?'

'I'll tell you what I fancy. Another half-dozen of those Whitstable natives.' He patted his stomach and laughed, so that Mrs Doggett couldn't help noticing that the poor lamb had lost most of his teeth. Mrs Bartlett turned away as though in disapproval, but said nothing.

At nine o'clock Alice brought up another half-dozen oysters. With them Edwin ate some of Colonel Skinner's mango chutney, and both he and Adelaide had slices of the fruit cake. When Alice came up and cleared away, she asked what he would like for breakfast. Red-faced and beaming, he said, 'A haddock, Alice. A nice large haddock.'

'A haddock, sir, very well.'

'But a big one. Like this.' He spread his arms wide. 'I shall get up an hour earlier at the thought.'

A very pleasant gentleman, Mr Bartlett, before he became ill, and now he was evidently well again. 'Is there anything else, ma'am?'

'Yes, Alice,' Mrs Bartlett said. 'Will you bring up some coals for the night. And that will be all.'

Alice brought up a scuttleful of coal, and said good night. The time was just after half past ten.

From that time onwards the Bartletts were alone. The Doggetts had a pleasant but quiet evening. They saw the New Year in, as they had said

they would, and then their guests went home.
At about twelve-thirty Mr Doggett, who was always last to bed, locked up, turned down the gas,
and went up to his room on the second floor. The
Bartletts' apartment, as he passed it, was perfectly
quiet.

AFTERWARDS (V)

From the day when she learned the result of
the post-mortem carried out in the back room
at Claverton Street, Adelaide recognized that everything had gone terribly wrong. She had made
mistakes, and none was greater than her trust in
Georgius Rex. From the time of that journey in
the hansom to Herne Hill she realized that he
was not in truth a king of men but only the Reverend George Dyson, a man timid and afraid. When
she understood that, her love for him died, and
afterwards she trusted in nobody but herself.

For George Dyson too that Saturday of the post-
mortem was crucial. The spell that had been cast
on him was lifted. He no longer contemplated a
life spent with Adelaide, but thought only of
escaping from the snare in which he felt himself
caught. As the weeks passed, these two moved
towards a disaster made more certain by their
attempts to avoid it, a disaster charted most easily
by the calendar.

January 3   This was Sunday, the day after the
post-mortem. Sunday, and George Dyson must go
to his chapel at Putney, must stand up and preach
to a congregation that would no longer include

Edwin nor, as he rightly guessed, Adelaide. He could think of nothing but the need to get rid of the four little bottles that stood on a shelf in his sitting-room. He put them in his overcoat pocket and threw them into some gorse bushes as he walked across Wandsworth Common on his way to chapel. He never knew what he said when he stood up to speak, but somehow he got through it, chatted and smiled afterwards. Yet although the bottles had gone, he still felt the shadow over him.

January 4 It was this threatening shadow that led him in the morning to Charlwood Street and Dr Leach. Could the doctor possibly tell him anything more about the likely cause of Edwin's death? Dr Leach reflected that although this kind of thing should be confidential, the man was a minister and a friend of the family. There could surely be no harm in telling him something of what Dr Green had said, that the lining of the stomach had been red and inflamed and, as the report put it, 'both stomach and intestines emitted a strong smell of chloroform.' He added, however, that he felt sure Dr Green was wrong. It would turn out to be that bottle of *chlorodyne* on the mantelpiece, not *chloroform*. George Dyson heard him in a daze, without understanding the difference, knowing only that there was reason for uneasiness. After leaving the doctor he suddenly remembered the poem he had given to Adelaide, something that she had said she would keep for ever. Supposing that it was found? The need to cancel out the past, to revoke his actions in these last months so that they should be totally erased just as the bottles had ceased to exist now that he had thrown them away, was obsessively strong in his mind. Edwin had given him a cheque for five pounds to cover the money he had spent down at Dover. If he paid this back, surely there would be no need to say it had ever been accepted? He had five gold sovereigns in his pocket when he went down in the train from Victoria to Peckham Rye and then walked to the Matthews' house. Alice Matthews was in the drawing-room with Adelaide when he entered, and thought how ill he looked. She left them together, because he obviously wished it.

He did not attempt an embrace as he would have done in the past, but stood looking at her, wondering what could have fascinated or even attracted him in her heavy face and coarse hair. 'I have just come from Dr Leach. There was nothing wrong with your husband's—with Edwin's—heart.' She said nothing. 'The doctor said that some drops of chlorodyne or chloroform had been found in the stomach.'

At that she said, 'Which was it?' He had been so shocked and confused that he could not remember, and had to say so. She stamped her foot. 'Oh, you are stupid. You must know which it was. Come now, tell me.'

He shook his head, and retreated slightly as she approached. He took the sovereigns from his pocket, and said that he must repay his debt. She told him scornfully to put them on the table.

'The poem I wrote to you, do you still have it?' She did not reply, and he blundered on, intent only on cancelling the past. 'I think it would be best if you returned it.'

'Those silly verses? You shall have them back by all means. Is there anything else?'

He had to pursue it, had to know the answer. 'You must tell me, what did you do with the chloroform?'

At that her calm broke. 'Oh, damn the chloroform.' She stamped her foot again, and turned her back on him.

'But I must know.'

'Go away,' she said. At that moment Alice returned, looked from one of them to the other, and asked what was the matter.

Dyson ignored her. 'You told me that Edwin was going to die soon.' She turned to face him now and shouted the reply. 'No, I did not.'

At that, as Mrs Matthews saw it, the tall clergyman seemed to crumple, so that she feared he might collapse. He was standing beside the piano and now bowed his head on it, saying softly, 'Oh, my God.'

It was a fascinating scene, and Alice tried to remember every detail of it to tell George afterwards, but it was also shocking. She said to Mr Dyson that he had better go. He nodded, and went to the door. As he went by she heard him say, as though to himself, 'I am a ruined man.'

Afterwards she asked Adelaide what had been the matter, but was told only that Mr Dyson had been bothering her about a piece of paper. When George came home she told him the whole story. They agreed that it was all very strange, but that they must stand by Mrs Bartlett. As George said, foreigners were excitable, and you couldn't judge them as you would English people.

January 5 On this day the law at last took some action in relation to the stomach contents and other parts of Edwin's body which had been left

in the sealed apartment at Claverton Street. Tom
Ralph, Coroner's Officer, took possession of 'four
glass vessels, jars or bottles, covered with brown
paper and sealed, with Dr Dudley's initials on the
seal.' He removed from the apartment also no
fewer than thirty-six medicine bottles. He put the
glass vessels into one hamper, the medicine bottles in another, and took them to the mortuary,
where he placed them in a large safe which stood
under cover in the back yard. There they stayed
for another six days.

Tom Ralph did not bother to look round the
rooms to see what else of importance might be
in them. He did not look for, and did not find, a
bottle of chloroform. He made, however, one
other discovery. In the front room, in the right-
hand pocket of one of Edwin Bartlett's suits, he
found 'four or five of what are popularly called
French letters.' The discovery went unremarked
at the time.

January 6   On this day the weather changed
again from its recent clemency, and snow fell.
Adelaide went to see Mr Wood, the solicitor who
had been present at the post-mortem. He told
her that at the inquest, which was to begin on
the following day, he had arranged that a young
barrister named Edward Beal should look after
her interests, and said also that the coroner had
now done with the Claverton Street rooms. Dr
Leach had the keys, and she could collect her
things.

George Dyson's alarm was turned to panic
when he received a subpoena calling on him to
appear on Thursday January 7 to give evidence
before the Deputy Coroner of Westminster on

matters touching upon the death of Edwin Thomas Bartlett. The past, it seemed, could not be erased as easily as he had hoped. What should he say when he gave evidence? He spent two hours on his knees in prayer before it was revealed to him that the best course (and perhaps also the safest) was to tell the truth. But supposing Adelaide contradicted him? It was clear that he must see her again.

Adelaide had returned from her visit to the solicitor. She received him coolly, and without the anger she had shown before. When he said that he would make what he called a clean breast of the whole affair she answered that it was a matter for him. He must do what he wished. She returned his poem.

He went then with Adelaide and Alice Matthews to see Dr Leach, and on to Claverton Street. Alice helped Adelaide pack, and Dyson made himself useful in buying cord for her boxes and in getting a cab. It was very far from the spirit of the old days.

This running about kept him from thinking, but no sooner was he left alone for a few minutes than his mind returned to the awful question of the chloroform. What could he say that would put it all in the right light, and show him as a man who had been doing his Christian best to help somebody in distress? He escorted Mrs Matthews back home (Adelaide was to come there later, after settling various matters with Mrs Doggett), and then went to Peckham Rye station to meet George Matthews off the train. George was surprised, and not pleased, to find the tall clergyman awaiting him in a state of great agitation, saying that he must speak to him and ask his advice.

That was a bit thick, George Matthews thought, considering that he hardly knew the man. But he was polite, as one had to be to a man of the cloth, and listened patiently to a semi-coherent gabble about bottles of chloroform bought at Mrs Bartlett's request, and then poured into another bottle and given to her. What the devil were you about, he wanted to ask the reverend gentleman, but the question could hardly be asked of a man in a state so near panic. He listened, and said 'H'm' and 'Yes' and 'I see,' as they trudged through the snow and slush.

'I should like you to understand my motives,' George Dyson said. He peered anxiously from under his black hat at his shorter companion. 'I have been duped, Mr Matthews, duped by a wicked woman. She deceived me.'

'Steady on now. Remember that Mrs Bartlett is our guest.'

'But it is true. Mr Bartlett threw us together— the Lord knows I do not wish to say a word against the poor man, I valued his friendship, but he threw us together. In consequence, I found myself attacked upon my weakest side.'

'Ha.' George Matthews felt an increasing contempt for his companion.

'And now tomorrow the inquest begins. I have to give evidence. If I tell them everything, Mr Matthews, they cannot possibly hold me at fault, don't you agree?'

'I don't know about that, but I'll tell you what I *do* think. I think you're crying out before you're hurt.'

'I beg your pardon?'

'You don't know the cause of Edwin's death, no more does anybody else until this Home Office man makes his report. Until you know, if I were you I'd keep my own counsel.' And not bother other people with your maunderings, he added to himself.

George Dyson said nothing to this, and refused an invitation to come in when they reached the house. Later that evening as he looked at Adelaide, demure and quiet, Matthews wondered whether she really was a wicked woman. He thought it quite likely. Had he not told his wife long ago that there was something unhealthy about her, and that she would come to a bad end?

January 7 Mr Braxton-Hicks, the Deputy Coroner, was a peppery little man. As soon as she saw him Adelaide knew he would be against her, and she saw that this was so when the first witness proved to be the Old Man. In the witness-box old Bartlett looked round, searching perhaps for a spittoon, and then began pouring out his tales full of hatred about her, saying that *he* had suspected poison, *he* had insisted that the post-mortem should be in the hands of an independent doctor, and so on. She whispered to young Mr Beal, asking if this should be allowed, if this was English justice. He whispered back that she would have her turn, and sure enough after the Old Man had stepped down she was called into the witness-box. She did not hear the first question, but she was determined anyway that the jury, who sat there like puddings, should know what sort of man he was.

'Mr Bartlett senior has always hated me, because I am of foreign birth, and—'

Mr Braxton-Hicks banged with his gavel. 'These

are family matters, and cannot be gone into here. In any case, I am adjourning the proceedings until the fourth of February, by which time we shall have the benefit of the Home Office expert's report.'

And that was that. It was over in half an hour. Afterwards, both Mr Wood and young Mr Beal warned her that she must take great care in what she said. But what harm could there be in telling the truth about that terrible Old Man? Mr Beal said that she should be guided by them. Perhaps it would be better if she did not go into the box at all. Perhaps, perhaps. It all seemed to her legal foolishness.

As she left the parochial boardroom where the hearing had taken place George Dyson, who had been sitting across the room, asked if he could speak to her alone. They had lunch at a little restaurant nearby, and as she considered the hollow-eyed pathetic figure across the table she wondered how she could ever have named him Georgius Rex. He spoke of nothing but his own position, his own problems, without a thought for her.

'You are distressing yourself unnecessarily,' she said.

'How can you say that?' He pushed aside his plate of roast beef almost untouched. 'What about the chloroform?'

'Oh, the chloroform. I am sick of hearing about it.'

'But I bought it for you. You must see that I have cause to be alarmed.'

Under the direct gaze of those eyes he had once thought irresistible, he felt bound to look away.

'I will promise you something. If you say nothing to—what is the word?—incriminate yourself, I will not incriminate you.'

'But I have done nothing wrong.'

'Then you have nothing to worry about. As for me, you know I am never afraid. I think we have finished.'

They parted, speaking hardly another word.

January 8 On this day Edwin Bartlett's body, lacking certain vital parts which reposed in the mortuary, was buried. His widow was present, accompanied by Mr Wood.

January 9 George Dyson had spent some more time on his knees in search of a way by which he might avoid making those admissions about the chloroform which, he knew, might be misinterpreted by those who did not understand his motives. He had also been summoned to a meeting with his Superintendent, from which he emerged in tears.

He presented himself once more on that Saturday afternoon at the Matthews', for the last time as it proved. When they made to leave him alone with Adelaide he checked them. It seemed to him that he had nothing to lose, perhaps something to gain, by speaking in their presence.

'This conversation is not of a private nature. I must tell you first that I am a ruined man.'

Adelaide made a derisive noise. George Matthews said, 'Hold on now, that's a bit steep.'

'It is the truth. In the Wesleyan faith there is a Superintendent appointed for each district, who is responsible for the conduct of the ministers. If I should be compelled to give evidence of a damaging kind at the inquest I shall have to resign. I was told so today. I could never take up another post in the Wesleyan ministry.'

You should have thought of that before, my lad, George Matthews thought but did not say.

'You are not compelled to give such evidence,' Adelaide said.

'I wish, I long not to do so. But don't you see that I must know about the chloroform, what you wanted it for, if it was used. Supposing that it turns out—'

He hesitated. Adelaide said indignantly, 'Don't mince matters. Say it if you wish. Say I gave him chloroform.'

He spread his hands in a gesture of appeal, not to her but to them all. 'To put it hypothetically—'

'Oh, hypothetically,' she flashed out. 'You are a great one for putting things hypothetically, are you not?'

'Supposing it was discovered that you gave him chloroform—and then that I gave it to you—I must know what you did with it.'

'And you will keep quiet, if you know?' He made an indeterminate hand-washing gesture. 'Very well, I will tell you. I said before that I never opened the bottle. It was in a drawer in the back room, and I found it when I collected my things. I put it in my pocket, and when I came back here on Wednesday evening I opened the bottle, poured out the chloroform from the train window, and threw the bottle into Peckham Rye pond as we passed it.'

Dyson said almost in a whisper, 'I do not believe you,' and as George said to Alice later on he had rarely heard an explanation that sounded less convincing. Adelaide shrugged, and went out of the room. Dyson made his apologies to George and Alice for the scene he had caused, and left the house.

Adelaide Bartlett and George Dyson, who had been Georgius Rex, never spoke to each other again.

January 11 Both George and Alice had felt increasingly uneasy about Adelaide's presence in the house. Was it because she sensed this that she insisted on paying for her board and lodging, and moved out when Alice said that she would not take a penny of payment? In any case she left, taking lodgings at Weymouth Street, just off Portland Place.

January 12 Now, at last, Dr Stevenson began his examination of the contents of those glass vessels. Dr Thomas Stevenson was the most famous medical toxicologist of the time, and the analyst most often consulted by the Home Office. He had succeeded the great Alfred Taylor as lecturer on forensic medicine at Guy's Hospital, and had brought up to date Taylor's standard work on medical jurisprudence. Of the eight bottles and packages he opened, one containing the lower jaw and another the tongue, those that held the stomach and the smaller bowel proved to be of prime importance.

When he opened the stoppered bottle that held a tablespoonful of thick semi-fluid matter from the stomach, there was a strong smell of chloroform, mixed with a slight odour of garlic which proved to come from mango chutney. He estimated the quantity of chloroform to be 11¼ grains, about five per cent of the amount analysed.

There was a small trace of alcohol, no sign of prussic acid or any other poison. And no chlorodyne.

Next Stevenson analysed the jar that contained the contents of the smaller bowel. This had not been tightly stoppered, so that the chloroform had to some extent evaporated. He found traces of it, less than half a grain, plus some chutney. And then the stomach itself. This was much inflamed. There was a patch of severe inflammation about the size of a crown piece, and around this the redness extended to a patch almost as large as his two hands. This large patch was that to which liquid would flow when a person was on his back. It was the usual place where inflammation showed after swallowing irritant poison.

He continued the examination over several days. He found no other poison but chloroform. The conclusion seemed inescapable. Edwin Bartlett had died from swallowing liquid chloroform.

There was an interesting corollary to this. It did not concern Stevenson at the time, because his interest was only in the cause of death and not in the manner by which it had been effected, but it later became a central point in the case.

The interesting point was this. Chloroform had been used for anaesthetic purposes since 1847. Since that time seventeen deaths had occurred through swallowing it, either by accident or suicide. There was, however, not a single recorded case of murder by the administration of liquid chloroform.

January 26 When she came to consider her own conduct later, more specifically when she thought about it in a cell at Clerkenwell, Adelaide realized that her confession to Dr Leach on this day had been a mistake. Shut up in those miserable Weymouth Street rooms, she suffered agonies while awaiting the verdict to be given by the Government analyst. If only all had gone as she expected, if only Dr Leach had signed the death certificate, how smoothly events would have flowed, how easily she could have shaped her future life. But she felt no ill-will towards the doctor, who was undoubtedly her friend. Almost her only friend now, for she had excised from her life the feeble and treacherous Dyson, and although she still saw George and Alice Matthews she felt distrust emanating from them. They seemed to be examining every word she said, like jewellers who suspected that she was trying to pass off paste for precious stones. And Mr Wood? No doubt he advised her well, but she did not feel the true current of trust flowing between them. He had said, with Mr Beal's approval, that when the inquest was reopened they should wait for the Home Office report before deciding whether or not she should give evidence. There seemed some reserve in his manner when he said this.

Dr Leach was different. She saw him frequently, and he prescribed for her nervous condition some of the tonics and sedatives that he had given so profusely to Edwin. She went to Pimlico, he visited her in Weymouth Street. He had no news of the analysis but offered several conjectures, all of them cheerful. When she visited him on this day he met her with a smiling face, then took her hands and held them.

'My dear Mrs Bartlett, I have news for you. Good news, I think.'

'You have seen the analyst's report?'

'No, but I have heard the nature of his findings
from one of his suborainates. He is going to give
cnloroform as the cause of death. That should set
your mind at rest. Had it been chlorodyne, or
one of those poisons that may be given secretly
in small amounts, I fear that some wretcned people might seriously have accused you of poisoning
him.'

'Chloroform.' She relinquished his hands. 'Oh
doctor, I wish anything but chloroform had been
found.'

He looked at her in surprise. 'What do you
mean? I do not understand.'

It was then that she made her confession, although that was hardly the name for it since she
did not confess to any sin. She had decided what
to say if things went as desperately wrong as they
had done. If Dyson was to say that he had given
chloroform to her that must be explained, and if
she did not give evidence at the inquest then Dr
Leach might tell the story for her in his own evidence. The story had been settled in her mind
for some days, but as she admitted to herself afterwards, she had not thought it through clearly.
When people called her tale 'marvellous,' meaning that they did not believe it, she realized that
a feeling for drama had led her away. The story,
many said, was preposterous. Perhaps so, and certainly she knew it was not literally true. Yet she
felt that a higher truth was embodied in what
she said, the kind of truth contained in Madame
Blavatsky's assertion that she was a virgin even
though she had had a husband and, as many said,
a child. Adelaide too felt that she was truly almost
a virgin.

Dr Leach heard the story, as she told it in his

surgery on that dark January afternoon. He listened with round eyes popping, his fingers pulling occasionally at his collar. When she had gone he made notes with a J-nibbed pen of what she had said. He had complete faith in Mrs Bartlett, and the astonishing nature of her story only proved to him once more the strangeness of all human creatures. At the inquest, and later at the Old Bailey, he repeated what had been said to him. This, in Dr Leach's own words, is the story he heard.

'Mrs Bartlett said that, being married young, she had been induced to enter into a marriage compact, scarcely understanding the meaning of its terms. The marriage compact was that the married relations of the pair were, in deference to certain peculiar views held by her husband, to be of an entirely platonic nature. Sexual intercourse was not to occur.

'The terms of this compact were adhered to, with a solitary exception, when a breach of the terms was permitted in consequence of her fondness for children and her anxiety to become a mother. After her confinement the former terms were resumed, she being indifferent on the matter. Her husband was affectionate, they strove in every way to fulfil each other's wishes, and lived upon the most amicable terms except when trouble was made by her husband's father. Yet her position had not been an easy one. Her husband always liked to surround her with male acquaintances. He thought her clever, wished her to be more clever, and the more attention given her by these male acquaintances the more delighted he appeared.

'During the last few months of his life her husband's nature seemed somewhat changed. They became acquainted with Mr Dyson, and her husband threw them together. He requested them to kiss in his presence, and seemed to enjoy it. He then gave her to Mr Dyson.'

When Dr Leach spoke this sentence there were gasps of amazement. At the Old Bailey he was pressed about it. Did it mean that Bartlett had 'given her' then and there, or in the event of his death? He could not be sure. And in what sense had he given her? Oh, the gift—or as it might perhaps be called the transfer—was entirely platonic, Dr Leach said.

'At this time, however, after the platonic transfer, Mr Bartlett showed signs of wishing to assume the marital rights that he had never previously claimed. This distressed his wife. "Edwin," she said, "you know you have given me to Mr Dyson. It is not right that you should do now what during all the married years of our life you have not done." He agreed, but in spite of his agreement these desires, these manifestations, became more urgent. She felt it necessary to prevent him putting these impulses into effect.

'With that in mind she obtained a bottle of chloroform. She intended, when the manifestations became apparent, to sprinkle some on a handkerchief and wave it in his face so that he would go peacefully to sleep.'

At this point in the confession Dr Leach shook his head, and told her what a risky thing she had had in mind. 'You see, Mrs Bartlett, putting chloroform upon your handkerchief and waving it in that way he would have resisted, there would have been a struggle, the bottle would have capsized and chloroformed the pair of you.'

She said with some impatience, 'I did not use it, so that did not happen.'

'No, but it *might* have happened if you *had* used it.'

With that point established, the narrative was resumed.

'She kept the chloroform in a drawer in the back bedroom, but was worried whether it would be right or wrong to use it. On the last night of the year, when he was in bed, she brought in the bottle, gave it to him and told him what she meant to do with it. He was not angry, but talked about it amicably and seriously. Then, perhaps sulkily, he turned over on his side and went to sleep, or pretended to do so. A little later she went to sleep herself. The large round bottle of chloroform, with a label on it, was left on the mantelpiece near the bed.'

That was the story. Dr Leach never thought of doubting it, but still there were some questions he asked when she had finished. Who had got the chloroform for her? he asked, but she would not name the person. And then, what had happened to it? She said that she had taken it from the mantelpiece at breakfast-time, and put it back in the bedroom drawer without looking to see whether or not it was full. Afterwards, she told him, as she had told Dyson and the Matthewses, she had poured it out of the train window and thrown away the bottle.

The implication of the story, of course, was that Edwin Bartlett had stretched up and taken the bottle in the night, uncorked it, and drunk enough of the contents to kill him. Dr Leach was prepared to believe this as a possibility, but one aspect of the story disturbed him, although it did not affect his perfect faith in Adelaide. If she had put the bottle back at breakfast-time, it must have been on the mantelpiece when the doctor first arrived after Edwin's death. Yet he had looked carefully round the room, and had seen no bottle of chloroform anywhere.

February 4   Mr Braxton-Hicks resumed his inquiry. Rumours of something scandalous about the affair had circulated widely, and the parochial boardroom was crowded. Everybody involved was now legally represented, not only Adelaide but also Dyson and Mr Bartlett senior. When Adelaide was called as a witness, Mr Beal refused to let her take the stand until Dr Stevenson's evidence had been heard. The Deputy Coroner said that he could not compel her to come forward, but that the jury might draw an unfavourable inference from her refusal. Mr Beal bowed.

The doctors then gave evidence, Dr Green who had noticed a strong smell of chloroform at the post-mortem, Dr Stevenson who said that Edwin Bartlett had taken a fatal dose of liquid chloroform. Dr Leach was in full flow when the hearing was adjourned for a week. From this time on, *The Times* called the affair 'The Pimlico Poisoning Case.'

February 11   Now the flood gates opened. Dr Leach told from his notes the 'marvellous' story. Then the Reverend George Dyson was called, and told how he had bought the chloroform and given it to Mrs Bartlett, after being attacked on his weakest side through Mr Bartlett's complaisance in relation to his wife. During this recital Adelaide

sat between Mr Beal and Mr Wood, not speaking,
hardly moving. Mr Beal asked Dyson no questions.
When he had finished a sigh of satisfaction, perhaps of pleasure, went round the boardroom.

Mr Braxton-Hicks took snuff. It was his moment,
and he meant to make the most of it.

'I ask again whether Mrs Bartlett intends to give
evidence? I ask for a very good reason.'

Mr Beal stood up. 'No, she does not. I make
that reply also for a very good reason.'

Mr Braxton-Hicks sniffed again, and looked at
the jury in a meaningful manner. They whispered
among themselves, and then the foreman rose.

'It is our unanimous opinion that Mrs Bartlett
should be taken into custody.'

Inspector Marshall then approached her. He
was in plain clothes, and therefore identified himself. 'After what has passed here today,' he said,
'I must take you into custody for the wilful murder
of your husband by administering to him about
midnight on the thirty-first December last a poi-
sonous dose of chloroform.' He gave the usual caution, to which she replied, 'I have nothing to say.'

She was taken to the House of Detention at
Clerkenwell.

February 18   On this day the jury, at the adjourned inquest, brought in a verdict against Adelaide Bartlett, and added that the Reverend
George Dyson was an accessory before the fact.
Inspector Marshall promptly arrested him. Dyson
sank into a chair and wept. A number of Wesleyan
ministers present tried to console him. It was, *The
Times* said on the following day, a very painful
scene.

PART FIVE
Trial and Verdict

CHAPTER 1
ADELAIDE IN CLERKENWELL

'The female prison extends on each side of the front of the prison, the two wings being connected together, and forming a continuous line in the upper galleries, over the entrance hall of the central main building.'

HENRY MAYHEW on the
House of Detention, Clerkenwell

She had not dreamed of this, much less expected it, and if she had been told that the course of her enterprise would place her in prison she would have been horrified, yet in some ways the experience was wonderfully tranquil. Because she was a prisoner awaiting trial she was housed in one of the ten reception cells which stood on either side of the female ward. She knew precisely the length of her foot, and by placing one foot before the other was able to say with certainty that her cell was a little more than eight feet long and a little less than six feet wide. There was an iron bedstead in one corner, a water closet in another, and a small wooden chair. The floor was of asphalt without any covering, and the walls had been recently whitewashed. The cell was very high, and the small window was placed far above her head. There was no gaslight, so that when it grew dark soon after six o'clock the day's activities were over.

These activities were few. They consisted of an
hour's exercise with other women awaiting trial,
which took place on the paved ground at the back
of the prison, and the eating of three daily meals.
There was bread in the morning, gristly beef or
other meat at midday on three days of the week,
and thick soup that clung to the inside of the
mouth on four, gruel for the last meal of the day.
Sometimes there was tea, more often cocoa. No
books were allowed, and no meals could be sent
in from outside. She was allowed to write only
two letters a week, but since there was nobody
with whom she wished to correspond, that was
not a great deprivation. She wrote to Mr Baxter,
saying that she thought it right in all the circumstances to dispose of the dogs, and suggesting that
the St Bernard's Club would find good homes for
them. He sent a note in reply, saying that this
had been done. She missed the use of writing materials at other times, for she would have liked
to keep her journal, but still she could not feel
indignant. She remembered Madame Blavatsky,
she remembered that it was possible to conquer
all outer circumstances by the power of the will.
Possible, that is, if you had the consciousness of
virtue, and she possessed that fully, knowing that
her actions had been taken not only in the fulfilment of her own destiny but for the benefit of
poor diseased Edwin, who was at last free of the
desires that had so long tormented him. She contemplated with serenity the trial that awaited her,
which she did not think of as one for a criminal
offence, but rather as one of those supreme trials
that exceptional people must endure at some time
in their lives.

There were moments when she thought of the convent, and of how pleased Sister Ursula would have been to see her so devoted to contemplation, and to things removed from the frivolity of the world.

So the days passed, not unpleasantly. There were periods when she almost forgot the reason for her presence in Clerkenwell, and it was a surprise to be told one day that she had a visitor. She assumed that this would be Mr Wood, but when she was taken into the reception room it was not her solicitor who rose stiffly from a chair, but the lean form of Mr Casumain. She sat down, separated from him by a table. A wardress stood beside the door.

It was years since she had seen him, and he was greatly changed. His hair had gone, and his head presented the appearance of wrinkled parchment. He had removed the thin long waxed moustache that she remembered, and was now clean-shaven. He sat forward on his hard chair in the attitude of a deaf man who is not quite able to hear what is being said. The hand he raised to put in his monocle was knotty as a tree-trunk. His voice, however, was just as she recalled it, with a warmth out of keeping with his appearance. She must have shown the shock she felt at the change in him, for his first words were a comment on it.

'Rheumatics,' he said. 'Rheumatics all over, legs, hands, every joint creaks. The doctor tells me I won't die of it, but I say to him what's the purpose in staying alive when it takes you half an hour to get out of bed in the morning? But I didn't come to talk about myself. What about you now,

Adelaide Bartlett, this is a pretty place you find yourself in. Did you never think to write to me to see if I could help?'

'I wrote to you before and received no encouragement.'

'So you did. Point is you were a wife then, now you're a widow. I must say you look well. And very composed, remarkably composed.'

'I am here in fulfilment of my destiny.'

He chuckled, and the sharp angles of his face were emphasized. 'You're here because Bartlett's dead, my girl, and the point is what to do about it.'

'I have every faith in Mr Wood, and in my counsel Mr Beal.'

'Beal is very well, but he's young. From what I read in the public press you'll need a man with more experience, more body to him. A man who's more expensive. I've spoken to Wood, and he agrees. No need to tell me you've no money, that will be provided for. The man we have in mind is Edward Clarke. You know his name?'

She shook her head, but the name did not concern her. Her mind had rushed back to the past. 'How is he, is he well?'

It was typical of Mr Casumain that he understood this oblique response. 'Older, like the rest of us. But happy in his wife and family, he has two more children now. However, as you see, he has not forgotten you.'

'But I shall never see him again? I shall never go back?'

Mr Casumain's voice might be warm but he could not say the simplest things without giving them a cutting edge, and the words themselves were sharp as a razor now.

'I told you long ago that there was no question of your going back. Such thoughts were dreams of your own. You should never have indulged yourself in them. But, as I say, he has not forgotten you. What do you say to Edward Clarke?'

'How can I say anything? I know nothing of lawyers.'

'Then accept him on my advice. Beal will be his junior. Your position is serious, you hardly seem to understand that.'

'My position, as you call it, is my destiny.'

'It is as well that we do not meet often, you would try my patience. But then you always did.' He reached for his stick, which was propped against the table, and with its help slowly hoisted himself to his feet. 'Is there anything you require? You cannot expect to be comfortable here, but if you will tell me what you would like, I dare say it can be arranged.'

'I may not be comfortable, but I am content. There is nothing, except that I should like to have the use of writing materials.'

'I will see what can be done.' He looked at her, shook his head, sighed. 'I wish you luck, Adelaide Bartlett. You will need it.'

On the day after the visit she was given paper, ink and scratchy pens, and was asked whether she would like to order food from outside. The Governor himself came to see her twice a week, asked about her health, and said that if there was anything she needed it could be supplied. But she ordered no meals, and used the paper very little. It seemed, after all, that there was nothing she wished to put down in her journal.

CHAPTER 2

THE DECISION

'The step which has been taken . . . was within the undoubted competence of the Crown.'

MR JUSTICE WILLS, summing up

It could be said with some plausibility that the fate of Adelaide Bartlett depended in large part upon the progress of Mr Gladstone's first Irish Home Rule Bill. The Bill, which as its name suggested, was designed to permit the Irish some measure of control over the country in which they lived, became a battleground in the House of Commons, and Sir Charles Russell was in the midst of that battle.* When in February the Conservative Government resigned and the Liberals under Mr Gladstone took office, it was natural that Russell should be appointed Attorney-General, since he was not only the first figure at the Bar but also an ardent Irish nationalist. As Attorney-General, however, he was also the Crown's chief counsel in the Pimlico Poisoning Case. Because of the time he had to spend on Irish matters, not only in the House of Commons but also in Committee, Russell prepared the case hastily, and left many of the details to his juniors.

It might be said also, a little more doubtfully, that Adelaide's fate depended in part on the fact that on a particular Thursday morning in early April Sir Augustus Stephenson did not have kid-

* For another case involving Sir Charles Russell see *The Blackheath Poisonings*.

neys for breakfast. Sir Augustus always ate kidneys
for breakfast on Thursdays. He might have bacon,
eggs or sausages with them, but the kidneys were
invariable. Sir Augustus was a quick-tempered
man. When no kidneys appeared among the
dishes on the hot tray he spoke to the maid so
sharply that she burst into tears, and then had
the very deuce of a row with his wife, in the course
of which he thumped a table so hard that a small
splinter of wood stuck in his palm. After reducing
his wife to tears as well, he left the house in a fury.

Sir Augustus Frederick William Stephenson had
been appointed Director of Public Prosecutions
rather more than two years earlier. The post had
been created in 1879, with the feeling that there
should be a department responsible for crimes
in which, as the Act passed in Parliament vaguely
put it, 'the ordinary mode of prosecution is insuffi-
cient.' What the drafters of the Act had in mind
was chiefly complicated cases of fraud but the first
Director, Sir John Maule, felt that the existing
state of affairs was so nearly perfect that it should
be interfered with as little as possible. After four
years he gave way to Stephenson, who had been
an adviser on criminal prosecutions for twenty
years, during the last eight of them as Solicitor
to the Treasury.

With Stephenson's appointment as Director the
two offices, one meant to advise and the other
to investigate, were embodied in one person. In
the eleven years he reigned before being compul-
sorily retired, Sir Augustus was a figure of power.
Even judges thought that he used this power auto-
cratically and with too much zest. One of them
said, after a man's acquittal on a manslaughter

charge that this, like other prosecutions under-
taken by the Director, had been pushed in a fash-
ion that made it hard to speak calmly about the
case. Stephenson was by no means dismayed by
such criticism, which made him feel that he was
doing his job efficiently.

His views were straightforward. He believed
that when a crime had been properly investigated
by the police, and somebody was then arrested
and accused, the accused person was almost certainly guilty. The police were responsible citizens
and represented the Queen's authority, and although of course it was proper for the accused
to be represented in Court he could not repress
a feeling of indignation when the result was an
acquittal. It was his view that hundreds of people
were walking the streets who should be in prison,
and when he was told that the prisons were already overcrowded, his solution was simple. 'Then
we'll have to build more of 'em, sir, shan't we?'
In his capacity as adviser in the Pimlico Poisoning
affair he had no doubt that both the accused
should be put on trial, and that both were guilty.

Stephenson was still brooding over the hopeless
inefficiency of a household regime that could not
provide kidneys regularly on Thursdays when he
reached the Royal Courts of Justice. He was not
pleased to find that Russell had been delayed, although his juniors Harry Poland and Roger Wright
were there. Poland had been involved in Treasury
cases as counsel for twenty years, and was sometimes called the Sleuth Hound of the Treasury.
Long-nosed, neatly bearded, elaborately polite,
and immensely industrious in checking points of
detail, he was an ideal junior. By nature he was

a cautious, even timid man, who remained a bachelor because, as he said, married life was nothing
but worry, and it was even possible that he might
have been bothered by children. Stephenson
knew Poland well, and regarded him as a bit of
an old maid, but still they exchanged a few words.
Wright he hardly knew, and acknowledged with
no more than a nod. He slapped down his papers
on a large mahogany table and went to the window, where he looked out on to the figures scurry-
ing about, lawyers, clerks, unidentifiable figures
with bundles of papers under their arms. He
looked at them, but he thought about the kidneys
and other domestic misadventures, his right foot
moving in a jig of irritation. Poland sat making
notes on documents in a file. He then passed them
over to Wright, who put them into three separate
groups. Stephenson turned, saw what they were
doing, and returned to looking out of the window.

It was a quarter of an hour before Russell arrived, and apologized for keeping them waiting.
They sat around the mahogany table.

'Bartlett and Dyson,' Russell said. 'What are
your views, Stephenson?'

Stephenson's irritation was now frantic. He
could have put down his views in a succinct mem-
orandum, but the Attorney-General had wanted
a conference, and of course could not be refused.
He had arrived late, and now asked for *views* as
though, Stephenson felt, he were speaking to
some clerk. Perhaps that had not been Russell's
intention, but there were many who thought his
manner overbearing.

'You have all the documents,' Stephenson said
curtly.

'Indeed. I was asking for an expression of opinion.'

'Opinion, yes. I've already put it down, it's in the papers.' He tapped the copy of them in the file before him. 'Both arrested, they should both be charged. Clear enough case, no question about it. Hope they both hang.'

The luminous eyes in Russell's strong square face looked at the Director in a way that made him feel uncomfortable. He did not comment, however, but only said, 'Mr Poland?'

'There is the problem of the means,' Harry Poland said in his quiet voice. 'I am not very happy about Dyson.'

'What do you say about the means?' Russell asked Stephenson. 'How, in your view, was the chloroform administered?'

Stephenson's face, which was always red, took on a tinge of purple. 'Not for me to say that. Damn it, the facts are plain enough. Man swallows enough chloroform to kill him. Wife has got her lover to buy enough of the stuff to kill half a dozen people. What more do you want? Up to the medical fellers to work out ways and means.'

'What about Stevenson?' The Director bristled. 'I'm sorry, Sir Augustus, I was referring to Dr Stevenson.'

Poland looked at his notes. 'He goes into a lot of detail. Some of it is very technical.'

'And what's the upshot?'

'His general conclusion is that administration was possible, although the results would have been uncertain.'

'And what does that mean, in plain English?' Russell had had a difficult morning.

More looking at notes, turning of pages. 'There was the possibility that he would vomit. A distinct possibility, Dr Stevenson says. Or he might have choked.'

'Yes.' Russell took snuff, sneezed, blew his nose. What a load of nonsense, Stephenson thought, how they fiddle about. He could not refrain from speaking.

'What does it matter? He *didn't* vomit and he *didn't* choke, he *did* swallow the stuff and it killed him. Stevenson's no doubt about that, has he?' No doubt at all, Poland said. 'There you are then. The defence fellers can be as clever as they like, they won't get round the facts'

'I agree that we need not say precisely how the chloroform was administered.' Russell's voice was beautifully rich and sonorous. 'I am not so happy about the question of Dyson.'

'The *question* of Dyson, what question?' The Director's face was purpling again. 'He goes out, buys the stuff from three different chemists, tells lies about why he wants it; I don't know what more you can ask.'

Would Stephenson have been quite so emphatic but for the missing kidneys? Would Russell have felt the urge to differ from him if Stephenson had been less dogmatic, and if his own morning had been less difficult? He said now, smoothly enough, 'That is just the kind of opinion I was hoping to elicit. Mr Poland?'

'No doubt there will be an application for the prisoners to be tried separately. Anything else might be prejudicial to them both. I am not sure that I think the case against Dyson is so strong that I would be confident of a conviction. His explanation that he was a tool in the hands of a designing woman, a wicked woman—' the Director gave a derisive snort— 'is a little far-fetched, but he is a man of the cloth and a jury might believe him. And then, if he is tried he may not give evidence.* We shall lose his account of what happened about buying the chloroform and the rest of it. Of course we shall have the chemists, but there is no doubt that without Dyson's evidence we shall lose a good deal.'

'You are against charging him?' Poland's reluctance to commit himself was well-known.

'I am doubtful.'

'Mr Wright?'

The young barrister cleared his throat. 'I think I agree, sir.'

'You *think* you agree?' Russell turned his torchlight gaze upon Wright, who shifted unhappily. 'Either you agree with Mr Poland or you do not.'

'I do agree. I am against charging Dyson. I think it risky, and we want to hear his story about his dealings with the Bartletts. We shall lose him as a witness if he is in the dock.'

'Although he will also be subject to what may be an uncomfortable cross-examination. Well, Stephenson, what do you say to these opinions that run contrary to yours?'

The Director felt that he was being goaded. 'What I have to say is that they are not merely contrary to my opinion, they are contrary to common sense. It's as plain as the nose on my face the feller was in it. He was her lover—'

---

* In England an accused person was not allowed to give evidence until the passing of the Criminal Evidence Act of 1898. Hence he or she could neither be examined nor cross-examined.

'That has not been established,' Poland inter-
jected.

'Did you expect him to admit it? He's already
admitted enough to hang him.'

Russell paused for a moment, got up, scratched
his back with an ivory tickler. 'I cannot agree with
you. Let me tell you the difference between Dyson and Bartlett as I see it. There are grounds
for strong suspicion against Dyson, he bought the
chloroform, he threw away the bottles, but remember that we heard much of this from Dyson
himself, that he revealed it quite voluntarily.
There is no doubt that he gave Mrs Bartlett the
chloroform. He may have had something to do
with the planning, but he cannot physically have
committed the crime. Can we bring home the
planning to him with certainty, are we sure that
a jury would not believe his story when they understand that it was told absolutely of his own
free will? I cannot feel sure of it. We will, if you
like, leave the question open, but my present
opinion is that we should offer no evidence against
the Reverend George Dyson.'

He might have known, Stephenson thought afterwards, that Russell would have his own way.
The Act that created the Director had said that
he was to work 'under the superintendence of
the Attorney-General,' and while the previous Attorney-General had been a compliant figure, Russell always made it plain that he was master.
Stephenson might just as well have sent a memo-
randum.

So it was settled. A decision had been taken
which was to prove of vital importance not only
to George Dyson, but also to Adelaide Bartlett.

CHAPTER 3
THE TRIAL AND THE PROBLEM

'No hypothesis can be put that is not attended
with difficulties so great that, if it stood by itself
and apart from surrounding circumstances, one
would say it could hardly be true; and yet we
know that Bartlett's death was caused by swallowing liquid chloroform, and therefore it must have
been caused by chloroform either criminally administered to him or not criminally administered
to him. There is no escaping from this dilemma.
If you take the evidence on either head alone,
you would say the thing could not be done. Yet
it has been done, and one of the two impossible
theories must be right.'

MR JUSTICE WILLS, summing up

Edward Clarke was in several respects the opposite of Charles Russell. He was a truly modest
man where Russell had his share of vanity, a strong
Conservative where Russell was an enthusiastic
Liberal, a Low Church Protestant from the West
country where Russell was an Irish Catholic. He
was proud of his rise to legal eminence after
leaving school at fourteen to act as assistant
in his father's silversmith's shop. He had read
in his spare time, gone to evening classes, saved
money, read for the Bar. Now, in his middle
forties, he was a rising silk, renowned for the care
with which he applied himself to every brief.
Like Russell, he was a Member of Parliament, and
had expected the post of Solicitor-General in
the Conservative Unionist Government very re-

cently defeated, although it had been denied him.

Clarke was not a sophisticated or worldly man—
how unworldly he showed a decade later in his
disastrously naïve defence of Oscar Wilde. He was
not a particularly brilliant speaker, nor did he
have an unusually quick or powerful mind. But
he was dogged, he worked hard, his serious look
and his mutton-chop whiskers were eloquent of
his sincerity. And he had some medical knowledge. Years earlier he had been involved in the
famous Penge case concerning the death of Har-
riet Staunton, when the medical evidence had
been vitally important, and he realized at once
that in the Pimlico Poisoning too the verdict
might hinge on questions of forensic medicine.
He postponed some cases and returned several
briefs, so that he could spend days in the British
Museum studying the qualities and effects of chloroform. He obtained all the textbooks, and when
trial began he was ready to use them.

t is unlikely that, in any circumstances, Russell
ould have spent days in studying medical textbooks, but in any case he did not have the time
Gladstone moved speedily on his Irish Home Rule
Bill, presenting it on April 8th, just four days before Adelaide Bartlett's trial began. In March Russell was in the midst of the preparations for the
Bill, on the first day of the trial he went to the
House in the evening and made a powerful speech
in reply to Lord Randolph Churchill's plea of 'No
Popery' in Ireland, and on most of the other days
he was bound to spend much time in the House.
Clarke, by contrast, was hardly present in Parlia-
ment during the week of the trial.

Interest in the case was intense. Crowds gath-

340 of 382 TRIAL AND VERDICT

ered outside the Old Bailey, and special tickets
of admission were issued by the sheriffs. Many
of those who obtained the tickets were women
in fashionable society, and for their benefit the
authorities provided additional accommodation in
the form of what *The Times* called a kind of hustings put up in Court, by the side of and very near
to the dock. When the prisoners, Adelaide Bartlett
and George Dyson, were brought up into the
dock, those ladies who had brought opera glasses
got a splendid view of them both. Adelaide did
not wear her widow's weeds but a black silk dress,
with a touch of white at the neck in the form of
a lace collar. She had no hat or bonnet, so that
what one paper called her shock of short black
hair was very visible. She did not look at Dyson,
nor he at her.

Dyson was not long in the dock. His counsel
made an application that the prisoners should be
tried separately, and Russell rose to say that the
application was unnecessary because the Crown
was offering no evidence against Dyson. They
would, however, be calling him as a witness. There
was a murmur of astonishment as Dyson stepped
down from the dock, and the little figure in black
silk was left alone. Her eyes were half-closed, but
she appeared composed. In truth she was not
afraid. The surroundings of the Court, the barris-
ters in their wigs, the Judge on high in his scarlet
gown, even the women peering through their
glasses, all strengthened her feeling that she was
the principal actress in a play, and that she must
play the part in which she had cast herself without
flinching, to the end. Yet although she was the
central character, hers must be a silent role. She
could say nothing, even though the whole trial

would be concerned with her life, her motives, above all her actions.

The trial moved slowly, like all trials. The shorthand writers had to take down every word of the Attorney-General's opening, every subsequent question and answer. Sometimes answers had to be repeated when a witness replied inaudibly, often counsel allowed a pause before his next question, when a reply had been lengthy or rapid. Slowly, slowly the form of the trial became apparent, as after scraping away earth from a piece of buried pottery one discovers the outline of a face.

Russell's opening showed the haste with which he had got up the case. He was unsure of Adelaide's age and equally of Dyson's who was, he said 'a man, I think, of some twenty-seven or thirty years of age', and over two or three points he had to be prompted by the assiduous Poland. After opening Russell left for the House, where his presence was urgently needed at the debate on Ireland, and appeared no more that day. It was Poland, urbane but not forceful, who examined old Bartlett and Mr Baxter and the Doggetts, and who tried in vain to check old Bartlett from showing very plainly his dislike of Adelaide, so that he was open to damaging cross-examination by Clarke. Had he disapproved of the marriage? Well, the old man said, he hadn't particularly approved or disapproved. He had not been asked to it, he lamely added, because they knew he was busy. Had he enjoyed the complete confidence of the married couple? 'I believe so,' he rashly said, and was at once confronted by the apology he had signed.

'I signed an apology but I knew it to be false.

I knew it to be the truth, what I said at the time.'

Clarke looked incredulous, something he managed very well. 'What, sir?'

'When I signed it, it was to make peace with my son.'

At that Clarke read out the apology with relish, saying 'You remember it well.' By the time he had finished, nobody could have doubted that Edwin Bartlett senior had a dislike amounting almost to hatred for his son's wife.

Adelaide listened with fascination. It was as good as a play, and indeed, as she had told herself at the beginning, it *was* a play. How splendid to see the Old Man given that kind of treatment, how good to know that a fine honest Englishman like Edward Clarke was her standard-bearer. She had been distressed when he did not come to see her at Clerkenwell, even though Mr Wood had explained that since she could not speak in Court Mr Clarke did not want to hear things from her that he might not be able to use, but now she forgave him. It would look well, she thought, if she showed herself unmoved, modest, with eyes cast down, and perhaps it would add to the impression of modesty if she did not look at her counsel.

On the following day Russell did not appear at all. He stayed at the House by Mr Gladstone's special request, so that again it was Poland who examined Alice Fulcher, the maid, and who led George Dyson through his story. Alice told them about finding Mrs Bartlett with her head on the clerical gentleman's knee, and said how strange she thought it that Mr Dyson had kept his old coat and slippers in the apartment. Clarke could not shake her, but persuaded her to agree that she had been rung for when she went in on that compromising occasion, so that Mrs Bartlett and Mr Dyson could not have felt themselves to be doing anything wrong.

With Dyson's examination Mr Justice Wills for the first time began to play an important part in the trial. George Dyson looked as wretched as he felt. He had come to regard the woman in the dock with loathing, believing as he did that her purpose had been to destroy him. He now regretted telling the full story of his purchase of the chloroform, but that was done and could not be undone. He was determined to show that he was not in any way a guilty man, but simply one who had foolishly allowed himself to be misled. His creation of this picture was badly damaged by the Judge.

Alfred Wills, Mr Justice Wills, was an almost super-typical English judge of his time. He was an excellent lawyer, and concerned to see that justice was even-handed—it was he who had rebuked Stephenson in that manslaughter case. But he was a puritan, with very firm ideas about a wife's proper subservience to her husband. He had also a positive horror of any public discussion dealing with sexual matters, and of any sexual activity conducted outside the marriage bed. When Oscar Wilde was defended by Edward Clarke, Alfred Wills was again the Judge, and in sentencing Wilde to the maximum of two years in prison he said that the guilty man had been the centre of 'a circle of extensive corruption of the most hideous kind', and that 'people who can do these things must be dead to all sense of shame.'

Mr Justice Wills did not regard the Reverend George Dyson's conduct with the disgust he later felt for Oscar Wilde's, but his sense of propriety was outraged. 'Did you kiss Mrs Bartlett only in her husband's presence?' he asked, and when the reply was 'And out of his presence', he made a note. And what was meant, he wondered, by Edwin Bartlett's remark that a man needed two wives, one for service?

'What do you mean by a wife for service? Is it household drudgery?' he asked, and when Dyson answered stumblingly that he thought the phrase meant that one wife should manage the household and the other be an intelligent companion, he pressed the point.

'I really want to understand what he meant. Were both of them to be his bedfellows? Or was neither of them to be his bedfellow?' The unhappy Dyson said that he had not referred to that side of the matter at all.

'Did it not strike you as an unwholesome sort of talk in the family circle?' the Judge asked wonderingly, and Dyson could only reply that Edwin Bartlett was a man who had strange ideas. Later, when Dyson spoke of Bartlett's contemplating his wife's eventual marriage to Dyson, Mr Justice Wills intervened again, to ask in a cuttingly ironical tone for the details of the conversation.

'It was a very remarkable conversation, probably such a one as never occurred in the experience of any man in Court before, and therefore must be impressed on your mind.' Dyson faltered through an account of it. Later, when the clergyman said in cross-examination by Clarke that his conversation with Bartlett was a very delicate matter to discuss, the Judge intervened again. 'No, no, we have long outstepped the bounds of delicacy.' In summing up he said to the jury that they should accept no statement of Dyson's unless it was confirmed by another witness, and then summarized his view of the clergyman in scathing terms:

At the time he first gave evidence, there can be no doubt that the Reverend George Dyson entertained very serious fears that his own life was in danger; and I should think there can be very little doubt on the part of anybody who has seen him here, that there is one person in this world that the Reverend George Dyson was determined should suffer as little as possible by this history—that is the Reverend George Dyson.

The clergyman was in the witness-box for most of the second day. Clarke dealt with him in a gentle, ostensibly sympathetic way, feeling that it was in his client's interests to associate her actions with Dyson's so that the jury might feel that she should not be in the dock if he was free, but after the Judge's questioning Dyson left the box an unhappy, discredited man. Adelaide thought that Mr Clarke had been too gentle, but was delighted by the discomfiture of the man whom she had thought of once—how mistakenly—as Georgius Rex. During the course of the day she wrote a note, and passed it to him. He read:

Monsieur, Forgive me that I do not look at you. It is not that I am ungrateful.

The 'Monsieur' she considered afterwards perhaps a mistaken touch, for she commonly used the standard English form of address, but Clarke was charmed, as she had intended. He thought the

note shy, delicate, and with the touch of something foreign that made him feel it a duty to protect this helpless lady. His concentration on the
case was total. He drove down to the Old Bailey
early each morning to make sure that he was in
his place when—as he later put it in his autobiog-
raphy—'the fragile, pale little woman came up
the prison stairs to take her place in the dock
and saw in the crowded Court at least one friendly
face.'

In the evening he drove straight back to his
house in Russell Square, went for an hour's walk,
ate his dinner, and then prepared for the next
day's cross-examination.

Day three. Again Russell was absent in the
morning, when Adelaide saw with a sense of wonder George and Alice Matthews in the witness-
box, telling of events that seemed to belong to
some other life, and dear Annie Walker who, although called by the prosecution, was staunch in
her defence, and white-bearded Dr Nichols,
whom she had never met, talking about *The Mysteries of Man*. They were followed by Mr Roberts
the dentist, who seemed to her neither here nor
there in what he had to say.

Then came another friend, her dear Dr Leach,
looking almost strangled by his high collar. Upon
occasion he gave evidence with a gasp, and with
beads of perspiration on his forehead, but always
he was quite obviously devoted to her and trying
to do his best on her behalf. Occasionally too he
looked towards her, as if to ask her approval of
one answer or to suggest that another had been
inevitable although he regretted making it. She
did not think it proper that she should look in
his direction, and so at times kept her eyes almost

closed, at others regarded the jury or the curious spectators. There was one woman who wore a blue bonnet and carried a bag containing knitting. She plied her needles throughout, except when there was questioning about such matters as the kisses or the two wives, when she put it down and stared intently at Adelaide. It would have been pleasant to grimace or put out her tongue in reply, but she did not do so.

In the afternoon Russell appeared, and took Dr Leach through his examination-in-chief. The doctor had spent many hours in the weeks since Mrs Bartlett's arrest in making notes of all that had happened, of the exact day and hour on which things had been said, of the medicines and treatment he had prescribed or thought of prescribing, of the worm's appearance and the subsequent intransigence of the patient's bowels against powerful aperients, of what had been said by everybody including himself on every occasion. He divided the notes into piles each of which covered a week, and then divided the weeks into days, so that little bundles of notes covered his desk like molehills. He had brought many of these notes with him, and his anxiety and uneasiness were so evident that at an early stage Clarke said that he had no objection if the doctor referred to his written memoranda, although he could not be permitted to read them. Dr Leach referred to them but that only made confusion worse, for there were things he could not find in the notes and thought he remembered but did not wish to commit himself to without a written reference. He took refuge in evasions, circumlocutions, obscure medical terms.

Within a quarter of an hour he had maddened Russell, who began almost to treat him as a hostile witness, and the Judge who asked him to translate his medical terms into English. Asked what treatment he had prescribed at the beginning, he said, 'A curative one.'

'So I should hope,' Russell responded, and asked for details. The doctor had no notes of that particular treatment, and although prepared to make a guess at what it had been, was careful to add that 'I am speaking from memory only, which is fallacious.'

As the afternoon wore on, his uncertainty regarding dates began to confuse Russell, who had expected the witness to have such details off pat. But the doctor was certain of what he had seen in the room after Bartlett's death, and his recollection did not favour the defendant. On the mantelpiece there was a looking-glass, a clock, some vases, the bottle of chlorodyne. No bottle of chloroform. Russell established this, then pressed it no further. When Dr Leach came to the story told him by Adelaide of her relationship with Edwin, his language became deeply veiled in obscurity.

'Her husband having fully effected the transfer to Mr Dyson—I mean in the platonic sense, mind—he now constantly developed symptoms of wishing to, I cannot say resume, but wishing to assume those married rights which he had never before claimed. You understand my meaning?'

Russell brutally pulled aside this web of words. 'You mean desiring to have sexual intercourse with his wife?'

'She put it in as delicate a manner as she could,' the doctor said reproachfully, 'but that is the meaning.'

By the time Russell sat down he was wishing himself back in the House of Commons. He had had enough of Dr Leach, and left his re-examination on the following day to Poland. But in the meantime Clarke, by cross-examination that was dexterously friendly, had begun to build up the idea that Edwin Bartlett was so worried about his condition that he was in a mood to kill himself. There had been the gastritis, the vomiting and dysentery, the worm, and finally the necrosis— were they not, altogether, enough to depress anybody? Dr Leach, his eyes fixed on the wistful figure in the dock, agreed that the patient's spirits had fluctuated remarkably, that at times he had certainly been very depressed, that necrosis was alarming, that once or twice as a medical man he had suspected insanity. But his natural desire to qualify any statement came to the fore, and he was soon insisting that too much stress must not be placed on any word or sentence he used.

'If you did not think so much of the literary effect, and would tell us what happened, it would be better for everybody,' the Judge said.

'My Lord, pardon me if I say that it is not the literary effect, but the accuracy, I strive to attain.'

'We do not strive to get any phenomenal accuracy,' Mr Justice Wills said. 'Just tell us what happened.'

Of this, however, Dr Leach was not capable. He was prepared to agree to almost anything, provided he was allowed to qualify the statement in the next breath. In re-examination he agreed with Poland that the degree of necrosis was slight. Then why had he said it was alarming?

'That word "alarming" has given rise to some misunderstanding. I used it for brevity's sake, without due consideration to accuracy, I am afraid.'

Altogether he spent more than a day in the box. When he left it he had created more confusion than he had cleared up. Yet all this, as both Russell and Clarke knew, was not the heart of the matter. At the centre of the case was the medical evidence, which should show how the chloroform had got into Edwin Bartlett's stomach. Russell knew the importance of Dr Stevenson's evidence, and conducted the examination himself.

No Victorian toxicologist had the national fame that was to be achieved much later by Sir Bernard Spilsbury and Sir Sydney Smith, but Stevenson was the greatest expert of his day, and his word could not be easily challenged. To drink liquid chloroform was exceedingly painful, and nobody would do it unless they wished to commit suicide. If murder had been committed, how was it done? What Russell wanted from his expert was an assurance that liquid chloroform could be poured down the throat of somebody rendered insensible by inhaling the narcotic. And he got it, or at least appeared to get it.

'Just describe, doctor, how you think it could be done,' Russell said. Stevenson said that he had himself poured liquid—although of course not liquid chloroform—down the throat of a man while chloroforming him by inhalation, passing the liquid to the back of the throat with a teaspoon. There was no insuperable difficulty in putting down chloroform.

Clarke intervened. 'Did you say insuperable?'
Stevenson amended the phrase hastily to 'no great difficulty.' Once the patient was insensible,

he added, he would have lost the capacity to swallow. A stimulant like chloroform would cause no muscular action, and hence could be poured down. The inadequate preparation made by the prosecution was shown once more, when Stevenson began to talk about experiments he had made upon animals. He was checked by Clarke, who said that the defence should have had a note of these experiments, and this line of questioning had to be abandoned. But still, Stevenson said that it was quite possible to chloroform a sleeping person with the use of a chloroform-soaked handkerchief. The actual swallowing of the liquid was often, but not always, followed by vomiting. Altogether, Stevenson gave Russell most of what he wanted.

How can a layman challenge an expert? In modern days this is done by producing other experts, but Stevenson and Dr Meymott Tidy who followed him in the box were unchallengeable in the sense that no figures of comparable stature could be put against them. Yet although Clarke was a layman he had a good deal of medical knowledge, and he had done his homework. Textbooks were piled in front of him in Court, the most recent edition of Guy and Ferrier on toxicology, Quimby and Elliott, Winter Blyth on poisons, Wharton and Stiller's *Medical Jurisprudence*, the *Annales d'Hygiène publique* of Dolbeau and a dozen others, including Stevenson's own up-to-date version of *Taylor's Principles and Practice of Medical Jurisprudence*. Clarke himself thought afterwards that his cross-examination of Stevenson was the finest thing of the kind he had ever done. There were limits to what he could hope to achieve. He did not attempt to challenge the specialist's supreme knowledge, but confined himself almost entirely to the practical impossibility of putting chloroform down the throat of an unconscious man, or even of administering it by inhalation to a sleeping person. Had Dr Stevenson done it? No, he had not. Did not the attempt to administer it by inhalation almost invariably wake a sleeping man? Not *invariably*, Stevenson said. And now the two slugged it out toe to toe, quoting cases to each other, with Stevenson (who of course had not been gathering details in the British Museum) by no means outclassing his opponent. Clarke triumphantly quoted from a textbook of Woodman and Tidy—Tidy was Stevenson's supporting expert:

We know that comparatively the insensibility from chloroform vapour is only slowly induced. It would be difficult therefore, to administer chloroform to persons forcibl and against their will.

The cross-examination lasted more than three hours, and although Stevenson did not give way on any point, his replies became more and more guarded. The last sets of questions and answers allowed Clarke to sit down feeling satisfied.

'Suppose you had to deal with a sleeping man, and it was your object to get down his throat, without his knowing it, a liquid the administration of which to the lips or throat would cause great pain, do you not agree it would be a very difficult or delicate operation?'

'I think it would often fail and might often succeed.'

'Would you look on it as a delicate operation?'

'Yes, because I should be afraid of pouring it down the windpipe.'

'If the patient had got into such a state of insensibility as not to reject it, it would go down his windpipe and burn that?'

'Probably some might go down his windpipe.'

'If it did so it would leave its traces?'

'I should expect to find traces after death unless the patient lived some hours.'

If Stevenson was doubtful of his own success in administering chloroform, what chance would Adelaide Bartlett have had?

Just before the end of the specialist's evidence there came an unexpected intervention from the jury. Stevenson had experimented with the effect of liquid chloroform in his own mouth, and had found it hot, sweet and burning. It left a red blotch or two on the tongue, which became a little numb, but that sensation soon passed and the blotch disappeared. What the foreman of the jury wanted to know was whether an unskilled person must not have poured down the chloroform very slowly, to avoid choking? And if that was true, would not some part of the chloroform remain in the mouth? If it stayed in the mouth, would there not be signs left in the gums and the throat? Signs which in fact had not been seen on examination? In reply to these intelligent questions Stevenson admitted that marks of irritation or inflammation would have been left, unless the chloroform had been swallowed very quickly, in a gulp or two. So how had Adelaide induced Edwin to gulp down the burning liquid?

That was the fifth day, and the end of the prosecution case. Clarke called no witnesses, and in-

deed had none to offer. During part of the morning and all the afternoon he made his final speech
for the defence.

In the speech, as he had done throughout,
Clarke made masterly use of those very aspects
of the case that seemed to tell most strongly
against Adelaide. He praised the authority of Drs
Stevenson and Tidy, but what had they said about
the central problem? 'Gentlemen, you have had
the best information which you could possibly get
on this subject, and what does it come to?—that
never, during the forty years it has been in use,
has there been a case of murder by chloroform.'
Accident, yes, suicide yes, but never murder. They
were being asked to find that Adelaide Bartlett
had 'committed an offence absolutely unknown
in the history of medical jurisprudence.'

On the way to Court in the police van that day
Adelaide had felt giddy, and on emerging from
the van had been hardly able to stand. Now she
had a strange feeling that although her body sat
in the dock some other part of her—should it be
called the spirit?—was floating somewhere above
them all, near the ceiling. She closed her eyes,
listened to her counsel's voice flowing gently as
a river, and seemed to see behind her closed lids
the Court spread out before her like a map. The
figures were all tiny, but she identified herself,
and the Attorney-General who sat with fingers
occasionally tapping the table in front of him, the
Judge impassive upon what looked very much like
a throne, and among them all the single standing
figure who sometimes turned his pages of notes.
Her being was suffused with love for Edward
Clarke, this noble Englishman. She felt a love pure

and ideal, the kind of feeling she had had for another who had soiled it by sensual greed. Edward Clarke was her single friend, and she needed nobody else.

Below Adelaide's dreaming spirit Clarke was telling the jury what they had to accept if they were to believe that Mrs Bartlett committed the crime. First she must have administered chloroform to her husband by inhalation while he was sleeping, and then 'poured the chloroform down the insensible and unresisting throat.' But, as he said, 'the moment that suggestion is made we have before us almost an impossibility.' He went over the ground of his battle with Stevenson to repeat that even 'skilled chloroformists' had had little success in chloroforming a sleeping person, and then came back to that phrase 'not insuperable' which Stevenson had incautiously used. Did not that mean the difficulties were *almost* insuperable?

On such delicate matters as what he called frankly the strange marital relations of Mr and Mrs Bartlett, and upon her 'marvellous story' to Dr Leach, he invited the jury to consider whether these were really so strange or the story so marvellous. He quoted a passage from *The Mysteries of Man* about avoiding the dangers and responsibilities of childbirth through abstinence. This, Clarke said, was easily done by most women and by many men. 'In every civilized community thousands live in celibacy, many from necessity, many from choice.' And the unusual story about giving her to Dyson seemed to him to be given force by the exchange of letters between Edwin Bartlett and George Dyson, especially the one written by

Dyson to Edwin at Dover, 'the letter so loving that Adelaide overflows with joy as she reads it.'

Other points he dealt with lightly, and came at last to telling the jury what had happened, or what had probably happened. Think of the husband's illness, of his depression as testified to by several witnesses, of his hypochondriacal concern about his health, of the worm, of the necrosis that may have been superficial but sounded extremely alarming. 'Necrosis means death. Necrosis of the jaw means the death of the bone, coming usually either from syphilis or from an administration of mercury.' And now Clarke sketched in imagination what must have taken place:

Suppose she left the room as usual to wash, and there was placed on the mantelpiece this bottle of chloroform. There was a wineglass there, that wineglass which was found afterwards, and while she was away it was perfectly easy for him, lifting himself only upon his elbow, to pour into this wineglass the less than half a wineglass of chloroform which may have constituted the fatal dose. If he then swallowed it, and swallowed it up quickly, there would be no appearance of exposure of the softer substances of the mouth and throat to the chloroform.

Two or three minutes later he would have passed into coma, and on Adelaide's return she would have thought him to be asleep. In all that, Clarke said, there was nothing unreasonable or extraordinary. It was what must have happened. And he went on to complete the picture of events, when the wife woke and found her husband's cold body.

She springs to his side; there is, close at the end of the mantelpiece, this wineglass from which he has taken the fatal draught. She pours into the glass some brandy and tries to pour it down his throat, with shaking hand she spills some brandy on his chest which the doctor smells afterwards. It is no use. She puts back on the mantelpiece, where it was found when they came into the room, the wineglass with the brandy in it. There was no admixture of chloroform with it, but it was a wineglass which her husband had used for chloroform.

Did this not explain everything, did it not make the whole story clear? 'There was no scientific miracle worked by the grocer's wife under circumstances where it could not have been worked by the most experienced doctor who ever gave himself to the study of this matter.' There was simply a bottle of chloroform left within reach of a sick and depressed man, a bottle that led to tragedy.

When Clarke sat down, wiping his brow, throwing back his head and closing his eyes like a man drained of energy, a murmur went through the Court that rose to a brief burst of applause, a sound quickly checked by the Judge.

The sixth day, the last day. The crowds waiting to get into the Court were larger than ever, even though there remained only the Attorney-General's final speech, the Judge's summing up, and the verdict. Ten pounds and more was paid for a good place in the queue, the windows and even the roofs of houses opposite the Court were filled with people, and when the doors had been opened and the Court was full, hundreds of people waited in the street. Hawkers did a good trade selling Adelaide's photograph. Russell spoke at less than half the length of Clarke. He still had Ireland on his mind, and it was a lacklustre performance marked by slips that Clarke eagerly corrected. He spoke

forcefully against the idea of suicide when Edwin
Bartlett was a man with 'years of life and prosper-
ity before him', and he summarized all the points
of suspicion connected with the purchase of the
chloroform, but in the end he was driven to ask
the jury for a verdict even though 'you may not
be able to state with accuracy to your own satisfaction the exact methods or means by which the
crime has been accomplished.'

After Russell's speech, and before the Judge's
summing up, there occurred what was in retrospect Clarke's only mistake in a case he had conducted with exemplary skill. He had learned that
Annie Walker was prepared to testify that Mrs
Bartlett had said long ago that her pregnancy was
the result of a single act, on a Sunday afternoon,
and asked for her to be recalled. She returned
to the box and agreed that Mrs Bartlett had told
her the pregnancy was the result of a single act.
Clarke sat down, but unhappily for him Mr Justice
Wills was not prepared to leave it there.

'Did Mrs Bartlett say so? That it happened only
once?' he asked. Annie Walker's innocent answer
caused a stir of astonishment, and caused Clarke
to cast his eyes heavenwards.

'Both of them said that,' she replied. 'Otherwise
there was always some preventive used.'

In summing up Mr Justice Wills was scrupulous
in mentioning every point of importance, and
careful to discuss in detail everything favourable
to the prisoner. When, near the beginning, he
referred contemptuously to the evidence of Mr
Bartlett senior, and said that the kiss with which
he parted from his daughter-in-law after looking
through her cloak brought to mind the name of

Judas, Adelaide thought that he was a friend. He said also that the original will had been a cruel one, and that the later will was wise, good and proper. More, he thought that to name as one of the executors George Dyson, 'a gentleman in whose ministrations he had found great comfort,' Edwin had behaved quite naturally. He stressed that Adelaide's anxiety for a post-mortem to be conducted immediately was a strong point in her favour. Yet, as he continued, the balance of his words became more and more unmistakably weighted on the side of a 'Guilty' verdict, and Adelaide realized that the man sitting above her and dropping his words slowly as through a sieve was in truth a bitter enemy.

The Judge's puritan heart found in the case what he called a curious and unpleasant blend of religion, coarseness, and a creeping, loathsome sexuality. What could one say about people who kept such a book as *The Mysteries of Man* as part of their domestic furniture without a feeling of shame? The book was garbage, and it was such books that helped to poison the modern mind. Without looking at the women who listened in the public gallery and the special stand, but raising his voice a little, the Judge said that women today were used to strange things. 'They are things that would have startled us in the days of my boyhood. And it is such reading as this that helps to unsex them, and to bring them to a place like this day after day to listen willingly to details which even to men of mature life are distasteful and disgusting.'

All of a piece with the garbage of the book was the fact, barely mentioned by counsel on either

side, that French letters had been found in the
dead man's pockets. Was a man's trouser-pocket
the place in which he would keep such articles
for *domestic* use, he wondered, did they point
to something in the dead man's habits which
might after all suggest that he suffered or thought
he suffered from syphilis? But suppose that the
French letters were for use at home—bearing in
mind that Annie Walker had been told by both
Bartletts that 'some preventive' was used except
upon the single occasion that made her pregnant—what then became of 'this morbid romance
about the non-sexual connection, and what becomes of the man with such exalted ideas about
matrimony that he thought the wife whom he
elected for his companion too sacred to be
touched'? He had already spoken contemptuously
of George Dyson, and had said of Dr Leach that
he was 'a not very strong-headed man painfully
haunted by the idea that he is the central per-
sonage in a drama of surpassing interest'. Now
he turned to the Bartletts, and again to the tale
of the solitary act of coition. After what they had
heard at the last moment from Annie Walker, how
could these people be elevated into figures of romance? 'It looks much more as if we had two
persons to deal with abundantly vulgar and commonplace in their habits and ways of life.' When
Adelaide heard these words, and in particular the
hateful word *vulgar*, she closed her eyes and tried
to absent herself from what was being said. In
this she was partly successful. She heard the
Judge's words, but they carried no meaning for
her.

This was fortunate, for when he came to discuss
Edwin Bartlett's death and how it had been

brought about, Mr Justice Wills returned again and again to the chloroform bottle. He thought there was strong evidence that the fatal dose had been contained in the glass found on the mantelpiece; that it was perhaps swallowed while not recumbent, but worked its effects while Bartlett was lying down; and that the examination had been made too late, and in circumstances too uncertain, to know exactly how much had been taken except that the dose was fatal.

It was right to say that to anaesthetize the victim when he was asleep, and then to pour chloroform down his throat was an operation 'open to so many chances of failure, that no skilled man would venture upon it unless he were a madman.' But what had happened to the bottle of chloroform, which must have been on the mantelpiece if Bartlett drank from its contents either by intention or by accident? Dr Leach had not seen it, Doggett had not seen it. Mrs Bartlett had said that she put it into the bedroom drawer about breakfast-time, but then why did not Dr Leach and Doggett see it?

'Where was it in the meantime? Why on earth should it be gone from that mantelpiece, and gone from any place where it could be readily found? It is difficult beyond measure to account for the disappearance of that bottle if all was right; if all was wrong, one can understand it.' He had waited anxiously for defence counsel's explanation of the matter, but none had been given. 'You will have to ask yourselves, when you retire to that room, what happened to the bottle?' With these words, as Mr Justice Wills hoped, imprinted upon their minds, the jury retired at seven minutes to three.

*   *

With judge and jury gone, leading counsel chatting with their juniors, and a general air of relaxation in Court, the ladies who made up almost the whole of the audience relaxed also, and tried to get a better view. As the *Daily Telegraph* put it:

The ladies crowded and stood up on the little hustings, and rudely peered through the glass panels into the dock, intently watching Mrs Bartlett's every movement. There, between two female attendants, she sat with drooping head. A warder spoke to her, and with a faint grateful smile she retreated below.

In the jury room a preliminary count by the foreman showed that few of the jurymen had been impressed by the Judge's words. There was agreement that Mrs Bartlett had told some untruths in the story she had given to Dr Leach, but that did not mean she was a poisoner. One man said that Dyson should be in the dock, another that Bartlett must have swallowed the stuff by accident. Most of them thought Bartlett had been occasionally confused and dejected, and in such a mood had taken chloroform deliberately. Only one juror held out for a guilty verdict, saying that the evidence was damning against Mrs Bartlett.

After an hour's discussion a majority of ten to two were in favour of a 'Not Guilty' verdict with, as the foreman later wrote to *The Times*, a rider saying that 'we were of opinion that, considering the state of health Mr Bartlett was in, or imagined he was in, and the state of mind the evidence showed him to be in, he administered the chloroform to himself with the view of obtaining sleep or committing suicide.' The other two jurors still held out. They did not convince the others, but persuaded them that the circumstances were suspicious. They obtained a concession that very much changed the tone of the rider added to the verdict.

The jury returned at five o'clock. The prisoner was brought up, Mr Justice Wills returned. The Clerk of the Court asked whether the jury had agreed on a verdict. The foreman stood up.

'We have well considered the evidence, and although we think grave suspicion is attached to the prisoner, we do not think there is sufficient evidence to show how or by whom the chloroform was administered.'

The Clerk waited, but the foreman said nothing more. 'Then you say that the prisoner is not guilty, gentlemen?'

'Not guilty,' the foreman said.

At that the ladies stood up, waved bags and hats, began to cheer. The news spread outside, and a great roar of approval could be heard, a roar that went on and on. The ushers scurried about, Mr Justice Wills said that such an indecent exhibition turned the Court into a theatre and that he would not have it. All in vain, for the cheering inside and outside the Court continued. Clarke broke down and wept, Russell shook him by the hand, the Judge retired. The small central figure heard the verdict calmly, although one paper noted that she had 'a hectic flush upon her usually colourless cheek.'

She drove away unrecognized in company with her solicitor, Edward Wood. It was, indeed, not her triumph but Edward Clarke's. When he had unrobed and come down to the courtyard he found the jury waiting at the foot of the steps to shake his hand. The crowd followed his brougham up the Old Bailey and along Holborn, and when he went to the Lyceum that night to see Irving and Ellen Terry in *Faust* the audience stood up to cheer as he entered the theatre.

So the Bartlett case ended, and the actors in it resumed their lives. Of the public figures, Russell became Lord Chief Justice and entered the peerage with the title of Lord Killowen. Clarke never went so high, but he became Solicitor-General and received a knighthood. Dr Leach wrote his article for *The Lancet*, and swelled with pride and pleasure when he saw his name below the heading 'The Case of Edwin Bartlett.' In the article he suggested that the dead man had voluntarily swallowed the chloroform 'in sheer mischief with the intention of alarming by his symptoms the wife who an hour or two previously had talked about using it.' He found nobody to support this view of the case.

And Adelaide? She stayed for a few days with the Wood family and then vanished from the London scene as mysteriously as she had appeared on it. No newspaper of the time was able to discover what had happened to her, although several tried. The rumours about her grew for a little while, and then withered for lack of information. Perhaps Edward Wood knew what had become of her, but if so he kept his own counsel.

MASSACHUSETTS, 1933

'Now it is all over she should tell us, in the interests
of science, how she did it.'

SIR JAMES PAGET,
sergeant-surgeon to Queen Victoria

A little village in the Berkshires. A small white
clapboard house in a street of similar houses. Neat
green verges, a patch of green in front of the
porch. Three o'clock, precisely three o'clock, on
a humid afternoon in late June. Young Ross Daniel
pushed the bell button, and heard a faint tinkle
within the house.

The woman who came to the door was in her
thirties, small and dark.

'I have an appointment to see Madame Bartlett.'
The woman did not reply, but stood aside for him
to enter. He hardly had time to notice what appeared to be some Indian carvings in the little
hall, when the woman tapped on a door and
opened it after a voice from within said, 'Come.'
The curtains in the room were drawn, so that the
only light was provided by a powerful electric
lamp which stood beside an armchair. A woman
sat in the chair, a book on a reading stand in
front of her. She did not rise, but extended a
hand to him, and spoke in a light musical voice.
'You are very welcome. Françoise, will you
please remove my book. I apologize for this
lighting arrangement. My sight is very bad, and

to read I must have a strong light focused on the page, but now that you are here the curtains shall be drawn. Will you do that for me, Françoise? Thank you, my dear. Then you may leave us.' When the woman had gone out she said, 'Françoise is half-French, half-Indian. She was once a medium, but alas the gift has left her. Will you please sit in that chair so that I can see you.'

The chair was so close that their two pairs of knees almost touched. The young man found it hard to believe that the woman facing him was Adelaide Bartlett. The photographs he had seen were all of the time of the trial, and that of course was nearly half a century ago. He had tried to make a mental allowance for the passing of time, but had not anticipated that the delicate and fragile creature he had read about might have turned into a fat woman. Adelaide Bartlett filled the easy chair in which she sat. The buttons of her dark green dress looked ready to burst, the material was tight across her thick thighs. The face above the dress was plump and round, and her pebble glasses made it impossible to see what were said to have been remarkable eyes. Her hair was still abundant, but it was now grey instead of black. Only her voice was as he had expected, light and youthful, with something exotic about the pronunciation.

'You are thinking I have changed, Mr Ross. But I had forgotten, your name is not Ross.' The letter he had written was on her lap, and now she took it from the envelope and held it close to her eyes. 'Your name is Ross Daniel, you work for the *Post-Intelligencer*, you are a young cousin of my dear

friend Dudley Wright,* and you would be grateful
if I could grant you an interview. And I know
what you want me to talk about, and where you
have seen my photograph.' She smiled, and looked
for a moment like a much younger woman. 'But
your name, I cannot say it. American names are
so often absurd, are they not? Why are you named
Ross Daniel when it should be Daniel Ross? I shall
call you Daniel, I hope you will not object. It
sounds more friendly and more natural. The picture you are looking at is a painting of H. B., done
from memory by one of her disciples and then
given to me. Do you know who H. B. is?' Ross
Daniel shook his head. The painting hung over
the mantelpiece. It was a large oil showing a
woman with powerful, ugly features. She was
wearing a sari and some kind of head-dress, and
she stood beside a river with her arm raised in
a gesture of benediction. At her feet several men
and women knelt with hands upraised to receive
her blessing.

'She was Helen Blavatsky, Madame Blavatsky,
the greatest and most martyred religious teacher
since Christ. You know of the Theosophical Movement, I am sure, you will have heard of it from
Dudley. Madame Blavatsky founded that great
movement. I am proud to call myself a humble
disciple.'

'Is that why you now call yourself Madame Bartlett?'

'Perhaps. You are quick, Daniel, you are quick.

* Dudley d'Auvergne Wright (1867–1948). Consulting surgeon to the London Homeopathic Hospital, senior surgeon
to Manor House Orthopaedic Hospital, theosophist, author of
The Evolution of the Human Consciousness.

But now tell me what you know about me, what Dudley has told you, and what you want to know.'

He explained, with a hesitancy that disappeared as he went on talking, that Dudley Wright had roused his interest by saying in one of his twice-yearly letters about family matters that a lady lived within the area covered by the *Post-Intelligencer* who had been the central figure, many years ago, in a famous British trial. He had asked for and been given details, had found the volume about the trial in the Famous British Trials series and been fascinated by it, and had asked his cousin for further information about Mrs Bartlett, in particular what had happened to her after the trial.

'Afterwards, afterwards I left England and came to this country. To Boston.'

'Was that perhaps to meet Fred Bartlett?'

'Fred? Good heavens no, did you believe the tales of that wicked Old Man? I had no interest in Fred, except that he was a little more like a gentleman than the rest of his family. My father thought it best that I should leave England for a time, and his agent made it possible for me to come to Boston.'

'Your father? His agent?'

She placed a finger to her lips in a coquettish gesture that, in spite of her bulk, had a kind of youthful charm. 'About that, as the old saying goes, my lips are sealed. You would be surprised, Daniel—no, more than surprised, amazed—if I told you the name of my father, who has never been able to acknowledge me. That is the true tragedy of my life, and it can never be revealed.'

'So you came to Boston.'

'And there for some years I taught young ladies

to play the piano. I played it very well, I had a true gift, everybody who heard me said so. I was also the leading member among the theosophical group in that great city. You will find that I am well known there among theosophical circles still.'

'Did you marry again?'

'Marry *again?* My dear young man, I was never married.' He stared at her in astonishment. 'Do you know what H. B. said once? She had a husband, it may be that she had a child, yet she kept her virginity unsullied. To do so is not a physical question, it is a matter of the will.'

'But, Madame Bartlett, was there not a child who was stillborn?'

'I see that you do not understand. In any real sense I was never married to Edwin. But never mind. Did you know that in the Great War I went back to England, worked with a unit that Dudley raised to help the wounded, was acclaimed as a heroine?' She pressed a switch beside the chair with her foot, and the electric light came on. Then, with a grunt, she levered herself out of the chair and waddled across the room to a bureau. She looked through the drawers of this bureau, found two large photographs and handed them to Ross Daniel before sinking back into the chair. 'My work for the Red Cross. I was in dear Dudley's surgical unit. I raised money for them by my speeches, travelled constantly between England and France. I thought nothing of facing the perils of the submarine and the Zeppelin.'

The pictures showed her as plump, but still recognizably the woman of the early photographs. In one she was on a platform addressing an audience of working men and women. She wore a cloak, and an enormous red cross was on her apron. The other picture showed her in a hospital ward, bending over a soldier's bed.

'If you wish to use them for anything you write about me, I shall be happy for you to keep them.'

The young man thanked her, and said that the photographs were fascinating. 'My cousin mentioned some kind of money trouble, something to do with your ordering of supplies for the unit.'

'Was there? Really I forget, and in any case it was nothing. With my war work done I returned to this country. And as you know, Dudley and I remained friends.'

'Yes. In any case it was really the period of the trial—'

He was interrupted by the sound of a bell. She laughed at his look of surprise.

'It is a little trick, the kind H. B. used. There would be the sound of a bell, and she would say it was one of the spirits. Naughty of her. For me, I tell you that I have just pressed—*there*—with my foot.' He saw another button on the floor, beside the one that had operated the electric light. 'Françoise will bring tea, then we shall talk.'

The tea was China, thin and fragrant. With it was served brown bread and butter and rich, creamy cakes. She ate two of the cakes, three slices of bread and butter. A smear of cream was left on her chin, which Françoise wiped away when she collected the tea things. During tea she spoke of her attempts to found a theosophical circle in the district, of the small response she had found, and of her difficulty now in moving about and attending meetings.

'You are not listening, Daniel. You are becoming

impatient, I can sense it. Madame Blanche has a sixth sense. Oh yes, I have been Madame Blanche Bartlett now for years. It is my true name, you know, Adelaide Bartlett was somebody different, less interesting. But it is Adelaide Bartlett you want to know about, impatient Daniel. Ask your questions.' She folded plump hands over her stomach. Ross Daniel was twenty-two, and had been a journalist for only eighteen months. He found it hard to begin.

'I should like to have your own story—of what happened on that last night. You could not give evidence, so you have never said what happened.'

'Shall I tell you something, Daniel? You remind me of him.'

He was taken aback. 'Of your husband?'

'No, no, foolish. Of Georgius Rex. That was what we called him, you know. Very well, I will tell you what Adelaide Bartlett did on that night so many years ago.' He took his notebook from his jacket. 'Oh no, no, you must not take notes, my Daniel.'

'But then I have to rely on my memory.'

'And I shall deny your memory, have no doubt of that, I shall sue your paper for millions of dollars. I am speaking now not to Daniel the newspaper man, but to Daniel who reminds me of Georgius Rex. I hope you are not truly like him, he was a fool and a coward. So notes are forbidden. Do you still want to hear the story?'

He said that he did. Perhaps something could be made of it, and what had he to lose? So he listened while she sat in the armchair with knees almost touching his. Over the mantelpiece Madame Blavatsky blessed the faithful.

'You will remember that the wise counsel and the medical experts had great arguments about how difficult it would be to make somebody inhale chloroform while they were sleeping because they were certain to wake, and how nearly impossible it would be for somebody unskilled to pour the liquid chloroform down a throat. But that was not what happened, not at all what happened.

'First I must tell you what kind of person this Adelaide Bartlett was, for you understand she was not myself, I am a different person. Yet like me she was very kind and gentle, she had learned something about medicine and liked to nurse the sick. But as she grew older she rejected the idea of the sensual relation between man and woman. She loved her husband, she loved Georgius Rex, but not in that way. Hers was a higher and purer emotion, like the loves of the saints. She tried to show these sensual men the way of saintliness, but in that she failed. Especially she failed with Edwin. I do not care to be indelicate, but you understand me, I am sure you do. She became aware also that Edwin suffered from a loathsome disease, a sexual disease that in time would destroy him.'

'But Dr Leach examined him, and—'

'And said the contrary. He did not make a proper, thorough examination. I tell you there was no doubt. Adelaide had no doubt.' He nodded, not wishing to interrupt again. She leaned forward, her hand touched his, and he felt a momentary shock like that from a naked electric cable 'She could no longer live with him, his demands were insupportable. Yet Adelaide was kind, she was always kind. Edwin was a diseased person,

but she did not wish him to suffer. She used her
medical knowledge for that end. You must believe
that, Daniel, Edwin never suffered.'

'What happened?' His voice came out as a croak.
He was conscious of her nearness, longed to move
away.

'She nursed Edwin in his illness, nursed him
devotedly, everybody said so. Then he recovered
and his only thoughts were to satisfy his sensuality.
You must see that she could not submit. She asked
Georgius Rex to obtain chloroform and he did,
without knowing the purpose for which it was
needed. It was not necessary for him to know anything except that she joined him in what was truly
a loving enterprise. And she paid a visit to John
Bell and Croyden, who are the most famous firm
of chemists in London, where she made a purchase of her own. Now she was ready for the next
time Edwin was—importunate. That came on
New Year's Eve. He had eaten a dozen oysters
that day, and they always affected him.'

Ross Daniel wished himself anywhere but
where he was. The reminiscent half-smile on her
face, the awful thought of anybody wishing to become importunate—ghastly circumlocution—
with this grotesque creature, combined to make
him feel physically sick. Yet he knew that he must
hear the tale to the end.

'Adelaide had told him of the pleasantness of
chloroform, and she mentioned it that evening
in the presence of Mrs Doggett. It is sweet, you
know, and subtle. She told him also, and this was
true, that just a tiny whiff of it would exhilarate
him and heighten the sensations he found so pleasant. Again I use delicate language, Daniel, but

you will understand. So that he was not asleep
but awake, and he did not reject but willingly
inhaled what he thought would be just one or
two whiffs of chloroform because he believed they
would increase his pleasure. Of course he inhaled
more, and within a few seconds he was asleep.'

The young man's mouth was dry. 'And then?'

'And then, Daniel. Do you know the nature of
a stomach pump? I see that you do not. It was a
Victorian invention, using a tube and a pump to
wash out the stomach in cases where some poison-
ous substance had been taken involuntarily. The
tube was put down the throat, and then the contents of the stomach were pumped out. But that
was not its only use. It could also be used to force
food *into* the stomach. Some of those poor suf-
fragettes were fed by it.'

'A hateful invention.'

'Yet useful in its time, and it interested Adelaide
Bartlett. She knew quite a lot about medical matters, more than people concerned with the case
ever realized. She knew how to make up a prescription, she was a wonderful nurse—you have
seen that photograph—she possessed not only a
companion to the pharmacopoeia, but also a very
good illustrated medical dictionary. She read
about chloroform and about the stomach pump.
One day she saw one of her beautiful St Bernard
dogs first chloroformed and then given gastric lavage. Do you know what that is?' Ross Daniel had
been brought up on a farm, and said he had a
pretty good idea. 'Then I will not explain. She
had a clever thought. You understand that for her
there were two purposes. Life with Edwin was
impossible, intolerable—'

'Could she not have left him?'

She stopped for a moment and stared at him. He could read nothing in her expression, yet he felt himself colouring as though he had belched in church. Then she said gently, 'He would not have permitted it. She felt this pure and perfect love for Georgius Rex and believed it to be returned. And Edwin was far, far gone in his sensuality. It was an act of mercy to end his life. She wished to be merciful, but not to suffer for her act of mercy. If you were a theosophist you would understand me.'

Ross Daniel gave private thanks that he was not a theosophist, but he did not interrupt again.

'The stomach pump was quite small, no more than eighteen inches long. It looked very neat there in the shop in its mahogany case, with the length of indiarubber tubing coiled round it, and it was sold freely to anybody because it could also be used as an enema. But there was one problem, and that was Mrs Doggett. Both she and the maid Alice were always looking out for anything unusual because they thought the Bartletts were such an odd couple. They were what the English call nosy. Not a nice word, but then it is not a nice thing to be nosy, don't you agree?

'So Adelaide had to make sure that the pump was not seen. How do you think she did it?' Ross Daniel shook his head. 'She bought the pump and had it packed up. Then she went to Hamley's the toy shop, and bought a Christmas present for Edwin, a big jigsaw puzzle of General Gordon at Khartoum. She asked the store to wrap the two packages in one and they did so, with the result that it was only one package Adelaide took back home. She told Mrs Doggett that it was the jigsaw, and showed it to her a little later. And it was a present Edwin enjoyed, for he liked jigsaws. Don't you think that was a good idea?'

The young man cleared his throat. 'Very good.'

'She had already taken the pump into the back room, of course, and she kept it there. Now I have to ask you to do something. I will show you something strange, Daniel. Will you please get up and fetch from the bookcase behind you a book bound in red cloth. I will not tell you the title, because you will recognize it.'

He found the book without trouble, next to what seemed to be the collected works of H. P. Blavatsky. It was *The Trial of Adelaide Bartlett,* the book he had read in the Famous British Trials series. She held out her hand, he gave it to her, and she turned the pages, talking as she did so.

'The strange thing is that something like what really happened was suggested, and that then the suggestion was dropped. It was when Dr Murray was giving evidence. He was the assistant to Dr Green, who carried out the post-mortem. Here it is. The jury foreman wanted to know how long it would take to pour chloroform down the throat of an unconscious person. "It would take some little time? You could not do it suddenly if the person was insensible?" he asked. Dr Murray answered: "Different methods might be employed. There might be a tube employed." And he added in reply to a question from the Judge that some mechanical means might have been used, and again mentioned a tube. But that line of questioning was dropped, I suppose because it was thought that too much skill would be needed. They did not

think of the stomach pump, of the chloroform not
being poured but forced down into the stomach.'

Ross Daniel shook his head. He felt like the
Wedding Guest spellbound by the Ancient Mari-
ner.

'So you are to imagine Edwin insensible. The
pump is filled with most of the liquid in the chloroform bottle, and is then carefully screwed up. The
tubing is already attached to the pump, and now
it must be put down the throat. And that is truly
the difficult part. If a mistake is made in passing
the tube down the gullet, the patient, for Adelaide
thinks of poor Edwin as a patient, will choke and
then wake. Do you know how this difficulty was
avoided?' She paused, inviting an answer, but he
was incapable of making one. 'By the use of some
butter, which had been warmed so that it was
soft. The whole of the end of the tube is greased
with it, the first few inches. Then gently, gently,
the mouth is opened and the tube put down, inch
by inch. Because of the butter there is no trouble,
it slips down easily, and since the patient is unconscious there is no trauma of the throat. There is
no need to use the whole length of the tubing,
because the pump will force the liquid into the
stomach.

'This also has to be done gently and quite slowly,
because none of the chloroform must come up
round the tube into the gullet. It took perhaps
two minutes. After that—' She made a pumping
gesture and laughed, a sound he found chilling
in its easy gaiety. 'After that there was perhaps
half a minute of worry. Just after the administration Edwin's skin grows pale, although his face
was generally so ruddy. Then it grows blotchy,

his breathing is shallow and quite rapid, almost as though he might shake. But then the rapid breathing fades so that the breath is hardly perceptible, although he remains alive. You will understand then that in all this Edwin did not suffer, not for a moment. That was Adelaide's chief concern. He was unconscious, and then he quickly passed into coma, just as the doctor said.'

'What happened to the pump?'

'It was put back in its case, and placed in the chest of drawers in the bedroom. To dispose of it was easier than bringing it into the apartment, because Adelaide had only to wait for a time when Mrs Doggett was occupied in her kitchen. This always happened in the late afternoon, when she was preparing her husband's dinner. So on the following afternoon—this was before the postmortem, you understand—Adelaide went out for a walk. The case was not very big, and she was able to carry it beneath her cloak, that cloak which the Old Man saw had no pockets. She had put into the case the chloroform bottle. Of course the bottle was never on the mantelpiece, and unfortunately Dr Leach remembered its absence. I am afraid the story she told of throwing it out of a railway carriage some days later was not true. It would have been too dangerous to keep the bottle in the bedroom. And she had also thought to put into the case two pound weights, of the kind used on kitchen scales. She took the very short walk to the Thames Embankment, and threw the box into the river. She looked down and saw nothing because of the darkness, but it must have sunk at once.' She spread her arms wide. 'Finish.'

'There is still something I do not understand.

You were anxious to have the post-mortem, it was something mentioned as a point in your favour. Yet the post-mortem showed the presence of chloroform. I should have thought you would have tried to delay it.'

Again her easy laugh. 'That shows the dangers of having limited knowledge. Adelaide knew about medicine, but she was an amateur and not a professional. It shows also that you should never trust a popular manual. Chloroform, she had read in all her medical books, is very volatile. If you pour out a little into a saucer it evaporates quickly. All books and articles tell you that, and she thought that this would also be true of chloroform taken internally. She thought all traces of it would disappear within an hour, and that the death would seem natural. It was a shock when Dr Leach, dear kind Dr Leach, said that he could not give a death certificate, but even then she believed that the chloroform must disappear within a day, and that the post-mortem would satisfy the doctors. So naturally she wanted it done at once. She was foolishly innocent, you must agree.'

Foolishly innocent indeed. Ross Daniel stood up. 'You thought you had found a foolproof way of committing murder.'

'The young are so censorious. I told you that Adelaide's chief concern was that Edwin should not suffer. And he did not do so, he had that brief sensation of pleasure, and knew nothing more. Why are you standing? Remember that all this happened long ago, and that Adelaide Bartlett was another person.' He moved towards the door. 'When your article appears I should like your paper to send me a copy. I hope you will use the photograph of me in hospital.'

He became aware that he was holding the photographs, and returned to thrust them into her hands. 'I don't want them. I shall write no article, I want nothing more to do with you.'

She began to laugh again. This laughter rang in his head after he had run out of the house and reached his car. It echoed still, after he had told his editor that Madame Bartlett had refused to talk to him about the past, and that accordingly there was no story. He heard her laugh that night in his dreams.

Two years later she died, still living in the same house, still attended by Françoise. He did not go to the funeral, but at the request of his editor wrote a couple of paragraphs headed: MADAME BARTLETT, WELL-KNOWN THEOSOPHIST, DIES.

It was the only obituary given to Adelaide Bartlett.

POSTSCRIPT
THE REALITY AND THE FICTION

This is a novel based on real life, introducing many people who actually lived, along with some fictional characters. Such books are not unusual nowadays, but it is rare for such an approach to be made to a case that was, and remains, a mystery. In that sense, this is an experimental crime story. If I were reading it I should want to know at the end what was true, and how much had been invented. This postscript is for readers who have similar feelings.

The essential story told here is true. Adelaide married Edwin Bartlett, and he received a sum of money which helped him to enlarge the grocery business of Baxter and Bartlett. She went to school, and then to a convent in Belgium, before beginning married life. She consulted Mrs Nichols when she became pregnant, and her child was stillborn. She and Edwin were equally fond of the St Bernard dogs, and they exhibited them at the Albert Palace.

Much of the detail surrounding Edwin's illness and death may sound unlikely, but it is true. Edwin did have that conversation with Dr Leach about mesmerism, said to the doctor that worms were wriggling about in his throat, and expressed the utmost reluctance to go out. He was delighted that Adelaide and Dyson should be so friendly, and although the story of his 'giving her' to Dyson rests only on the words of Adelaide and Dyson, his behaviour makes it seem likely enough. The details of the trial, and the principal figures included in it, are taken from the trial transcripts and from biographies or memoirs of Russell, Clarke and Poland.

For information about Adelaide's activities in World War I, and of her friendship with Dudley Wright, I am in debt to Yseult Bridges's *Poison and Adelaide Bartlett.* In 1932 Adelaide wrote to Wright that she was almost blind. The year of her death is not known.

So far runs reality, but much fiction is intertwined with it. Nothing more is known of her ancestry than Clarke's careful statement that she was the natural daughter of 'an Englishman of good social position' and he, or his agents, arranged the marriage.' There have been rumours that the Englishman was royal, but they are no more than rumours, although the fact that her protector was rich and powerful was made clear at the time of her trial. The background provided for her here is wholly invented, and so is her Journal. I have tried by their use to create a psychological background for her later actions which, as it seems to me, must have been connected with repressed or partly fulfilled sexual desires. The conduct of all the chief actors, Edwin, Dyson, and Adelaide, gives off a strong whiff of the sexuality that bubbled constantly below the surface of Victorian life, something sensed with disapproval by Mr Justice Wills. So far as I know, Adelaide did not meet Madame Blavatsky, but she might have done so, and certainly in her later years she was preoccupied by theosophy. The account of Madame Blavatsky's behaviour in the presence of a disciple is derived from V. S. Solovyoff's *A Modern Priestess of Isis*. Blavatsky told him that, in spite of her marriage, she had always been a virgin.

And finally, the trial and the puzzle. The decision not to prefer charges against Dyson seems surprising in retrospect. Sir Augustus Stephenson was, from contemporary accounts, the kind of autocrat shown here, although the conference at which the decision was taken is imaginary. Russell's preoccupation with the Irish Home Rule Bill and his absence from Court for so much of the time undoubtedly damaged the presentation of the prosecution case. The foreman of the jury wrote the letter to *The Times* quoted here, but the sketch of what took place in the jury room is invented

And the puzzle? Very few theories have been advanced to explain it. There are some who believe that Edwin committed suicide in sudden despair about his necrosis of the jaw, but if so he is the first suicide who ordered an extra-large haddock for his breakfast and said that he would get up an hour early to eat it. Mrs Bridges in *Poison and Adelaide Bartlett* suggested that Adelaide had caused Edwin's illness by administering sugar of lead to him, and when that did not work had hypnotized him with Dyson's help, so that under hypnotic influence he took up the wineglass which she had filled with brandy and chloroform, and drained it down 'without pain or vomiting.' There is much, both in the trial evidence and in works on hypnotism, to contradict this theory.

The interview in the Epilogue is imaginary, although we know from her correspondence that Adelaide was alive, and in America, in the early nineteen thirties, and that she had for some years called herself Madame Bartlett.

My own view is that Adelaide certainly poisoned her husband, and that the method suggested here is more plausible than any other. I do not pretend that it is without difficulty, particularly the introduction of the stomach pump into the apartment and its later disposal. The General Gordon jigsaw is an invention, but some similar means may have been used—or it is quite possible that Adelaide simply took a chance, as she did when asking Dyson to obtain the chloroform. It is possible also that she used only a tube and a funnel, which could have been disposed of more easily although they would have made the actual administration of the poison more risky . . . arguments about the possibilities in the actual case remain unending. But although I have respected almost all the facts I should emphasize that this is a work of fiction concerning an imaginary character named Adelaide Bartlett who also had a real existence. It is not a 'documentary,' although it is based on documents, but a novel.